Wishes & WINGS

The Birdsong Trilogy
Book Three

New York Times & USA Today Bestselling Author

NINA LANE

SNOW QUEEN
PUBLISHING

Wishes & Wings
The Birdsong Trilogy: Book Three
Copyright © 2022 by Nina Lane
All rights reserved.

Cover design: Najla Qamber Designs

Published by Snow Queen Publishing

ISBN: 978-1-954185-23-4

I am seeking, I am striving, I am in it with all my heart.

—*Vincent van Gogh*

PART I

CHAPTER 1

Nell

I'D CALLED my father first. The earth was still shaking from the thud of my mother's body hitting the concrete floor of the garage. The only instinct that penetrated my terror was to reach my father.

He'd called 911 before rushing home from campus. The medics and police arrived before he did. A police officer had taken me aside and was talking, but I couldn't hear him past the shock roaring in my ears.

My father hadn't said anything. He'd just grabbed me and held me tighter than he ever had before. Only then had I been able to breathe again.

When he meets me at the San Francisco airport after my sleepless flight from Frankfurt, his embrace is as forceful as it was that day over ten years ago. Except this time, I'm still unable to breathe properly.

I lock my arms around him. His constancy, at least, is reassuring in this world that has shattered into infinite pieces.

"Thank god you're back." Easing away, he puts his hands on my shoulders and looks me over. "These past two months have felt like a thousand lifetimes. You have no word on Darius yet?"

I shake my head.

"I've called a few friends of his, but they hadn't even heard he was still in Varaz," my father says, taking my arm as we walk away from the arrivals gate. "I'm so thankful he was there with you. Now that we know what happened, I'm sure we'll find out something soon."

After a stop at baggage claim, we drive north to Grenville. It's a warm summer day, the sun casting a golden light over the undulating hills and the distant strip of the Pacific. The house on Dearborne Street is brighter, with repainted rooms; fresh, colorful artwork, and several pieces of newly refurbished furniture. Fern's touch, I know.

"Fern will be over later this evening for dinner, after you've had a chance to settle in." My father carries my travel bag upstairs. "When you were in Varaz, I bought a new computer, and she figured out how to get better Wi-Fi installed to improve access speed or whatever it is. So you shouldn't have a problem connecting."

"What's the Wi-Fi password?"

Given his history of blocking my access to the internet, I half expect him not to tell me. But he rattles off the password without hesitation, and I input it into my phone. He starts climbing the narrow staircase leading to my old attic bedroom.

"Actually, I'd like to stay here, if that's okay." I push open the door of the guest bedroom where Darius lived. "It's more convenient."

My father shrugs in assent and puts my bag on a bench in the guest bedroom. "Can I get you anything?"

"No, thank you." Not even the jet lag can extinguish the burning sensation in my chest. "I'll probably take a nap, so I'll be down at dinner."

"Sounds good." He approaches and pushes my hair away from my forehead, studying the wound I'd sustained in the landslide. "That looks worse than you'd said over the phone."

"It's okay. I'll have a scar, but the doctor stitched it up well. It doesn't hurt anymore."

He lets my hair fall back into place and gives me a faint smile. "You have some stories to tell, don't you?"

"Some better than others."

"You're safe now." He embraces me again. "Welcome home, Nell."

My throat constricts. "Thank you."

He leaves. I close the door and unlock my phone. My hands shake as I check email and text messages—most from Darius's friend Lindsey Harris, whom I'd contacted shortly after arriving in Telina.

She and her husband Tom hadn't known Darius was in Krasnovar, but after hearing my jumbled, stuttering recap of events, they'd launched into doing whatever they could to find out what happened to him. I'd spent the days before my flight to California contacting whomever I could think of—Darius's friends and colleagues, as well as government officials—in the hopes that I'd know something before I left.

Instead, there is a gaping black hole of information that

no one can fill. Though news agencies are reporting from the southern provinces of Krasnovar, all anyone knows is that the Krasnovian army has launched an offensive attack in Varaz and surrounding areas.

I scroll through the messages. *Nothing yet. Trying a friend of his in Bulgaria. Might be able to get through to the press in Saldem.*

No message from Savko. I manage to get a few rings on Alexei's cell phone, but he doesn't pick up and his voicemail isn't working.

I leave another message for the State Department official I was routed to when I first called about Darius. The official was outwardly concerned and promised to help, but despite the intense urgency of the situation, two days later, he still hasn't returned my calls.

I toss the phone onto the bed and go into the bathroom to wash off the grime of travel. I can't distinguish the shower spray from the tears rolling down my face. Though I've cried only once in the past two weeks, my grief feels endless, with each passing second obliterating whatever hope I've tried clinging to.

I hadn't wanted to leave Frankfurt. Hell, I hadn't wanted to leave Krasnovar, not without Darius. For hours after driving away from Varaz, I'd managed to block the horror of what had happened—the vision of him walking toward the factory flanked by PLF soldiers, the rusted metal doors slamming shut behind them.

Instead, I'd forced my brain onto a razor-thin, narrow path that allowed no room for deviation. *Shift gears. Get Alexei and Jacob to safety. Get Hazel and Brian back home. Press the gas pedal. Turn right.*

I'd been terrified beyond reason. Convinced the PLF soldiers at the base of the mountain would fire their AK-47s at us the instant we stepped out of the truck.

Though they hadn't, they also hadn't let us through easily —taunting Alexei, threatening Jacob, insulting me, Hazel, and Brian. We'd all complied with their demands to record videos praising the PLF, though that didn't make them treat us any better.

Sickeningly, I'd been almost resigned to a sexual assault, while at the same time my burning rage left me in no doubt that I'd kill anyone who touched me. No one did. We'd endured shoving and harassment, but the abuse hadn't exploded into extreme violation.

As we'd navigated the gauntlet, Private Tarek had barked out warnings to the other men about Captain Lenkov. Though I never fully understood what he'd said, he was the one soldier who didn't flood me with complete fear.

Tarek had also given us the passes to get us through the checkpoints and accompanied us to Kolchava before taking the PLF truck back to the camp. Brian, Hazel, and I had managed to get Alexei to the local doctor, who was able to treat the bullet wound. No one in town whom we spoke to knew anything about Marcus, Sofia, and Tomas.

Per Darius's instructions, I'd contacted Savko, who ordered me not to leave Kolchava. He arrived several days later with transportation to Telina, where Alexei was able to receive further care at the hospital.

Savko also arranged a temporary apartment for Alexei and Jacob, as they awaited news from the rest of their family. Though he'd also gotten me, Hazel, and Brian rooms at a nearby hotel, I'd spent most of my time with Jacob at the hospital while Alexei underwent surgery.

"Your flight leaves at six p.m.," Savko told me, after he'd translated the doctor's report that Alexei might lose some mobility in his left arm, but otherwise would fully recover.

I almost couldn't understand the remark. What flight? It had been over two weeks since we'd left Varaz and made the arduous trek to Telina. Alexei would be in the hospital for at least another few days. Darius was—

I shook my head. Savko looked at me worriedly. He was in his fifties, a man with a kind, open face and a reassuring confidence in his ability to get things done.

"You and your two American friends are all booked," he continued. "No standby. Very complicated to get you the tickets. You must be there early so they do not give the seats to someone else."

"I...I can't leave." The words tasted like dust.

He frowned. "Nell, this is not an option. You must leave tonight. The airport is only allowing sporadic flights. This is why you could not leave sooner. We do not know when there will be another flight out of Krasnovar."

Out of Krasnovar.

Away from Darius.

Leaving him in the custody of the PLF. Not knowing what had happened to him and all the other people of Varaz.

Savko gently touched my arm. "I promise you I will try to find him."

Him? Or his remains?

I ran to vomit into a garbage bin.

"It's not just him." Shaking, I wiped my mouth and took

the bottle of water Savko offered me. "There are other people. So many. Alexei needs to find his wife."

"I know. The military is likely disrupting the communications, but a good friend of mine is trained in how to access encrypted information through the internet. He's been working on decoding the PLF's messages in and around Varaz. We hope to learn the situation soon, and you know I will do whatever I can to locate Darius."

As if worried I might bolt, Savko didn't leave my side for the rest of the afternoon. I knew he'd promised Darius he would get me on a plane, if it came to that—which it had.

I said goodbye to Alexei and Jacob, even if I didn't believe it was really *goodbye*. Of course I wasn't getting on a plane. How could I leave now?

Savko drove me to the airport. Everything inside me was knotted, tangled, frayed.

I stared out the window at the parts of the city that had been scarred by both the civil war and the current conflict—burned-out stores, gutted apartment buildings. I knew Savko wouldn't let me go with him back to Varaz, if he could even get there himself, and I had no way of finding out anything about Darius if I stayed in Krasnovar.

Maybe leaving was my best chance, difficult though that was to believe. If nothing else, it would be the fulfillment of Darius's goal, the reason he'd come to Varaz in the first place. He'd desperately wanted to get me to safety.

Hazel and Brian had been at the airport since early afternoon awaiting the flight. Savko carried my small travel bag, gave my passport to the gate agent, walked me all the way to the security line. His expression was grave.

"I do not break promise," he said. "To him or to you."

I opened my backpack to show him Darius's camera still tucked inside. "I'll keep it for him this time."

Savko smiled. "God willing, you will not have to hold it for long."

I hadn't cried until I was alone in a Frankfurt hotel room, waiting for my flight to San Francisco the following day. Then, the tears had welled up and spilled out in an utter deluge, wrenching sobs from a dark pit in the middle of my soul.

The PLF wouldn't have killed him—not right away. Not only did they have a score to settle, Darius had information they wanted about their financing channels and what the UN Office of Counterterrorism knew about their entire organization.

But Darius won't ever willingly tell them anything. He hadn't when they'd held him hostage six years ago, and he won't now. No matter what they do to him.

Hazel and Brian were flying into LaGuardia, so we'd parted ways at the gates. They'd both promised to use whatever resources they could to find out what was going on in Varaz.

The news was scarce. The Krasnovian army had been gaining ground in the southern provinces, and the counterattack on Varaz was part of a renewed offensive in the north. Though preliminary reports were cautiously optimistic, no one knew how successful the strategy would be or how long the offensive would last.

No one knew how many people had been or would be killed.

I'd gotten on a flight to San Francisco. I wished hard for Poe's safety too. It seemed self-indulgent to worry about my dog when the lives of thousands of people were at stake, but Poe had first chosen me, and then he'd chosen Darius. He was the first creature who understood we were inextricably bound.

Which means that I'd *know* if Darius was no longer alive. If the vital force of his being had been extinguished from the world, I'd feel it to my bones.

Wouldn't I?

I hadn't known my mother was dead until I saw her hanging in the garage. Up until that moment, I'd had an ordinary day at school. A math test, pizza for lunch in the cafeteria, dodgeball in gym. On the bus ride home, I'd been thinking of a new drawing I wanted to work on and hoping there was butter pecan ice cream for dessert.

I hadn't sensed the slightest rip in the universe, much less a shattering chasm.

But this is different. This has to be different.

After getting out of the shower, I dress in yoga pants and a T-shirt, then check my phone for the millionth time. Darius's friend Patrick O'Hare is also working to get news out of Krasnovar, but the media is blocked. He reports that he's heading to Krasnovar now in the hopes of getting into the country himself. Lindsey and Tom have contacted international rescue organizations, and several of Darius's longtime editors and colleagues are using "alternative" methods to trace his whereabouts.

The messages are both chilling and reassuring at the same time—though I see him disappear through the factory doors every time I close my eyes, and even when I don't, the people convening on Darius's behalf have vast resources and avenues. They have to be able to find out *something*.

My phone in hand, all notifications turned on, I go downstairs. The smell of marinara sauce wafts through the air. Fern is in the kitchen, and her enveloping embrace brings another lump to my throat.

"You had us all shaking in our boots." She pulls back to look at me, her smile warm, her blue eyes creased with concern. She puts her hand on my cheek. "There are no words for how relieved we are that you're safe. Come and sit down."

I sit at the table—a new cherrywood table and chair set that Fern helped my father pick out last year—and watch as she moves around the kitchen, taking down plates and checking on something in the oven.

"Clover messaged me that she'll be home early tomorrow morning," I say.

"Yes, she's driving up to see you, but unfortunately Simon has to work so he can't join her." Fern sets a glass of wine in front of me.

"She said she has an internship this summer."

"With an animation studio." Fern picks up a couple of potholders. "Thankfully it starts next week, so she's able to make a quick trip back here. She'd have been crushed if she hadn't been able to see you."

She takes a baked ziti out of the oven and sets it on the counter. Her remark brings up the realization that I have no idea how long I'll be in Grenville. I can stay with friends in New York if I have to, but I don't know if it's better for me to be there or here. I also don't know what else to do. I have no plan.

"Any word about Darius?" Fern looks at me. "The last we heard, Varaz was still…in trouble."

Under siege.

I shake my head, unable to say the words, *"I haven't heard anything yet."*

"Henry got ahold of a reporter in Saldem whom Darius worked with once." Fern sets the plates on the table. "He said he's trying to get to Varaz."

A familiar refrain. A lot of people are trying. No one has yet succeeded.

"The problem is that it's so remote." I rise to take silverware out of a drawer. "We almost couldn't get out, so chances of anyone getting in are pretty slim."

"The UN sent in relief organizations," Fern says. "And I hear they're finally getting some international aid."

"Too late for a lot of people." I set the knives down hard enough to clink. "The country could have used the help when this whole mess first broke out. And it wasn't as if the UN didn't know about the People's Liberation Front. Darius has been warning them about it for years."

She squeezes my arm because there's nothing either of us can say that will make any of this easier to bear.

My father comes in for dinner, and the three of us sit down. Though in the early stages of their relationship, I'd found it a bit strange to have Fern be part of our household, I came to welcome her presence on my visits home. I'd tried not to get too used to it in the event things didn't work out, but as her bond with my father strengthened, I let myself accept and be grateful for her role in our lives.

Over dinner, I stick to talking about the good things in Varaz and the people I met. I don't want either of them to think my volunteering in Krasnovar was a mistake. God knows I feel guilty enough for having been the reason Darius was there.

I blame my lack of appetite on jet lag. Fern waves me away when I try to help with the dishes.

"I'll take care of it," she says. "Go pool your resources with your father's. I know he contacted the senator again."

Though I'm not convinced contacting politicians will get us anywhere, I join my father in his office to find out about his continued efforts to first, get me out of Varaz, and now to find out where the PLF has taken Darius.

"They could kill him." The words scrape my throat. "Or hold him hostage indefinitely. After he escaped once, they'll manacle him to the wall this time."

My father's expression darkens. "It's certainly not the first time he's been in a tough situation."

"This is a little more than a *tough situation*."

My father glances up at the caustic edge to my voice. "I'm just saying he knows how to take care of himself. There's still hope."

Is there? Darius doesn't even have his lucky sea glass anymore. And he's escaped countless close calls throughout his life. At some point, even his allotment of luck has to run out.

I give my father a list of people I've called, as well as the contact information for the State Department officials who have proven as useless as a screen door on a submarine.

"Lindsey Harris." My father lifts his eyebrows in recognition. "I met her and Tom a while back. Good people. She was involved with the hostage aid organization Darius was donating to."

"She still is. She's sent out a bunch of messages to the staff and board of directors about Darius."

Despite our combined efforts, by midnight we still don't know anything. My father heads up to bed, and I stay by the computer and phone. There's no way I can sleep. My eyes burn. I check and recheck my messages, search the internet, send out emails and texts. I post on message boards and social media.

Finally, when a thin layer of light begins to diffuse the darkness, a text notification from Savko appears on my phone screen. *Alexei and Jacob doing well. Nothing on Darius. PLF front lines retreating from south.*

I have no response. If the PLF is also retreating in the northern province, they'll take Darius with them to God knows where.

I drop my phone onto the desk and press my hands against my eyes. If I didn't feel guilty enough about having been the reason Darius was in Varaz, I feel even worse knowing he wouldn't have turned himself back over to the PLF if it hadn't been for me.

A gut-wrenching ache rips open my insides. Tears slips past my fingers and fall onto the desk.

"Nell?"

I startle, looking up sharply. My father is at the door, dressed in a T-shirt and pajama pants.

"Have you been here all night?" He approaches, eyeing me with concern.

I grab a tissue and wipe my eyes. "Couldn't sleep."

"It won't do you any good to make yourself sick over this." He pauses. "In fact, you might want to see a doctor after all you've been through, at least for a checkup."

"I don't need a doctor." I gesture to my phone. "Savko says the PLF is retreating from the southern province. They might be leaving Varaz too, but that would mean Darius could be anywhere. He might even be dead already."

The lines on his forehead deepen. "I'm as upset and worried about him as you are. But you need to remember his line of work. He's gone into the worst conflicts in the world for well over twenty years. Every time, he knows he might not come back. We *all* know that."

Irritation scrapes my chest. "This is not the same thing. He was in Varaz because of me. He turned himself over to the PLF because of *me*."

"And he'd do it again. He wouldn't want you to feel guilty about what he did to get you to safety. He probably felt terrible that he didn't get you out sooner."

"Yes, he did." I rub my eyes. "That's the only reason I got on the plane. Even though I didn't want to. In fact, I wish I was still there."

My father frowns. "Given what happened and how difficult it was to even get in touch with you, you're extremely fortunate to have gotten out unhurt."

I swallow past the lump in my throat. I'm physically unhurt, but this pain and fear goes deep into the marrow of my bones. "I know I'm fortunate. But I *need* to find Darius."

The intensity of my voice echoes in the room. I feel the pressure of my father's gaze. My heart punches my chest.

I lift my head. Throughout my life, my father's constancy has been a grounding force. His face—the strong angles framed by his trimmed beard, his brown eyes crinkling in thought behind his glasses—has remained the same for me, even over almost twenty-three years. He is as secure, as stable as a pyramid.

For the first time, I realize that must be one of the reasons Darius has relied on their friendship for so long. When your life is built on recklessness and danger, you need at least one thing, one person, who is unchanging.

"Dad, I love him." The confession bursts out of me like a firework, sparks flaring, smoke burning.

My father doesn't move. "I love him too. He's a brother to me."

"No." I dig my fingers into my palms, deflecting a sharp stab of pain and guilt over divulging this without Darius here. But I can no longer hide it. "I'm *in* love with him."

Silence. Still no movement, no change of expression aside from the slow darkness creeping into his eyes.

"I fell in love with him back when he was staying with us, but he didn't...he refused to admit what was happening." The words tumble out, tripping over each other as if they've been straining for release. "That was the reason he left Grenville sooner than he'd intended. It's why he's stayed away all these years. But in Varaz—"

I stop. A muscle twitches in my father's cheek.

"Darius fought it." The weight of the battle descends on me. "He didn't want it to happen, not at first. But it did. *We* did."

I don't need to say anything else. My father is still for a moment that feels like an eternity. I see him absorbing the wave of shock. An ache pushes against my chest. I don't want to hurt him. I've never wanted that.

But aren't lies and subterfuge a kind of weapon? How can I pretend that Darius is still just *Uncle Darius* to me? How can I act as if he hasn't opened my world, filled my existence with possibilities, shown me that I can be or do anything? How can I conceal the fact that I love him with every cell in my body, every beat of my heart?

"Did he...what did he..." My father's voice is strangled. I've never known him to fight for words.

"He didn't do anything he shouldn't have. Just the opposite. For the longest time, he thought our feelings for each other were wrong. But what we went through in Varaz...it changed things. Changed us."

My father unclenches his fists, spreads out his hands. For an instant, I think he's going to say something, but instead he turns and leaves the room.

I let out my breath slowly. My relationship with my father has endured many twists and turns, some of which I've feared would drive us apart, but we have always navigated our way back to each other. He knows in his blood what it's like to be disowned, dismissed, and rejected by your own family, and he never wanted that to happen to us.

He still won't...I don't think. But he will likely consider Darius's role to be unforgivable.

I push away from the desk and rise. My father would have to have learned the truth at some point. No matter what has happened to Darius, my love for him won't just go away.

I drag myself upstairs and manage to doze off for an hour before showering and pulling on clean clothes. My father has left for campus to teach his summer classes, and there's an envelope on the kitchen table with a stack of twenties inside. I put them in my wallet and grab the car key for the old Toyota. I slip it onto my keyring and head outside.

After driving to downtown Grenville, I park along the sidewalk and walk to Dream Bean. I order several frothy coffee drinks and set them in a tray to bring to Comic Castle.

Walking in the door of the comic book shop with its bright, airy interior and neatly organized shelves elicits a wave of both pleasure and sorrow. I'd found a home here at the exact same time I'd started to become aware of my strange, intense new feelings for Darius. Now everything—Comic Castle, the house on Dearborne Street, even Grenville itself—is different, as if I've walked back into a world where I no longer belong.

Now, I belong to only one place, one person. Wherever he is.

Fern looks up from taking graphic novels out of a box. She smiles, but her eyes are cloudy.

"He told you." I approach and set the coffee tray on the counter.

"He stopped by on his way to campus." A line of worry creases her forehead. "He's pretty upset."

My chest tightens. "I know what it might look like from the outside, and I know it's unconventional. But there has never, not once, been anything manipulative or inappropriate about my relationship with Darius."

"Nell, honey, I'm not judging you." She sets a stack of books on the counter. "And I know Darius is a good man. Henry wouldn't have been lifelong friends with him if he weren't. But surely you can understand your father's concern. There's a huge gulf between you and Darius, and not just in age."

There was a time when I'd have nodded and then tried to

assure her that none of it mattered. Nothing mattered except how we feel about each other.

But now? After the mazes and battlefields Darius and I have been through together, I don't owe anyone a justification. I don't have to explain why I love him so deeply. I don't need to reason or rationalize anything about my love for him.

I pull my arm from Fern's. "Is Clover here?"

"She's upstairs." Her forehead still creased, Fern returns to unpacking the graphic novels. "She was going to text you as soon as she got out of the shower. Go on up."

I head upstairs to the apartment above the store and knock. The door flies open, and I'm almost knocked backward by Clover's ambushing hug.

"Oh my god, I can't even believe it." She tightens her grip. "I'm so glad you're alive."

I laugh as fresh tears fill my eyes. I wrap my arms around her, and we hug for a long time before disentangling ourselves. She indicates the scar on my forehead.

"You should give Winsome Swift one of those now, as a symbol of strength," she says. "Especially since you're even stronger than she is."

Though I don't feel that way, Clover's belief in me boosts my badly damaged courage.

We go into the apartment to talk. Aside from longer hair, Clover looks the same as she did in high school—she's wearing torn jeans and a *Sesame Street* T-shirt, and her whole face lights up as she tells me about her upcoming internship. She has a new confidence that makes me both happy and proud of her.

We soon head back downstairs to have coffee with Fern,

who thankfully doesn't bring up Darius again. Though I don't know what kind of long-term repercussions my revelation will have, I'm glad that the truth is no longer a secret.

After a couple of hours, I leave to make a stop at Monarch High School so I can say hello to my former art teacher, Hannah Meadows. Clover walks me out to my car, and we make plans to meet for dinner that night.

"You sure you'll be up for it?" She puts her hand on my arm. "I can't even imagine what you went through. What you're still going through. So I totally get it if you don't want to go out."

"You're one of the few people in the world I want to go out with right now." I take my keys out of my pocket. "As long as you don't mind me checking my phone every so often."

She smiles faintly. "I encourage it. Friendly's at seven?"

"I'll be there."

We exchange another hug, and she returns to the store. I get into the car, glancing down at my keyring as I fish for the unfamiliar key fob. I fan all the keys out into my palm.

Not only do I still have the key to Darius's apartment in Krasnovar, I have the two keys to his apartment in New York. I'd put them on my keyring because I hadn't known what else to do with them.

My body surges with a memory of the night he'd given them to me—when I'd been unable to stop myself from confessing how much I still needed him. When he'd pushed me up against the wall and kissed me with a hot, angry desperation that flooded me with lust.

He has always made me *feel* beyond what I thought possible. Before him, I hadn't known so many feelings and emotions even existed, much less that I could ever experience them.

I love you, Nell. I love you so much.

I press a hand to my mouth, holding back a painful sob. I'm tired of crying and not being able to do anything useful. And I refuse to believe that Darius has just disappeared into a void, that there isn't a single person who can determine if he's even still alive.

I know his friends will turn the world upside down trying to find out where he is and what happened to him, but no one had been able to get him out of PLF custody six years ago. Why would they be able to do anything now? For all the negotiating and—

My heart slams against my chest. I struggle to pull in a breath.

There's one man who might be powerful enough to get some answers.

Conrad Hawke had refused to pay Darius's ransom six years ago, but the PLF isn't after a ransom this time. And Conrad certainly has the resources and the money to buy information or hire people to look for Darius.

I start the car and drive down Main Street. A fierce, growing determination overcomes my despair.

Conrad Hawke owes his son. He doesn't know it yet, but it's time for him to pay.

CHAPTER 2

Nell

To my everlasting gratitude, my father pays for my flight to New York and drives me back to the airport only a week later. He parks and carries my travel bag and suitcase to the security line. We face each other; his eyes are unreadable. Mine, I know, are bloodshot and swollen.

"I'm so sorry." The apology comes out choked and raw. I will never apologize for loving Darius, but I hate that my feelings are causing my father pain. That I will be the reason their decades-long friendship will break apart.

"Let me know when you arrive," he says. "And what you find out."

"I will."

A brief, tense silence falls. He clears his throat. "This isn't what I want for you."

"It wasn't what I wanted either, not at first. But it's the truth. *My* truth. It's not going away."

The muscles around his jaw tighten. I sense the anger he's keeping in check—both at Darius for crossing a line that should have been forbidden, and at himself for being unable to do anything about it. I'm sure some of his anger is also directed at me, but likely for being—in his perception—too naive to know my own mind.

Not anymore, Dad. This is me now.

I touch his arm. "I don't want to hurt you."

"Too late." He stares at something in the distance, his features tense and his eyes glittering. "But whatever happened, you weren't the one at fault."

"Neither of us was at *fault*." An ache of love and frustration swells in my chest. "Darius did nothing wrong. Nothing coercive or manipulative, *ever*. If you believe nothing else, please believe that. He's always been exactly who you know he is."

My father shifts his gaze to mine. "The man I know would never have taken advantage of my daughter. Much less in a situation where her *life* was at stake."

"You're right. Darius would never take advantage of anyone. And he didn't take advantage of me."

"Given the circumstances, I find that impossible to believe." My father steps back and gestures to the security line. "You'd better get checked in."

I swallow the countless protests, explanations, arguments. All of that will have to wait for...I don't even know when.

We embrace, though my father's hug isn't as tight as it was when I'd arrived. I promise to text him frequently, but I don't ask him to keep me updated about what he might learn. I don't want to know if he intends to stop searching for news about Darius.

When I arrive in New York, I take the subway to my friend Alice's place in the Bronx. She'd said I could stay the night on her sofa since I have no idea if the keys Darius gave me will still work to access his building and apartment.

After I get settled, Alice and I meet a few other friends for drinks and dinner. They all want the details of my so-called "adventure," and I give them just enough to sate both their curiosity and concern. After that, it's easy to shift the conversation to their various jobs and activities.

While I enjoy the company of my old friends, I experience a strange disconnect, as if I'm no longer the young woman I'd been just a few weeks ago—the one who'd have been right in the thick of the chatter about job searching and the art scene. It's the same feeling of unbelonging that I'd had in Grenville.

Though I know beyond a doubt that I belong to Darius, what happens if I never find him? Will I spend the rest of my life looking, even when everyone else has given up? And if I do find him, he and I had clearly established the boundaries of our relationship. His declaration of love is a living thing inside me, nourishing and sustaining, but it doesn't erase the impossibility of a future together.

Which begs the question...either way, who will I be without him?

"Hey, Nell like bell."

I look up at the familiar voice to see Jonah making his way across the crowded bar to our table. The sight of him—

chipped-tooth smile, blue eyes, sandy hair—relieves my darker thoughts. I stand to return his tight hug.

"You look great." He indicates the scar on my forehead. "That gives you a lot of character."

I manage to smile. "I wish I'd acquired character an easier way, but thanks."

He grins and joins us at the table. We spend another hour filling in the past couple of months, and I'm thrilled to hear about both the successful defense of his master's thesis and the potential for a job offer at the architectural firm where he's been interning.

Alice and I return to her place close to one. The following morning, after she plies me with croissants and coffee from her favorite bakery, I head into Manhattan. Darius's apartment is on West 95th Street, a few blocks from Central Park.

When he'd given me the keys, he'd told me he didn't sublet the apartment, but that a colleague was staying there and would be vacating it soon. To Darius's frustration, even though I was about to lose my lease, I'd declined his offer to move into the apartment...an argument that had led to the up-against-a-wall kiss and my decision to take the volunteer position in Krasnovar.

It feels like that night happened a thousand years ago.

I exit the subway and shade my eyes against the unsea-sonably hot June sun. It's not yet nine, but heat is rising off the pavement, and humidity clings to the air. Traffic clogs the streets—cars and taxis spewing exhaust, buses jolting and hissing.

I walk to the Upper West Side apartment building. I'd found the address in my father's ancient Rolodex, which leads me to believe that Darius has owned the apartment for a number of years. It's an older stone building the color of sand with symmetrical, pointed pediments and foliated molding over the doorways.

Crossing the street, I pass between a dark blue sedan and a sleek Lexus. I climb the steps and test the security key in the front door lock. Somewhat to my surprise, it turns. My heartbeat increases as I go inside. I pass the mailboxes and climb the stairs to the top floor. The corridor is painted a soft cream color that complements the dark wood doors.

Apartment 510. My courage falters. I have no idea if another friend of his is living here or not. I don't think Darius would have had time to arrange for someone else to stay here, but he could have turned over the task to a property management company.

I stop outside apartment 510 just as a door down the hall opens. A woman with bright red hair and glasses comes out, a large tote bag slung over her shoulder. She locks her door and heads toward the stairs, meeting my gaze. She nods in acknowledgment.

"Morning." My voice sounds thin and uncertain.

"Morning." She glances at the apartment. "Moving in?"

"Oh, I'm not sure. I was looking for the guy who was staying here, actually. Is he…?"

"Dan?" She frowns. "He moved out a couple of months ago. He was a reporter or something, said he was heading down to a job in DC."

"Right. I mean, no one else has moved in?"

She shakes her head. "Not that I know of. Far as I can tell, the place is empty most of the time. I'm not sure who owns it, but whoever they are, they're losing a fortune by not subletting. Are you looking for the owner?"

I almost laugh. If only she knew.

"No, I have his contact info. Thanks."

"Sure." She gives me an odd look, then shrugs and continues walking to the stairs.

I wait until she's out of sight before letting myself into the apartment. I'm not sure what I'd expected, but my heart jumps at the sudden realization that I'm walking into *his* space.

It's a lovely, well-lit one-bedroom with hardwood floors and crown molding. A sofa and comfortable chairs in forest-green and rust are arranged in the living room, and large windows display a view of the street and buildings on the opposite side. The kitchen has stainless steel appliances and granite countertops, and the cupboards are stocked with plates and cooking pans.

Since Darius isn't here often, and he lets other people use the apartment when they're in town, the personal items are mostly books, a few pieces of artwork and framed photographs, and several old cameras. Articles of clothing—dress shirts, two suit jackets, trousers—hang at one side of the bedroom closet, while stacks of his T-shirts and jeans are folded in the bottom drawer of the dresser.

I touch the clothes, almost as if I can feel his body heat clinging to the material, smell his warm, masculine scent. It might not technically be *right* for me even to be here, but if none of his friends have used the apartment since April, I doubt anyone is going to be moving in soon.

And Darius had said he just lets people stay here when they need to, so if there is an issue, I can explain that he'd given me the key. It wouldn't be difficult to verify that we know each other. Plus, if I do need to turn the place back over to someone else, I can couch-surf with Alice and the others.

With that rationale in mind, I retrieve my backpack and travel bag from Alice's, then buy enough food to last me for the next few days. After I'm settled in the apartment, I take the subway to the Lower East Side and a street lined with rowhouses, one outfitted with a ramp. Before I can ring the bell, the front door opens and Tom Harris appears.

"Nell, it's great to see you again." He gives me a smile, ushering me into the foyer. "We were really relieved to hear you'd made it back safely. Come on in."

Lindsey is waiting in the front room, and she greets me with such effusive pleasure and concern that I almost can't believe this is only the second time we've ever seen each other. I love that she makes it feel as if we're lifelong friends.

"I'm so glad you're here." She gestures for me to sit down, maneuvering her wheelchair to face me. "And that you called. We had no idea that you'd gone to Krasnovar."

"Darius didn't tell us that he was in Varaz either." Tom returns from the kitchen with a tray of coffee and cookies, which he sets on the table. "I think he'd contacted Patrick O'Hare, but Patrick had been in the Sudan for several weeks. He's in London now."

Tom pours me a cup of coffee and gives me a plate for the cookies. They update me on the details of the search-and-find communications, though Lindsey has been keeping me in the loop so well that there's nothing I don't already know.

"The problem is that everything we've heard is specula-tion rather than fact," Lindsey explains. "The communications haven't been restored in any of the towns in the Opala mountain range. Patrick said the rumor is that at least one of the PLF platoons in Varaz has retreated. Of course, we don't know if they're the ones who are holding Darius."

Frustration squeezes my chest. This is ridiculous. With all the resources and technology the world has, there is no reason we should be so cut off from what's happening in Varaz.

Lindsey touches my arm. Her eyes are sympathetic. "Aid and relief organizations are finally being allowed in, so we should know more soon."

Though I nod, I'm not convinced. Krasnovar is a small, Eastern European country that has little, if any, importance on the world stage. There are salt and mineral mines, and plenty of forests, but as far as I know, Krasnovar has no major natural resources like oil or coal. Aside from bordering countries who don't want to get caught in the crossfire, no government has a vested interest in Krasnovar.

Which is why the national military and the PLF are duking it out on their own. If the PLF wins, they'll reestablish the horrific dictatorship responsible for repressive laws, censorship, and genocide. Darius has presented lengthy reports to the UN about the dictatorship's war crimes, which had been executed by the People's Liberation Front.

Though everything the PLF has done makes me sick, at this point I'd send them flowers if it meant we'd get word about Darius.

I don't tell the Harrises that I'm staying in Darius's apartment. I don't tell them about my plan to talk to Conrad Hawke. Or at least, try and talk to him.

In my imagination, he's like a despotic mastermind,

accessible only through steel doors that open with complex codes and retina scans. I don't know what makes me think I can get anywhere near him. I only know that I have to try.

The next day, after I make coffee in Darius's kitchen and try not to feel like a trespasser, I take the bus to the other side of Central Park, where a massive, chrome-and-steel skyscraper houses Hawke Financial.

I assume Conrad Hawke sits on the very top floor, though the security guards won't even let me into the lobby without either a company ID or my name on their list.

I walk back outside and sit on a bench, pulling out my phone. I bring up the cell number of my old friend Simon, who has been living in Los Angeles for the past few years.

"Hey, Wonder Woman." He sounds like he's smiling. "I'm sorry I couldn't drive up with Clover, but hopefully we can get together later this summer. How are you?"

"Surprised I'm still alive, I think." I give a small laugh. "It's good to hear your voice."

"Yours too. Man, you were in some serious shit, huh?"

"That's one way of putting it. Did you hear about Darius Hawke?"

"Yeah, Clover told me. Is he okay?"

"I don't know yet. I'm not sure anyone knows, but I'm trying to find out. I'm hoping to get in and talk to his father."

"Mr. Hawke's father? Like the Hawke Financial guy?"

"Yes."

"Whoa. Does your dad know?"

"No." I press the bridge of my nose between my fingers. "He wouldn't approve."

For so long, there has been so much my father hasn't approved of or wanted. Things that have gone against his wishes, his plans, his values. For the past five years, I've loaded even more onto him, topping it off with my confession of love for his once-closest friend. A lesser man would rage against so much perceived wrongness, or buckle under its weight.

And yet my father has done neither. He's just still there. Like a tree withstanding every shift in the weather, from sunny days to intense, destructive storms. Bending, maybe, but not breaking.

"What about Conrad Hawke?" Simon asks. "He doesn't know you want to talk to him?"

"No. He might not even know that Darius has been captured again." I tighten my grip on the phone. "Of course the Hawke Financial building is guarded like Fort Knox. I was hoping you could call on your internet-savvy friends and see if you can get me some personal contact info for him?"

"No problem. Phone number, email, whatever?"

"Anything. I don't even know exactly where he lives."

"On it. I'll call you back."

In less than half an hour, he texts me the name and cell number of Conrad's personal assistant, with an added *still looking*.

While I wait, I call the assistant's number. A woman with a crisply musical voice responds. "Lenora White."

My heart suddenly starts pounding. "Ms. White, my

name is Nell Fairchild. I'm trying to reach Conrad Hawke about an urgent situation."

An audible sigh comes through the phone. "Mr. Hawke is unavailable."

"Could you please tell him I called?" I have no idea if it would help or hurt to mention that the "situation" involves his son. Or that I'm related to Conrad by marriage.

Does he even know who I am? Has he ever known anything about me? Even though he and Odette had divorced, my mother was still his stepdaughter. Which makes me my—

"Mr. Hawke is very busy," Lenora White says sharply.

"I realize that. I'll only take a few minutes of his time."

"He doesn't have a few minutes to give you. Goodbye."

"Wait!" Panic flickers. I have the awful feeling she might be my only chance. "This is about his son. Darius Hawke is missing."

Silence falls for a second before she says, "Do you know how many calls we get every month from people attempting to extort money from Mr. Hawke?"

"That's not what I'm doing."

"How did you get this number?"

"Through a friend. Please. I need to speak to him."

Lenora clicks her tongue sharply. "I'll be putting you on the blacklist. Call this number again, and you'll be arrested for harassment."

"Ms. White." I take a breath. "I'm Conrad Hawke's granddaughter."

CHAPTER 3

Darius

"Darius."

Her voice was raspy, like crushed paper, broken glass. It made his throat hurt.

He wanted to leave. He wanted to stay forever.

She turned her head toward him. The wrap on her head shifted crookedly. Under it, her scalp was smooth and shiny. He wanted to straighten the wrap, kind of like a bandage, but he was afraid she'd break if he touched her.

Her hand lay palm-up at her side. Blue veins against her white skin. Like rivers on the wall map hanging in Mrs. Akerman's third-grade classroom. Spilling into oceans.

"It's okay." The nurse gave him a gentle smile from the other side of the bed. "You can come closer."

He edged toward the bed. The room felt too small, like it

could squeeze him to death. White walls, mechanical bed, hard chair.

She'd been here for months, breathing the antiseptic air into her failing lungs, closing her eyes against the fluorescent lights. The curtains were always drawn, blocking out any sun, any hint of the outside. Not like her room back in the east wing of the house.

That room was filled with flower-patterned furniture and had huge windows that let in a ton of light. It always smelled good too, like vanilla, and even when she spent more and more time in bed—a big, comfortable bed with lots of floral pillows and a canopy—she had a music player close by so she could listen to the piano concertos she loved so much.

He hated that she was here now, in this horrible little room with the linoleum floor and the stupid picture of the ocean on the opposite wall. Too many other people were around—staff and other patients and the doctors and nurses who'd gone from talking about "next steps" to saying nothing at all. They just checked the machines and looked at her charts, then walked away.

He hated that they walked away.

As far as he knew, he was the only person who visited her anymore. At the house, she'd always had lots of friends and people coming over, but since his father moved her here, no one came. His father sure didn't, but then he'd never visited her in the east wing room either.

He'd put her here after telling the doctor to "stop her treatment." The boy had heard them talking. They'd used a lot of medical words he didn't understand.

But he knew the "treatment" was keeping his mother

alive. He didn't want it to stop. She didn't either; he knew that. But two days later, an ambulance came and took her away from the flower bedroom.

He hadn't known where she was going. When he'd asked, his father had given him an irritated frown. "Forget about her. She's done."

Done? The boy was enraged.

Schoolwork was done. Dinner was done.

His mother was *still here*.

How long had it been? Time was so weird. It felt like one day, she'd been her usual self, and the next day she was telling him that she had an illness that meant she'd lose her hair because of the medicine. Then, before the school year was even over, she started having trouble getting out of bed.

"I want to see her," he'd told his father.

His father's frown deepened. He was like a volcano—all hard, cold rock with a burning core that could kill you dead if it erupted.

"You don't need to see her."

"I want to." He'd clenched his fists. He'd avoided battles with his father by staying away from him, but no more.

He'd been ready to fight. But his father had only shrugged. The next day, the nanny drove him to an ordinary building somewhere in Brooklyn. The sign on the outside said it was *Grace Hospice Care*.

The first times he'd visited, his mother had smiled, played cards with him. Once she'd read him a story. But she got tired so fast. Twice she'd fallen asleep before he'd left. Her face was thin, her cheeks hollowed out, her eyes strangely large.

The last time he was there, the last time she and he were

both there, she didn't stop looking at him. Like she was memorizing him to take with her when she left.

She lifted her hand and put her fingers on his cheek. Her hand was cold and skeletal.

"I'm so sorry," she whispered. "I…I tried to take care of you, Darius. The best I could. Didn't…didn't want him to know."

Didn't want who to know what?

The boy couldn't push any words out. Everything in him was burning. Like a volcano.

"Remember…" She lowered her arm and took his hand. "Remember that I love you more than all the stars in the sky."

He still couldn't speak. He tightened his fingers around hers, scared he might break them. They felt as fragile as twigs.

Her breath was so thin. Almost not there at all.

The nurse leaned over her, forehead crinkling.

His mother's fingers slackened. Her eyes closed. Then her breath was gone.

CHAPTER 4

Nell

Several hours after my phone call with Lenora White, I enter a sleek elevator that glides silently up to the top floor of the Hawke Financial building.

After the security guards searched my bag and took an "identification photo" of me, they'd asked me so many questions that I'm sure they even know the exact length of my fingernails. But I'd pay any price to be where I am now. Never mind that I'm shaking so hard my teeth almost rattle.

The elevator doors open onto a vast office surrounded by windows overlooking the city. Aside from a glass-topped desk, an elegant bar lined with gleaming bottles, and several modern chairs, the room is austere and sterile. Only the afternoon sunlight and the distant blue of the Hudson River lend any warmth.

A tall man with steel-colored hair rises from behind the

desk. Any illusions I'd harbored that maybe Darius isn't really related to Conrad Hawke dissolve.

The man standing in front of me is an older version of his son. Though his strong features are weathered with lines and creases, and his brown eyes glint with hardness, there is no question he is Darius's father.

Given the gauntlet of security, I'd expected him to be surrounded by bodyguards, but he and I are the only ones in the room.

"Come in." His voice is as deep as a well.

I take a few steps closer to the desk. My low-heeled pumps sink into the plush carpet. My heartbeat hammers in my ears.

I'm as scared as I was facing the PLF soldiers wielding their AK-47s and Kalashnikovs. Maybe even more so. At least then, I'd known exactly what their weapons were and what they could do.

I can't say the same for Conrad Hawke. He has more power than the majority of people in the world, but I have no idea how or if he would use it against me.

"I'm Nell Fairchild." He knows I'm telling the truth; his chief of security ran my driver's license through the system and conducted a background check that probably unearthed a copy of my birth certificate. "Katherine Hawke was my mother."

"So I understand." He narrows his eyes. "What do you want? Money?"

"No." My spine tenses. "I want your help finding your son."

"Call his cell."

"It's not quite that easy. The People's Liberation Front

has taken Darius hostage again."

A flash of shock appears behind his eyes—so quick that I wouldn't have noticed it if I hadn't been watching him closely for a reaction. But that one millisecond tells me that Conrad Hawke hadn't known anything about Darius's situation until now.

He strides around the desk. I try not to shrink back as he approaches, his wide shoulders blocking out the view of the skyline, his height forcing me to tilt my head to look him in the eye. Everything about him, from his deep voice to his physicality, is made for intimidation.

"Explain," he orders.

I take a breath. "Darius was back in Krasnovar because I was there when the attacks started several weeks ago. We weren't able to get help from the embassy or anyone else. Darius came to Varaz to help me get out, but we were unable to escape in time. He ended up surrendering to the PLF so that I and several of our friends could get to safety."

Conrad's mouth thins. "Surrendering."

"Yes. This all happened at the end of May. I just got back last week. The State Department isn't bothering to investigate. Darius's friends and colleagues sprang into action as soon as I called, but the media is having a hard time reaching anyone in Varaz. So I'm here because I'm desperate, and you're the only one powerful enough to do *something*."

He looks at me for a long minute that stretches into an eternity. I'm suddenly and uncomfortably reminded of the way Darius can peel away all my layers with only the force of his gaze.

"What were you doing in that shithole anyway?" Conrad asks.

"I was working for a rebuilding organization. I was supposed to be in Krasnovar for four weeks as a volunteer."

"When did Darius get there?"

"The middle of May. He arrived right before the city was put into lockdown."

"How did you end up in a position where he could *surrender* to the PLF?" He says the word as if it leaves a bad taste in his mouth. I don't imagine Conrad Hawke has ever surrendered in his life.

I explain how we were trying to leave Varaz in the midst of the siege when we were stopped by the PLF blockade led by Captain Lenkov.

"Darius had been using an alias, but when the situation started deteriorating, he finally revealed that he's Darius Hawke."

"Why did he do that?"

Conrad should know...shouldn't he? Or maybe not. He and Darius have been estranged for I don't know how many years. Conrad might not even know anything about Darius's photojournalism, much less his counterterrorism initiatives.

"I think Lenkov knew how valuable Darius is to the PLF," I finally say.

"Valuable enough to trade for...how many of you?"

"Five." I swallow hard. "I think Captain Lenkov agreed to the deal because of Darius's knowledge."

Conrad frowns. "Do you think or do you know?"

"Well, I assume that was the reason."

"What kind of information do you assume this...Captain Lenkov wanted?"

"Whatever Darius has." I spread my hands. "Lenkov knew that Darius has been doing a lot of counterterrorism work with the UN. He told Lenkov he has evidence about the PLF's financing channels, that he knows where they're getting their funding. That was when Lenkov agreed to the deal. I guess they—the PLF—want to find out what else Darius knows so they can cover their tracks."

Conrad folds his arms, his gaze steely. "What else did he say?"

"That's all I can remember. They spoke in both English and Krasnovian, so I couldn't understand it all."

"Where did they take him?"

"To a deserted factory just outside of Varaz. The Krasnovian army was starting its offensive right about then, so there was even more fighting. My friends and I managed to get to safety, but I haven't been able to find out what happened to Darius or where he is. No one has."

"And you think I can?"

"I think you can, and I hope you will. He's your *son*."

"I'm surprised my *son* wasn't killed years ago." He walks back to his desk and punches a few keys on the keyboard.

Though my heart is still racing, I feel a bit steadier. At least I'm not shaking like a scared cat anymore. Most importantly, I've explained why I'm here, and while it might not get me any results, I've done one more thing to find Darius.

Conrad straightens. He pushes back his cuff and looks at the thick silver watch on his wrist. "Have you eaten lunch?"

It takes me a second to process the mundane question. "No."

He makes an abrupt gesture that seems to indicate *come with me*. After striding to the elevator, he punches the button. The doors slide open. He extends a hand and waits for me to precede him.

We're going to lunch?

It seems like a ridiculous question, so I just step into the elevator. He follows. As soon as we reach the ground floor, another large, stone-faced man comes forward to escort us down a corridor.

A massive black Bentley SUV is waiting in the alley, as if the driver was expecting us. He opens the back door. I climb onto the butter-soft seat, my nose filling with the scents of leather and scotch.

Conrad gets in next to me, and I edge closer to the opposite door. Classical music drifts from a sound system. The windows are tinted black, making the interior shadowy and almost oppressive.

The driver whisks us into the traffic of downtown Manhattan. The engine is silent, the vehicle so smooth it almost doesn't feel like we're moving, but I experience a sudden surge of nausea like seasickness. I curl my fingers into my skirt. A trickle of sweat rolls down my spine.

I'm no longer in a luxury car. The gritty smells of rock, smoke, dirt, and blood assault my senses. I'm trapped in a cave, buried alive under tons of wreckage that could shift any second and crush me to—

"Drink?"

I startle, forcing my brain back to the present. "What?"

Conrad indicates the contents of a refrigerator tucked into the rear console. I shake my head, unable to make my voice work to thank him for the offer.

I sit back and inhale. *Stay calm. Just a bad memory. Well, a shitty, terrifying memory—but a memory nonetheless.*

"You okay?" He's looking at me, his eyes two slits in the darkness.

"Fine." I force a light note into my tone. "So where are we going?"

"A local place."

I fully expect to end up at an expensive, fine-dining restaurant with Wagyu beefsteaks and a mile-long list of cocktails. Instead the car glides to a stop in front of a small café with ivy-covered stone walls. The boho chic interior is filled with mismatched tables, and the customers are a combination of hipsters and college students.

After the hostess leads us to a table, Conrad pulls my chair out for me before taking the opposite seat.

"Do you...um, come here often?" I take a sip of cold water and glance around at the other customers. Conrad is the only one here over thirty. He's also the only one wearing a suit.

"No." He sits back and opens the menu. "I've heard their wraps are good."

I study the sandwich offerings, feeling off-kilter. I'd steeled myself for a major confrontation. I was prepared to argue further, plead, make a case. I'd expected him to banish me from his office, not take me out for a chicken-bacon wrap.

After we've placed our orders, Conrad gives me another penetrating look. "So you're from California."

"I grew up in a town called Grenville. It's north of San Francisco."

"When did you move to New York?"

"Four years ago. I was a student at the Art Institute."

He lifts his eyebrows slightly, almost as if he's impressed. But there's no way Conrad Hawke would be impressed by my art degree.

"What were you doing before you ended up in a damned war?" he asks.

"Waitressing. Trying and failing to find an arts-related job. Worrying about how to pay my next rent check." I shrug and give him a faint smile. "Oddly enough, none of that seems quite as dire now as it did two months ago."

He chuckles, a low deep sound that almost surprises me. I hadn't imagined him capable of smiling, much less laughing.

"And how did Darius know where to find you in Eastern Europe?" he asks.

"He's been a...a family friend for many years, so he'd heard I was there. He introduced Katherine to my father."

Conrad nods, as if recalling things he'd once forgotten. "Henry. Smart man. What does he do?"

"He's a professor at a college in Grenville. Greek and Roman history."

He takes a swallow of the beer he'd ordered. "Too bad he got mixed up with Katherine."

"He never saw it that way."

Conrad settles his gaze on my face. "You don't look like her."

"I know."

"She was a stunner, even as a kid. Like her mother. Odette was a model. Born in Russia, moved here as a teenager."

"Where did you meet her?"

He gives me a close-lipped smile. "Where men like me meet women like her. She'd have been perfect if she hadn't had a daughter. I made the mistake of overlooking that imperfection. That girl caused me no end of trouble."

My stomach knots. I'm saved from having to respond by

the arrival of our food. Though I'm not hungry, I eat a few bites of chicken as Conrad digs into his cheesesteak wrap.

Questions push at the back of my head. I'm not sure I should be pursuing this conversation, but I'm increasingly aware that I don't know that much about Darius and my mother's childhoods. Throughout my life, his visits with us had always been filled with outings, trips to the beach, discussions about his travels. I'd never heard him talk about his parents, especially not his father.

"How old was Katherine when you married Odette?" I ask.

He bites into the wrap and speaks around a mouthful. "Ten or eleven. Didn't know something was wrong with her at first. Darius was…what, nine? Unruly little bastard ever since his mother died. But he always felt like he had to look out for Katherine. Not that that did any good. Hanged herself, didn't she?"

My fingernails dig into my palm. I manage to nod.

"Total waste." He reaches for his beer, eyeing me as he takes a swig. "You seem pretty levelheaded. Must take after your father. He ever remarry?"

"No. He's been in a serious relationship for a few years. I don't know if they'll get married, though."

He sits back, tapping his fingers against the bottle. "What about you? Got a boyfriend?"

Heat rises up my neck. I shake my head, stuffing a french fry into my mouth to avoid answering.

"Any job plans?"

"I'll probably see if I can get my old job back at the Golden Biscuit." I pick up the chicken wrap. "At least, until we get some news about Darius. That's honestly all I care about right now. I'm the reason he was there in the first place, and I'd do anything to find out if he's…"

Still alive. Safe.

My eyes burn. I set the wrap down and lift my head. Conrad is watching me, deep brackets carved into either side of his mouth. Frustration squeezes my chest.

"Why didn't you pay his ransom six years ago?" I ask.

His eyes harden, and I think I've gone too far.

"Those negotiations were not made public." His voice is tight, like a steel cable.

"Darius told me. He said you'd claimed it was company policy."

"That was the truth. Not a claim."

"But he's your son. Not your company."

He twists his mouth. "You seem to know a lot about him. What else did he tell you?"

"That he was tortured in captivity. Beaten. Subjected to mock executions. You could have spared him all that trauma by handing over a few million dollars."

"It's not my job to *spare* people."

I inhale a heavy breath, reminding myself that I can't afford to antagonize him any more than I already have.

"What's happening in Krasnovar right now is horrific," I say in an attempt to appeal to his social conscience—if he has one. "The country had finally established a democratic government and was rebuilding after the civil war, and now they've been thrown back into chaos because of the PLF."

Conrad studies me. "What do you know about the PLF?"

"They used to be the main military branch under the dictatorship. Balakin was the top general both then and now. The PLF took Darius hostage because he'd been embedded with the Resistance Army, and the PLF wanted intel—which he never gave them. Obviously, they also wanted money from you, which you never gave them either."

He arches an eyebrow, but makes no response.

"After the dictatorship was overthrown in the civil war, the PLF was disbanded, or so everyone thought," I continue. "Turns out they went underground and somehow refinanced and rearmed themselves, all in preparation for this attempted coup. I've heard that General Balakin wants to install himself as the country's new leader. And Darius's knowledge of both counterterrorism tactics and the PLF's operations and financing will help Balakin strategize."

Conrad stabs his fork into a tomato. "What else do you know about Darius's counterterrorism work?"

"Not much. I didn't know anything about it until a few months ago when he was in New York. He was here to talk to a UN subcommittee. He said he'd been working with the UN and some other organizations. Not in an official capacity, but as more of a private consultant. You didn't know?"

He drops the fork with a clatter. "I cut him off two decades ago. He's an adrenaline junkie who deserves whatever end he meets."

"And you think he deserves to die? Even though you might be able to do something to prevent it?"

Conrad's eyes flash. He leans closer to me. "You're pretty fixated on this. Got a schoolgirl crush on him?"

"I've known him my whole life. He walked back into a torture chamber because of me." I swallow a surge of nausea. "How could I *not* be fixated on finding him?"

Conrad sits back and lifts his hand for the bill. I push away my mostly uneaten food and pick up my bag.

After he pays, we walk out to the sidewalk. The SUV is idling at the curb, double-parked. The driver jumps out to open the back door.

Conrad turns to me. "Where are you staying? Isaac will drop you off."

I can't stand the thought of getting back into the dark, cavernous space of the SUV. I back up a few steps. "I have some errands to run, so I'll take the subway."

He takes out his cell and unlocks the screen. "Give me your number."

Though I can't imagine him ever calling or texting me, I have a faint surge of hope. If he wants my number, that means he's not dismissing me entirely. I tell him my cell number, and he inputs it into his phone.

He starts to get into the car, then looks at me. A shadow from the door cuts across his face.

"Everything going on now?" he says. "It's way out of your league. You were in the wrong place at the wrong time. Now you're safe. Get back to your job and your friends. Leave this kind of shit to the people who know what they're doing."

"Thank you for the advice, but I won't stop until I know Darius is safe too."

He studies me for a moment before getting into the car. "I'll see what I can do."

The door slams shut. A few seconds later, the SUV pushes into the traffic clogging the streets.

CHAPTER 5

Henry

ROUTINE HAS ALWAYS BEEN Henry Fairchild's gravity, the force that keeps him from losing his foothold in the world.

Only one time in his life had he spun into a whirlwind—exhilarating and wondrous—and while he would not change marrying Katherine for anything, he'd known early on that he had to be the grounding force against her wild, untamed spirit. He was the rock, the anchor. For Katherine, yes, but mostly for Nell.

Nell.

His chest aches every time her name passes through his mind, which is—has always been—often. Even now, it catches him unaware, these passing thoughts of his daughter. He's spent half his life with her swimming right beneath his consciousness, breaking the surface like a dolphin.

More than Katherine, Nell has been Henry's focus. He's

always wanted—needed—to ensure her well-being, her safety, her stability.

He'd failed her in the most brutal way possible when he hadn't recognized the signs leading to Katherine's last act of unfathomable despair. He would never forgive himself for the faults—lack of foresight, ignoring his instincts—that had led to Nell finding her mother hanging in the garage.

She was forever changed by that discovery, of course. And Henry has always wondered how different his daughter might have been if that shock and horror hadn't been embedded in her very cells. If she hadn't known a pain so great she'd cut herself open to try and get rid of it.

If he'd found another way to help her that didn't mean sending her away from him. He still hears her screams of hatred on the day he'd told her she was going to Harbor View. That she'd be there for months. And after she'd come home from the psychiatric facility, she'd closed in on herself, quiet and skittish. Always afraid he'd make her go back.

Until—

He stares out at the grassy expanse of the campus quad, peppered with summer school students and faculty. He is to blame. He missed something—a clue, a signal, a cry for help.

Or did he?

He remembers the night four years ago when Darius came to Grenville. His friend's contained, shadowed energy had filled Henry with both sorrow and joy. He'd disliked the changes in Darius—the psychic scars from his captivity—but he was so relieved that the other man had made it through, survived, and that he was here again.

Henry had seen the way Nell looked at Darius with wary caution and hope. He'd noticed the affection that softened

Darius's features as his friend and his daughter greeted each other for the first time after so many years apart.

Henry understood Nell's hero worship of Darius Hawke. He had the same kind of awe for his friend. He'd first experienced it when he was sixteen, the day Darius had beaten down the three bullies who were tormenting him.

In less than a minute, two of the assholes were bleeding on the ground, and the third had run off crying. Big, unruly Darius wasn't even breathing hard.

Henry had known exactly who Darius Hawke was; all the boys at Harkson Academy did. They knew about Darius's father Conrad—far wealthier than any other boy's father—and Darius's failing grades. They knew he snuck off school grounds at night, had a girlfriend named Claire in the next town over, and that he frequented places where even the most daring senior boys didn't go—seedy bars, drug-fueled neighborhoods, strip clubs.

Later, Henry would learn that Darius's excursions were about his photography—some of the time, anyway—but back then, they'd all been in awe of the reckless, defiant young man.

Henry had made the offer right after Darius had dispatched the bullies—Darius's protection in exchange for Henry's tutoring. To his surprise, Darius had agreed.

More to his surprise—even now—that agreement had solidified into a twenty-five-year friendship. A brotherhood. When Henry had married Darius's stepsister, he and Darius had become family.

So how could…?

Nell?

Betrayal clenches his gut, hot and thick. Henry has

always been slow to anger, the opposite of Katherine and her sudden, sharp temper. But now, every thought of Darius incites a flare of rage, like a match scraping against a strip of phosphorous.

The heat burns away the reminder that Darius is missing again. A cold part of Henry thinks that could be his solution —if Darius never returns or is found dead, this whole business will be over and done with.

But Henry knows his daughter. She feels too deeply, right to her marrow. This, too, will change her forever. Darius had to know that when he—

Henry shakes his head to rid himself of the inevitable speculations that have jammed into his brain ever since his daughter's confession.

He didn't want it to happen, she'd said. *But it did. We did.*

"She's an adult," Fern had reminded him gently.

"She's my daughter."

"Those things aren't mutually exclusive," Fern said. "She's an adult *and* your daughter. She's not only capable of making her own decisions, she's entitled to them. And Darius is her decision."

But for *what?* Henry can unravel the most complex rhetoric in ancient philosophy, but he doesn't know where to begin identifying what either Nell or Darius expected from their...*happening.*

Was it just sex? He forces himself to confront the question. For all his anger toward Darius, his conviction that the other man is in the wrong, Henry can't imagine that Darius would go after Nell for no other reason than sex.

Darius has plummeted in Henry's esteem, but Henry still doesn't think he'd use a woman callously. Moreover, if

Darius just wanted to get laid, he'd have his pick of many willing women. He wouldn't have fixated on *Nell*.

Jesus. Henry drags a hand down his face.

I'm in love with him, Nell had said.

Did she think they were going to get married? Did *Darius* think that? What kind of life would that be for Nell anyway, married to a man two decades older who spent all his time dodging death and destruction in the world's worst places?

And what did Darius expect—that he'd bring her along? Leave her at home? What about all her plans, her career?

Nell had fought so hard to get into art school, to move away from Grenville, to be independent. Henry had struggled against her defiance, fearing all the imagined horrors and disappointments that could hurt his beloved daughter. But she'd been determined, and he'd slowly managed to let go.

Over the years, because of both Nell's accomplishments and Henry's expanded view of the world through his relationship with Fern, an unbearable pride in Nell had emerged. He'd become so proud of her talent, her courage, her strength. He began to see the future that awaited her— one in which she carved her own path, made the most of her creativity, changed the way people saw the world.

What of that?

Henry stares out the window of his office. A gray-haired man sits on a bench in the quad. A young woman crosses to the brick library. Two students lounge under a tree with paper coffee cups.

As Henry watches the mundane scene, the worst, most shameful thought rises. He tries to force it down, but it breaks the surface like a hot bubble of tar.

He'd sensed it. He hadn't known at the time what *it* was, but he'd felt the occasional strange tension between Darius and Nell. He'd seen Nell look at Darius with a new kind of intense curiosity. When he'd found the naked pictures of his daughter, his first thought was that Darius had taken them. He'd walked in on them one night in the living room and while nothing had looked amiss, the air had been so thick with...*something* that Henry had stopped in his tracks and wondered what the hell was going on.

Nothing.

He'd ignored whatever it was he thought he'd sensed or felt. Smothered it.

Of course, it was nothing. Not Nell. Not Darius.

Never.

Henry tightens his hand on the windowsill. He'd failed Katherine and Nell in the worst way imaginable by not seeing the severity of Katherine's final descent into darkness. After she'd died, he'd told himself he'd never again ignore or smother his instincts.

Then he went and did the same thing with Nell and this mess with Darius. Except now, Henry still has a chance to fix it. He's spent his life looking out for and protecting his daughter.

He won't fail her again.

CHAPTER 6

Nell

THE NEXT FEW days pass with no contact from Conrad. I hold on to the belief that my visit was still a success—I hadn't even expected to get into the Hawke Financial building, much less talk to him face-to-face.

Not only had I done that, he'd taken my number and indicated he'd look into the situation. He can probably get more information in five minutes than I can in a full week.

Since I'm back again relying on my father for money—a fact that makes me feel worse than it ever has before—I stop at the Golden Biscuit and plead with Gus to give me a few shifts a week, but he apologetically says his staff is full and he can't find room for me.

I spend an afternoon applying to other restaurants and shops. Living in Darius's apartment, I'm spared from having to pay rent, but I still have expenses—not to mention loans and credit cards to pay off.

Then Lindsey tells me she's looking for part-time help at her bookstore, Pen and Paper, and though I suspect she conveniently created the position for me, I'm not too proud to take the offer.

In the hours between my bookstore shifts, I continue scouring the internet. The video that Hazel, Brian, and I had made at the PLF camp surfaces on several Eastern European websites, but doesn't break through to US news agencies. I send countless emails and make dozens of phone calls trying to get answers. I run foreign websites through online translators and parse the articles for information.

A ray of hope comes from international news sources, who report that the Krasnovian national military is gaining ground in its offensive, as most of the PLF troops have retreated from the capital city and several other urban centers. There have also been at least two major victories in the west.

But the northern province and mountain ranges remain in severe crisis, with fighting continuing across the region. Civilians have fled toward the borders, and the refugee camps set up in the south are already at capacity. Aside from rumors, the situation in Varaz is still obscured.

My father and I speak twice—stilted conversations about the bookstore, the city, his classes. Neither of us mentions Darius, though our silences reverberate with both his presence and absence.

In phone calls and emails, Fern assures me that my father is "dealing with it," though we all know our relationship has changed forever. No matter what's happened to Darius.

A week after my return to New York, I finally manage to connect to a video call with Alexei and Jacob. We've spoken on the phone several times, but seeing their faces onscreen creates a wave of both pleasure and sorrow. They've had no word from or about Sofia, Marcus, and Tomas, and so we share the pain of uncertainty.

"Were you able to speak with the humanitarian aid representative I contacted?" I ask. "She's in Telina, and she said she'd try and call you to see if she could help."

Alexei shakes his head. He's pale and gaunt, the angular lines of his face made sharper by his beard. Though he'd shrugged off my concerns about his health, assuring me he'd been patched up in "no time," I suspect he was in worse shape than he let on. Beside him, Jacob also looks too thin, his eyes darting back and forth as if he's afraid of another attack.

"There are so many displaced people." Alexei waves his hand. "So many left without homes yet again. I am sure this aid worker is occupied with many other tasks."

I acknowledge that with a nod. Alexei has entered his personal information into several "reunification" apps and databases that seek to reunite families who have lost contact due to war or natural disasters. The sheer number of people using such programs is discouraging at best and horrifying at worst. The vast majority of refugees and migrants will never see their family members again.

It's so gut-wrenchingly *wrong*.

"Jacob, have you been practicing your checkers strategy?" I ask, forcing a lighter note into my voice.

His eyes brighten a little as he tells me about the board games he and Alexei often play. They are living in a one-room apartment near the hospital, owing to Alexei's loss of function in his arm and need for rehabilitation. Because they can't travel, they spend much of their time playing games and listening to the radio for news.

Alexei tells me about a book he recently read, and we indulge in some blue-sky talking about him and his family visiting New York one day.

After we end the call, I head off for a shift at Pen and Paper. The bookstore is neat and tidy—a bright, open space filled with wooden shelves displaying classic novels, new releases, nonfiction, and children's books. Lindsey has developed a loyal clientele who keep the place busy, some of them lingering for a few hours.

I clip on my name tag and get to work stocking books. Lindsey comes in around three to take over the afternoon shift, but I stay and continue helping. I like being around Lindsey with her effusive warmth and her way of making it seem like everything will turn out okay.

I stay until six, when she tells me to clock out and go call a friend.

"You still need to have a bit of fun, Nell." She guides her wheelchair toward the front counter. "Or normalcy, at least. Get a drink or go to a movie, okay?"

Though that's the last thing I want to do, I nod and collect my bag. "I'll see you tomorrow."

"Can you come over for dinner Friday night?"

"I'd love to, thanks."

"Great. I'll text you." She gives me a warm smile before turning her attention to a customer.

I leave the bookstore, slinging my bag over my shoulder.

As I start toward the subway, I notice a monstrous black SUV at the curb.

My heart bumps. The driver, Isaac, gets out and holds open the back door. Like all of the security men surrounding Conrad Hawke, he's big and beefy with square, expressionless features.

"Ms. Fairchild," he says. "Mr. Hawke asked me to pick you up and bring you to his residence."

"What for?"

"You'll have to ask him that, miss." He gestures to the backseat.

Just the sight of the cavernous interior makes my chest tighten.

"I'd actually prefer to walk or take the subway, if it's all the same to you," I say.

Isaac blinks. "I have orders, miss. He's expecting you."

"Where does he live?"

"It's not my position to give that kind of information."

I look at the SUV again. "If I go, can I ride in the front?"

He stares at me, as if I've just asked him if he can take me to Mars. "You want to ride in the front?"

"Yes. Please," I add.

With a shrug, he closes the back door and opens the passenger side door. I climb into the seat. Though the tinted windows still make the space darker than I'd like, at least I don't feel as if I'm about to have a panic attack.

Isaac maneuvers the big vehicle deftly through the crowded midtown streets before approaching a limestone skyscraper at least seventy stories high. He pulls into an ornate courtyard, and a doorman descends the stone steps.

"Welcome, Ms. Fairchild," he says. "Please come with me."

It's ridiculous, of course—the marble ocean in the foyer, the elevator like a silent space shuttle, the sheer, dizzying height. A maid opens the double-doors of Conrad's apartment and ushers me inside, where blinding views of the city and Central Park spill into the room. Everything is clean and modern—chrome, white, gray. A rush of vertigo forces me to sink onto the elegant sofa.

"Need a drink?" Conrad walks into the room, his tone clipped. He's dressed casually in dark trousers and a white shirt that fit the décor of the place. He stops at a sidebar and pours ice cubes and liquor into two crystal glasses.

"No, I—"

"Take it." He shoves the glass into my hand.

I could probably use the reinforcement right now. I take a sip. The burn of the alcohol spreads across my chest. Conrad tilts his head back and downs his drink in a couple of gulps.

"Why am I here?" I set the glass on the circular coffee table. My stomach is knotted. Something is wrong, but I don't know what. "Did you find something about Darius? Do you know where he is?"

He studies me for a second, then turns and pours himself another drink. "No."

My heart plummets. "Did you find out anything at all?"

He takes a folder off the sideboard and approaches me. He doesn't sit, and I'm forced to crane my neck back to look up at him. His height and breadth fill my vision.

"You said they'd taken him into a factory." Conrad takes another swallow of his drink. "Outside of the town."

"Yes. It used to be a cheese factory before the civil war. I don't think there were any plans to reopen it."

"How many soldiers did you see there?"

"There were about half a dozen when they stopped us." I try to think back objectively, to block the image of Darius on that dirt road, all those rifles pointed at us, Alexei bleeding in the back of the truck.

"A lot more of them were at the factory," I continue. "At least, the parking lot was filled with PLF trucks. I thought they might have taken it over as a headquarters or something."

"You're not the only one who thought that." He drops the folder onto my lap, his mouth compressing. "The Krasnovian army intelligence discovered the PLF had been using the factory as their command base. It was one of their first targets during the offensive attack."

A sick feeling clogs my throat. I open the folder to reveal an 8x10 aerial photograph.

Black spots swarm in my vision. The image is of the factory...or rather, what was once the factory. Now it's a twisted mess of bricks and metal. Heavy black smoke rises from the charred remains. Trucks are overturned in the lot. Bodies of PLF soldiers lie sprawled around the perimeter, as if they were thrown from the building.

"Concerted bomb attack." Conrad twirls his glass, making the ice cubes click together. A muscle twitches in his jaw. "Don't know how many, but it turned the tide of the battle in Varaz. The Krasnovian army has had the upper hand ever since."

Though part of my brain recognizes the good news in his statement, I can't think past the horror. Conrad seems equally affected—despite his coldness toward Darius, his face is tight with frustration and anger.

"When…" I stare at the photo and swallow the bile choking my throat. "When did this happen?"

"First week of June." He takes the photo from me and puts it back in the folder, dropping it on the sideboard. "Best as we can tell."

I'd been in Telina by then. The factory was bombed less than a week after we'd left Varaz? After the metal doors closed and locked behind Darius?

I can barely make my voice work to ask the question. "Do you know if Darius was still there?"

"There's been no recovery effort, but chances are high he was there. Word is that a number of the PLF soldiers were killed, including Lenkov and several other so-called officials. It's doubtful there were any survivors."

"But he…he could have been somewhere else."

"Also doubtful given the amount of fighting going on at the time. They wouldn't have risked moving him. I wouldn't have, at any rate."

"There has to be a way to verify if he was there or not."

Conrad's look is faintly pitying. "You came to me for answers, yes? Now you have them."

"This isn't proof that he's dead." My whole body is cold. He is not somewhere in that burning, bombed-out wreckage. He can't be.

Conrad sets his glass on the table and sits on a chair in front of me. For the first time, his features soften, giving him an expression that is almost paternal.

"You're upset," he says. "Give yourself time to process this. Go back to your bookstore, have drinks with friends. Do the things a girl your age should be doing. Stop obsessing over a situation you can't control. Over a man who probably should've been killed years ago."

My hands curl into fists. I want to yell, cry, beg him to keep looking for his son—but I can't even move past the shock.

Conrad's cell phone buzzes. He glances at the screen, then pushes to his feet and stalks into the other room, closing the door behind him. I hear his low voice, but can't make out any words.

The photo sits on the sideboard like a ticking time bomb. With shaking hands, I dig my phone out of my bag and hurry to open the folder. I snap a couple pictures of the photo and slip the phone into my pocket the instant before the door clicks open.

I turn to face Conrad, my heart thumping. I don't know if he saw me take the picture, but my instincts are telling me he wouldn't like it.

"You have your answer, Nell," he says.

I grip my phone tighter. I have nothing of the sort.

Poe. Was he inside the factory too? He'd jumped out of the truck and run to Darius, but Darius was already behind locked doors when Poe got there. Did he find a way in? Or did one of the soldiers—

I stop that train of thought, reminding myself that Poe knows every street and alleyway of Varaz and its surroundings. He'd know where to run, where to hide. Where to stay safe.

"Listen to what I'm telling you." Conrad narrows his eyes. "Forget about him. Leave it alone."

I want to scream at him that I couldn't *forget* Darius even if I tried. But making a scene won't do any good.

"I'm sure this has all come as a shock to you too." I manage to keep my voice even. "I appreciate your efforts."

He gestures toward the door in a clear indication that it's time for me to leave. I slip my bag strap over my shoulder, and we walk to the door.

A hollowed-out pit opens inside me. I sense this is it—that Conrad Hawke will take no further action—and part of me is aware that he's done more than I'd expected. He did get information no one else could.

"How did you do this?" I indicate the photo on the sideboard. "Find out about the bombing?"

A slight, humorless smile curves his mouth. "That's why you came to me, isn't it? Because, in your words, I'm the only one *powerful* enough to do something."

"Yes, but even the media can't get into Varaz. Who gave you that photo?"

"It's not relevant."

"Yes, it is. What if they can help us find out who was in the factory at the time?"

He makes a noise of impatience. "They can't help *us* with anything else because *we* are done here."

"Was it someone in the government? Because I've contacted every agency from the FBI to the Department of Defense, and everyone I talk to tells me they don't know anything. Which is obviously a lie, right?" I point to the photo. "Because they know about *that*."

For an instant, darkness flashes in his eyes, something malevolent and ugly. My breath stutters. I've been worried before that I might have gone too far with him, but now I know I have.

"I've told you what you need to do." The edge of his jaw is like iron. "Pay attention."

Gripping my bag, I force down another retort. Conrad pulls the door open for me, his gaze on my face.

"Your mother was beautiful, but she relied on Darius to do her dirty work," he remarks. "She didn't have a spine. You do. Even though we don't share blood, you must've somehow inherited that from me. But don't let stubbornness get you into trouble, understand? The car is waiting downstairs for you."

I extend my hand, trying to keep it from shaking. "Thank you for your help."

His big hand closes around mine. His expression turns grave. "He's dead, Nell. I'm sorry, but that's the truth."

I tug my hand from his and leave the apartment, walking swiftly toward the elevator.

I can't believe it. I *refuse* to believe Darius is no longer part of this world.

But I have no idea how to prove it.

CHAPTER 7

Nell

WHEN I GET HOME, I power up my laptop and do numerous searches for "Conrad Hawke."

The results yield his biographies and articles about his businesses and investments. I click on the images and scroll through dozens of headshots of Conrad and pictures of him shaking hands with other businessmen, politicians, the president.

There are photos of him on conference panels and speaking at podiums, and a seemingly endless array of him at high-society parties and galas. In several of them, a tall, stunning blond woman is at his side, her slender figure clad in sleek gowns, her aquiline features displaying a practiced smile of enjoyment.

Odette.

It takes me a second to realize this woman is my biological *grandmother*.

An odd hitch rises to my throat. After she'd divorced Conrad, Odette had moved back to Russia when my mother was still a teenager, which was one of the reasons Darius felt even more obligated to look out for her. I don't think Katherine stayed in touch with her mother—if she did, she'd never mentioned it. Last I heard, Odette had passed away several years ago.

I keep scrolling, unable to reconcile the glamorous woman in the pictures with either my mother or myself. Far down on the pages, there are a few older photos of a younger Conrad with a pretty, dark-haired woman. One of the pictures is from a magazine spread about their Hamptons estate, and they're both sitting on a vast expanse of lawn with a brick mansion in the background.

Victoria Hawke. Darius's mother. I knew she'd died of cancer when he was young, but I've never seen pictures of her until now.

Unsettled, I push away from my laptop, which I'd set up at the desk in Darius's living room. The apartment is dim, with only the glow of the exterior lights providing any illumination.

I stare out the window at the cars parked along the street. A dark blue sedan is right in front of the building, the shadow of the driver in the front seat. I've seen that same car parked there before.

Not that that's significant. There are thousands of cars in Manhattan and probably thousands of dark blue sedans. I don't even know why I noticed it.

Closing the curtain, I step away from the windows. I

unlock my phone and bring up the photo of the bombing. My vision blurs.

There's no question it's the factory—even in the charred wreckage, the basic structure is still evident. The wall surrounding Varaz is visible in the distance. In addition to the PLF soldiers lying around the factory grounds, a closer look reveals what appear to be bodies twisted under the debris.

Nausea roils in my stomach.

I swipe the screen and bring up Savko's number. His voicemail picks up. "Savko, it's Nell. I hope you're all right. I wanted to find out if you've heard about the factory, and I also need to ask you about…something else. Give me a call back, if you can."

I end the call and go into the kitchen, thinking I should eat something even though I'm not hungry. I'm halfway through making a sandwich when my phone buzzes.

"Savko?"

"Yes, you can hear me?"

"Yes." I raise my voice over the interference. "Where are you? Are you all right?"

"I am fine. Back in Kolchava, which is safe for now. The road to Varaz is still blocked, but it appears the fighting has lessened considerably. I have yet to find news on our friend."

"Did you hear that the Krasnovian army bombed the factory?" I ask.

"There was rumor, but I could not confirm."

"I've seen a photograph. I have a copy of it, in fact. I'm pretty sure it's not doctored, and I can't think of a reason why it would be. Most of the factory is obliterated. I don't know if Darius was still there, but he must have been. It happened less than a week after the rest of us escaped."

Savko lets out a heavy breath. "I am so terribly sorry to hear this."

"I won't believe he's dead until we know it for a fact. If there hasn't been anything in the media about it, then the exact casualties are still speculation."

"How did you obtain the photograph?"

"Well, it's actually a photo of a photo. I got it from Darius's father. Conrad Hawke."

There's a second of silence. "What did...how did this happen?"

"I'm not exactly sure myself." I can't help a humorless laugh. "I went to ask him for help, and...well, he gave it to me. At least, he found out about the bombing. But he wouldn't tell me where he got the photo."

"He has many connections, no?"

"More than I can imagine. But he made it clear that he won't do any further searching. And whoever gave him the photo obviously knows about the situation in Varaz. If they could obtain a photo of the factory, then they might know about the number of casualties and who, exactly, was there at the time."

"You make a good point. You do not have an idea from where he obtained it?"

"No. But it's an aerial photo, so it has to be someone from the military or government. I don't think anyone from the media could have gotten this kind of photograph in the middle of a siege."

Then again, I have no idea. After all, Darius has spent his life getting photographic evidence of war.

"I wish I could tell you I can help you with this," Savko says. "I can often do much within the borders of Krasnovar, but unfortunately not so far beyond. You said you have the photo?"

"I took a picture of the print, which was an 8x10 black and white."

"Can you email it to me? I cannot promise I can be helpful, but you remember I told you about Martin?"

"Your friend who knows how to intercept internet communications."

"That is just one of the things he can do, but he is not always successful," Savko says. "People and groups who wish to keep their correspondence untraceable know well enough not to leave a digital footprint."

"Do you think he can trace the photo to its source?"

"I can ask him." Savko's voice holds a shrug. "It would be easier with the original digital file, of course, if the metadata is intact. But perhaps Martin can locate it if he knows what he is looking for."

Relief prickles my skin. Again, it might be fruitless, but at least we're *doing* something. The only thing any of us can do is try. If I hadn't attempted to talk to Conrad, I wouldn't have even known about the bombing. Every piece of information will help us put the puzzle together.

"Thank you, Savko. I'll send it to you right now. And please feel free to give Martin my number."

After we end the call, I forward him the photo-of-the-photo and sit back down at my laptop. My phone buzzes with a text from Jonah—*drinks? dinner? ice cream sundaes?*

Though I'm tired, I know it's healthy for me to have short

breaks from constantly thinking and worrying about Darius.
I pick up my phone to respond. *Sundaes, definitely.*

Awesome. Serendipity's in half an hour?

I respond with a thumbs-up emoji before going to get
ready. Ice cream with a friend won't solve all my problems,
but it will definitely make me feel better.

Jonah is already waiting at a table when I arrive at the ice-
cream parlor. We greet each other warmly, and I sit across
from him as we peruse the sugar-laden menu. We place our
orders and chat about his recent trip back to California to
visit his family.

"So are you looking for a new job yet?" he asks after
we've both been served elaborate silver dishes of ice cream
drenched in hot fudge, nuts, and toffee.

"Not really." I pick up my spoon. "I don't want to commit
to a brand-new job when I don't even know how long I'll be
here."

He lifts his eyebrows. "You're not staying?"

"I don't know." My stomach tenses. "I'd like to, but if I hit
too many dead-ends about Darius's whereabouts, I might
have to go back to Europe to see if I can make any headway
there."

How I'd afford to go back to Europe, I have no idea. My
father's generosity will have a limit at some point, especially
now with our relationship strained over Darius.

Jonah pauses in the motion of lifting his spoon to his
mouth. "You'd go back just to find out what happened to
Darius Hawke?"

I'd go to the end of the universe. And beyond.

"Of course I would." I eat a piece of toffee, wary of telling him the truth and then annoyed with myself for hesitating. "I love him, Jonah."

Jonah blinks. "Well, he's like your uncle, right?"

"No. We're in a relationship. In love." I mash the ice cream with my spoon. "I've actually been in love with him for years, which is the reason I couldn't make a relationship work with you. It had nothing to do with you and everything to do with the fact that I couldn't get Darius out of my head or my heart. I never will."

Jonah focuses on his sundae as he processes this. "He's kind of—"

"It doesn't matter. That's the thing. I figured that out in Varaz when we were under attack. What does age or anything else matter? Honestly, when you know you could die any second, when your only instinct is survival and yet you're still thankful to feel so much for one person alone, nothing else matters. Nothing."

"Whoa. Sounds like you need to write a book or something."

I smile. "Didn't know I was so poetic, did you?"

"Actually, I'm pretty sure I did." He digs a spoonful of hot fudge out of his dish. "I don't enjoy knowing I couldn't compete with some badass war photographer—actually, I get why I couldn't—but I'm glad you found him. Found each other. I guess."

Two spots of color appear on his cheeks, and he eats a piece of brownie off his sundae.

"Thank you." The tightness in my chest eases. I spent so long trying to understand and then suppress my feelings for

Darius, to deny them, to try and get rid of them. Admitting to the world that I love Darius Hawke is a relief, like a sunrise breaking through the clouds.

"Sometimes people say that the heart follows a path that doesn't make sense," I say. "But this is just the opposite. My feelings might not make sense to anyone else, but they make perfect sense to me. That's why I know it's right."

"You think you'd marry him?" Jonah asks.

Marry him.

"I couldn't..." A piece of toffee sticks in my throat. I take a sip of water and shake my head again. "We could never get married."

"Why not?"

"Because he...neither one of us is the marrying kind." Even before the words are out, they sound completely stupid. My face warms. "I mean, this not knowing if he's dead or alive...this is his life. It's how he exists. Whenever he goes away, his family and friends live with the fear that he won't come back."

I will always come to you.

His promise lives under my skin. He's never broken a promise to me. To anyone, as far as I know.

"He could quit and do something else," Jonah offers.

"No. Then he wouldn't be who he is. He wouldn't be doing his life's work."

He'd be like a hawk with clipped wings.

Jonah polishes off the last of his ice cream and scrapes the bowl. "So you're basically expending all this effort looking for the man you love, even though you can't actually be with him once you find him?"

A hoarse chuckle breaks from my throat. "I guess so."

"That's pretty magnanimous." He takes out his wallet, waving away my attempt to pay. "What happens if you can't find him?"

"I'd rather not think about that."

Except the answer is—*I'll keep looking.*

For all I know, this search for Darius could be *my* new life's work.

We head back out into the sweltering evening and part ways at the subway station. I walk the eight blocks back to Darius's apartment, maneuvering around other pedestrians and hawkers.

As I wait to cross the street, I check my phone, pleased to find a text from Alexei that the humanitarian aid representative has contacted him about helping to locate Marcus, Sofia, and Tomas.

The light turns green, and the walk sign appears. I glance over my shoulder to ensure no cars are turning right. I start to cross. Someone behind me shouts.

A dark blue sedan swerves around the corner, speeding so close that I almost feel it brush against me. I gasp and stumble backward. The car continues down the street and disappears around another corner.

A hand closes on my arm, pulling me back to the sidewalk.

"You okay?" An older man peers at me, and a few other people gather around. "That was a damned close call."

"Maniac, speeding like that with people about," adds the woman next to him. "Sure you're okay, hon?"

I assure them I'm fine—certainly it's not the first time I've been involved in a close call in the city—though I'm still shaking a little as I continue walking.

A dark blue sedan. Not the same as the one that I've seen parked outside the apartment building. Or was it? I don't know.

Could someone have deliberately been trying to hurt or scare me? And if so, that "someone" could only be Conrad Hawke.

I think.

Who else could it be? Did Conrad see me take the picture of the bombing photo? But why would that even matter to him, much less give him a reason to want to scare me?

Then again, why had I felt like I needed to hide the fact that I wanted a copy of the photo?

He'd been insistent that I stop digging and "leave it alone," but isn't he the least bit *curious* about what happened to his son, even if he doesn't care? And why does it matter to him whether or not I keep searching for information when he'd said "we're done"?

The questions ricochet through my brain, intensifying my unease.

Relieved when the building comes into view, I quicken my pace. There's no blue sedan parked anywhere on this side of the street. I hurry inside and climb to the fifth floor.

A tall man wearing jeans and a T-shirt is standing outside apartment 510, his blond head bent as he searches for something in his pocket.

I blink. "Patrick?"

He looks up, his eyes widening. "Nell?"

With a laugh that dilutes my lingering apprehension, I approach him. "What are you doing here? I thought you were in London."

"I was. I just got in." He stares at me and shakes his head.

"I had no idea you were in New York. When…uh, when did you get here?"

"Last week." I'm somewhat perplexed by his uncharacteristic stammering before I realize he must be confused about the apartment. "I thought I could do more from here than from California."

"Oh." He scratches his head and glances at the door. "Uh…"

"I haven't even told Lindsey that I'm staying here." I dig my keys from my purse and unlock the door. "Technically, I probably shouldn't be, but Darius gave me a key a few months ago and I figured it'd be okay. But if you'd been planning to stay here, I'll get a hotel room."

"No need. I'm only in town for a couple of days. I'll get a room at the Marriott."

I thank him, both grateful and relieved. No sense protesting, especially since I can't afford a hotel room and I'd rather not impose on my friends if I don't have to.

"Come in for a coffee." I push open the door, thinking I wouldn't mind not being alone right now. "Or a drink. I just had a close call with a speeding car, so I could use both the company and something to steady my nerves."

He picks up his travel bag and follows me in. "The perils of living in the city, huh?"

I don't want him to know I'm still shaken from more than just the car, so I shrug and say, "I'll still take it any day over living in a war zone."

"Wise choice."

"Would you like a gin-and-tonic?" I cross the room to the bar cart.

"Sure."

He remains standing by the door as I mix the drinks.

"Sit down." I indicate the sofa and hand him a glass. "Are you here for work?"

"Yeah, a few meetings." He takes a swallow of the drink and sits, running a hand over his thigh. "I couldn't get into Krasnovar."

"Lindsey told me. She said it's probably better that you're not there. More resources outside of the country. But thanks for trying."

He nods, looking past me to the windows. "So I guess you don't know anything new either?"

I take my phone out of my bag. Even if Patrick couldn't get into Krasnovar, he might be able to shed some light on the situation.

"I don't know if you've heard about this yet." I pull up the photo on the screen. "Remember I told you they'd taken Darius to an old factory outside of Varaz? It was bombed in the offensive attack."

He stares at the image with a frown. "Where did you get this?"

I tell him about my meetings with Conrad Hawke. "I really thought he'd just have me thrown out, but he agreed to talk with me and used his contacts to find out about the bombing."

Patrick puts the phone on the coffee table and shakes his head. "You met with Conrad Hawke."

"Not only that, we had lunch together. It was his idea. He wasn't as terrifying as I'd expected him to be, though I wouldn't want to just hang out and have a beer with him."

Patrick looks at me for a moment, then lets out a huff of

laughter. "That was damned ballsy of you. Most people are scared of him."

"I am too…or I was. And I didn't think he'd want anything to do with Darius, but he did look into the situation. Though he also made it clear that he doesn't intend to do anything more. So I'm trying to find out about this bombing. Conrad was pretty convinced that Darius was there, but he couldn't confirm it. I won't believe he's dead unless there's proof."

Unless there's a body.

I block the horrific images constantly threatening to seep into the forefront of my thoughts.

"I've been in touch with Savko about this." I indicate the photo and explain that Savko's friend Martin is trying to find out who supplied it to Conrad. "I figure the more information we have, the better."

Patrick frowns. "I don't know that it's a great idea for you to be digging into Hawke's business."

"I'm not. I just want to find out where he got a military or government photo. Whoever has the means to obtain evidence of a strategic attack might know which officials were actually killed. General Balakin is the one they want to take down, right? So they'd want to verify his death, or at least find out if he was even in the factory when it was bombed."

Patrick leans forward, resting his elbows on his thighs. A light from the street slants across his face, illuminating the lines around his eyes.

"Look, Nell, I know this has been rough on you—"

"Oh, don't even go there." A bolt of irritation shoots

through me. "Don't be condescending. Yes, it's been *rough* on me. It's been even worse on Darius."

"Darius is an experienced—"

"And I'm a naive little art school graduate," I snap. "I get it. But that didn't stop him from falling in love with me."

Patrick doesn't seem shocked or even mildly surprised by my revelation. He links his hands together, his gaze on my phone.

"What I'm trying to say is that it would be more productive if you left this up to the authorities," he says.

I sit back and shake my head, not quite believing what I'm hearing. It's as if he's reading from the script of my former life, when other people had constantly tried to push me in directions I didn't want to go. And I'd obeyed.

Yeah, well...fuck that noise.

"What authorities?" I ask sharply. "The *authorities* couldn't get Darius out of PLF custody six years ago, could they? He was a hostage for well over a *year*, Patrick. If he hadn't escaped, he'd probably still be locked in the compound. What makes you think the so-called authorities even care where he is now?"

He rubs his hands over his face, the brackets around his mouth deepening. "There are at least a dozen of us trying to find out what happened to him. Probably a lot more."

"I know that, and yet so far I'm the only one who's learned anything useful. So don't you dare pat me on the head and tell me to let the grown-ups handle it."

Patrick's eyes are dark, his features set, but a faint glimmer of admiration appears in his expression. "I apologize. I didn't mean to be condescending. But Darius would kick my ass from here to eternity if he thought I wasn't looking out for you in his stead."

I sigh, knowing that's the truth. "Looking out for me and trying to stop me are two different things entirely. You're one of his best friends, Patrick. I love him. Surely you understand there's nothing that will stop me from trying to find him. *Nothing*."

He's silent for a long minute before he pulls a hand through his hair. "Could you at least do me a favor?"

"I'll try."

"Keep me informed, okay?" He pushes to his feet. "Let me know what you're doing, who you're talking to and contacting, what you find out. It'll make it easier to pool all our resources and information."

"Yes, of course." I pick up my phone and double-check that I have his current email and cell number. "You'll do the same for me?"

He bends to pick up his travel bag. "I have a bunch of meetings and appointments tomorrow, but I'll text you before I leave. Unfortunately, I won't have time to take you out to dinner."

"Next time." I rise and walk with him to the door. "Thanks again for letting me stay here. I haven't even started looking for a full-time job yet, but I'm planning to soon. I hope I can find another apartment sometime in July."

"Don't rush it." He opens the door. "Darius would want you to stay here for as long as you need to. I'll let people know the place is occupied indefinitely."

"Thank you, Patrick."

We exchange an embrace before he leaves.

I close the door. Only after turning the lock do I realize that I have no idea how many people have the key to the apartment. Obviously if they're all friends of Darius and Patrick, I have no reason for concern, but I don't know that they are.

I shake my head. I'm being silly. Of course Darius wouldn't give a key to someone he didn't trust implicitly. Or even to anyone else at all. Patrick is probably the only other person who has one.

A wave of fatigue washes over me. I've been up since four this morning, and now it's past midnight. Not to mention, an encounter with a speeding car—malicious intent or not—is enough to spook anyone. No wonder my imagination is getting the better of me.

I take a quick shower, letting the hot water ease the tension in my neck. After drying off, I pull on one of the massive, worn T-shirts I'd found in the dresser.

I recognize that it's a little obsessive to wear Darius's T-shirt to bed, but the soft, well-washed material feels so good against my skin. I love the reminder that he wore it countless times, that it was close to his body. I also sleep better with it on, imagining his scent is still woven into the frayed threads.

But tonight, the shirt doesn't provide its usual soporific comfort. I lie awake, staring at the shadows crawling across the ceiling.

I'm still unsettled by Patrick's visit, and I don't know why.

CHAPTER 8

Nell

JULY ARRIVES IN A SLUGGISH, humid torpor. The heat is already relentless, coursing in waves off the pavement, and the constant noise of the city adds to the oppressive atmosphere. Any leads about Darius hit wall after wall.

I try again to get into the Hawke Financial building to talk to Conrad, but the security guards order me to leave. When I call his assistant, she informs me that he's in Europe on business.

Although I'd given Conrad my number, I have no way of reaching him—not that further contact would do any good. But I have an incessant urge to be doing something. If I have to wait around for other people or the media to keep me informed, I'll explode with frustration.

I make a large red X over today's date on the wall

calendar I'd hung in the kitchen. Over a month since I left Varaz…and Darius didn't.

A Krasnovian media crew made it into Varaz a few days ago and have given reports of continued sporadic fighting. The news ran video footage of gun-riddled buildings, shattered windows, overturned statues in Harmony Square. Debris littered the cobblestones, and smoke rose from the charred remains of structures damaged by fires and pipe bombs.

I'd hardly recognized some of the streets. A number of residents were still there, hurrying in the background with their heads down, as if expecting to have to dodge a sniper bullet.

After watching the reports, I'd cried so hard my throat ached. The Krasnovian military might have the upper hand, but the destruction appears endless. Aside from contacting the humanitarian agencies, I don't know how else to find the friends I'd left behind—Ivan, Lara, Anna, Mr. Becherov, Josef, all the children who'd attended the school.

The media had reported the factory bombing, but aside from confirming that "top PLF officials" had been killed in the attack—one of them had *not* been General Balakin—there were no further details. Nothing about an American photojournalist.

In another video call, Alexei tells me the aid worker is looking for a "family of three" in the southern refugee camps. A new energy lights his eyes as he explains that there might not be many older men traveling with their daughter and grandson.

"There is good chance that if Marcus, Sofia, and Tomas

are in one of the camps, they will not be difficult to find," he says. "Especially if their names are in the registry."

Increasing the chance is the fact that Marcus and Sofia are also looking for Alexei and Jacob—so at some point, their efforts, like magnets, will hopefully connect.

Alexei's positive news lightens the heaviness that has settled in my bones. Despite all my emails, phone calls, and endless searching, I'm no closer to finding Darius than I was the day I drove away from him. I've even contacted private hostage rescue services, but they're not inclined to do anything since we don't even know where Darius is. Not to mention, Conrad Hawke is the only person who could afford the massive price tag.

After an afternoon shift at the bookstore, I stop and get a take-out sandwich and salad before returning to the apartment. I sit at the table with my laptop, eating a few bites while doing yet another in-depth search of websites.

In addition to searching for deeper content, I've also learned how to access the "dark web." Unfortunately, my browsing doesn't yield anything that seems useful, and most of the content is probably in code anyway. I'm not even sure what I expected to find there—a PLF chat room?

My phone buzzes. Savko.

We exchange greetings, and he confirms that the situation in parts of Krasnovar is improving, with the PLF having sustained three successive defeats in the southern province.

"That's great news," I tell him.

"Yes, but I have less good news for you," he says. "Martin was able to locate a digital image of the photo, but it is stripped of metadata, and he could not trace it back to any specific person."

I sigh. "Well, I know it was a long shot, but please thank him for trying. Where did he find it?"

Savko pauses. "Through a private server, I believe. He said there were four more images of the bombing site. He also accessed some information about transactions Conrad Hawke might have made. Unfortunately, I have not been able to examine the files in much depth."

"Considering that you're in the middle of a war, I won't hold it against you. Corporate reports should be the least of your concerns."

He chuckles. "I will send them to you, if you have interest. It's possible that the contact is listed somewhere in the files."

"Sure, I'll take a look at them."

He hesitates for a second. "There also appear to be details about Hawke Financial's business in Krasnovar."

"I didn't know Hawke Financial even had any business in Krasnovar." I shake my head at myself. There's no reason I should have known that.

"I guess it shouldn't be a surprise," I add. "They probably work all over the world. Maybe that's why Conrad was able to get the photos."

"True. I will send you what Martin found along with the digital files of the photos. I should send it via courier, but I have no idea when it would reach you. Courier and mail services are severely disrupted. So I'll send it through a secure server, but you must download it and transfer it to a flash drive right away. Then erase it from your computer."

"Wow. I feel like an international spy."

"Nell, I am not making a joke. This is important procedure."

I remind myself that Savko is a fixer who is frequently involved in illicit dealings. It's his default to be overly cautious.

"Do this right away, Nell," he insists.

"Okay, I promise."

"Anything else Martin finds, I will try and get it to you a different way."

A few minutes after we end the call, a message from him pings on my email with a link to access the files. Since he knows far more about subterfuge and things like "digital footprints," I follow his orders and download the files. After transferring them to a flash drive, I delete them from the laptop, then open them through the flash drive.

The other four photos are different angles of the bombed-out factory—curls of smoke rising, bodies littering the ground alongside the debris. I spare them a cursory glance this time, not wanting to imagine Darius among the rubble.

I put the photos aside and scan the other files. I have very little idea what I'm looking at—documents and spreadsheets littered with numbers. Many of them are in other languages. They all appear to lack any company name or address, and none of them have the Hawke Financial logo. There are different kinds of maps and multiple reports with phrases like *lithium hydroxide - 4.4% to $8,825/t.*

I scroll through a few of the other documents. There are more than I'd expected—several hundred at least.

Though I don't know what it all means, an uneasy sensation begins to collect in my chest. This is clearly private, if not classified, information about various business transactions, which means Martin obtained them by hacking into the Hawke Financial databases or whatever computer system they have.

Which also means he took my request to a whole different level.

I open my web browser and delete my search history and the messages from Savko, then I delete his texts from my phone.

Overkill and paranoia, no doubt, but I'm still on edge after the close encounter with the blue sedan, not to mention all these increasingly fraught questions. And after Patrick's visit, I've been sleeping even worse than usual now that I've realized other people might have a key to the apartment. There's a security chain on the inside of the door, but it's not much of a barricade.

I put the flash drive in a pouch on the front of my backpack. With so much talk about secure Wi-Fi networks, I probably shouldn't look at the files here on my laptop. I have no idea if someone would be able to "see" what I was doing, but given that an expert like Martin could get records from Hawke Financial, which probably has top-of-the-line cybersecurity, I'd rather not take the chance.

Tomorrow before work, I'll go to the library and use one of the public computers to search the documents more closely for a possible contact connected to the photos. Then I'll throw the flash drive away since I'm sure this is all information I'm not supposed to have.

I close my laptop and get ready for bed, pulling on one of Darius's T-shirts. Before I turn off the living room lights, I make sure the security chain on the door is firmly locked in place. I start toward the bedroom, then stop and take hold of a large, overstuffed armchair.

I drag the chair across the floor and wedge it securely against the door. It's not exactly an armed guard, but at least now no one can get in without making a lot of noise.

"You're a disgrace to international spydom, Nell Fairchild," I mutter to myself as I double-check the locks. "Where are the lasers and secret codes?"

My attempt at lighthearted thinking doesn't ease my tension. I've always been self-protective, guarded, cautious. I've often had reason to be apprehensive. During the siege in Varaz, I learned the true meaning of the word *terror*.

But I'm safe now. I'm back at home, which is what Darius wanted for me all along.

I pull his T-shirt more closely around me. I have no reason to be scared for anyone but him. I don't need to be scared for my own safety anymore.

So why am I?

CHAPTER 9

Darius

"YOU HAVE TO FIND HER." The boy dug his fingers into his palms.

His father stood beside the fireplace, arms folded and his gaze on the hand-carved ebony and boxwood chess set on the table in front of him. The older the boy got—he'd just turned sixteen—the more he noticed how much he looked like his father. And the more he hated the resemblance.

Silence lay heavy in the room. The rest of the house was filled with ribboned garlands, wreaths, and elegant Christmas trees. Magazine perfect for the exclusive holiday party his father hosted for the top Hawke Financial executives and their spouses.

The boy had returned yesterday for winter break. Odette and Katherine were the only reasons he hadn't stayed at boarding school, which was saying something considering how much he disliked Harkson Academy.

Slowly his father moved the black rook.

"I don't," he said, "*have* to do anything."

"She's been missing for four days."

Conrad Hawke's expression didn't change. The boy's heart punched his ribs. He hadn't heard from his sister in over a week. Neither had Odette. Katherine hadn't returned their calls and texts.

His father hadn't called the police. He'd forbidden anyone else to either. For years, he'd done everything in his power to prevent anyone from knowing about Katherine's increasingly unmanageable behavior. Even if the police did know that Katherine was missing, they wouldn't do anything about it. Not with Conrad Hawke calling the shots.

"You *have to* find her," the boy repeated.

His father smirked. "Like you *have to* stay in school? Doing a shit job of that, aren't you? The headmaster said you were protecting some weakass coward from bullies, but you and I know differently, don't we? You have no control. No self-restraint. You just love to fight. That's only one of the things that makes you such a fucking disappointment."

The boy swallowed a flame of anger. His father was right —there was freedom in the explosive rush of fighting. It was a way of taking control and letting loose at the same time. His father would never understand that.

"Katherine is your daughter." The boy forced the conversation back to his sister.

"She is not my daughter." His father's voice twisted around the last word, and he thumped the white knight a little too hard on the board. "She's a pain in the ass and a liability. If I'd known she'd turn out like this, I'd never have married her mother."

The boy didn't know if any of them would be better or worse off if Conrad hadn't married Odette.

"It'll be down to fifteen degrees tonight," he said. "What if she's outside?"

His father shrugged and moved a black pawn. "Then she'd better find a way to get inside."

The boy stepped closer. Anger burned low in his gut. He hadn't expected his father to do anything for Katherine. He'd never done a damned good thing for anyone. But he wouldn't let his father throw Katherine away. Not without a fight.

"If you don't look for her," he said, his voice cold, "if you don't *find* her, I'll go to the press. I'll call every fucking news-paper and wire service on the east coast and tell them Conrad Hawke's seventeen-year-old *daughter* is missing. That she has mental health issues and is on medication, but he can't be bothered to give a flying fuck that she walked out of his house four days ago and hasn't been heard from since."

His father's eyes iced over. "Don't you fucking threaten me."

"I'll do more than threaten you." The boy stopped on the other side of the chessboard. He was almost as tall as his father now and looked him in the eye. "I'll blackmail you. What'll it do for your name and reputation if news spreads that you couldn't give a shit about your daughter? What'll your investors and partners think? And what would they think about the stories I could tell them? Do you really want the world to know what a sick fuck you are?"

His father's arm came up swiftly. Hard satisfaction filled

the boy's chest. Provoking Conrad Hawke to physical violence meant you'd gotten to him. Usually he left the dirty work to his associates. Like the dickhead he'd hired nearly every year to kidnap his son and dump him in a desert or a forest for "survival training."

The boy shot his hand out and grabbed his father's wrist, stopping the upward arc of his arm the instant before it made contact. Brief surprise flicked over Conrad's face. His muscles tightened. The boy shoved him away.

They stared at each other. The air thickened. Hot and oppressive.

"So." The boy smirked. "Who's the disappointment now? No, you're worse than that. You're a failure."

His father's eyes burned. "Get out."

The boy grabbed the chessboard and upended it. The pieces scattered and spilled over the thick carpet. He threw the board at the fireplace and stalked to the door.

"Find her," he snapped. "Or you'll regret it."

His stepmother was waiting in the corridor, her hand at her throat, still as a statue. Her aquiline features were enhanced with makeup, her blond hair pulled into a smooth, fancy twist. She'd always been beautiful, but in the seven years she'd been married to Conrad, her blue eyes had dulled, and lines cracked across her smooth skin.

"What did he say?" Her voice was barely a whisper. She was afraid to move near her husband, lest she disturb the air around him.

The boy tightened his jaw. Odette's struggles with both her husband and her daughter were wearing her down, like a board bowing under too much weight.

"You don't have to stay," he said again. He'd lost track of

the number of times he'd told her that. *Leave. Get out. Divorce him.*

Her answer was always the same. *Where would I go? What would I do? The prenup doesn't leave me with much. And what about Katherine?*

Now Odette didn't reply, only darted her gaze to the office as if her husband's shadow were watching.

The boy put his hand on her arm. "He won't get away with this."

Relief softened her features, and she embraced him. "Thank god you're home."

If his father did send out people to search for Katherine, the boy never knew. He was the one who found her two days later, after scouring all the places he thought she might be. Only after remembering her rambling talk about a cross-country road trip did he track her down to a shithole bus stop in West Virginia.

She was out of money, sleeping on a bench, hungry and unwashed. It made him sick—his delicate, vulnerable sister at the mercy of the world. She wasn't good at taking care of herself. Odette didn't know how to take care of her. His father had a whole other definition of "take care of."

The boy sat next to Katherine on the bench. "You need to come home."

She rested her head on his shoulder. Her blond hair was tangled and greasy. "I hate it there. He locked me in the basement again."

The boy's spine tensed. The dark scared her, made her scream. His father knew it. But he put her there so he wouldn't hear her.

"Mom can't do anything." Katherine rubbed her temple. "No one can."

I can.

"I'll take care of it." He rose to his feet, picking up the plastic bag that held her belongings. He'd been battling his father for years, ever since his mother died. But he wasn't going to fight anymore. He could break away, sever all ties with the man who darkened every corner of his life. Conrad Hawke wasn't worth it. He had nothing the boy wanted or needed.

"He won't hurt you or your mother again," he told his sister. "I promise."

Even then, he knew the promise would come with a brutal price. And to drag it out, keep him on edge, his father might wait years to make him pay.

CHAPTER 10

Nell

As FAR AS I can tell, aside from the digital photos of the factory bombing, the Hawke Financial files contain no information about the war or anyone who might have been able to obtain military photographs—not that I can even understand most of the documents.

I do learn that *lithium hydroxide* is a compound used in lithium ion batteries, and it and other mineral deposits can be found in underground mines. I also figure out that the documents are written in Russian and several Eastern European languages—mostly Moldovan and Krasnovian.

I run them through a few online translation sites, but the results are incomprehensible since the verbiage is dense and appears to be incredibly technical. Far beyond my limited knowledge.

I take the flash drive out of the library computer. My overall takeaway is that Hawke Financial has an interest in mining, possibly for battery minerals. My search on "battery minerals" yields articles about supply chains and the use of the minerals for clean energy.

So maybe Conrad Hawke is doing something progressive. And if he's not, I don't care. I'm only interested in how he can help Darius. Whatever else he does with his corporation—and I have no doubt it's not all legal—is his business.

I slip the drive into the zippered pouch in my backpack, not ready to discard it yet as I haven't scrutinized all the documents, and I don't want to throw the photo files away.

I should feel guilty about not caring if Conrad Hawke is laundering money or whatever other white-collar crimes men like him engage in, but the vast infrastructure of corporate transactions is probably rife with corruption and misconduct. Taking that on in any capacity whatsoever is not what I need to do right now. Or ever. I'm far more concerned about Darius and the people living through yet another war.

I leave the library and walk down the stone steps, squinting against the glaring sun. The air is so thick with humidity that it's like breathing through a wet paper tissue.

I descend to the subway and take the next train to the 96th Street station. I walk a couple of blocks to Pen and Paper and am sweating by the time I arrive. Lindsey is arranging new releases at a counter near the front.

"Hey, I got you an iced coffee." She nods toward the back room. "I put it in the freezer so the ice wouldn't melt."

"You're a goddess, thank you so much." With a groan, I

stop in front of the air-conditioning vent and let the cold air wash over me.

"How was the library?" Lindsey stacks several biographies on the table.

"Good. I found listings for some new full-time job openings, so I'll get the applications filled out later tonight." I deflect a pang of guilt over the lie. Though I showed her and Tom the factory photos, I haven't mentioned the files Savko sent. I'm still troubled by the way they were obtained, and I don't want Lindsey thinking I'm getting involved in something underhanded.

After stashing my backpack in my locker and retrieving the iced coffee, I spend the rest of the afternoon helping customers, finalizing details for an author's book signing, and stocking books.

I open a box to reveal stacks of artist's sketchbooks, which make my heart clench. I can hardly remember the last time I drew or sketched anything. I'd had my sketchbooks in my backpack when we were getting out of Varaz, so I still have all the drawings I'd done while I was there, but I haven't even thought about my art in what feels like ages.

I leaf through one of the sketchbooks, all the thick, crisp pages waiting to be filled with images of whatever strikes my fancy—portraits of people on the subway, flowers in Central Park, the front of a café.

During my break, I purchase the sketchbook and a new set of pens. As I put both in my backpack, a current of anticipation goes through me. Returning to my art might be just what I need to steady myself, regain my balance, feel like Nell again.

Lindsey leaves early to attend a movie screening with Tom, so I close up the shop by myself. At nine thirty, I turn off the lights and head outside, locking the door behind me.

I start back to the apartment, then spot an all-night diner across the street. If I go back to the apartment now, I'll fall again into the rabbit hole of searching for news about Krasnovar.

I cross to the diner and request a booth. After the waitress brings me water, I order a salad and a bowl of mac and cheese. As I'm waiting for the food, I open the new sketchbook and pen set.

I start to draw, letting my hand make the shapes that have always been so familiar to me. My original character Winsome Swift begins to appear on the page, her red cloak swirling around her legs, her long hair whipping in an unseen wind.

I end up staying at the diner for two hours. I fill five pages with sketches of Winsome Swift, then treat myself to a slice of apple pie with ice cream. I'd been right—getting back to my artwork, one of the core things that makes me *me*— will keep me anchored and strong.

After paying the bill and adding a generous tip, I wait for the bus that goes through Central Park to the west side. It's close to midnight, and only one other person—a stocky man in a gray suit—is waiting. When the bus rolls to a stop, he waits for me to board first.

I pass him and climb the steps. For some reason, a slight chill runs down my spine. I show the driver my card and take a seat close to the front. The man gets on and walks to the back.

I'm accustomed to being on guard in the city, especially late at night, but my recent wariness feels deeper, like it's an extension of how terrified I'd been in Varaz. As the bus cuts through Central Park, I resist the urge to look back at the man, to see how far away he's sitting.

It's not a long drive, and I stand to exit through the back doors. As I walk forward, I sense his gaze on me, but when I look his way, he's staring out the window at the darkness.

Have I seen him before? He has the same build as the security guards at Hawke Financial—heavyset and jowly—but was he one of them? Or am I letting my imagination get the better of me again?

Praying he doesn't get off at my stop, I hurry down the steps. The doors shut behind me. The air brakes hiss, and the bus lumbers forward.

Though the man didn't follow me off the bus, the peace that I'd found again while drawing shatters. I walk quickly back to Darius's apartment building. I don't know if I'm more afraid of the reality that someone could be out to cause me harm or the idea that I might be imagining it.

My mother had suffered from paranoid delusions. More than once, she'd believed people were out to get her and—

No. Stop. You are not your mother.

My eyes burn. I break into a jog, not stopping until I'm inside and locked behind the security doors. I climb to the fifth floor and let myself into the darkened apartment.

I toss my backpack on the sofa and hurry into the kitchen to splash water on my face. The cold water helps jolt me back to my senses, but my chest is so tight it's hard to pull in a breath. I pour water into a glass and take a long gulp. Maybe I should—

My heart jams into my throat. *What was that noise?*

It sounded like the creak of a door hinge.

Coming from the bedroom.

Holy shit.

I grip the glass tighter. My skin prickles with fear. I've been so concerned with keeping the door locked while I'm here that I hadn't thought about anyone entering when I'm away.

Get out, Nell. Get. Out. Now.

The order fires through my brain, jolting me into action. I put the glass down and start across the living room to the front door.

My peripheral vision catches a sudden movement. A big, male silhouette appears in the bedroom doorway, cloaked in shadows.

A scream lodges in my throat. I bolt toward the door, scrambling to unlatch the security chain. My heartbeat pounds in my ears. A deep voice resounds behind me, echoing like thunder, but I can't make out any words past the terror.

I get the chain unfastened and have my hand on the doorknob when two muscular arms clamp around me from behind, hauling me backward. I start to fight, to kick and yell, when something inside me suddenly unknots and loosens.

He's still talking. His voice isn't harsh or threatening. It's low and soothing and—

Oh my god.

I squeeze my eyes shut. My breath burns my lungs. The thumping sound decreases, letting in the meaning of his words.

"Nell...baby, it's okay. It's me. It's me."

I go still. My acute fear drains away. His arms are locked tight around me, his torso an inflexible wall against my back. Everything about him—his body, his arms, his scent, his voice—shocks me with both disbelief and unbearable warmth.

"Turn around." His grip loosens. "Look at me."

Tears flood my eyes. A sharp longing spreads through me, tangling with the love I've clung to so desperately for days, weeks, months, years. Everything inside me hurts from wanting this to be true and yet—

"Nell." The rumble of his voice spills right to my soul. "Please."

I turn, unable to breathe, my mind fogging. I stare at his chest clad in a worn blue T-shirt, and then slowly force my gaze upward—past the strong column of his throat, his jaw dusted with stubble, his beautiful mouth.

He's looking at me, into me. His brown eyes are blood-shot, etched with lines of fatigue, and filled with a deep, aching tenderness.

I can't speak. But I don't have to. He cups my face in both of his hands and brushes his thumbs across my cheeks before bringing his mouth down on mine.

A thousand sensations explode inside me—stars bursting open, oceans surging with light, the moon spinning across the sky. His kiss is so warm, gentle at first and then increasingly possessive.

Dizziness washes over me. My pulse races. He moves his lips over mine with both care and intensity, as if he's imprinting himself on me all over again. The familiarity of him begins to penetrate my shock, melting the ice in my veins.

I don't dare touch him, fearing this illusion will shatter if I do, but I let myself absorb the sheer pleasure of his kiss, his touch, his overpowering presence. In my darker moments, I'd thought I would only ever again feel his lips on mine in a dream.

Then he lifts his head, and I open my eyes, and he's still there, as solid and powerful as a mountain. He rubs his thumb across my lower lip, tracking his gaze over my face almost as if he can't believe I'm real any more than I can believe he's actually here.

"I love you," he says.

I burst into tears. He slides his hands under my rear and lifts me against him. He walks to the sofa and sits, pulling me closer. I straddle his lap and bury my face in his shoulder as all my anguish and wild, intense joy come pouring out in a deluge of sobs.

Darius.

He tightens his arms around me, anchoring one hand against the back of my head. I cry until his shirt is wet with my tears, until my chest aches and my throat is scraped raw.

When the storm begins to ease and my sobs lessen to hiccups, I close my eyes and savor the feeling of his body against mine. His heartbeat thumps against my breasts. His arms are pillars of strength and security. I press my face to his neck and inhale—no spices or citrus now, just the warm, clean scent of him.

I ease back slowly, meeting his gaze. His eyes are glittering, the angles of his face sharpened by his scruff. A long scratch cuts down his temple and dark circles ring his eyes, but he is undoubtedly the man who holds my heart in the palm of his hand.

He brushes his fingers against the scar on my forehead and wipes away the tears still dampening my cheeks. A tremble courses through me.

"Darius." His name escapes me on a breath. "How...what did..."

"I'll tell you everything." He settles his palm against the side of my neck. "But first I need to know that you're okay."

I nod, though I'm not sure *okay* can describe how I've been these past few weeks. It certainly can't describe how I am right now—caught in this spiraling whirlwind of exhilaration and disbelief. There are no words for this feeling.

"I'm okay," I manage to say. "I can't...I can't believe you're here. I was so scared for you, this whole time. How did you...when did you get here? What hap—"

"Nell, have you felt unsafe at all?" he interrupts. "Threatened in any way?"

I sit back on his thighs and stare at him. How would he know that? "I...a few times, I've gotten a little spooked, but I haven't been threatened. Why are you asking?"

"I've heard about your investigation, and I don't like where it's going."

"You mean my search for you?" Baffled, I shake my head. "All I've done since I left Varaz is try to find out what happened to you."

His expression darkens slightly, even as he leans forward to press his lips against mine. I let the brief contact flood me with light before pulling back to look at him again.

"Darius, what happened?" I spread my hands over his chest, struck by the solidness of his muscles through his shirt, his sheer physical presence. Warmth pulses up my arms. "Are *you* all right? How are you even here?"

"I managed to get out after the Krasnovian army bombed the factory. I'd memorized several maps of the mountain when we were in Varaz in case you and I had to cross the range to get to safety. So I more or less knew the route to the border of Moldova."

"You *walked* all the way to Moldova?"

He nods, pulling his hand away from my neck to look at his watch. "I'll tell you the rest of it later. Right now, we need to go."

"Go? Go where?"

He lifts me at the same time that he stands, then he sets me gently back on my feet. "Get all your important stuff together. Anything you don't need, you can leave here."

I have a sudden, unwelcome flashback to our escape from Varaz, when we'd grabbed whatever we could before running. "Darius, what's going on?"

He presses another swift, hard kiss to my lips. "Later. I promise."

I untangle myself from him and go into the bathroom. Part of my brain is still clouded with shock—maybe when I walk back out, he'll have disappeared like an apparition—but I am also sharply aware of the fact that I'd stalled when he first showed up in Varaz and asked me to leave with him. As a result—

With a groan, I splash cold water on my face. None of that matters anymore.

Darius is here. Alive. It's as if my heart is repeating those words with every beat, like a mantra. *He's alive. He's safe. He's here. Here.*

He looks up from his phone when I emerge from the bathroom. I didn't bring a lot with me when I came to New York, so I throw a few clothes and toiletries into my travel bag and stuff my other sketchbooks and laptop in my backpack.

Darius picks up the bag, and we leave the apartment. Though I'm burning with questions, I keep quiet and follow him down into the subway.

He grabs my hand as we exit at the 42nd Street Times Square station. Maneuvering through the Friday night crowd, we pass partygoers, theater patrons, and aggressive hawkers.

We end up at a dingy hotel smashed between a fast-food restaurant and a strip joint. Graffiti covers the facade, and the foyer is dark and musty.

Darius guides me ahead of him as we climb the narrow stairwell to the sixth floor. He reaches around me to unlock the beat-up door of a room at the end of the hallway.

The instant the door opens, a cry breaks from my throat. I fall to my knees.

Poe lunges into my arms, almost knocking me backward, his body wiggling wildly with joy, his tail thumping so hard it hits the sides of the doorframe. I start to laugh and cry at the same time as he licks my face, my arms, my hands.

"Oh, Poe. My beautiful boy." I press my face into his soft, thick fur and hug him as tight as I can, ensuring he, too, is really here.

"I can't believe it." I look at Darius in astonishment and rise to my feet. "How did this happen?"

"We ended up partners on quite a journey." He rubs Poe's head affectionately as we enter the room. "It took some logistical work to get him out of the country, but no way was I coming back to you without him."

After locking the door, he sets the travel bag and my backpack on a chair. I sit on the bed with Poe as the dog continues wiggling and panting with excitement. I hug him close, still reeling with both disbelief and joy at having both him and Darius back again, whole and healthy.

I scratch his ears and glance around the room, which is no better than the rest of the hotel—peeling paint, thread-bare carpet, rusty sink. In good news, the sheets and towels all look clean, and there's a wrapped bar of soap on the counter.

Darius's duffel bag is on a luggage rack, and one of his T-shirts is crumpled at the foot of the bed.

"How long have you been staying here?" I ask. "Why didn't you call me?"

"I couldn't risk anyone tracing a call or a text." He strides to the window and peers down at the street. "I just got in a couple of hours ago. I wanted to check in before coming to get you."

"Why here instead of the Eastlake Hotel?"

I couldn't care less about the room—I'd stay in a roach motel if it meant I could be with him and Poe—but none of this makes any sense.

He turns from the window. A neon light flashes from the opposite building, creating a pattern of light and dark across his face.

My heart clenches with a combination of relief, trepidation, and wild, desperate love. Though in some ways the lockdown in Varaz had felt like an eternity, for Darius and me, for us, it had been almost no time at all. A second in the span of the years we'd been apart, all the hours and days I'd longed for him so desperately while fearing I would never have him. That he would never come back.

He opens his arms. "Come here."

I cross the distance between us in three strides. Warmth floods me the instant he encloses me in his unbreakable grip. Our mouths crash together. A thousand sparks light the air. He steps toward the bed, pausing to give Poe a narrow look. He points at a corner of the room, where there is a nest of pillows and blankets. The dog lumbers off to paw at his own bed.

I wrap my arms around Darius's shoulders as he lowers me onto the mattress and braces himself above me. My whole body surges with hot anticipation. He covers me like a thundercloud, his powerful frame pressing against every inch of me. He tracks his gaze over my face, his eyes dark and glittering, then brings his mouth down on mine.

I part my lips and drive my fingers into his hair. My arousal fires up like a match set to dry timber. We seek, explore, and devour each other with urgent hunger, as if we need to reaffirm our reunion, being together again. He presses his lips to my cheek, his scruff prickly against my skin, and down to the pulse pounding in my neck. His breath is hot.

"Christ, you feel amazing." He presses one hand between my legs. My blood goes into full boil. I arch into his palm, aching to feel his touch on my bare skin.

"Hurry," I whisper.

He has never been rough with me, never yanked off my clothes in a frenzy of need, no matter how much I might have wanted him to, but now a sudden, feral energy radiates from him.

He lifts himself away from me to strip off my shoes, jeans, and shirt, raking his gaze over my near-naked body. He unfastens my bra with a quick twist of his fingers, then sits back between my legs and stares at me, his eyes brewing with heat.

"Fucking perfect." He strokes his hands over my breasts, cupping their weight and thumbing my stiff nipples. Sparks ripple across my skin. We both watch the movement of his hands, the response of my body, as our breathing increases and the air thickens with lust.

"Oh." I want to squeeze my thighs together to ease the burgeoning ache, but my legs are splayed over his lap. "I think you could make me come just by doing that."

A smile tugs at his mouth. He trails his hand between my breasts, across my belly and down between my legs. When he presses his finger into my cleft and rubs my damp underwear against me, I buck my hips upward with an involuntary moan.

He presses harder, watching me. The heavy bulge in his jeans is tantalizingly close to my sex, and I try to writhe against him, but he stills me with a hand on my thigh and slips his forefinger beneath the cotton.

"Oh my god." The bright thread of tension coiling around me tightens. I fumble for his other hand, desperate now for something to hold on to. "Please."

He moves back only long enough to strip off my under-wear, dropping it to the floor. I grip his left hand as he resumes his caresses with his right, shifting his gaze from my face over my body. My nipples are sticking straight up, aching for his touch or his mouth, but I don't want him to stop what he's doing.

"Darius." I close my eyes, everything in me straining toward that break in pressure, the flood of relief.

"Come on, honey." He probes his finger inside me and eases it back and forth while circling my clit with his thumb. "Nice and hard."

Squirming, I pump my hips upward to encourage his deeper penetration, fisting my other hand in the bedcovers. One more stroke, and shocks of pleasure fly through me. I whimper, shaking and trembling as he continues urging every last delicious sensation from my body.

"Please." I disentangle our hands and fist the front of his shirt. "Take off your clothes. Fuck me."

His breath escapes on a low hiss. He pulls his shirt over his head, revealing his hard muscles and scarred skin. The shadows and neon lights move across his smooth, broad shoulders like wings.

A gasp catches in my throat at the sight of the heavy, dark bruise crawling from his ribcage all the way up his side. I reach out to touch it carefully, and he lets me, as he always does—no part of him is off-limits to my curiosity. Not even the damaged parts.

I trace the uneven edges of the bruise, an ugly black, green, and purple like a rotten plum. My heart aches at the bleak speculation of how he'd sustained the wound.

As if sensing my encroaching despair, he catches my wrist and brings my palm to his lips. Then he sheds his jeans, and my attention snaps to the length of his erection pressing against his boxer briefs.

Licking my dry lips, I sit up and pull the briefs down over

his hips. His shaft emerges as if it has a life of its own, rising upward, thick and hard as steel, yet malleable at the same time. I want to taste him, to run my tongue across the veined length, but he pushes me back onto the bed and slants his mouth over mine again.

"Can't wait," he murmurs against my lips.

"Neither can I." I curve my legs around his thighs, reveling in the sensation of my breasts crushing against his bare chest.

With a groan, he reaches down and pushes into me with a single hard stroke. A sharp cry tears from my chest as he sinks deep inside, stretching me, filling me.

This time, there's no pause, no waiting for me to adjust— he pulls back and pushes forward immediately, again and again, repeated thrusts that jostle me so hard my breasts bounce and my thighs ache. Never before has he fucked me with such determined possession, as if he's claiming me as his all over again.

But he doesn't have to claim me at all. I will always be his.

I wind my arms around him, digging my fingers into his shoulder blades as he surges back and forth, his mouth on mine, open and hot. His eyes are black, on fire with lust. He's everywhere, consuming me, his breath rasping against my skin, his hands clutching my hips, his hair-roughened thighs abrading mine.

It won't last long, we're both too worked up, but oh my god, the feel of his thick cock stroking me from the inside out has me writhing and crying out with every plunge. Arousal whips through me again, pulling me upward, but this time I force it under control and open my eyes so I can watch him—his mouth set, his eyes burning, sweat dampening his hard-edged features.

Our rhythm gets faster. The air floods with the sounds of our gasps and moans, our bodies slapping together, his deep, low refrain of *you feel so damned good, so tight and hot,* that drives my need to unbearable heights.

I grip his biceps, opening my mouth to pull in air. His penetration almost starts to hurt, the raw friction and sheer effort of taking him in. As if sensing my discomfort, he slows and pauses, his hot gaze searching mine. With a moan, I bend my body toward him in a silent plea. In the past, he has been almost too careful with me, and I'm desperate for him to keep going, to give me all that he has.

"Harder." I grab his hair, tugging him down to me and pressing my lips against his. "Oh, you feel so good. Give it to me, please."

I sense his grab at self-restraint, his brief hesitation. I clutch him and tighten my inner muscles around his shaft, drawing him in deeper. He groans into my mouth and pushes forward, his pace increasing again.

"Come inside me." I sink my teeth into his shoulder, gripping his muscular back, my whole body rolling and quivering under the force of his thrusts. "I want to feel you."

His rough shout reverberates clear down to my bones the instant before he drives into me and stills, his body tensing and flexing. As if incited by his release, I start coming before he's even done, another wave of explosions billowing through me, lighting up every nerve.

After we both slide down the other side, Darius rolls off me, chest heaving.

"Goddamn." He pulls me closer and buries his face in my hair. "I missed you."

I give a choked laugh, even as sudden tears sting my eyes. Still trembling, I spread my hand over his chest and tuck myself against his side.

He settles his arm heavily over me. Part of my mind prickles with the knowledge that this haven is only tempo-rary—that something is wrong—but I force the unease aside and let myself sink into his endless strength.

CHAPTER 11

Nell

I PUSH TO MY ELBOW, blinking away the threads of sleep. My blood is still pulsing gently. The room is dim, only the incessant glow of the neon signs appearing through the curtains.

Sometime during the night, Poe clambered onto the bed, and his weight is heavy against my leg. The faint sound of his snoring mixes with the rumble of a garbage truck from the street.

Darius is sitting in a chair by the window, clad only in a pair of worn jeans, one foot on the windowsill. He is breathtakingly beautiful—his messy dark hair falling over his forehead, his chest sculpted in shadows, his features sharp against the white wall. He's gazing at me. His eyes are pensive and opaque.

"Did you sleep okay?" He moves to sit on the side of the bed and reaches out to drag his fingers through my hair.

I nod, shifting to rest my head in his lap. I still feel the echoing throb of him inside me. "What time is it?"

"Almost four." He settles his big hand against my neck. "We have to leave soon."

A slight tension in his tone makes me look up. His eyes crease with concern, and there's a faint line between his brows. Goose bumps rise over my skin. I sit up slowly and reach for his discarded T-shirt, pulling it over my head.

"Why do we have to leave?" I shake my head and huff out a laugh. "I guess my question should be...why are we here in the first place?"

He presses a kiss to my forehead before easing away. He takes two bottles of water out of his backpack and returns to hand me one.

"What, exactly, happened back in Varaz?" I sit up against the pillows and twist the cap off the bottle. "How did you get away?"

He sits down again, his chest heaving with a sigh. "A few days after you and the others left, the PLF was planning to take me to General Balakin. I didn't know where he was, but I assumed it was near Telina. I was in the backseat of one of the PLF trucks when the Krasnovian fighters bombed the factory. The blast threw the truck sideways. I lost consciousness for...I don't know how long.

"When I came to, there was chaos everywhere. The factory was demolished, parts of it on fire, soldiers were dead or injured, others were mobilizing for a counterattack. I knew it was my only chance, so I hauled myself out of the truck and ran...well, stumbled back to the road.

"I saw Poe crouched behind a pile of bricks, and I realized he'd been roaming around the area ever since you left. I managed to grab him by the collar, and we headed into the woods. I'd hoped the PLF wouldn't think to look for me there."

"Did they?"

"Not that I know of. Poe and I hauled ass to get as deep into the forest as we could. Reaching Moldova was our best chance of escape. I tracked our route and timing via the sun and the stars, plus whatever I could remember about the terrain."

"How long were you out there?"

"Four days or so, based on what I figured out." He pauses and reaches out to pet the dog, who is still snoring gently. "Poe was a champ. Didn't stop, even when his paws started bleeding. One day after we crossed a valley, I saw an asphalt road winding around the side of a mountain. We made it up the side of the cliff, and a truck driver saw us and stopped. He took us to a border town where we were both able to get medical care and food."

My throat tightens. I can't even fathom him and Poe slogging day and night through the wilderness.

"How did you survive?"

"I knew what plants and berries were edible. We found a few creeks for fresh water. Caught a fish a couple of times. It was rough but kept us going." He smiles faintly. "We'd never been so glad to see beef stew and bread, though. Not to mention people. And we were lucky that neither of us was badly injured."

"How long did you stay in the border town?"

"Three days. Then we took a bus to the capital city. That's where I've been for the past few weeks."

"When did you call the US embassy?"

He shakes his head. "I didn't."

"You didn't contact the embassy at all? Why not?"

"I called Patrick instead."

"So he helped you to…wait a minute." I stare at him as the truth begins to dawn. I quickly do the calculations in my head. "I saw Patrick in New York ten or eleven days ago. He's known almost this whole time that you were alive? He knew when he came to your apartment?"

Darius nods, his jaw tightening. "He's the one who told me you were there."

I shake my head. That must have been why Patrick had been acting so strange that night—he knew Darius was alive, had even been in contact with him, but he was keeping those facts from me. Even though he also knew what I'd been going through trying to find Darius.

"But why didn't Patrick tell me you were safe and in Moldova?" Though his and Poe's return is all that matters, I can't prevent my utter confusion. "Why didn't he tell me? Why didn't *you*? I was trying so hard to…to find out where you were…so scared you'd been in the factory when the bombs dropped, and instead of—"

"Nell." He captures my wrist in his hand. Faint desperation rises to his eyes. "Believe me, you were the first person I wanted to call. The *only* person. But I couldn't."

"Why not?"

"Because I didn't want you to know I was alive."

He didn't want me to know he was alive.

My mind repeats that bizarre notion several times, but it still makes no sense.

"No one could know." Darius tightens his grip on my wrist. "The whole time Poe and I were in the forest, I expected the PLF to come after me. Especially once Balakin discovered I'd escaped the bombing. They wouldn't give up just because I crossed the border, especially if their forces were taking a hit."

"Why not?"

"Because they think I know too much about the structure of their organization and how they're getting financed."

"You do, right? That's what you told Lenkov."

"I was bluffing." He shrugs. "We don't know much of anything about the PLF financing or how they managed to reorganize after the civil war. No international agency has ever done a full investigation of them because they weren't considered a big threat. Until now, of course."

"But Lenkov believed you. Or at least he wanted to find out exactly what information you have on them."

Darius nods. "That's why I don't want them to know I'm still alive. They wouldn't want me to take any action against them from the outside. And for all I know they've put a bounty on my head. So my best bet was to lie low and hope that they thought I'd been killed in the blast."

"And that meant not contacting anyone." My breathing eases a little as I process his explanation.

"Except Patrick. I had to know if you'd made it out, if you and the others were okay. I knew he'd know. I also needed his help getting out of Moldova without a passport or any kind of ID. Between that and the logistics of bringing Poe with me, it took longer than I wanted."

No wonder Patrick hadn't been surprised when I'd told him I was in love with Darius. He already knew.

"Why didn't you just stay in Moldova?" I ask. "It was safe, wasn't it? No one knew who you were."

A shadow cuts across his face. "Patrick called me after he'd talked to you. He said you went to my father."

I nod, twisting the water bottle cap between my fingers. "I understand that you wouldn't have wanted me to, but *no one* could find out anything about where you were or what had happened to you after I left Varaz. Your father was the only person I knew of who had the kind of resources we needed."

The muscles around his jaw tighten. He pushes to his feet and paces to the door.

"Please don't be angry." I move to sit on the side of the bed. "You have to know I'd have gone to the queen of England if I'd thought she could help find you."

He shakes his head. "I'm not mad. It makes me love you even more, that you'd go to such lengths for me. But you shouldn't have been able to get anywhere near Conrad Hawke. Or he should've refused to talk to you. Had you banned from his office."

"I expected him to. Honestly, I didn't think I'd even get into the building, much less talk to him face-to-face. And when I did, I thought he'd refuse to do anything, so I was kind of shocked when he did."

"Which makes me wonder about his motives. It wasn't from concern about me." Darius looks at me, his gaze hooded. A strange tension laces his shoulders. "He told you about the factory bombing?"

"Yes, and I got a copy of one of the photos from him."

"He gave you a photo?"

"Not exactly. He showed it to me and tried to convince me you were dead. I think he thought that if he threw me a bone, I'd stop looking for you. At least, he kept telling me to stop." I take a sip of water. "I took a picture of the photo when he left the room. I still have it on my phone."

"And that's what you sent to Savko?"

"Yes. I wanted to see if he could find out where your father got it. He couldn't, but he did find the digital file, plus a few others."

I explain the phone call with Savko, and how he'd recruited his IT friend Martin to try and identify the mysterious source.

"I had no idea if it'd do any good, but I figured it wouldn't hurt to follow the lead." I rest my hand on Poe's back as he shifts and settles against my hip. "I didn't learn anything new, though. Martin came up with a bunch of Hawke Financial files, and Savko sent them to me."

Darius turns, his gaze suddenly as sharp as a laser. "He sent you what Martin found?"

"Yes. He thought the contact might be mentioned somewhere in the documents. I looked, but couldn't find anything. It was a bunch of financial reports, maps, graphs. I don't know what else. I couldn't make much sense of it, but I had a bad feeling about keeping them. It looked like classified corporate stuff."

"And the factory photos were from the same computer system?"

"I assume so, yes."

"What did you do with the files?"

"They're on a flash drive in my backpack. Savko told me to delete them from my laptop."

He lets out a long breath, his hands curling into fists. His spine is rigid, like a metal rod. A flicker of alarm rises in me.

"Darius, what does this have to do with you being back here?"

"Nell." He approaches, reaching out to press his hand against the side of my neck. "Savko is dead."

I recoil. Shock bolts through me, freezing my blood. "What?"

"He was found in Kolchava." Darius's grip tightens. "Shot through the head."

"Oh my god." I stare at him through a flood of tears. "I just talked to him. How did...was it the PLF?"

"Possibly, though no one was caught. And Martin is missing." He crouches in front of me, his features hard, his mouth compressed. "When Patrick told me you'd talked to my father and then Savko, and he also said something about a close call with a speeding car..."

"No." A sense of horror begins to encroach on me. "You think someone is after me? That I really am in danger?"

A muscle works in his jaw. "The Hawke Financial security system has intrusion alarms and tracking programs set up in the event of hacking. My guess is that they tracked the break-in back to Martin and then Savko. I can't prove that's connected to his death, but after what Patrick told me, I wasn't taking any chances. I got back here as fast as I could."

"And you think your *father* is somehow responsible?"

"I don't know. But the circumstances are suspicious. He wouldn't take that kind of breach lightly."

I bring a hand to my mouth, sickened at the thought that my brief call to Savko might have resulted in his death. In his being *shot in the head.*

"Nell, I can't confirm any of this." Darius pushes a lock of hair away from my forehead. "I just had a bad feeling about it. I've learned over the years to listen to my instincts. Now that I know you have a physical copy of the files, it's even more critical that we leave New York."

"Where are we going to go?" I ask.

"Somewhere safe." Darius rises to his feet. "No one knows I'm here. In fact, you and Patrick are the only ones who know I'm alive. I plan to keep it that way for as long as possible. No one will think that you might be with me."

Everything tangles and snarls in my brain, making it difficult to grab a coherent thought.

"We'll head out as soon as you're ready." He follows the line of my cheekbone with his thumb, his expression gentling. "You did nothing wrong."

I'm not so sure about that. I might not intentionally have done anything wrong, but if a man is missing and another one is dead because I pulled them into something dangerous...

A burning sensation fills my throat.

And if the Hawke Financial cybersecurity team traced the hacking to Martin and then Savko, they won't stop until they find the person at the end of the trail.

Me.

God in heaven.

After all Darius and I have gone through—from battling others' expectations to battling in an actual goddamn war— we're still not safe.

PART II

CHAPTER 12

Darius

I WANT TO DO EVERYTHING. Kiss her, hold her, fuck her, protect her, save her. Kill for her again. I want to lock myself around her and never let go.

I can't be apart from her. I'm constantly in her space, only inches away, as we check out of the hotel and pick up the old SUV I'd paid cash for yesterday. She doesn't put any distance between us, doesn't seem to mind that I'm sticking to her like a magnet, that my arm, my shoulder, or my hand is always touching her. It's as if she knows I need to keep reassuring myself that she's here.

She's scared, terrified even—I see the storm brewing in her gray eyes—but outwardly she's quiet and calm. She doesn't ask any questions, just gets into the passenger seat of the car and pulls on her seat belt.

I toss our bags into the trunk and open the back door for

Poe. He jumps inside and stretches out on the seat. After shutting the door, I get behind the wheel.

"Turn off the location tracker on your phone." I navigate out of the parking lot. "You'll have to get rid of it, so we'll back up any data you want to save. Don't even turn on your laptop."

She pulls her phone from her hoodie pocket and unlocks the screen, working through the settings.

The sun begins a slow ascent over the horizon, spilling a reddish light over the city. It's early enough that the traffic isn't bad, and before long we're driving through the Lincoln Tunnel.

"Where are we going?" Nell finally asks as we cross into New Jersey.

"South Dakota."

She glances at me. "Really? Why?"

"I know a guy there who can help us out." I don't, however, know if he will.

"What guy?"

"An old friend." *For lack of a better word.* "He's resourceful. If anyone can find whatever trail Hawke Financial has left behind, he can."

"Does he know we're coming?"

"No."

"Why not?"

"Because he'd set out booby traps." I throw her a half-hearted grin. "Kidding."

Sort of.

Nell huffs out a laugh. "I'll say one thing. Being with you is never boring."

I try to ignore a stab of regret. Part of me still wants her back in New York, oblivious to anything going on in Kras-novar. I wish she'd never gone there at all, that she'd never seen the things she saw or experienced the true horror of war. I want her safe in her dingy apartment, going out with friends, working at the greasy spoon diner and hoping for a better job.

I also don't want anything to have been different. I don't want to be anywhere but here, with her. Walking away from her on that dirt road outside of Varaz had ripped me apart. Only when I'd closed my arms around her again had the pieces started to come back together.

I can't think about what will happen later. *Together* isn't a word I should ever associate with Nell. Not if I want to survive loving her.

She reaches over and settles her hand on my thigh. "Are you all right?"

I shouldn't be surprised by the question. Even when Varaz was under siege, she was thinking about everyone else.

"Now that you're with me, I'm fine." I shoot her a quick smile.

"I mean, after having been in the PLF's clutches again." She tightens her hand on my thigh. "What if it makes things worse for you? The nightmares, I mean."

"It won't." I don't know how to explain my certainty. But the night she witnessed my flashback and didn't flinch—just the opposite; she moved even closer—my old demons shattered into oblivion. None of them have power over me anymore. Nothing does.

Except her.

"All that stuff is over." I shrug, as if I'm talking about a movie. "What happened in Varaz...and what's happening with us…is all that matters. I don't have room for anything else. I won't be controlled by the PLF anymore or by what happened years ago. I promise." I take one hand off the wheel and put it over hers. "I'm all right."

She turns her palm and squeezes my hand just as a canine whine of hunger comes from the backseat. I pull off the highway to a drive-thru coffeehouse and order breakfast sandwiches, muffins, and coffee.

After taking Poe for a quick walk, we eat at a table next to the parking lot. Poe sits in the shade and wolfs down two sandwiches and half a bottle of water.

"How long will it take us to get to South Dakota?" Nell sips her coffee and squints against the sunshine. Her hair is loose and messy, her skin pale aside from a faint reddish burn on her neck from my stubble. Purplish circles line her eyes.

"Couple of days." I push a blueberry muffin toward her, indicating she needs to eat something. "I'm going to avoid the toll roads and highways, so it'll take us a little longer. Right now we need to get rid of your cell. I have a burner phone, but other than that, we're not using cell data or any online accounts."

Nell pulls her phone out of her pocket and slides it across the table toward me.

"Any data you want to save?"

"No." She starts to bring her cup to her mouth again. Then she stops, her eyes widening.

"Nell?"

"My father." She sets her cup down. Her throat ripples. "What should I tell him?"

My insides twist with guilt. "Text him that you're going

out of town for a few days and will have limited email and phone access."

It's a shitty excuse that Henry is smart enough to see through, but I can't think of anything else. No way do I want him or Fern to know anything about this—for their own protection as much as Nell's.

She looks at her phone like it's a poisonous snake. A crease mars her smooth forehead.

"Nell?" I close my hand around her wrist. "What's wrong?"

"I told him." She lifts her gaze to mine, her eyes the color of rainclouds. "About us."

My jaw clenches involuntarily. I'd half expected that she'd tell Henry what was going on—she would never be able to stand lying to her father. But I'd blocked any thought of his reaction.

"Are you upset?" Nell asks.

"Not with you. But I should have been there."

"I'm sorry I didn't wait until you could be." She looks down at my hand gripping her wrist. "But I had to explain why I was so desperate to find you. It wasn't enough that I was just looking for *Uncle Darius,* not when I was up all night scouring websites and sending emails. So I...I told him."

"What did he say?" Stupid question. What the fuck do I *think* he said?

"Nothing good." Nell shrugs and reaches for her coffee, her expression darkening. "He was shocked, of course. Angry. Convinced that I'm the innocent, and you're the wolf."

He's right.

The old, ugly thought claws at the back of my mind.

"No." Nell leans forward, her eyes suddenly sparking like flint striking metal. "Don't you dare go there again, Darius Hawke. We're so fucking past that we can't even see it anymore. *I love you.* I'm glad I told my father. I also told my friends. I want to tell the world because I'm not—I never will be—ashamed of what I feel for you and what we have. Never. And if you still feel guilty, even after all we've been through, then I swear to God, I will walk away right now and take my chances alone with whatever boogeymen are after me."

She fills my vision—silver sparks, tumble of gold-streaked hair, flushed cheeks. The righteous fury and determination in her blood.

What am I without her?

I no longer know. I don't even want to know. But one day, probably sooner than I can stand, I'll be forced to find out. I've dragged her into way too much darkness already, and all I want now is to get her back into both safety and light.

"I love you." I tighten my hand on her wrist, feeling her pulse thumping against my fingers. "You were all I could think about when Poe and I were slogging over the mountain. The only reason we both had to survive was to get back to you. I told you I'd navigated via the stars, but more than that, it was *you*. You were my north star. You always will be."

She turns her hand and curls her fingers into mine. But her eyes are still guarded, her mouth tight.

"Then don't make me defend *us* again, least of all to you," she says. "It took so long for you to finally see that our feelings for each other are rare and beautiful and worth cherishing. I would fight into eternity to protect what we have. But I need to know that you will too."

"I will." The vow burns through my chest like a shooting star and lands right under my heart.

"Promise?" Nell asks.

"I promise. And I'll stop being an ass."

She rolls her eyes. "Well, you don't have to aim *that* high yet."

"Watch it." I reach over to tweak her nose, and her brief smile is like a second sunrise.

I can't help my regret about Henry—friends since we were sixteen, as close as brothers—but Nell overpowers everything else. And keeping her safe is the only thing that matters right now.

"Come on." I stand, tugging her to her feet. "We need to get going."

After dropping our empty paper wrappers into a nearby recycling bin, she picks up her phone. She types out quick messages to her father and a couple of friends before handing the phone back to me.

I erase all the data and restore the factory settings, then remove the SIM card. After snapping it into a few pieces, I throw one in the trashcan and the other two in the dumpster behind the restaurant.

We get back on the road, driving for a couple of hours before stopping to let Poe out and take him for a short walk. Navigating with an old road atlas, I stay off the highway and stick to smaller county roads and towns.

It's close to evening by the time we reach the outskirts of Cleveland. I pull into the parking lot of a standard roadside motel and park a distance from the glass-fronted office.

"Will they let us book a room without IDs?" Nell asks.

"For extra cash, sure." Good thing I have plenty of it, too —I borrowed a lot of money from Patrick so I won't have to touch any of my accounts or credit cards. "Stay in the car. I'll get the room."

I walk to the office and pull open the glass door. A woman in her midfifties is sitting behind the laminate counter, her hair scraped into a bun, her glasses halfway down her nose as she peers at her phone.

She looks up at the sound of the bell attached to the door.

"Evening." I dig into my pocket for my wallet. "I need a room for the night, please."

The woman, whose name tag reads *Annette*, punches a few keys on the computer. "Single or double?"

"Whatever's available."

"King or two queens?"

"Either."

She glances past me out the window to the car, then turns back to the computer. "Double with one king is eighty-five a night."

"That's fine."

"Driver's license and credit card, please." She taps her finger on the counter.

"I'll pay cash." I take a hundred from my wallet and slide it over to her. "I also have a dog."

"We're a pet-free establishment."

My shoulders tighten. There's something about this— about her—that's making me uneasy. But leaving now might seem suspicious. I take out another fifty and put it on top of the hundred.

"If there's a problem," I say, "I'll go elsewhere."

Given that there are only three other cars in the parking lot, I'm guessing Annette could use the business. She picks up the bills and hands me two keycards. "Room 142, halfway down on the left. Office is open twenty-four seven."

I thank her and leave, getting back in the SUV. After giving Nell one of the keycards, I maneuver the car to a parking space in front of the room. She gets out and opens the back door for Poe, who leaps to the pavement with a bark of joy at being freed from confinement.

"He needs a walk," Nell says, rubbing the dog's head.

"Later." I open the room door and usher them both inside, then bring in the bags. "I'm going to fill up the tank, and I'll grab us some dinner from the take-out place down the street. Won't take more than half an hour. Poe will stay here with you."

I don't want to leave her alone, but the fewer people who see us together, the better. After pulling the curtains and locking the door behind me, I drive to a gas station. I fill up the tank, then buy a bunch of toiletries and snacks at the convenience store.

I pick up food and sodas at the restaurant before returning to the motel. As I pull into the lot, I catch sight of Nell striding toward the room from the direction of the office, Poe at her side. She's carrying a couple bottles of water. Her body is rigid with anger.

My heartbeat kicks up. I park and get out of the car. "What's wrong?"

She shakes her head and turns to unlock the room door. I follow her in, slamming the door shut. "Nell, what happened?"

"God. Stupid, narrow-minded people." She puts the water

next to the TV and sits on the bed, her fists clenching. "I took Poe out for a quick walk and stopped at the vending machine to get some water. That woman from the office saw me and asked me to come and sign a registration form. I told her you'd already taken care of it. Then she asked me if I was *all right* and if I needed help. At first, I didn't even understand what she was talking about. Then I realized she thought I might be in trouble. Needless to say, I set her straight."

My gut wrenches. Of all the things I've considered both about this situation and my relationship with Nell—*that* has never been one of them. Not once have I thought someone might suspect I was coercing or trafficking her.

But I should have. A young woman traveling with an older man, no ID, booking into a cheap motel and paying cash...

Fuck. There's no way to keep her completely out of sight. And even if we hit the seediest, most out-of-the-way places, even if people don't care who we are or what we do, they'll remember us. They'll be able to describe us.

"I'm sorry." Nell drags her hands through her hair with a sigh. "I was so enraged, I just reacted. I told her in no uncertain terms that we're together and she should mind her own damned business. But I have no idea if going on the offense just made it worse."

"You don't need to be sorry." I stop beside her and run my fingers over the scar on her forehead. "You're right. It's none of her business. But it'll be better from now on if you don't interact with anyone else. We have to avoid being seen together."

Her expression darkens. She doesn't like the stark fact

that other people might have the same suspicions. I don't like it either, even if I do have a grudging respect for Annette because at least she tried to take action when most people wouldn't get involved.

"We'll get a few hours' sleep and be out of here early," I say.

Nell pushes to her feet, her body still tense as she grabs a robe from her bag and disappears into the bathroom.

I go out to the SUV to bring in the food. I'm half tempted to get back on the road right now, but Annette will be even more suspicious if we leave an hour after checking in.

Fuck. Fuck. Fuck.

No more motels. I'm driving straight through to the Black Hills. We'll sleep in the SUV if we have to.

When I go back into the room, Poe is lolling on the bed, licking his paw. The bathroom door is closed, the shower running.

I put the bags on the table and take clean clothes out of my duffel. I've kept my Glock pistol under a couple pairs of jeans, but now I take it out and check the magazine and chamber. Fully loaded. Best to keep it close at hand.

The bathroom door opens, and Nell comes out in her robe, her long, wet hair falling around her shoulders. The fragrant steam carries her scent of vanilla and cinnamon. That smell alone heats my blood. Not to mention the sight of her—legs bare under her short robe, the neckline open to reveal a V of damp, tempting skin, a drop of water winding over her collarbone...

Christ. I turn away, willing my erection to subside. Not a surprise that she fires me up in two seconds flat, especially after Varaz. The thought of losing her, of never seeing her again, had carved a massive black hole inside me. Now all I want to do is fill it back up with her. As much of her as I can get.

I open the bag of food and set the containers out on the table.

"I got you a chicken sandwich." I nod to the opposite chair. "And a slice of chocolate cake for dessert."

She comes to the table, rubbing her hair with a towel. "Do you think maybe I should dye my hair? I'd be less recognizable as a blonde."

Though I don't like the idea of her changing her sparrow-wing hair in any way, I nod. "Might be a good idea, but we're not interacting with anyone until we get to the Black Hills."

I put Poe's box of meatloaf on the floor and add some kibble that I'd picked up at the convenience store. He jumps off the bed and lumbers over to investigate.

"This friend of yours…" Nell nibbles at a french fry and eyes me somewhat warily. "What does he know about us?"

"Nothing yet." I bite into a barbecue sandwich. "He doesn't know we're coming."

"Shouldn't you tell him in advance?"

"I'm not sure how to reach him."

She frowns. "What, does he live in a cave?"

"He's off the grid—more or less."

"What's his name?"

"Banks."

"Banks what?"

"Just Banks. Like Adele or Bono."

"Or Satan," Nell mutters.

I laugh. The sound makes her look up, amusement flashing in her gray eyes.

"He'd take that as a compliment," I assure her.

"But he's not going to give us any crap, right? He's your friend."

"He's an acquaintance." I nod toward her untouched sandwich. "You've picked at your food all day. You need to eat."

"I'm not hungry." She drops the fry she's holding. "I still can't believe that Savko is dead because of my stupid phone call."

My chest constricts. "We don't know if that's why he was killed. You didn't cause his death."

"But he wouldn't have been in the line of fire if he hadn't done me that favor."

"Nell, Savko was always in the line of fire. It's how he lived."

She lifts her gaze to mine. Shadows circle her eyes. "Like you."

I have no response because it's the truth. I push the food container aside and reach for her hand, pulling her to her feet.

She steps into my arms, pressing her forehead against my chest with a sigh. She's a warm, little bundle of softness and good smells.

"The world can be a shitty place, no question." I rub my cheek on her wet hair. "But do you remember when we went to the castle, and you reminded me about all the good I'd experienced? That's still true. It'll always be true."

"Sometimes the good is really hard to find." Her voice is muffled against my shirtfront.

"I don't know about that." I pat her back and slide my hands down to squeeze her round ass. "I've got the goods right here."

She gives a small laugh that makes me feel like I won the lottery. I ease away to look at her. Some of the darkness has faded from her eyes, leaving them a soft gray like a dove's wings. I put my hand under her chin, tilting her face up to mine.

When our lips meet, her sigh of pleasure sinks into my blood. I urge her lips apart and deepen the kiss. She opens up like a flower bud, touching her tongue to mine, drawing me into her. She rises to her tiptoes and wraps her arms around my neck. Her body goes pliant, fusing against mine.

"You taste delicious," she murmurs. "Spicy and sweet at the same time. Maybe I'm hungry after all."

"I know I am, but not for food."

Without breaking our contact, I turn and lower her onto the bed. I'm already hard, my dick pressing uncomfortably against my fly.

One touch, one kiss, and my lust for her goes from zero to a thousand in two seconds flat. I used to be able to control it—or tried to—but since getting a taste of her in Varaz, I'll never have enough. I'm greedy and ravenous for her. An eternity isn't long enough to sate my hunger.

I pull away from her and tug at the loose belt of her robe. The folds fall open, revealing her naked body. All the breath escapes my lungs. She's so fucking gorgeous—pale and smooth, her nipples like berries, her skin still damp and shiny with shower water.

I run my palms over her breasts, her hips, her legs. I love

the way she watches me touch her, as if she's astonished by the sight of my rough, ugly hands on her perfect curves.

"God, Darius." She squirms, pushing farther back onto the bed and reaching for a pillow. "I'm already so aroused. How do you do that to me so fast?"

I grab her hand and bring it to the front of my jeans. "I was just thinking the same thing about you."

She draws in a breath as she palms my erection. "Let me see."

I take off my shirt and jeans, but before pulling off my boxer briefs, I push her legs apart and press my mouth to her inner thigh, stroking my tongue along the crease beneath her hip. She rises to her elbows, her eyes widening. "What are you…"

I rub her thighs gently, not wanting to unnerve her. Aside from my need to treat her carefully, there hadn't been enough time in Varaz to do all the things I want to do with her.

"Do you want me to stop?" I curve my hands around her thighs.

"No, of course not. I've just never…" She pauses and licks her lips. "I mean, I'll probably come."

I grin. I can't imagine it's possible to love her more than I do. "That's my end goal, baby."

She returns my smile, a flush rising to her cheeks. I brace my hands on either side of her and kiss her again, biting down on her lower lip. She moans a little and relaxes against the bed.

I kiss her chin, her nose, her cheeks, trailing a slow path over her neck and the arch of her collarbone. I press my mouth to her breasts, stroking her nipples, and make a line down the center of her soft belly. She twitches, gasps, wiggles. Every move, every sound, ratchets up my lust another level.

I ease between her legs again and kiss her inner thigh, working my way to her cleft. A tremble rocks through her. She fists the bedcovers. I open her up with my fingers and lick her slowly. She arches upward with a choked moan.

"Oh my god…" She twists her hips and lifts her head to look at me. "That's so…*oh!*"

Her pleasure is enough—almost—to keep my own urgency in check. I suck and lick her until she's writhing under my mouth. I ease one finger, then another inside her. She clenches around my fingers and reaches down to grab my hair.

"Darius." Her voice strains to breaking.

"Come on, honey." I thrust my fingers gently and close my lips around her clit. She cries out the instant before she starts to come, her body shaking and vibrating as she pushes upward against my mouth. I don't pull away from her until the sensations ease and she falls back into the pillows, dazed and panting.

"That was…oh my goodness." She opens her eyes and stares at me. "Why on earth haven't you done that to me before?"

"Not from lack of wanting to."

She presses her hand to my jaw. "You don't have to be careful with me. After all we've been through, you should know that by now."

Without answering, I pull myself up to lie beside her. She runs her thumb along my collarbone.

"There are a lot of things I wish hadn't happened," she

murmurs. "But there is nowhere else I would rather be than with you."

I brush my lips across hers and run my hand over her breasts. Little ripples of pleasure course through her body. She sighs and turns toward me, then glances down at my erection, which is pushing against her thigh through my briefs. She squeezes it, the warmth of her palm sending a shockwave through me.

"I want to do the same thing to you," she whispers.

Though my blood burns at the thought of her full lips closing around my cock, I shake my head.

"But—"

I stop her with another kiss, maneuvering to get my briefs off. "I'm going to fuck you now."

A breathless little gasp catches in her throat. She winds her arms around me and shifts onto her back, spreading her legs. "I want to do *this* all the different ways too."

I want to show her how. For years, my mind has blistered with fantasies—Nell on her hands and knees as I thrust into her from behind, her straddling my hips and riding me. Pushing her up against a wall, bending her over the back of a sofa.

But now...I ease on top of her and bury myself in her tight, wet heat.

So. Fucking. Perfect.

I grit my teeth, battling back a surge of uncontrollable lust before I start to thrust. Forcing myself to keep the pace easy and moderate. Everything about her goes straight to my blood—her gasps of pleasure, the way she writhes and twists her body, her grip on my shoulders, her fingernails digging into my back.

I want to sink into her forever and dissolve. Become a piece of her. She parts her legs wider, opens her mouth, pushes her tongue against mine. It's enough to break my restraint, but I manage to hold on and slow the pace of my thrusts.

"Harder." She rakes her hands down my spine, her lust-dark eyes searching mine. "Don't hold back."

My jaw clenches at her obvious invitation. I'd hurt her the other day; I could tell by the way she arched her body as if she were trying to escape, even as she begged me not to stop. Being with her again after getting out of that hellhole had stripped me of all self-control. I'd wanted to fuck her so hard she'd feel me inside her for the next month.

But I hate that I hurt her.

"Darius, do it." She strains upward, cupping her breasts in her hands. "Make my tits bounce."

Jesus.

Pressing my forehead to hers, I sink deeper inside her, a rhythm that pushes me to the edge. She wraps herself around me, matching every surge with a thrust of her hips.

"I feel it again," she whispers against my mouth. "I'm going to…oh, god."

She lets out another of her little cries as her body ripples and clenches around me. Urgency obliterates my hesitation. I thrust faster, jolting her against the bed as the pressure builds and builds—

"Fuck." I pull out of her and grasp my shaft the instant before shooting over her smooth belly.

She watches me, her body trembling, her face flushed and eyes hot. "That is so sexy."

I ease away from her, swiping my arm across my forehead as the pleasure ebbs. My pulse is still pounding as I climb off the bed and start toward the bathroom to dampen a washcloth. Nell grabs my wrist and pulls me to a stop.

"You don't always have to wash yourself off me right away." She strokes her hand over her belly, rubbing my semen into her skin. "I love the way you feel on me. I love it even more when you come inside me."

I press my lips against her forehead and detach her grip. "You're going to get cold and sticky if you don't clean up."

After wetting a cloth with hot water, I wipe her skin and rub the cloth between her legs. She opens her thighs, her gaze on my face.

"Do you not want me to be dirty?" she asks.

The question is so unexpected, so strange, that I don't know what to say. "Uh…what?"

"You always get a washcloth for me right after we make love, and I know you're still holding back. I mean, don't get me wrong," she adds hastily. "I absolutely *love* everything we've done. Everything we do. In fact, I love it so much that I want more. I want everything you have to give. But I feel like you treat me with such caution, like you don't want to take me too close to the edge. Like you're putting limits on how far you're willing to go with me."

I still have no idea what to say. No idea if that's true.

I bunch the washcloth in my fist and walk back to the bathroom. "Sorry, Nell. I don't overthink sex."

"I wasn't—"

I close the door with a hard click, cutting off her voice.

CHAPTER 13

Nell

As Darius navigates the car through the maze of back roads, I gaze out the side window at the Ohio landscape. Dawn sunlight falls over the rolling, farm-dotted hills, pale yellow mixing with multiple shades of green. A ribbon of clouds unfurls across the horizon, but the sky above is turning cornflower blue.

Looking at the scenery, I can pretend like we're a normal couple enjoying a countryside road trip. We're staying in quaint little inns and bed and breakfasts. We stop to browse antique shops, visit landmarks, tour historical museums tucked into small towns. We try all the local specialties of the Midwest—cheesesteaks, shoofly pie, buckeyes, cream puffs. We laugh, take pictures, make spontaneous detours. We hold hands and kiss a lot.

Then what? You go home to your cottage with the white picket fence and big picture window overlooking the lake, where you create art and Darius...owns a portrait photography studio?

Hah.

In case you forgot, Nell—you're on the run from people who might want to kill you, driving to the Badlands to talk to a man who sounds like the Unabomber, and there's not an antique shop or a cream puff in sight.

Not to mention, Darius is shutting himself off again because you dared to bring up the fact that you'd like to get a little dirty, sexually speaking.

Which should actually crank his engine, right? Don't men like to take their women for a walk on the wild side? Especially when the woman is already halfway out the door?

I glance at him in the driver's seat, his hands tight on the wheel. His features are hard-edged and inscrutable. He's been almost silent since he woke me up an hour ago and told me to get ready to leave.

A sigh collects in my chest. Sex should be the last thing on our minds, but it seems to be what we both desperately want right now. Especially after our painful separation when we didn't even know if the other person was still alive. And we've come so far from where we began that there's no way I'm going to let us backslide now.

"Hey." I reach out to touch his thigh. "Sorry for what I said last night. I didn't mean to offend you."

He lets out his breath slowly. "You didn't. I'm sorry I reacted the way I did."

He falls silent again, his gaze on the black stretch of road in front of us.

Much as I'd like to press the issue, I leave it alone for now. It's part of who he is, I know, this need to protect me—

even from himself. Though I don't want or need to be protected from him, he's still guided by his moral compass. Back in Varaz, I'd known he wasn't unrestrained in his love-making, that he was keeping himself and his deeper desires in check.

At the time, I'd accepted that. God knows it took long enough to convince him it was okay to kiss me, much less strip me and fuck me. But I still secretly wish he'd be less restrained. Now more than ever.

It's as if these past few months—the beauty of Varaz followed by the horrific destruction, the brutal reality of war, the running for our lives, the terror of thinking Darius might be dead and then the joy at discovering he was alive—have heightened my emotions to unfathomable levels. All my fears, desires, and longings are sharpened to knifepoints. I want to feel and experience everything.

With him. He's the only person in the world who under-stands how horrific events can somehow flick a switch on inside you. Inciting you to live.

Or at the very least…to eat a world-famous cream puff.

Since it'll be hours before we reach Wisconsin, I convince him to stop in a town near Toledo for lunch and ice cream. We take Poe for a walk in a grassy park, and Darius reluc-tantly agrees to let me use the local library's computer to check news websites as long as I don't log in to my email account.

The news from Krasnovar only adds to my anxiety. Though the fighting has eased up in the south and west, with skirmishes continuing in sporadic bursts, the PLF forces have moved relentlessly across the northern province and continue to battle for control of Varaz.

My only hope is that Sofia, Marcus, and Tomas made it out of the north and are hopefully either in a refugee camp or near Saldem where Alexei's mother and sister live. Which means they might have more resources to reach Alexei, even if he can't contact them.

As I read the articles, Darius checks the documents on the flash drive, scrolling through them with a distinct frown.

"I didn't understand most of them," I tell him. "But I figured out they have something to do with battery minerals and mines."

"You're right. They're reports about the mineral grades, plus predictions for future demand of things like lithium ore." His frown deepens. "They focus on Eastern European mines, especially in Romania, Krasnovar, and Moldova. Hawke Financial might be interested in potential investments, but there's no mention of a mining company. No precedent for an interest in minerals either."

He navigates to the security exchange website, where there is a list of Hawke Financial's holdings. After scanning the list, he shakes his head. "If they are getting into mineral investing, it makes sense that they wouldn't want it to be public knowledge yet. But…"

His voice trails off. *But would they kill to prevent it? Have they already? Why?*

The questions roll around in my head as we return to the car, though neither of us has any answers.

We continue driving, making occasional stops for either food or bathroom use, but there's definitely no sightseeing or lunches at quaint hometown cafés. Darius avoids the Illinois tolls, continuing to stick to county highways and smaller roads as we head north toward Wisconsin.

Though he stops near Madison to buy me a cream puff from a local bakery, he continues driving into the night—putting as much distance as possible between us and New York. Only once somewhere in Minnesota does he pull into a rest stop, where we climb into the back of the SUV for a few hours' sleep.

We pass through the Badlands the following afternoon, and it's another hour and a half before we arrive in the Black Hills. The surrounding towns are crowded with cars, RVs, and motorcycles, but Darius bypasses the tourist spots and takes a narrow, winding road into the mountains.

The pine trees appear in increasingly thick clusters alongside craggy granite rock formations. We don't see another car for at least an hour before he turns off onto a rutted dirt road punctuated with rocky potholes.

Several miles in, the road all but disappears. Darius keeps driving through the brush until we reach a tree-enclosed clearing dotted with a dilapidated cabin, an old pickup truck, and an ancient-looking camper/trailer on cinder blocks.

The camper windows are smudged with dirt and cobwebs, the screen door broken off the hinges. A stack of tires sits on the ground alongside a few ragged lawn chairs. In the center, a rock-encircled campfire exhales plumes of dirty smoke.

The whole place shouts *creepy loner survivalist.*

"You're kidding, right?" I peer through the front windshield. "Is he—?"

The cabin door suddenly flies open and slams against the siding. I startle as a big, hulking man steps out, a long, curved hunting knife held like Thor's hammer in front of him. From the backseat, Poe growls and barks.

"Wait here." Darius stops the car and turns off the engine. He gets out, holding up both hands. Poe's bark turns into the staccato rhythm of warning.

My heart pounds in my throat. Darius kicks the car door shut and approaches the man—who I assume is Banks. Even in an ancient Rolling Stones T-shirt and torn cargo shorts, he's scary. He looks almost as tall as Darius with a powerful build and a weird, pent-up energy that feels as if it could go haywire any second. His dirty blond hair is long and lanky, and an unruly beard covers half his face.

He'll be delighted to help us out, I'm sure.

With a flick of his wrist, he throws the knife. The blade embeds in the ground inches from Darius's feet.

"You sonuvabitch." The man's deep, gravelly voice resounds through the windows of the SUV. "What the fuck are you doing here?"

"I need to talk to you." Darius walks forward, his hands still up at his chest but his body relaxed.

"Stop right there." Banks pulls another knife from his boot and positions it to throw. "What about?"

"We're in some trouble." Darius gestures to the car, and Banks's gaze swivels to me.

I give him a little wave through the windshield and attempt a smile that probably looks more like an appeal of *"Please don't kill us."*

Banks lowers the knife slightly, his eyes narrow. Darius walks around to the passenger side and pulls open the door, extending one hand to me and holding up the other to Poe in a "stay" gesture. Poe barks, pacing back and forth on the seat, his tail swishing.

"It's okay." Darius closes his hand around mine as I get out of the car. Even in the shade of the evergreens, the hot air hits me like a furnace blast.

I eye Banks warily. "I'm pretty sure he doesn't want us here."

"If it weren't for you, he'd have aimed higher." Darius gives me a rueful smile and turns to the big man by the cabin. "Banks, this is Nell. I'm here for her, not me."

Banks gives me a cold once-over. "What do you want?"

Something inside me snaps, like a wire stretched too tight. I'm sick to death of getting ordered around and snapped at, of being scared, of forcing myself to keep my guard up. The last thing I need is some big, freakish knife-thrower trying to intimidate me. No matter how well he does it.

"I want you to stop throwing knives around," I tell him bluntly. "And you'd better not threaten me with a rifle instead. I've dodged more than enough bullets in the past couple of months...and from guns much bigger than anything you might have."

Darius laughs.

Banks stares at me for a second, then snorts. The knife lowers an inch. "What kind of trouble you in?"

"Stop snarling and we'll tell you."

Banks snaps his gaze to Darius, his frown deepening. Darius responds with a shrug.

"Look." Taking a chance that if Banks really did plan to hurt us, he'd have done so already, I walk a few more steps toward him. "I don't know what the deal is with you and

Darius, but we've been driving for the past two days. It's…
what, ninety degrees out here? Our dog needs a drink, and
frankly, so do I. Can you at least spare us some cold
water?"

Banks glances at the car again, then steps back into the
cabin. "Wait."

He disappears inside with the knife. I let out a breath I
hadn't realized I was holding. When he emerges again, he's
carrying a glass and a plastic dish full of murky-looking
water. No knife. He sets the bowl beside the porch steps and
jerks his chin at me.

"Come and get it." He holds out the glass.

I sense Darius bristle at the order. I approach Banks, my
heartbeat kicking up again with every step. As I get closer, I
realize he's bigger than he seemed from a distance, and he
has shockingly green eyes that, given his icy stare, feel as if
they can turn a person to stone.

Behind me, there's a click as Darius opens the car door.
Poe bounds up in front of me, barking ceaselessly at Banks.

"It's okay, boy." I dart forward to grab the water dish and
bring it back to him, setting it closer. He bends his head and
laps thirstily.

I take the glass from Banks and down a couple of gulps.

"So, talk," he orders.

I'm half-tempted to tell him he's still snarling, but I'd
better not push it. "We need your help…uh, deciphering
some computer files."

"I don't do that kind of shit anymore." He glares at
Darius. "You know that."

"I took a chance."

"You failed."

Darius nods toward the cabin. "What've you got in there?"

"None of your fucking business." Banks crosses his arms. "What kind of files?"

"We don't know." I put my hand on Poe's head. "That's why they need to be deciphered."

"And traced," Darius adds. "We want to find out where they lead."

"What for?" Banks snaps.

"Because the man who helped acquire them is dead," Darius says.

And Nell might be next. He doesn't have to say that part.

Banks stares at me, like he's trying to determine whether or not I matter enough to help. Darius takes a bottle of Jack Daniels from the back of the SUV and holds it out.

Banks thrusts his finger toward the lawn chairs beside the campfire. Darius and I walk over. I'm glad to sit down because my knees are still shaking.

After stoking the fire and tossing another log onto the flames—why he does this, given the heat, I have no idea—Banks disappears back into the cabin. He returns with two more jelly glasses and hands one to Darius.

He slouches in a chair on the opposite side of the fire, his gaze on me. "How'd a little girl like you get caught up in shit like this?"

"Bad luck?" I offer.

A faint grin ghosts over his mouth.

"How'd a big brute like you get stuck in a place like this?" I wave a hand at the cabin.

Banks watches Darius pour the whiskey. "He didn't tell you?"

"Should he have?" I ask.

With a shrug, Banks lifts the glass to his lips and downs a long swallow. "You still taking pictures, Hawke?"

Darius nods. Only now do I remember I still have his camera in my backpack. I'd completely forgotten about it.

"But my jobs are on hold until we get this figured out," he says.

He pulls the flash drive out of his jeans pocket and hands it to Banks. Though I know this is the reason we're here, I can't help a twist of unease. Banks didn't exactly put out the welcome wagon, so I find it hard to fully trust him. But if Darius does…

Banks flips the flash drive through his fingers while Darius tells him the whole story—from my volunteer job in Krasnovar to the siege and our escape from Varaz. He tells Banks about his surrender to the PLF, the factory bombing, and the fact that Patrick and I—and now Banks—are the only people who know that Darius is still alive. He explains how I got in to see his father and ended up with the Hawke Financial files—which appear to have been traced back to Martin and Savko.

Banks listens without comment, his gaze still unnervingly on me. I'm sharply aware that he could use all this information against us. That would probably be worse than being on the other end of his knife-throwing.

I let out my breath and bend to pet Poe, who is at my feet, his ears pointed and his attention on Banks. If Poe were more accepting of him, I might be too—but the dog's lingering wariness heightens my own.

Banks leans toward the fire, still flipping the flash drive. "Mining reports? Doesn't sound too damning."

"Could be nothing at all," Darius admits. "Or it could be the reason a man is dead. That's why we need your help."

"Did you make copies of the files?"

"No."

"Send them to anyone else?"

"No."

"Good." Banks studies the drive. "They're probably embedded with tracking codes. Don't copy or send them to anyone. Did they come through email?"

"A large file server," I tell him. "I transferred them to the flash drive and deleted them from my laptop."

He nods. "Tracking system is how they found you."

"So what do we do now?" I ask.

"You could just destroy the flash drive." Banks nods at the fire, the logs popping and cracking. "If someone's after it, then get rid of it."

"Then we've got no leverage," Darius points out.

"Or knowledge of where it might lead," I add. "And whoever wants it won't know we destroyed it. So they'd still be looking for us."

Banks meets my gaze through the smoke. In one fluid motion, he tosses the flash drive into the air right above the fire.

I draw in a sharp gasp, half rising to try and grab the drive before it falls into the flames. Then, just as fast, Banks shoots his arm straight out. The flash drive lands in his palm.

"Asshole," Darius mutters.

I sit back, my heart pounding. Banks's mouth twists into a smile. He shoves to his feet and points at the camper. "You can sleep there. Stay out of my house."

He strides back to the cabin, the flash drive clenched in one hand and the liquor bottle dangling from the other.

"What a charming, personable human being," I mutter. "If he's a friend of yours, I really don't want to meet your enemies."

Darius gives a humorless laugh. "I wouldn't call him a friend. Obviously."

"How do you know him?"

"We go back a good fifteen years. Haven't seen him in about that long either."

"So he's not a friend, and you haven't seen him in years, but you trust him with our lives."

"Yeah."

Okay, then.

Darius stands, lifting his arms over his head in a long stretch. The movement pulls his T-shirt up at the waist, exposing his granite-like abs—smooth muscles and taut skin.

"I'll grab the stuff from the car," he says.

I drag my attention from his torso to his face. "How long do we have to stay here?"

"Could be a month." He shrugs. "Could be a year."

"Darius."

His expression softens, and he approaches to pull me into his arms. "Hopefully not more than a few days, as long as Banks starts digging into the files right away. If he doesn't, we have to wait."

"Can't you pay him to speed it up a little?"

"He won't take money from me." He presses his lips to my forehead. "He won't be rushed either."

"So what if he doesn't do it at all?"

"I think he will."

"You *think* he will."

"Nothing is ever guaranteed with Banks." He pats my ass. "Go on into the camper. I'll bring our bags in."

Clicking my fingers for Poe, I start toward the ancient vehicle. Until now, I've never seen a camper that actually looks haunted. The interior is dusty and old (*retro*, I tell myself) with a lime-green sofa, peeling linoleum, Formica table and bench seats, and scarred wood paneling. A door leads to a tiny bathroom, and the back section holds a bed and shelves.

Darkness falls more swiftly this deep in the woods. As I attempt to clean off the counters and table, Darius gets the dedicated generator working so we have electricity. There's running water for washing, but he tells me only to drink the bottled water. We eat packaged sandwiches for dinner, and I fill a bowl with kibble for Poe.

Darius had had the foresight to purchase new sheets, which is good considering the mattress is bare. After I finish making up the bed, I start to close the curtains. A light is on in the cabin on the other side of the clearing.

"How long has Banks been here?" I ask.

"At least ten years." Darius turns up the wall-unit air conditioner. "Last I heard, he makes a fortune hacking and testing computer security systems."

I lift an eyebrow. "Out *here*?"

"As a teenager, he was a genius-level computer expert. Used to hack into corporate and bank systems, then negotiate a deal to help them fix the holes. After high school, he joined the military."

The cabin door opens, and Banks emerges—his Bigfootlike silhouette illuminated by a single porch light. He crosses to the campfire and flops down in a chair.

"What did he do in the military?" I ask.

"He became a special ops officer." Darius folds his arms as he stares out the window at Banks. "High-level intelligence work, top secret clearance. About eleven years ago, he was with a unit in Baghdad, routine recon in a heavily trafficked, commercial district. He was on the fifth floor of a parking garage when he intercepted communication about a suicide bomber. From where he was, Banks could see the guy in a truck right outside a hotel. His CO said to take the guy out. Banks knew he could do it—he was trained to kill with one shot. But when he scoped in on the bomber, he didn't shoot."

"Why not?"

"It was a kid. No more than fifteen. Sitting in the front seat, wearing a suicide vest. Banks couldn't pull the trigger. Ten seconds later, the bomb exploded. Tore off the front of the hotel. Eighteen people died. Including the kid."

I stare at him. "How do you know all that?"

Darius's mouth tightens. "I was there."

CHAPTER 14

Darius

NELL FALLS SILENT. Her dismay is tangible. I brush my fingers against her arm and leave the trailer, crossing the distance to the campfire.

Smoke still billows from the logs, but the flames are dying, the bright glow turning to ash. Banks is sitting with one foot on the rocks, staring at the embers. He doesn't look up as I approach and sit down.

"You still got good taste." He indicates the whiskey bottle.

"At least one of us does."

He stabs at the logs with a stick. "Where're you going after this?"

"Depends on what we learn."

Banks slants his gaze to the camper. "You fucking her?"

"Don't talk about her like that."

He snorts. "Guess that answers my question."

"*Don't* talk about her like that." My voice is a razor blade.

He holds up one hand in a gesture of truce. "Seems like she can stand up for herself, huh?"

Yeah, she can. She can do anything.

I lean forward, resting my elbows on my thighs. "You going to look at the files?"

"Already did." He takes a swig of the liquor. "A few. I'll do some digital forensics. You said they came from the Hawke Financial system?"

"Yeah, but no idea which one. The guy who found them has gone missing."

"You get any of the papers translated?"

"Not yet. I can make out some of it, but not the context."

"I can get that done." Banks squints at the fire. "You really went back into the shithole?"

"It was the only way. But now the PLF thinks I know more about their organization and funding than I actually do. That's why I don't want anyone to know I made it out of there alive."

"You must know more than most people."

"Sure, but the UN and other counterterrorism organizations haven't thought the PLF was much of a threat. All the research and energy has been directed toward the higher-profile groups. I've been telling the UN for years that the PLF hadn't disbanded, that they were probably reorganizing. Now they might finally listen."

"At what cost?" Banks jabs at the fire again, conjuring up sparks and smoke.

"One that's too damned high."

An owl hoots in the distance. I look up at the sky, where a few stars gleam through the dark canopy of trees.

"How long've you been here?" I ask. "Thirteen, fourteen years?"

He shrugs. "I don't keep track."

"Civilization isn't so bad."

Banks laughs. "This from an asshole who was tortured in captivity and makes a living taking pictures of people slaughtering each other. Not so bad, huh?"

I catch sight of Nell passing in front of the camper window, the overhead light sliding across her chestnut hair.

"If it weren't for the bad..." I push to my feet. "I'd never have known how good it can be."

I walk to the camper and go inside. The old, dusty smell is gone, replaced with the scents of Nell—vanilla and a bunch of sweet, fruit-like things. Peaches and plums. She's sitting cross-legged on the bed, a camera in her hands.

"Everything okay?" She glances up, her gaze darting outside to Banks just before the camper door closes.

"Yeah." It takes me a second to realize she's holding my old Nikon. "You've had that all this time?"

"Of course." She holds out the camera, her lips curving into a faint smile. "I put it in my backpack when we were getting out of the apartment. And before I got on the plane, I told Savko I'd keep it for you this time."

Grief tightens my chest. Savko had brought me my camera when I was in the hospital after escaping the PLF the first time. He'd kept it for the duration of my captivity.

"I knew you would need it again one day," he'd told me, his grin wide behind his beard.

I'd barely been able to hold the camera after he'd handed it to me. Froze up when I tried to use it. I hadn't taken a single picture until two years later—on a Wednesday morning in Grenville when I'd fixed Nell in the lens and pressed the shutter button.

Now, as I take the camera from her, my hands fold around the body automatically. The weight of it is easy and comforting.

I scroll through the photos in the LED window—Varaz before the siege. Jacob and Tomas running through the street. Lara holding out a heart-shaped gingerbread cookie, beaming with pride. Children painting a mural at the school. Men clustered around the bar at the Koroleva Café. A faded fresco on a wall opposite the town hall. Alexei and Sofia's wedding, and the joyful celebration afterward.

Nell, of course. Dozens of pictures of her. Crossing Harmony Square. Coming toward me from the museum, laughing as Poe bounds up to greet her. Playing Shepherds and Sheep with a group of children. Dancing in the parade, a vision in the vibrant, colorful Krasnovian costume. Her hair long and disheveled, skin flushed with exertion, eyes bright. Her smile that looks as if it's meant for me alone.

Just a couple of hours later, on that very night, she was naked and open underneath me. Easing inside her had been both a mind-blowing relief and a shock that hit me like an exploding star. I still can't reconcile loving her this much and knowing it can't last.

"You look like you're thinking very hard," she remarks.

I put the camera aside and approach to smooth her hair away from her face. "There's a lot to think about."

She takes my hand and kisses my palm. "Speaking of thinking…I'm worried about my father. Because I know he'll be worried about me. Obviously we've had a recent falling out, but we still text and talk on the phone. He's not going to believe that I just wanted a few days off the grid, especially since he thinks I'm still looking for you."

I thread my fingers into her thick hair. Henry is a tight, frayed knot in the middle of my chest. I hate what I did to him, what he thinks of me now.

"Darius." Nell tugs on my hand. "Don't go there. Focus on what's *here*. Whatever happens, my father is going to have to deal with our relationship one way or another. But right now, I want him to know that I'm okay."

"I'll try to find a safe way we can contact him," I promise, though I don't know what that will be. I don't want to risk Henry's safety any more than I do Nell's. "Maybe we can get word to him through the college. I'll figure something out."

"Thank you." She edges forward on the bed and slips her arms around my waist, pressing her head to my torso. "He's had more than enough surprises recently without needing to worry about my safety again."

Or that you're with me.

I rub the back of her neck. Her arms tighten around me. She brings one hand to the front of my shorts and flicks open the button.

My blood goes hot. She glances up at me, her eyes darkening to a deep silver. The image flashes in my mind again— pushing my cock into her mouth, watching her lips slide over the shaft.

Smothering the urge to let her unbutton my fly, I stroke my hand down her cheek and ease away. "I'm going to take Poe for a walk. You need to get some sleep."

She drops her arms from me, disappointment shadowing her lovely features. I turn and snap my fingers for Poe. He ambles up from the sofa and follows me back outside.

I start walking, then break into a jog. Her voice is a constant stream in my head—*don't stop, keep going, fuck me.* Never before has a woman flooded my whole being so completely, all the sharp corners and crevices. She makes me want to break down every last guard I still have. To let her in all the way.

But if I do, I'll never be able to let her go. She'll be trapped forever.

CHAPTER 15

Henry

EVERY PART of Henry relaxes at the sight of Fern's car parked in the driveway of the Dearborne Street house. And when he walks inside and sees her, all lingering tension slides like water from his spine. She smiles, her cornflower blue eyes creasing, and crosses the kitchen to greet him with a warm kiss.

"I thought we'd just heat up the enchiladas you made the other day." She pats his lapel. "I still have a lot to do before I leave for the comic convention on Friday, so I need to get back to the store after dinner."

He slides his hand around her waist and pulls her in for a harder kiss. "I'll come with you and help."

"That would be great, but this isn't allowed." She tugs at his necktie playfully—she still teases him about his suits and ties being so "old-school professor."

Last Christmas, she'd gotten him a wool cardigan with leather elbow patches. She'd meant it as a joke, but he wears the sweater every weekend. And he suspects she secretly likes his suits and ties—though she never misses the chance to take them off him.

"Don't worry." He pats her ass as she turns to open the fridge. "I'll put on the official Comic Castle uniform."

Thanks to her, he now has an impressive supply of T-shirts emblazoned with superhero logos and silk-screened images of vintage comic books. And he never teases Fern about the jeans and T-shirts she wears all the time—he loves the way the denim hugs her hips and ass, loves the curves of her breasts under the cotton, loves watching her trim, lithe body move and flex as she shelves books or works in the garden.

It catches him by surprise sometimes—Fern here, in his house, in his life. Embedded so deeply in his heart. For years, he'd felt like his marriage to Katherine had used up his allotment of both love and fury. After her, he was destined to a life of quiet solitude and taking care of Nell.

Truth be told, that was what he'd wanted—or so he'd told himself. He'd certainly never imagined falling hard for a pixie-like beauty whose knowledge of comic book history rivals his expertise about the ancient Romans.

Fern is everything Katherine wasn't—always so easy to be with, comfortable in the world, and unwavering in her loyalty and care for the people she loves. Until now, Henry hadn't known how peaceful, how right, a relationship could be.

If only…

"Clover says she's getting to work on a storyboard for a new kids' TV show." Fern takes plates out of the cupboard.

"Good for her. Unfortunately, she mocked my ingenious idea for an animated version of Virgil's *Georgics*."

"She didn't mock you," Fern reprimands with an arch of her eyebrows. "She just knows that an allegorical treatise about agriculture won't play well for the under-five set."

Henry has to acknowledge that point.

"We should go visit her," he suggests. "Make a detour to Vegas."

Fern tosses him an affectionate smile. "So you can lure me to a quickie wedding chapel?"

"Of course. I've always wanted Elvis as a witness. Maybe even as the officiant."

She rolls her eyes, then crosses to kiss him again. "I love you, Henry Fairchild. You are the man and the relationship I never thought I'd find."

Though her words are poetry, he has to smother a sting of frustration. "So prove it by marrying me."

She backs off, her eyes narrowing.

Shit. Wrong thing to say.

"I wasn't aware you needed proof of my love," she says, her voice tinged with cold.

Henry sighs and drags his palm over his beard. "That's not what I meant. We've been together for four years. I just don't get why you don't want to be my wife."

"It's not that I don't *want* to be." Turning her back, Fern pulls open the silverware drawer. "I don't see the point. Both of us had challenging marriages. And things are so good with us. What if getting married to each other messes up what we have?"

"Honey, marriage will only strengthen what we have." Even as he says the words, Henry resigns himself to her response—as he has for several years now. He's lost track of the number of times they've had this discussion. "If a quickie Vegas wedding and Elvis aren't your thing, then we'll have a lavish gala in San Francisco and invite everyone we know. I'll give you whatever you want. Just say yes."

She stares at him for a second, as if surprised by the intensity in his voice. He's surprised by it too. He hadn't expected to make his case again five minutes after walking in the door. He's been on edge these past few days, uneasy for reasons he can't fully name. Fern's reluctance only adds to his disquiet.

But because he can't explain that even to himself, he holds up his hands in a gesture of truce. "The offer stands. Always."

Her shoulders relax, and she smiles. "I know, and I love you. Always."

The declaration softens the brief tension, though Henry knows this is only a détente, not a resolution or agreement. He takes the silverware from her and sets the table while Fern continues heating up leftovers.

"Any word from Nell?" She removes the enchiladas from the microwave. Her voice is light, but he hears the undercurrent of concern.

He shakes his head, picking up the glass of scotch she'd put on the table for him. He takes a swallow, but the liquor doesn't burn away the sick feeling in his gut.

In early June, he and Nell hadn't parted well at the airport. She'd been on the verge of tears; he'd been smothering his anger. But after she left, they'd both made an effort to stay in touch through texts and occasional phone calls. Their messages skimmed the surface—the weather, work, Nell's friends—but at least they were in contact. He knew where she was, more or less what she was doing, and that she was all right.

But now...she'd said she was going "out of town" with a friend for a few days and wouldn't have good internet access.

Okay. Henry thought it odd that she was leaving New York at all given her obsession with finding Darius, but he'd also been glad that she was doing something besides searching for him. She hadn't said where she was going—and given the new fragility of their relationship, he hadn't asked—but Nell wasn't particularly outdoorsy or into going off the grid.

So even if she had spotty cell service and Wi-Fi, she'd still have *some* access. At least enough to download her messages and tap out quick replies—if for no other reason than to assure him she was fine.

Since her last text almost four days ago, Henry has sent her seven or eight messages. She hasn't replied to any of them. Even if Nell were deliberately not responding to him, she'd never cut Fern or Clover off without explanation. But they haven't heard from her either.

He glances at Fern. She's looking at him warily, and then she voices the question that has been ricocheting through his mind all day.

"Should we call the police?"

Henry stares at his glass, swirling the liquor around. "Not yet."

He can't begin to imagine what Nell went through in

Krasnovar. Every time he thinks about it, the horror of *what could have happened* hits him with the force of a blow. Then the nightmare followed her home, forcing her to plunge into a search for a man who should be dead.

"Henry, I'm worried about her." With a frown, Fern taps her fingers on the counter. "What if she's in trouble?"

That's the problem.

Henry suspects his daughter *is* in trouble. He also suspects that calling the police could cause more problems. Nell might not want him to come looking for her, or he might make it worse if he does. Because there is only one reason she would cut off all contact with her family—and that reason is Darius Hawke.

And while Henry's rage at Darius is like a living thing inside him, he's sharply aware of the ways in which he's failed or hurt his daughter, no matter his good intentions.

Not this time. If Nell wants him to know where she is, she'll contact him. But Henry won't risk her safety by calling the authorities or looking for her on his own.

This time, he will trust his daughter.

CHAPTER 16

Nell

EARLY MORNING LIGHT falls through the trees, and the air carries the sound of birdsong and the rustle of forest creatures.

I set a bowl of food down for Poe and peer out the window. The campfire is dead, covered with white ash, and the cabin across the clearing appears cold and silent.

The SUV is gone—Darius woke me briefly to murmur that he was going to the store and would be back soon. I've taken great comfort in the fact that he no longer has any hesitations about literally sleeping with me. He would only trust himself to do so if he knows beyond a doubt that he's defeated his nightmares.

Pulling on a lightweight hoodie, I open the camper door. Ears perked, Poe bounds out in front of me and sniffs the air as if he's doing reconnaissance.

We take a short walk around the area, making sure to keep either the cabin or the camper in sight. The morning air is nice and cool, with dew sprinkled over the leaves, though the rising sun carries the promise of another scorcher.

Poe emits a low growl as we return to the camper. Banks is sitting on the cabin steps, his long legs planted like Doric columns on the ground. A paperback is folded in his big hands, the cover bent and torn.

Reminding myself that Darius would never have left me alone with this knife-slinging giant if he didn't trust him implicitly, I stop a short distance away. "Morning."

Banks peers at me through a tangle of hair. "You still here?"

"Am I supposed to be somewhere else?"

He picks up a blue ceramic mug emblazoned with the phrase *Rise & Grind.* "Thought you were with Hawke."

"Darius just went to the grocery store. We have to avoid being seen in public together." I push my hands into my hoodie pockets. "It's all very James Bond, Jason Bourne. Except a lot more terrifying."

With a grunt, he lifts the mug. "You want some coffee?"

"Is that *coffee*"—I make air quotes—"or coffee as in a regular, non-spiked, caffeinated morning beverage?"

He stares at me for a second, then barks out a rusty laugh. "Organic Sumatran dark roast. French-pressed."

I lift my eyebrows. "Yes, please."

He thunks his mug back down on the porch step and disappears inside. He returns with another chipped ceramic mug—this one orange and bearing a grinning jack o' lantern.

"Thank you." I approach to take it from him.

He points his chin toward a tree stump at the base of the porch steps. I sit and sip the coffee, which is rich and delicious.

We're silent for a few minutes. His gaze snags on my thigh. I'm wearing shorts long enough to cover my self-inflicted cutting scars, but now I realize the hem has ridden up far enough to expose several of the thick, raised lines. It's obvious they're not accidental—they're straight, symmetrical, and all the same length, slicing across the expanse of my bare thigh like the rungs of a ladder.

Banks looks away. I grab the hem of the shorts and tug them down farther. Though I'd shown the world my scars in my self-portrait collage at the Monarch High School art competition, Darius is the only other person besides my doctor who has seen them in actuality.

But I'm surprised to realize I'm not too troubled by Banks's observation. He too has plenty of deep scars of his own. Maybe some are also self-inflicted.

"It's nice out here," I offer, taking another sip of coffee. "I see the appeal. You don't have to deal with anyone."

"What about *you*?" he mutters.

"Anyone irritating, I mean."

He chuckles.

"What's the book?" I glance at the tattered paperback resting on the step.

He tosses it to me. I catch it with one hand and scan the cover—an old detective novel with an illustration of a private eye in suspenders and a fedora hat.

"A friend of mine in art school once did a collage of old pulp fiction covers." I hand him the book back. "They were pretty creative, like movie posters."

"You went to art school, huh?"

I nod, though it feels like I graduated a lifetime ago. "I thought it would be relatively easy to get an arts-related job. I was wrong. That's part of the reason I ended up volunteering in Krasnovar. I'd never even been out of the States before that."

"Good thing you got out when you did."

"Because of Darius." I tighten my grip on the mug. "He said he knows you from way back when."

Banks doesn't respond. His green eyes are cloudy. His relationship with Darius is none of my business, but it's obviously the reason Darius trusts him with our lives.

I can't help wondering if the feeling is reciprocated. Though Banks's welcome was hardly warm and fuzzy—or even a *welcome*—it seems like he's going to help us. Maybe.

"What'd he tell you?" His voice is gruff.

"Not much, at first. Then about Baghdad." I pause, watching his face for signs of anger, but he's closed-off and unreadable. "I think Darius has always understood things like that...impossible choices. Especially in war. I never did. I lived a sheltered life before I moved to New York, and even then, I was protected and privileged in a lot of ways. It wasn't until I went to Krasnovar that I had any sense of the actual impact of war on people's lives. The choices it forces them to make. I only saw and lived through a tiny part of it, but it felt like a thousand years."

Banks stares off into the distance, his silence almost louder than the sounds of the forest. Then he says, "He had pictures."

I shake my head, not understanding.

"I fucking hated that he was even there." He takes a gulp

of coffee. "He was a photographer embedded with our unit. What the hell was that? We didn't need an asshole following us around with his camera, taking pictures of everything we did. *Information warfare*, the lieutenant called it. Hawke wasn't the first, of course, but it stuck in my craw. Not that there was anything I could do about it."

He leans forward, elbows on his knees and his mug grasped in both hands. I get the sense that he's almost talking to himself rather than me.

"Hawke was good, though." He drags one hand over his beard. "He knew what to do, how to move. None of us felt like we had to watch out for him because he could take care of himself. He and I were the only ones there, on the fifth floor of the parking garage. He was taking pictures the whole fucking time, even when the bomb went off. I don't know how long it was. We'd run down to the scene and... Jesus, what a mess. It was after the ambulances arrived and the area was secured...Hawke gave me the memory card from his camera."

I swallow. "With all the pictures on it?"

"He was the only one there."

I gaze at a little sparrow hopping across the porch. I know what photos were on that memory card. Dead bodies sprawled on the street. The destroyed hotel—flames ripping through the interior, smoke billowing out from the scorched remains. People running toward the chaos, running away. Faces contorted in anguish and terror. Maybe even an image of the teenage bomber.

And photos of Banks, both before and during the hesitation that shattered his world and drove him into hiding. From people, from society, and maybe even from himself.

Not for anything would Darius ever have published those photos, even if he'd kept the memory card. But he'd wanted to assure Banks that no one would ever see them and to give him back a measure of control.

"I could've been court-martialed," Banks says.

I look up in surprise. "Why? What for?"

"I disobeyed an order." He drains the last of the coffee and sets the mug on the step. "I got a direct order to take the bomber out. I didn't do it."

"But it was understandable. For heaven's sake, anyone would...you didn't *consciously* disobey." My voice trails off as I realize how naive I must sound. "What did your superior officer say?"

"Nothing. He never knew." He runs his hand over his thigh. "Hawke is the only one who knows that seventeen...*eighteen* people died because I didn't pull the trigger when I was ordered to."

Another dimension to their dark, shared secret. No wonder Banks has a conflict of love and hate for Darius. When only one other person knows your worst, most wrenching pain, you're stripped to the bone. Defenseless. And Banks is not a man who wants to be vulnerable or indebted to anyone.

He pushes to his feet and turns to go back into the cabin. The weathered door slams shut behind him.

I rub my thumb over the pumpkin on the mug. Maybe helping us is Banks's way of making things even between him and Darius—though I know Darius doesn't think there was ever an imbalance to begin with. He proved Banks can trust him. And he knows he can trust Banks.

The sound of the SUV engine rumbles through the air.

Darius parks near the camper and gets out, his shoes thumping against the leaf-strewn dirt.

He goes around to open the hatch. He's wearing khaki shorts and a faded gray T-shirt that shifts across his chest and shoulders. His movements are both purposeful and efficient, edged with the masculine grace of a man at home in his body.

He glances up, catching me staring at him. In a swift assessment, he notices the coffee I'm holding, the paperback still on the porch, Banks's mug beside it. His eyes narrow.

"Everything okay?" he asks.

I nod, setting the mug down and rising to approach him. I slide my arms around his waist and press my face against his T-shirt. Soap, morning air, pine needles.

He folds his arms around me. "You sure?"

"Yes. Did you bring me some ice cream?"

"Butter pecan, still cold in the cooler." He kisses the top of my head and releases me to pick up the cooler. "And pickles. They're not Krasnovian pickles, but hopefully they're a worthy substitute."

I smile. "Ice cream and pickles. Anyone would think I was—"

He looks up sharply.

I stop, horrified. The word shrivels in my throat. Embarrassment crawls up my neck.

"Oh my god." I press my hands to my cheeks. "I didn't...I wasn't implying...I mean, I'm *not*, I assure you..."

He laughs, the booming sound startling me into silence. I stand there, my face still hot, as he steps over and presses his lips to mine.

"It's okay," he murmurs. "Of the things that could scare me right now, *that* is definitely not one of them."

He turns, carrying the cooler up the steps and into the camper. I stare after him, my embarrassment easing. Though I'm not about to start harboring any illusions, least of all one about us having a baby and living in domestic bliss, it's a relief to discover that the hypothetical possibility doesn't rattle him.

Then again, there's not much that rattles him—except, as he'd confessed in Varaz, the idea of losing me.

I grab the grocery bags from the SUV and follow him inside. We unpack and put the food away, and he takes a newspaper out of one of the bags.

"Patrick told me that Savko's friend Martin has been found safe in a village near Polvik," he says. "Sounds like he knew he was in trouble, and he got out of Saldem as soon as he could."

I breathe a sigh of relief. "That's good to know."

"There's more good news out of Krasnovar." Darius opens the paper and points to a short article. "The army has taken back control of Kolchava."

"Really?" I scan the article.

"They're still battling across the entire northern province, and the PLF has Varaz in a chokehold again," he says. "But it's something."

"What about Telina?"

"The PLF broke through a defensive line in the eastern part of the city." He puts the ice cream in the freezer. "But the army has held them back from a full invasion. So far."

"I don't suppose we can contact Alexei?" I ask. "See if he's been able to find Sofia?"

Regret flashes in Darius's eyes. He shakes his head, reaching out to touch my hair. "Not yet. I'm sorry. Patrick is still trying to find out whatever he can."

At least Patrick is one link to the rest of the world. I'm not sure yet if Banks counts as a link or not. Unless it's a missing one.

I fold the newspaper and head back outside. Though I hate what's happened in Krasnovar, I feel better knowing that at least the PLF hasn't overrun the country entirely, despite their surprise nationwide attacks. Maybe soon the war will shift in favor of the people.

How will Conrad Hawke react to this news?

The question appears unexpectedly in my mind. When Conrad had told me about the bombing, he'd seemed almost angry, his frustration barely contained.

At the time, I'd thought he was upset about Darius, but a man who refuses to pay ransom for his hostage son wouldn't react that emotionally to his possible death. God knows Conrad hadn't even been moved when I'd told him Darius was missing. He'd said that Darius should have been killed years ago. That he "deserves whatever end he meets."

I shake my head to dislodge the unsettling thoughts. If Hawke Financial is doing business in Krasnovar, it makes sense that he'd be invested in the outcome of the war.

It's just strange that no one, not even Darius, seems to have known about Conrad's Eastern European interests until now.

CHAPTER 17

Nell

DARIUS CAN'T STAND BEING inactive. And since we're stuck in Banks's lair, he prowls around for the next two days looking for things to do, just like he did in both Grenville and Varaz.

He repairs an old generator, changes a flat tire on an ancient car that Banks doesn't even use, and fixes everything broken in the camper—the hotplate, a curtain rod, a cabinet door. He replaces rotten boards on the cabin steps and rebuilds the rock circle around the campfire—which means he has to scour the forest for bigger, *better* rocks than the ones currently in use.

Banks, narrow-eyed and thin-lipped, tolerates Darius's industrious labor until Darius starts climbing a ladder to tear out old shingles on the roof. Then Banks orders him to "Get down from there, you motherfucker, and leave my shit alone."

After a short but heated argument which ends with Banks threatening to kick his ass out of the Black Hills altogether, Darius grudgingly abandons the roof repairs. Then he takes out his anger on several dead tree trunks by splitting them into firewood.

Since Banks always needs firewood, he stalks back into the cabin and slams the door, leaving Darius to hack away at the logs.

It's a barrel of laughs. I stay out of the testosterone-fueled tornado whipping around the forest, occupying myself with reading one of Banks's detective novels, sketching, playing with Poe, and conducting a moderately successful attempt to make popcorn over the campfire.

It would be fun in a *Little House on the Prairie* kind of way if we weren't in hiding and on the run at the same time.

Every ten minutes, I glance at the cabin, hoping Banks will emerge to tell us something useful rather than bluster around defending his kingdom from Mr. Fix-It.

And while Darius continues stomping through the campsite like an angry bear, I can't help secretly admiring his vigorous, determined energy. Watching him chop wood becomes my favorite pastime, especially since he's so unaware of my attention. I sit by the campfire, pretending to be engrossed in my sketchbook while actually gazing at him out of the corner of my eye.

He wields the axe with fluid ease, like it's an extension of his body—swinging it around and lifting it over his head before bringing the blade down with a heavy thwack. The wood just surrenders, falling into neat, equal pieces that he tosses on the pile before dragging another log to the tree stump.

Again, the effortless lift of the axe, the flex and pull of his muscles, and a heavy grunt as the blade descends and the wood splits in half.

He's sweaty. His T-shirt is plastered to his chest, his hair is damp, and drops of sweat roll down his neck before disappearing under his collar. His biceps bulge with power, and his leg muscles are as strong and corded as the logs. Sawdust and flecks of wood cling to his clothes and hair.

He must smell like pine sap, the copper tang of exertion, hot summer air. And *him*, that warm, delicious scent of salt and citrus that makes me—

"Seen enough?"

His dry voice breaks through my reverie, forcing my gaze to his. He's paused in his work, his grip loose on the axe handle and his chest heaving.

I give him a weak smile. "Just...um, admiring the view."

"Take a picture," he deadpans. "It'll last longer."

"I already have." I tap my finger against my temple. "Up here."

A smile tugs at his mouth. It's the most amusement I've seen from him in two days, so it feels like seeing a rainbow through the clouds.

He picks up a split log and throws it onto the woodpile, which is now almost the size of a minivan. After setting the axe down, he approaches and sits in the lawn chair next to mine.

I'm right—his clean, sweaty, woodsy smell hits me like a drug. I want to move closer and inhale a deep lungful, filling myself with both his scent and everything it contains—strength, determination, courage, resolve, dedication.

He reaches for a water bottle and twists the cap off,

tilting his head back to take several huge gulps. Even the movement of his throat muscles is captivating.

"So what do you think your frenemy is doing in there?" I gesture toward the cabin. "Besides plotting world domination?"

Darius lowers the bottle and wipes the back of his hand across his mouth. "I hope he's breaking through firewalls and decrypting ciphertext."

"And if he's not?"

"I'll have to buy him another bottle of whiskey." He sets the water down and picks up my sketchbook from the top of my backpack. "Do you need a new sketchbook?"

"No, I have quite a few pages left in that one."

"Let me know when you need new supplies, and we'll stop at an art store." He flips through the pages of the book, pausing to examine my drawings of Poe, a ladybug on a leaf, the old pickup truck. He turns another page and stops.

I glance over at the quick colored-pencil sketch I'd done of Banks—all dark scowl, bushy beard, tangled hair, and bright green eyes.

Darius frowns. "When did you draw *this*?"

He stabs his finger at Banks's face as if it's a cockroach.

"Yesterday. It was just from memory. He has interesting features."

Darius's frown deepens. "What do you mean *interesting*?"

I elbow him in the side. "I mean *interesting* the way a woolly mammoth is interesting."

His eyebrows snap together. "You told me I was the only man you've ever drawn."

"Oh. Well, that is...you *were*. I mean, obviously you're my favorite," I add hastily. "But when I was trying to forget...er, focus on other things, I started making an effort to draw different men…ah, *people*. I've done portraits of Alexei, Ivan, my friend Jonah. It's very important for an artist to expand her creative capabilities."

"Fine." He slams the book shut. "But you don't need to be expanding a damned thing with Banks."

"Hmm. Considering it took you four long years to finally fuck me, I'm not sure you're in a position to be giving orders."

He shoves to his feet, rising to his full height so fast that a little thrill of excitement zings through me. He reaches down and hauls me against him, a menacing glower darkening his features.

"Let's get one thing straight." He lifts me into his arms so that we're eye level. "I'm in charge."

I wrap my legs around his waist and brush a speck of wood off his cheek. His body heat—intense and thick with adrenaline—sinks into me.

"You're in charge." I kiss his chin. "When I say so."

A growl rumbles from his chest. I can feel the vibration through his entire body, and the flicker of excitement grows into a firestorm. He slides his hands under my ass and stalks to the camper.

After yanking the door open and kicking it shut, he deposits me on the bed and stands there glaring at me, all seething, grimy male.

I am so turned on. It's like with one flick of his wrist, he dialed a burner up as high as it can possibly go. I push to my elbows and lift my eyebrows in an attempt at nonchalance, though it's impossible to quell my trembling.

He snaps open the button on his fly. I lick my lips. He

draws in a heavy breath. Slowly I sit up on the edge of the bed and grab the waistband of his shorts, pulling him closer. My head fills with his earthy scent.

He's hard already—his shaft a long thick ridge against the front of his pants. I ease down the zipper, my heartbeat kicking up at just the sound of the metal rasping open. Then I push his shorts and boxer briefs off, and his erection rises.

I half expect him to stop me, but this time he doesn't. I lean forward and enclose him in my mouth. Arousal and a touch of trepidation fill my blood. He spears one hand into my hair, and I feel his burning gaze as I slide my lips over his shaft.

I've never experienced anything like this before—the pulsing heat against my tongue, the salty taste of him, the strange feeling of both power and submission.

Though his hand tightens against my scalp, I know he'll let me do this for as long as I want. So I take my time figuring it out on my own—gauging by the tension in his body and the sound of his breath what he likes the most—before pulling away. Though he's *in charge,* I suspect I'm the one who gets to dictate where this goes.

I get to my knees on the bed and wind one arm around his neck. He grasps my hips, his hot breath stirring my hair.

"Darius." I press my lips against his warm neck and murmur, "Do you remember that night at the beach house?"

He goes still. His eyes darken...with regret or lust, I can't tell. But he's never flinched from his own past, and I won't let him retreat now—not from our shared history, and especially not from me.

"Do you remember what you said when you were so mad?" I rub my thumb across his lower lip. "About the things you'd do to me? That you'd grab my hair and spank me and—"

"I remember." He averts his gaze.

"Hey." I tighten my arm around him. "I'm not reminding you to make you feel guilty. I don't think you ever realized how much that speech turned me on."

He doesn't move, but a muscle twitches in his jaw.

"I even relived it in my fantasies." I stroke my hand down his arm and take hold of his wrist. "I'd touch myself while imagining getting on my hands and knees so you could fuck me from behind...like an animal, you said."

He still doesn't move, but his breathing increases.

"Just thinking about it now makes me wet again," I whisper, parting my thighs and pressing his fingers up under the hem of my shorts. "I'd come so hard when I'd think about you doing those things to me. About us doing them together."

"Jesus, Nell." A hoarse chuckle breaks from his throat, even as he works his finger past the elastic of my underwear. "You test every limit I've ever possessed."

"That's my point." I rotate my hips against his hand. "I don't want to test your limits. I want to break them down."

His jaw clenches. The heat in his eyes belies the tense set of his features, the attempt at self-control.

"I told you I wasn't scared of you or anything inside you." I let go of him to pull off my T-shirt. "Just the opposite. I know you've been holding back because you think parts of me are still fragile, that you don't want to hurt or scare me. And God knows I love you for that because it's sweet and so *you*, but you don't have to treat me with kid gloves. I want everything you can give me. I'll take it. I waited for you for so long, and now—"

I push back on the bed and wiggle out of my shoes and shorts. My pulse is pounding, my blood hot. The taste of him still lingers on my tongue.

Without a word, I strip off my bra and underwear and turn around, getting to my hands and knees. Behind me, his breath expels in a heavy rush. He settles his hand on my ass. An instant later, his finger trails down the cleft.

A shudder rocks through me. His adrenaline is charging the air, lighting it with flames. He runs his big, callused hands all over my body—my thighs, my hips, reaching underneath me to my breasts. His touch is rough, urgent, like he's filling his palms with me. His cock brushes against my thigh, then he moves away to pull off the rest of his clothes.

I grab the bedcovers, my breathing shallow, my body arching toward him. He pushes his knee between my thighs.

A pluck of anxiety twinges through me—I have never felt this exposed, not even with him, and he's jacked up from more than just lust—but then he presses a kiss to my shoulder blade, and the knot unloosens.

"Okay?" His deep voice vibrates against my skin.

"Oh, yes."

He eases into me. I tighten my grip on the bedcovers. Sweat rolls down my neck and between my breasts. In this position, he feels bigger than ever, his shaft throbbing against my inner flesh, firing my nerves.

He digs his fingers into my ass. His breath saws through the air above me. I squeeze my eyes shut when he starts to thrust. Though he's moving slowly, still tense with self-restraint, the impact jolts me forward. I push back, crying out as our bodies flex and collide together hard. Darius stills.

"More," I whisper.

He groans, sliding his hands to clutch my waist, and increases the pace.

God. It's like he's driving into me even deeper than he has before, stimulating places I hadn't known existed. I'm hot everywhere, inside and out. My senses flood with the sensation of his thrusts and everything else—the abrasion of his hair-roughened thighs, the grip of his fingers, the slam of his hard stomach against my ass. He grunts heavily with every stroke, the guttural rumble intensifying the heat in the air.

I start coming before I even realize it's happening—the explosions bursting through me so fiercely I can barely choke out a gasp of pleasure. Darius slows, waiting for the sensations to ease before he pushes into me again.

Through the fog of bliss, I expect him to drive toward his own release—but no. He slides his hand under me and adeptly rubs my aching clit, pulling me again toward that bright pinnacle. I bury my face in a pillow, barely aware of the pleas streaming from my throat—*yes, please, more, harder*—as another orgasm breaks over me like a sunrise.

His rhythm shifts. He closes his fist around the length of my hair, pulling my head back. Delicious prickles skate over my scalp and down my spine.

I brace myself, arching against him as his thrusts speed up again. Sweat drips from my breasts, and my muscles lock against the increasing force. A low groan fills the air. His body stiffens, shuddering against mine as he comes deep inside me.

With a muttered curse of satisfaction, he lowers me to

the bed and sinks beside me, stroking his hand down my back. His skin is damp with sweat, his dark hair sticking to his forehead. I edge closer, still absorbing the aftershocks of pleasure.

"See?" I poke his steel-like upper arm. "I can take it."

He gives me a half smile, though darkness invades his brown eyes.

"Come on, Darius." I push to my elbow and rest my hand on his chest. "It's not like we're getting into whips and chains here. At least, not yet," I add, giving him another teasing poke. "Last time I checked, this is pretty normal stuff we're doing. I know it's nothing you haven't done with other women. In fact, you've probably done a heck of a lot more."

He doesn't respond, but he doesn't have to. I've never been under any illusions about the number of relationships he's had or the women he's slept with. But I also know that only with me has he felt the need to stay in check.

"You're not going to hurt me," I tell him. "We both know that. So why have you had this barrier?"

He brushes his hand through my hair, pushing it away from my face.

"I love you," he says. "Hard."

"Good." I kiss his shoulder. "I like it that way."

"But I can't have you forever." He runs his thumb over the line of my cheekbone.

Though my heart twinges, I attempt a rueful smile. "So that means we can't have crazy, wild sex?"

"It means I don't want to get any more addicted to you than I already am." He lowers his hand. "If that's possible."

I spread my fingers over his chest, feeling his heartbeat. Though I don't want to admit it, I understand what he means. He's been a part of me for so long—embedded in my cells and my blood and all the invisible, intangible things that constitute *me*—that I don't think I've ever fully imagined life without him.

Even during the four years we were apart, he was still there, a presence in his very absence. I hadn't gone a day without at least a passing thought of him; more often, he'd invaded my fantasies, my attempted relationships with other men, my dreams.

But though I'd been devastated when we separated in Grenville, his leaving had also—in ways I still can't fully measure—strengthened and challenged me. I'd woken up, broken free. I'd started to become the woman I'd always wished I could be. And then Varaz had shown me I'm even more than that.

How will it feel to walk away from Darius again—now, after all we've endured, after we've fallen so deeply into each other? How will I bear watching him walk away from me?

In Varaz, I'd assured him I didn't expect anything more. That I knew our lives weren't a fairy tale. That a future for us was an impossible tangle of desires and wishes pushing against reality. I couldn't imagine, would never want him to quit his life's work for my sake any more than I could imagine staying behind and waiting for him. I didn't want to live with the fear that he might not come back.

And yet...isn't that what I've done my entire life? What we've both done? He's always lived on the razor's edge while I've waited for and reaped the joy of his return.

Now, of course, I'm a different person. Even without him, I have a rich, fulfilling life with my art, my friends, my activities. Darius and I are far more balanced than we've ever been before.

He'll always be older and more experienced, but he's no longer an authority figure. The power dynamic is on him only if we both want it to be.

Maybe that bodes well. Maybe despite all that's happened —or perhaps because of it—we're growing and entwining like the roots of a plant.

What if that means we can reshape our future together? What if we could build a life on this new symmetry? On this powerful love and intimacy that has no end? On trust, devotion, and knowing he will always come back to me? What if we allow truth and honesty to overpower fear?

The questions burrow inside me. I have no answers, and I shouldn't even speculate on them—at least, not when we're in such a precarious situation. We don't know what will happen in the next five seconds, so ruminating on a hypothetical future is both silly and a waste of time.

Still, it's there. A tiny kernel. A seed that might, one day with enough care and sunlight, flourish into something that could outlast time itself.

CHAPTER 18

Nell

I WAKE TO A RHYTHMIC THUMP, like the sound of metal embedding into wood, but it's not the heavy *thwack* of Darius's axe.

Pushing myself out of bed, I pull on shorts and a white cotton shirt, pausing to splash water on my face and brush my teeth before going outside. I've overslept considerably; it's already late morning, and the sun burns through the canopy of trees.

Darius is nowhere in sight, and Poe is flopped beside the burned-out fire, his ears perked and head moving back and forth as he watches Banks. Who is standing about twenty feet from a grove of pines, flinging knives.

One by one, the sharp blades sink deep into the tree trunks. He crosses to yank them out, then returns to throwing. Though there aren't any targets, his aim is flawless. I have no doubt the knives are landing exactly where he wants them to.

What is it with men and this primal urge for sharp blades and wood?

Banks stops at the sound of the camper door closing. I smile and wave hello.

He grunts, holding a knife by the blade before flinging it at a pine tree. The knife spins and lands solidly in the wood.

I'm not even going to ask. Whether Banks's knife-throwing prowess is a hobby, actual self-defense, therapy, whatever...it's his business. I've pushed far enough into his private life. There's a reason he chooses to live out here alone in the wilderness, and chatting with an inquisitive young woman on the run isn't one of them.

I walk to the campfire and give Poe a hug and an ear-scratch. On a tree stump beside the chair I usually sit in, there is a ceramic Christmas mug and a metal carafe.

I sit down, pouring myself a cup of hot fragrant coffee. In addition to having a potential career as a knife-throwing circus performer, Banks would make an excellent barista.

Darius emerges from the woods with a large, jagged rock, which he drops beside the campfire before kissing my fore-head in greeting. Banks stomps past him to the cabin, knives in hand. The wooden door slams shut behind him.

"He's quite a blade-slinger," I remark.

"He was picturing me as his target."

I grin. Darius grabs another rock from a small pile and starts rearranging the circle, widening the fire bed's diame-ter. I take another sip of coffee, enjoying watching him work.

"Were you a Boy Scout?" I ask.

He chuckles and shoves another stone into place. "Not even close."

"So how did you learn to do all this lumberjack wilderness stuff?"

He straightens, studying the rock circle. "I spent many summers in an outdoor survival program for rebellious kids. Well, my father's version of that kind of program. He'd hired a guy—former Marine—who'd come grab me in the middle of the night and drop me off in some isolated forest or desert for two or three weeks."

"Alone?"

"With a walkie-talkie, yeah." Darius's tone is matter-of-fact, as if he'd just gone away to summer camp. "I think the guy was close by, but I never saw him, and he didn't help me out. By the time I was ten, I was on my own."

I shake my head. "But it had to be illegal to do that to a child."

"Probably. But Conrad Hawke has never thought laws apply to him."

"How old were you?"

"Around eight to…I don't know. Fourteen, fifteen. Before I was shipped off to boarding school."

"Your father made you do that every summer?"

"Guess he figured it wasn't working." Darius gives me a humorless grin. "It was tough, but I didn't mind getting away from him. Except that also meant being away from Odette and Katherine. Odette tried talking my father out of it, but that didn't do any good. Not that I ever expected it to."

I stare at the ash-coated logs on the fire. "Was he physically abusive? Your father?"

"He knocked me around a few times, but he had plenty of

other ways of terrorizing people without resorting to physical violence." Darius picks up another mug and pours fresh
coffee into it. "He let other people get their hands dirty on
his behalf. That's how he's always operated."

"What about your mother?" I ask. "Victoria."

A shadow crosses his features. He's silent for a long
moment before he says, "She died when I was seven.
Cancer."

"Do you remember her?"

"Yeah." He rubs his thumb over the handle of the mug.
"My father didn't want me to, though. He'd ordered the
doctors to stop her treatment."

I stare at him. "Did *she* want to stop?"

He shakes his head, his gaze on the burned-out fire. "She
was a fighter. But what she wanted didn't matter to Conrad.
She'd always been the perfect wife, the hostess, the woman
who completed his image. And when she couldn't fulfill that
role any longer, he moved on. She was expendable, like
everyone else in his life. After she died, he got rid of all her
clothes, possessions, everything that had belonged to her.
Erasing her. Or trying to."

It would sound like a harsh assessment if I didn't know it
was true. "How could he order the doctors to stop treating
her? Wasn't it her choice?"

"Conrad has spent his life ripping choices away from
people." Darius brings his cup to his mouth. "Of course, I
didn't figure all that out as a seven-year-old. Back then, I just
felt like I was going to explode."

My heart constricts. Despite our vastly different
upbringings, I think Darius had a much lonelier childhood
than I did. And I could turn to both my father and him for

comfort and stability. Darius eventually had Odette and Katherine, but they'd also relied on him, not the other way around. He's always been everyone else's protector.

But now, I hope he knows he can depend on me. That our differences and similarities balance the scale. That together we might even be powerful enough to reshape the future.

The cabin door opens, the slam of wood against wood shaking the thought out of my head. Banks emerges, carrying an old black laptop with the flash drive attached to a port.

"No device is entirely secure when you're connected to a network." He thrusts the computer at Darius. "But this is as tight as I could make it. Log into any of your accounts, and you might as well roll out the red carpet for the fuckers."

While I suspect Banks handed over the burner laptop to thwart Darius from tearing down and then rebuilding his entire cabin, it's a relief to have a tool that connects us to the rest of the world.

Instead of collecting rocks or chopping firewood, Darius spends the rest of the morning frowning at the laptop screen as he tries to track down the origins of the factory bombing photos. He also examines the digital photos from so many different angles and resolutions that it's like he's deciphering an unknown language.

I peer over his shoulder at the grainy images.

"I told Savko I thought they had to be from a government or military source." I still don't like looking at the photos—the black smoke and shapes of dead and wounded bodies. I really hate the memory of wondering if Darius was one of them. "When your father showed the first photo to me,

Varaz was still under siege. Communications were out, the fighting was worse than ever, and not even the media had reported the bombing. So the photos had to come from someone with connections or influence."

Darius zooms in on the factory again. "What did my father say when you asked him where he got the photo?"

"He didn't like that I was asking. He told me to stay out of it, which obviously I didn't do." I twist my mouth, old regret stabbing me. "Maybe I should have heeded his advice."

"You didn't do anything wrong." Darius pats my thigh. "It's admirable how much you were able to get out of him. He's not one for helping people, but you had an impact on him."

"I assumed it was because I'm Katherine's daughter."

Darius shakes his head. "He wrote Katherine off years ago. And he sure as hell didn't do it for me. You were the reason. Which means you impressed him. He doesn't impress easily either."

I don't know what to make of that. I don't like Conrad Hawke one bit—and I'll never forgive him for leaving Darius to be tortured—but he was different from what I'd expected. Less supervillain and more...complicated.

"Well, despite all his connections, your father didn't seem to know much about your counterterrorism work."

"Not surprising. He never much cared what I did."

"Maybe he got the photos from someone involved with his mining interests in Krasnovar." I shrug. "Can you trace them any further if they don't have metadata?"

"Not much. Unless they have some other identifying feature..."

He squints at the image with a frown. I can almost see the

wheels and gears clicking together in his mind, like the mechanisms of a finely tuned clock.

Leaving him to his studying, I take our empty cups back into the camper. I've gone over my conversations with Conrad Hawke a thousand times in the hopes of gleaning some insight into this whole mess, but none of it makes sense.

With Banks holed up in his cabin, and Darius fixated on the laptop, I spend the afternoon cleaning up the camper and handwashing some clothes. When I go back outside to pin them up on a clothesline, Banks is building the fire, which he does every afternoon around five.

He lights the kindling, and Darius brings a few logs over from the woodpile. The two men converse for a couple of minutes as I hang the clothes.

I can't hear what they're saying, which is a decided relief. For the past few days, my ears have been ringing with all the rough shouts and insults ping-ponging between them.

"Nell, come in." Banks jerks his thumb to the weathered cabin door before disappearing inside.

My heart knocks against my ribs. Darius crosses to the porch and pulls open the screen door, ushering me into the cabin ahead of him.

I have no idea what I expected to find—a hoarder's nightmare, maybe—but the place is spare and clean, with shabby furniture and shelves stuffed with books. A low counter separates the living room from the kitchen, and aside from a few modern appliances like a microwave and coffee maker, it could be a nineteenth-century cabin.

Then I glance through an open door to another room, and the illusion shatters.

Multiple computers, keyboards, and monitors are set up on various desks, and two TVs are mounted on the walls. The room has an eerie glow from all the screens. Wires, consoles, antennas, connectors, and switches link everything together in an intricate, high-tech maze.

Banks sits down in a red-and-black swivel chair positioned in the middle of the setup. He's like a spaceship captain on the bridge, about to order a jump into hyperspace.

He plugs the flash drive into a port on the computer and brings up an image of what looks like a legal document in Krasnovian. "Like you thought, Hawke Financial is getting into mining investments. Conrad Hawke is doing business in Krasnovar through a shell corporation."

"Is that legal?" I ask.

"It's not necessarily *illegal*," Banks replies. "Shell companies can legitimately be used to disguise transactions. The question is why Hawke would want to. And what he's doing with other shells."

"Laundering money, most likely." Darius crosses his arms and stares at the screen.

"He's making payments, not getting dirty money. From what I can tell so far."

"Who's he paying?"

"Several mining companies." Banks brings up strings of numbers and stock market abbreviations on another screen. "In return, he's getting exclusive mining rights throughout Krasnovar."

Darius grabs a couple of folding chairs and pulls them up closer to Banks. He and I sit down as Banks scrolls through the documents and images on the flash drive, explaining what he's been able to decipher.

There are permits for mining rights, graphs and charts about mineral ore and grades, future predictions, import and export laws, maps about Krasnovian mining belts, and dozens of reports.

All of it has to do with the shell corporations through which Hawke Financial has been making transactions to mining companies.

"How long has my father been doing this?" Darius asks.

"Oldest date I could find goes back about six or seven years, but I'm guessing he started before that." Banks points out a series of colored maps. "The maps show that Krasnovar has reservoirs of traditional metals like copper and iron, but there are huge untapped deposits of lithium and other rare earth metals. They're in massive demand for use in phones, laptops, tablets, cameras, electric vehicles. All told, the Krasnovar deposits could be worth over a trillion dollars."

"A *trillion?*" I look at Darius in surprise. "Wouldn't everyone want in on that? Why haven't other big international companies invested in Krasnovar's mines if that much money is involved?"

"They were probably thwarted by the civil war," he says, "then political instability and security challenges. It hasn't been easy for any company to do business in Krasnovar for almost fifteen years."

"Or the companies might not even have known about the deposits," Banks adds.

Darius frowns. "But somehow, my father did."

"The country's problems haven't stopped him." Banks

reaches for a soda beside the computer and takes a swallow. "But extracting lithium and rare earth minerals is a shit ton more complicated than mining copper. Requires a lot more money, technical knowledge, and time. It could take half a dozen years, if not longer, between the discovery of a lithium deposit and the start of extraction."

"Do we know if the mining companies found the deposits?" Darius asks.

"Oh, yeah. A few of them. That's why your father wanted the mining rights and started pouring money into production. Probably wanted to get a foothold before anyone else."

"So if he started six or seven years ago, then they might be getting close to extraction now," Darius says.

"Right." Banks settles into his captain's chair and rocks back and forth. "The stakes are going up. Big time."

"That must be why he doesn't want anyone to know about his investments," I suggest. "If there's potential to make over a trillion dollars, he probably wants to keep it all as confidential as possible so he won't have to share the wealth."

Darius and Banks both nod. Banks takes another gulp of soda.

"But how did he find out about the mineral deposits in the first place?" Darius asks. "And why was Hawke Financial the only company to invest?"

None of us have an answer to that.

"How did you track all of this?" Darius leans forward to study the string of numbers on the computer screen.

Banks launches into a lengthy explanation of his "digital forensics," though I don't understand most—okay, any—of what he's saying about attribution, password cracking, and cross-drive analyses. Given the sheer stealth and clue-following involved, however, it's no wonder he likes detective novels.

As he and Darius talk about firewalls, Poe trots over to scratch at the door. I touch Darius's arm and indicate that I'm going to take the dog out. He nods.

I open the door and follow Poe outside. He crosses to the camper, and I fill his bowl with kibble and some leftover turkey.

Dusk has started to fall, creating long shadows across the forest floor. Poe gobbles down his food and wanders around the campfire, sniffing and pacing. He picks up a stick and pads over to drop it at my feet.

"Haven't gotten much exercise these past few days, have you?" I scratch his ears and toss the stick a short distance away. With a bark, he bounds after it and returns it to me.

I throw the stick again, and we start an energetic game of fetch that leads us deeper into the forest. I'm careful to keep the camper in sight as Poe runs farther and farther, his tail wagging and his body wiggling with happy dog energy. I run after him, also enjoying the chance to stretch my muscles and breathe in the cooler evening air.

Poe races back and forth, retrieving the stick and dropping it at my feet. I throw it, then follow while he fetches and pauses every now and then to sniff at a tree or chase a squirrel.

After a particularly energetic toss, the stick lands on the other side of a small incline. Poe hurries to grab it and disappears from my sight.

"Poe!" I climb up after him, my breathing fast.

I stop at the top of the hill, peering into a thicket of

increasingly dense pine trees and brush. "Come on, Poe, let's not go too far."

Turning, I glance back toward the campsite. A twinge of disorientation goes through me before I spot the weathered side of the cabin through the trees.

"Poe! Come on, boy."

He growls. My heart jumps. "Poe?"

The leaves rustle. Poe darts out of the brush, barking in a sudden frenzy, his ears flattening as he comes toward me. Alarmed, I put my hand out.

"Poe, what in…"

He stops a short distance in front of me in his protective guard dog stance, his body stiff with warning, his barks sharp and short.

Is there another animal or—

Another noise slices through the air—a click, a low whoosh, and then a *thump*. Poe's barking cuts off abruptly, like a plug was pulled. His legs crumple underneath him. He falls to the ground.

Uncomprehending, I rush toward him. Another click stops me in my tracks.

A massive man in black pants and a lightweight jacket emerges from a dense grove of trees. He's carrying a pistol outfitted with what I think is a silencer.

A gun he just used to shoot Poe.

CHAPTER 19

Nell

A SCREAM CLAWS up my throat and stops. I run to Poe and drop to my knees beside him. His fur is getting matted with blood, his body unmoving.

No no no...

"Get up." The man's voice is cold and quiet.

I stare at him through unfocused, blurred vision. No recognition fires past my terror. Is he Conrad Hawke's bodyguard or security officer or...?

"I do not want to hurt you." He holds up his other hand, but the gun is still unwaveringly pointed at my head. "Let's go."

Ice spills through my veins and prickles over my skin. Somehow I manage to get back to my feet. My hands are sticky with Poe's blood. I can't breathe.

"Where is Hawke?" he snaps.

Oh god. My heart hammers. He knows Darius is alive.

I shake my head, like I don't understand the question.

The man steps closer. He's huge with flat, hard features and the steely eyes of a person who knows how to kill. Every instinct yells at me to run, but looking at the gun is like staring into a black hole. He might not *want* to hurt me, but he will.

He advances. "Do not try and run or fight."

I can't even move. Something about his voice stings the back of my mind, but it doesn't form into anything meaningful.

"Where…where are you taking me?"

If I scream, will Darius and Banks hear me? Or will this killer shoot me like he shot Poe?

He waves the gun, impatience tightening his features.

I tell myself to walk, but my limbs won't obey. I'm too terrified to even look at Poe.

The man closes in on me, wrapping his meaty hand around my arm and pulling me forward. I stumble. Before I can regain my balance, a large shadow falls over both of us.

Darius.

He yanks the man backward. His grip breaks away from me. Darius clamps his arm over the man's forehead from behind, twisting his neck hard enough to wrench him to the ground. Bone cracks like the strike of a whip.

The man grunts. The gun falls. Before Darius can reach for it, the guy turns, one hand disappearing beneath his jacket. The waning sun glints off the metal of another pistol.

I open my mouth to shout a warning when Darius dives for the fallen gun. He grabs it, aims, and fires. Another whoosh, and the bullet slams into the man's skull. Blood splatters. He hits the ground, his eyes wide and unblinking.

Bile chokes my throat. My head spins with a wave of dizziness. Darius grabs my shoulders. His mouth is a hard line, his eyes burning.

"Okay?" he asks.

I manage to nod. "P-Poe."

He releases me and turns. With a low curse, he crouches beside Poe and runs his hands over the dog's body. "He's still breathing."

Lifting Poe into his arms, he starts back to the campsite. I follow, sick with dread and overwhelming fear.

As we near the campsite, Banks runs toward us, his gaze going from me to Poe in one quick assessment.

"Fuck," he says.

"He's alive, but he took a bullet to the side." Darius sets Poe down beside the campfire, pulling the dog's fur aside in a search for the bullet hole. I pick up my hoodie from a chair and drape it over Poe. Darius grabs the sleeve and presses it against the wound to stop the bleeding.

"How many were there?" Banks bends to lift Poe's eyelids and peer at his pupils.

"One." Darius's eyes harden. "But not for long. Nell, did you recognize him?"

"No. He wasn't one of the security men from the Hawke Financial building. At least, not one that I'd encountered. But he asked where you were. They know you're alive and with me."

Over Poe's head, Banks and Darius exchange glances that seem to speak volumes.

"Man, you gotta get out of here." Banks turns, meeting my gaze. "Nell, get your stuff together. *Now*."

The sharp note in his voice spurs me into action. Blocking my terror, I run to the camper and throw my belongings into my travel bag. When I go back outside, Banks and Darius are speaking in low, urgent tones. I toss the bag and my backpack into the SUV.

I hurry back to Poe and kneel beside him. Tears sting my eyes. His breath is shallow and faint, his tongue hanging out, his whole body shivering. I put my hand on his head.

"We need to take him to an emergency vet." My voice breaks.

"What you *need* is to get the hell out of here," Banks replies tightly. "Somehow those fuckers tracked you here. I guarantee more of them are on the way."

"There's gotta be a tracker on the car." Darius starts toward the SUV.

"Don't waste time looking for it." Banks runs to his old pickup truck and yanks something out of the dashboard. He returns to hand it to Darius. "And take the laptop. It's as untraceable as I could make it, but be careful."

"I'm taking the flash drive too."

"You could leave it with me," Banks suggests. "Keep them off your trail."

"No way, man. It's what they're after, and you've done enough."

The two men exchange a quick handshake before Darius runs to the camper.

Banks approaches me and Poe. I stare at him, stricken by the level of danger we've put him in. "What about you?"

"Don't worry about me." He picks Poe up and stands, striding back to his truck. "I'll take him to the vet. Hawke, get her *out of here*."

Darius is already loading up the SUV with his stuff. His Glock is tucked at the small of his back. "Nell, get in the car."

"But we left that man..."

"I'll take care of it," Banks snaps. *"Go."*

There's no time to say goodbye to either him or Poe. Darius hauls me into the passenger seat, pausing only to fold me into a swift, hard embrace.

"Hold on," he whispers in my ear.

He lets me go and slams the door, hurrying to get behind the wheel. After pushing a small, cylindrical device into the car's electrical socket, he starts driving. The SUV skids over leaves and branches, cutting a path through the brush before we reach the dirt road leading to the highway.

I wipe the tears from my cheeks and struggle to contain the sobs wrenching through me. Darius reaches over and puts his hand on my knee. He doesn't say anything. His anguish is as deep as mine.

We reach the two-lane highway winding through the hills. Signs point the way to several towns; Darius goes in the opposite direction. The heavy silence is broken only by the low hum of the engine and the rush of an occasional passing car.

"Will he be okay?" I dig into my backpack for a package of tissues.

"Banks will be fine." Darius flexes his hands on the wheel. His profile is inflexible, a single muscle twitching in his jaw. "I don't know about Poe."

My tears overflow again. "How did they find us?"

He doesn't respond, his mouth compressing.

"What if they're still tracking us?" I ask.

"That's a GPS blocker." Darius indicates the device plugged into the electrical socket. "It jams the signal so they can't track us."

"But how were they able to put a tracker on the car in the first place? How did they find us?"

"Shitty luck," he mutters, pulling off the road and into the half-circle of a small rest stop.

He takes out his burner phone and checks the messages. My heartbeat accelerates.

"Banks says Poe is in surgery." He hits the call button and waits for Banks to pick up, putting the phone on speaker.

"Yeah, man." Banks's voice comes through, distorted but audible. "I had to leave him with the vet to get back here. No one in a five-mile radius of the cabin, but I'm not taking any chances. Couldn't find any identification on the dead guy, and the serial number on his gun had been drilled off. Any idea how the fuckers found you?"

"Possibly." Darius drags a hand over his jaw. "Look, could you check the law enforcement databases over the past few days? See what kind of info and alerts they've gotten."

"Local or federal?"

"Both. The FBI and the...the human trafficking center. Check their tip line, if you can."

Nausea surges in my stomach.

Banks doesn't hesitate. "On it. I'll call you back."

"No," Darius says. "I'm going to get another phone. I'll be in touch."

He ends the call and tosses the phone in the console.

I swallow past the tightness in my throat. "You think that woman at the motel had something to do with this?"

"She might've reported us." He starts the car and backs out of the parking space.

"But how would your father know it was *us*?"

"He didn't. He just knew it was you. Then he probably guessed who was with you. He was likely getting intel from different sources, which is how that bastard found us in the Black Hills."

I don't know what to make of this until later in the evening, after we've driven halfway to Wyoming. In the parking lot of a fast-food restaurant, Darius contacts Banks from a new burner phone he picked up at an electronics store earlier in the day.

Over the speaker, Banks first reports that Poe is in recovery—not out of the woods yet, but the vet is cautiously optimistic. For the first time all day, I'm able to breathe a little easier. Then Banks confirms what Darius suspected.

"The Ohio state police got a tip about you and Nell. Security camera footage of her. Your license plate number and description. It took me about three mouse clicks to learn that, so the hired guns probably got the info the second it was reported."

"That's how they found the car." Darius presses the bridge of his nose between his thumb and forefinger. "He probably put the tracker on it when I was in town. Followed us right to the cabin."

"And made his move when he saw Nell alone." Banks mutters a noise of disgust. "What d'you want me to do next?"

"Look after Poe and keep digging into those files. There's

a reason my father wants them back. I want to know what it is."

"Where are you heading?"

"We're going to keep moving." Darius turns the key in the ignition. "Better for us not to stay in one spot."

"Nell there?"

"I'm here," I say.

"Poe said to tell you he misses you a pawful lot," Banks reports. "But he'll see you soon."

I laugh, even as my eyes spill over with fresh tears. "Thank you, Banks."

"Take care of her, Hawke."

Darius meets my gaze. Beneath the determination in his eyes is the deep tenderness that I have known my entire life.

"Always," he promises.

He ends the call and starts driving again. Though his vow thaws some of the ice in my blood, I'm still cold.

I wrap my arms around my torso as I stare out the side window. Something pushes at the back of my mind, like a fish struggling to the surface of a pond.

"He had an accent," I say.

I feel Darius glance at me. I bite my thumbnail, not sure if I even know how to articulate why I feel like this is important.

"The hitman?" he asks.

"Yes. I just remembered. I didn't process it at the time, but I was thinking about your father's security officers…and I dealt with over half a dozen of them before I even met him. I was wondering if I'd seen this guy before, but I hadn't. And none of the other security men had accents."

Darius frowns as he processes this. "My father only hires

highly trained bodyguards and security. Some of them are former Mossad, Alpha Group, SAS. He could've sent any one of them after us."

"I figured." I rub my hand over my throat. "But we don't have evidence that the man was sent by your father, do we? I was trying to think of something that would definitively tie him to Hawke Financial, and now that I remember his accent...I don't know. Maybe I just got used to hearing accents in Krasnovar."

Darius shoots me a sharp look. "That guy's accent was Krasnovian?"

"I don't know." The cadence of his words was vaguely familiar, but he hadn't said nearly enough to make me sure of it. And it's not as if I can easily distinguish a Krasnovian accent from so many others. "I might have been able to place it if I'd noticed it at first, but in retrospect, it could have been Russian or Romanian or Polish or one of any dozen languages."

"There's a possibility my father is hiring men from Krasnovar," Darius says, "especially given his investments in Eastern European mines. But he has plenty of high-level security units in the US already. If he's hiring Krasnovian military, it would probably be to protect his mining interests in Krasnovar, not to carry out contract orders."

The pieces click in my brain. I look at Darius. He meets my gaze briefly. We're both thinking the same thing.

There's no evidence connecting the hitman to Conrad Hawke. But with more news finally coming out of Krasnovar, it's likely that everyone who died or was wounded in the factory bombing has been identified.

And Darius Hawke, Pulitzer Prize-winning American

war photographer, former PLF hostage, international counterterrorism expert who supposedly knows about the PLF
financing and funding sources, was not among them.

The People's Liberation Front might know he escaped.

And they're the ones who might have found us.

CHAPTER 20

Darius

THOUGH SHE'S TRYING to hide it, Nell is close to her breaking point.

We've been on the road for twenty-three hours since leaving the Black Hills, and the truth—the hard reality of what we're facing—has slammed into her like a train. Her eyes are bruised with dark circles, her skin devoid of all color.

She'd been even more terrified during the siege in Varaz, but back then we'd been focused on getting to safety. We knew who the enemy was. She'd had other people to think about. She could see the city wall, the eastern gate we were heading toward. She had to watch out for Jacob and Tomas. Poe was at her side.

Now, we're driving without a destination, escaping from an enemy we can neither see nor fight. Poe is hundreds of miles away in a vet's office, recovering from a bullet wound. Nell can't contact her father or her friends. It's like a horror movie—midnight, no moon, pitch-black. She knows something is out there, waiting to pounce, but she has nowhere to run or hide.

After a night of no sleep, I stop at a big-box store for an air mattress, extra pillows, and a mobile hotspot. I drive for another hour before pulling off the road into a grove of trees and high grass behind an abandoned barn.

It's close to eleven. In the passenger seat, Nell stirs and opens her eyes.

"What are we doing here?" Her voice is hoarse and scratchy.

"Hoping to get a decent night's sleep." I get out and open the hatch to move things around and make room for the air mattress. I'd switched out the SUV's license plates for two old junked ones, but it's a flimsy cover—and though I wish Nell could sleep in a hotel again, there's no way I'll take the risk.

After I get the mattress inflated and made up with sheets and pillows, Nell crawls over the console into the back. She sinks onto the bed with a sigh of pleasure, as if it's made of the finest goose down.

"Get some sleep." I pull a cotton blanket over her and tuck her in. "I'll wake you when it's time to leave."

"Don't go anywhere."

"I'll be here." After locking the doors, I crack open the windows to let in the cooler night air, then sit beside her as she settles her head against the pillow. In seconds, her breathing shifts into the rhythm of sleep.

I pull the burner laptop out of my pack, connect to a

weak signal, and log in. Banks has been sending me his findings through a proxy server, and I scroll through them before pulling up the photos of the factory bombing. Though Banks hadn't found any information about their source, Nell's instincts were right. The photos lead to someone or something important.

I study them again, magnifying the multicolored pixels, the amorphous shapes. They were taken with a high-quality camera and a zoom lens, though the photographer hadn't gotten any close shots.

But photos always hold a clue, a piece of the story. I just have to find it.

I create a new anonymous email address and send all five of the photos to a colleague and friend at a science and technology institute in India. Vidya and I have corresponded multiple times over the years about the technical aspects of digital photography.

Although I wish I could explain that I'm Darius Hawke, I invent a pseudonym and ask if she can please run the attached images through the watermark extraction system that she's been developing. I have no idea if she'll comply, but it's worth a shot.

I text Patrick on the prepaid phone he'd bought for our communication, letting him know that we're okay but telling him nothing else. I owe him a lot, and I don't want him involved any more than he already is.

Tossing the phone aside, I press the heels of my hands to my eyes. It's been ten days since we left New York. Henry and Fern must be out of their minds with worry about why Nell hasn't responded to their messages. Her friends too. This can't last much longer.

Beside me, Nell stirs and tucks her body closer to mine. She's like a bite of warm chocolate cake nestled into a spoon.

I rest my hand on her hair, smoothing a few strands away from her face. A patch of moonlight illuminates her features and turns the scar on her forehead silver.

She rubs her cheek against my chest. She blinks, focusing her sleep-hooded eyes and reprocessing where she is and why she's here.

"Anything?" she asks.

"Banks texted that Poe is stable and the vet expects a slow but complete recovery."

"Thank god." Nell heaves a sigh. "And Banks is okay? No one's bothered him?"

"No." I stroke her hair gently. "But you've seen how Banks deals with people bothering him. He'll be fine."

"I feel awful that his lair was invaded because of me."

"Nell, look at me."

She lifts her head. Her eyes are cloudy, her skin still pale.

"None of this is your fault." I slide my hand to the back of her neck. "There was no way for you...for anyone...to know that Krasnovar was about to be overrun by terrorists in an attempted coup. And that the shitshow would follow us here."

She acknowledges that with a wry nod and rises to one elbow.

"Like I said"—she leans closer and presses her lips against mine—"being with you is never boring."

I pull her closer, deepening the kiss. Lust fires through me, quick and hot. Her effect on me is a constant burn of desire, like a fuse before it ignites an explosion. But as much as I want her right now, I pull away and stroke my thumb across her lower lip.

"You should get some more sleep. I want to get back on the road before sunrise."

She settles her head on my chest, easing her hand under my T-shirt. "Maybe we should make our way to Mexico. Disappear. We could find a little adobe house in the middle of nowhere. Learn Spanish, drink hot chocolate with chili, raise chickens."

It sounds as close to heaven as I've ever imagined.

"But I'd miss my family and friends." She smooths her palm over my abdomen before tugging her hand out from under my shirt. "And you'd be incredibly bored."

"I don't know about that." I run my hand down her side to her curved hip. "Hot chocolate and chickens sound pretty good right about now."

"Do they?" She settles her arms on my chest and rests her chin on her hands, her gaze on me. "Even for an adrenaline-chasing war photographer?"

"I don't do it just for the rush."

"I know, but that's part of it, right?"

I shrug, though we both know the truth. It's not one I'm proud of but it's there, buried under all the scar tissue.

"The rush doesn't mean I don't like chickens," I tell her.

Nell smiles, and suddenly it feels like we're the only two people in the world.

"Good to know, tough guy." She pats my chest. "Maybe one day you'll find another place where you can take a deep breath."

I twist a lock of her hair around my finger. "You remembered."

"Arkenos? Of course. Your favorite place in the world."

I study the strands of her hair in the moonlight. "What's your favorite place?"

"You." She responds with no hesitation. As if the word just flew out of her.

I don't know what to say. It feels like my heart is trying to escape a cage.

"Darius." Nell touches my cheek, her eyes softening to dove-gray. "I will always love you. And I won't lie and tell you I haven't thought about what we could have together, if we tried. But now more than ever, I know that life isn't a fairy tale with a happy ending. Or at least, not necessarily the one we dream of."

I want to ask her what kind of "happy ending" she dreams of, but I hate the thought that I can't—won't—be the one to give it to her.

"Besides," she adds, "having a favorite place doesn't mean you need to live there."

"You do, though." I spread her hand over my heart. "Right here."

She smiles again. "Keep me there for a little while longer, would you?"

Forever.

The promise sticks in my throat. As useless as it is to think beyond what's happening right now and what I need to do to keep Nell safe, she makes it impossible for me *not* to imagine the future.

Or at least, a version of the future where I can kiss her whenever I want. Where no one bothers us and time doesn't matter. Where I can look up and see her sitting by the window, her head bent over a sketchbook, the sunlight pouring over her like melted honey.

Where every day I put a vase of fresh wildflowers on the table for her. Where all we need to think about is how late we should sleep in, when we're going to make love next, and whether or not we need more feed for the chickens.

But the world doesn't allow such places of blissful peace. At least, not for any length of time.

I wrap my arm around Nell and pull her closer, pressing my lips against her hair.

I'll keep her here, all right. Hold on as tight as I can. For as long as I can.

CHAPTER 21

Nell

THE SUN IS like an egg yolk on a white-blue china plate. Heat rises from the asphalt, almost visible against the crisp, dried prairie grasses covering the fields on either side of the highway. The stereo hums with Simple Minds' "Don't You Forget About Me," the lyrics floating on the air-conditioned currents streaming from the vents.

This morning when I woke up, Darius told me that we're going to drive to Los Angeles. Apparently there is a computer/hacker conference starting at a Hollywood hotel tomorrow, and Banks gave him the name of a guy who has a device that can further muffle internet traffic. Darius hopes it will enable me to safely contact my father.

I'm both anxious and relieved. I desperately want to talk to or at least text my father. It's been two days since we left the Black Hills—ten days since we left New York—and aside from my time in Varaz, my father and I have never gone this long without any kind of communication.

I know the destination also gives Darius a plan of action. We still have no solid evidence that the hitman was connected to either Conrad Hawke or the PLF. And Darius is limited with what he can do on the burner laptop, so he's still forced to rely on Banks for information. It's gnawing at him hard, this aimless driving and lack of ability to control everything.

We're well into the dry valleys and mountain ranges of central Nevada when he pulls off the highway to a rest stop. Several other cars are parked in front of a large, wooden building, and a few kids are running around a playground outfitted with swings and a slide.

Darius and I have developed an automatic routine at rest stops—he gets out of the car first, and I wait until he's either gone into the building or walked a distance away before I get out to stretch my legs and use the bathroom. He doesn't get back into the car until I've returned and am sitting in the passenger seat. We never even make eye contact when we're in public.

"I need to get ahold of Patrick and check for a return email." Darius picks up his backpack and phone and pushes the SUV door open.

He squints at the building, where a family of four is coming out the door. The parents are carrying frothy iced coffees, and the two kids are eating packaged ice-cream bars.

"Looks like there's vending machines or a shop inside." He pulls out his wallet and hands me a couple of twenties. "Grab a few snacks for the road."

I nod, stuffing the bills into my shorts pocket as he gets

out and heads into the building. I wait a couple of minutes before following.

The interior is big and airy with overhead fans circulating. A little alcove contains a snack shop, where an older woman is ringing things up on the cash register. A few more families and couples are seated at round tables or are looking at the big information posters that detail the area's history, flora, and fauna.

I use the bathroom and stop to peruse the shop's offerings, stocking up on trail mix, chips, and protein bars. Out of the corner of my eye, I see Darius go back outside—I assume to find a cell signal, which has often been spotty at the various rest stops.

Since he usually takes at least half an hour both looking for a signal and talking to Banks or Patrick, I treat myself to a dark chocolate Klondike bar and eat it while reading the info posters paneling the walls. After I've finished learning about a 15,000-year-old glacial lake, a birds-of-prey conservation area, and the formation of a canyon, I toss the crushed ice-cream wrapper into the trash and head back out.

I'm halfway to the SUV when I see the police car parked in the spot on the other side, the vehicle dwarfed by the bigger SUV. A uniformed officer is standing by the police car's trunk and another is beside the open driver's side door, his head bent over a tablet.

My heart stutters. I stop and back up a step the instant one of the officers glances over at me.

I tighten my grip on the plastic bag of snacks. It's obvious I was walking toward the SUV, so will it be suspicious if I turn around now and go back inside?

Before I can even make the decision, the officer approaches me.

"This your car?" He jerks a thumb at the SUV. His name tag reads *Burton*.

I don't know what to say. "No" would be accurate, but then he'll ask whose car it is, and I'll be forced to tell him about Darius—who I hope is well out of both sight and earshot.

"Why?" I finally ask. "Is there a problem?"

"Looks as if your registration is long expired." He peers at me from beneath the brim of his hat. He's youngish, probably not that much older than me, with coarse skin and a few pimples. Beads of sweat dot his upper lip. "Could you step over to the vehicle, please?"

Telling myself to stay calm, I walk with him to the SUV. I sense a few passersby glancing at us. The second officer looks up from his tablet, his eyes narrow. "Name and identification, please."

"Natalie Fleming." I dig out my wallet and hand over the fake driver's license that Patrick and Darius had somehow procured for me.

The second officer—Ramirez—studies the license. Ramirez is older with a graying beard and a sharp, assessing gaze that seems to indicate he's both seen and heard it all before.

"Not only is your registration expired," he tells me, "your license plate isn't linked to your vehicle. In fact, it's not in the system at all. Can you explain that?"

I can, but I sure as hell don't want to. I won't.

"I'm sorry, but I don't know anything about that." I shrug,

maintaining a pleasant tone of voice even as my heart sinks lower and lower. This isn't going to end well.

Burton is peering into the windows of the SUV, noting the travel bags, the two take-out coffee cups in the front console, the package of bottled water.

Ramirez studies me, tapping the fake ID on the edge of his tablet. "Where are you heading?"

"California."

"Alone?"

Shit.

"No. I…my…my husband is still inside." I'm starting to shake. They can't question Darius. No one can even see us together. But how do I explain the evidence of two people, the junked and likely stolen license plates, or the fact that I don't even have the keys?

Ramirez hands my fake ID over to Burton, who opens the passenger door of the police car and pulls out a heavy laptop. After less than thirty seconds of tapping on the keyboard, he shakes his head at Ramirez, who walks over to look at the screen.

Sweat rolls down my spine. I glance back at the building. No sign of Darius, but he never leaves me alone for long. I can't even imagine what he'll do if he sees me talking to two police officers.

"Miss, I'm going to have to ask you to come down to the station with us." Ramirez straightens. His expression has gone from suspicious to…concerned? "Don't worry. You're not in any trouble."

I swallow past the growing lump in my throat. "Then why do I need to come with you?"

"We just want to ask you a few questions." Burton puts

the computer away, but not before I catch a glimpse of the screen—a grainy security camera still shot of me outside the Ohio motel.

If I run, will they chase me down? How do I warn Darius? What the fuck should I do?

"Let's go." Ramirez pulls open the door of the SUV. "Go ahead and grab your belongings."

I reach into the SUV and take my backpack from the floorboard. Ramirez holds open the back door of the police car.

"Am I under arrest?" I ask.

"No," he says. "This shouldn't take long."

Shouldn't does not mean *won't*.

Burton has moved behind me, blocking whatever escape I might try to make. I'm boxed in between him and the two vehicles. Running would be utterly useless—and if I leave with them, maybe that will turn their focus away from Darius.

I get into the backseat of the police car. Burton closes the door. The click shatters through me, splintering my insides. I half expect one of them to wait for my "husband" to come out of the building. Burton is talking on his radio, but I can't hear his words past the thunderous roar in my ears.

Another police car pulls off the highway and into the rest stop. Ramirez approaches the driver, and the two officers converse through the open window for a few minutes. Ramirez points at the SUV, nods, and returns to his vehicle.

I clench my fists. I'm terrified. If they see Darius, they'll probably arrest him. Then what?

Ramirez pushes the car into reverse and maneuvers out of the spot. The other police car pulls up, blocking the SUV.

As we drive toward the exit leading to the highway, I look back.

My breath stops. Darius is standing in the shadows behind the building, tension lining his body as he watches me leave.

The police station smells like ink and stale coffee. It's small, housing a lobby and a few offices lined with metal desks. Several officers and a couple of men in suits are lounging in swivel chairs, shuffling through papers or working on computers.

None of them glance up as Ramirez and Burton lead me to a separate office. A woman is sitting beside the desk, and she rises as we enter. She's tall and pretty, with long hair pulled into a braid and kind eyes.

"I'm Greta Atkinson." She extends her hand to me with a smile. "I'm here to support you however you need."

I don't respond. Ramirez closes the door and gestures to a chair in front of the desk.

"Sit down," he offers. "Would you like some coffee or water? Anything to eat?"

I shake my head. I'm still holding the bag of snacks, which suddenly seems absurd.

"There's…" My voice comes out dry and raspy. "There's been a terrible mistake. I'm not—"

"You're safe here," Greta says soothingly.

The hell I am.

"Let's just get some facts down." Ramirez sits behind the

desk and picks up a pen. Burton stands by the door, his arms crossed. "Tell us your name. Your *real* name," he adds.

I feel sick. Again, I don't know what to do. They know I'm not *Natalie Fleming*. But have they identified the woman in the security camera footage?

Greta answers that question. "You're Nell, aren't you? Nell Fairchild."

My spine stiffens. "I don't want you to contact anyone."

"We won't. We just want you to tell us the truth."

"Listen." I pull in a deep breath. My lungs burn. "I realize you think I'm the victim of an abduction or something horrible like that, but I assure you that couldn't be further from the truth. And I'm almost twenty-three, not thirteen. I'm an adult. I'm not being coerced. I'm not in danger. The woman who called the hotline or whatever was flat-out wrong about her suspicions. And I honestly don't think I'm obligated to answer any questions *or* that you have any right to keep me here against my will."

"Considering that you appear to have been traveling in a potentially stolen vehicle, we have every right," Burton replies.

"That isn't a stolen vehicle."

"Then why isn't it registered?" Burton counters. "Where did you get the plates?"

I am so screwed. My only consolation is that Darius wasn't caught off guard. He knows where I went, and he saw the other two officers arriving at the rest stop. He'll know what to do.

I might be stuck here, but at the very least, I can keep my mouth shut. I turn my attention back to Ramirez.

"I don't intend to answer any further questions without a lawyer," I say.

He sighs. "Do you have a lawyer?"

"No."

Another sigh. "Look, we'll have to keep you here until we can secure you counsel. But if you answer our questions, we might be able to let you go today. You said you were traveling with your husband? The other officers are going to question him too, so you're not doing either yourself or him any favors by not cooperating."

He glances at my left hand, one eyebrow arching. I curl my fingers into my palms.

"As I stated," I reply curtly. "No further questions."

Ramirez looks almost pained. He flicks his hand toward Burton, who approaches and steers me out of the office. We walk down a narrow, concrete corridor to the back of the station.

Five seconds later, a holding cell door closes and locks behind me.

CHAPTER 22

Darius

AFTER WALKING BACK out to the highway, I hitch a ride to a town called Woodpine, over twenty miles from the rest stop.

The only advantageous part of this fuckup is that I have my laptop, phone, gun, and all my cash—none of which I've ever left in the car. I also have the flash drive. When the cops are forced to tow and search the SUV, they'll find clothes and travel bags, but nothing that could identify me.

Nell, on the other hand—

I clench my jaw and hand over a stack of cash to a junkyard dealer. He pushes a car key across the counter. I grab it and walk out to the old beater sedan sitting outside the gates.

Based on the area map, I've figured out that the cops probably took Nell to a station in Arlington, about thirty miles southwest.

After starting the car, I head north. When I'd told Banks what had happened, he'd cursed so vehemently the airwaves blistered. Though he'd promised to hack his way into the police system to try and find out what, exactly, had happened to her, I have a sick feeling there's nothing I can do to get her back.

Not yet. If the police connect her with the woman in the hotline tip, then they'll intensify their search for me. Hell, even if they don't—we were in an unregistered car with probably stolen plates.

I could make them a deal. I'll turn myself in for the stolen plates if they let her go. But then I won't be able to protect her, much less figure out what the fuck is going on.

At the very least, Nell is somewhat safe with the police. There might be less chance of either my father or the PLF getting to her if the police keep her at the station.

It's a small consolation at best—I don't want her anywhere except with me—but I have to take it.

A call from Banks buzzes. I hit the speaker on my phone.

"I don't know what happened to her," he says.

"What?" I turn up the speaker volume, sure I didn't hear him right.

"She's not in the system."

"There's no arrest record?"

"No. She wasn't booked. No fingerprints, no mug shot. At least, not yet."

"Did they even take her to the station?"

"From what I heard on the recording, yeah," Banks says. "But either they didn't book her or they didn't keep her there."

"Then where the fuck is she?"

"I don't know, man."

I bite back a thousand curses. Banks has done far more than I'd ever expected or even wanted—as much as I've needed his help, I hate having to stay underground and not do it myself. But now more than ever, I need to be strategic about my next move.

"Okay." I drum my fingers on the steering wheel. "Anything on Conrad?"

"Ever since his system was hacked, he pulled up the drawbridge and locked it all down. I can't get into any of his shit right now."

"Yeah. I can't even get a read on where he is."

"I'll keep digging," Banks assures me. "And I've got Poe back. He's still recovering and on pain meds, but he's walking and eating well."

"Good." It's no small relief—and one that I need right now. "Thank you."

After ending the call, I keep driving, cutting a path through the deserts of Nevada. I stop in another small town and pull up in front of the local library to connect to their free Wi-Fi. I log in to my anonymous email. There's a message from Vidya, the professor at the technology institute in India.

Since there's only one person I know of who would ask this kind of question with these kinds of photographs, I've run them through the extraction program for you.

The results are attached. I hope everything is all right. Let me know if you need anything else.

I don't want to put Vidya at further risk by replying, but after this shitshow is over with, I'll send her both flowers and a sizable donation for her department.

I download the attachments and delete the email account. In addition to the photos that she put through her computer program, Vidya also sent me a report about the results of the watermark extraction process.

There's always a lot of talk in the photography industry about the watermarking of images to prevent theft and preserve copyright protection. Most photographers and photo sites layer visible, transparent text over an image to identify the photo's owner.

But there's an increasing use of hidden watermarks that are imperceptible to the human eye, even through extremely close analysis and magnification.

I've used spatial watermarks on my own photos in the past—a unique identification signal embedded into the pixels of an image that can only be seen through color separation and extraction algorithms. Vidya's computer program is designed to find a hidden watermark—if one is embedded in the photographs in the first place.

According to her report, that is indeed the case with the photos of the Varaz factory bombing.

I stare at the mark Vidya found in the top left corner of each photo. It's an outline of a fingerprint, embedded so deep into the pixels that it's invisible on the surface.

A fingerprint.

I know exactly what organization uses a fingerprint logo as an identification mark—the Granite Intelligence

Agency, a private company that infiltrates terrorist units, conducts full-scale operations, and investigates potential threats.

The watermark is a breadcrumb they use to trace activity. By tracking who sends and receives their watermarked photos, they can pinpoint key operators both within and outside of terrorist organizations.

The photos of the bombed factory were taken by a Granite Intelligence agent who'd infiltrated the PLF. The watermark proves it.

It also proves that my father got the photos directly from the PLF—only he didn't know he was getting them from a Granite Intelligence spy. He thought he was getting them from a PLF captain or another secret contact. Someone he's been in league with for years.

I pull up a document from the Hawke Financial files—one involving a transaction my father made with a mining company in Krasnovar. I dig further into the company's name and employees. One surname jumps out at me.

Balakin.

In Krasnovar, it's as common a surname as Smith is in the United States.

But this is no coincidence.

What had Captain Lenkov said on the road by the factory?

"Your father has interests far greater than you."

He'd known about Conrad's goals. The top PLF officials were as invested in the mining company as they were in terrorism.

All the fragments of information I've collected start moving, like pieces shifting around a chessboard.

Krasnovar has over a trillion dollars' worth of untapped battery mineral mines.

Six years ago, my father began obtaining exclusive rights to Krasnovar's mines, but he did so covertly through shell corporations, money laundering, and other illegal transactions that were not supposed to lead back to him or Hawke Financial.

It takes six or seven years for a lithium mine to start production and extraction—which means my father's long-term investments are now close to paying off.

The dates of several contracts are from the same year when I was being held hostage.

The same year my father refused to pay the PLF a five-million-dollar ransom for my release. Because of company policy, he'd said.

I close the laptop and stare out the windshield at the library.

There was no "company policy." My father was cutting a deal with the PLF for mining rights. That was why he didn't pay the ransom—instead of giving in to the terrorists' demands, he started collaborating with them.

And he left me in their custody either to rot or as part of their negotiation. The PLF had also been demanding the release of political prisoners, so keeping me a hostage meant they'd still have leverage. And plenty of money.

Conrad Hawke has been financing the PLF for the past six years, helping them rearm and regroup as they prepared to violently take back control of Krasnovar.

He *needs* the coup to succeed and for the dictatorship to return to power. Otherwise, he'll lose all his rights to the mines...and the billions of dollars they could produce.

No fucking wonder he wants the Hawke Financial files to stay hidden. The contents of the flash drive are a grenade that could destroy him and his empire with one yank of the pin—or click of a mouse button.

I shake my head. I've always known my father was ruthless. Corrupt. Greedy for money and power. But I've never thought him capable of terrorism and war crimes. Of funding a military coup to reinstate a brutal dictatorship for his own gains.

I copy the watermarked images and extraction report onto the flash drive, then take the drive out of the laptop and put it in my pocket. The two-inch piece of plastic now has all the evidence I need to take my father down.

Checkmate, asshole.

CHAPTER 23

Nell

TIME COMPRESSES. I no longer know how long I've been in the holding cell—two hours or twenty?

It's a walled, enclosed space with only a small window in the door. I hear yelling from the adjoining cell—a deep-voiced man who sounds either drunk or high. Probably both.

I hate the claustrophobia, the bare walls, the lack of space. I hate someone else being in control of my freedom. I hate not knowing what comes next. But I remember that Darius survived far worse circumstances for so much longer. I can get through this.

At some point, one of the officers brings me a tray bearing watery spaghetti, gray green beans, and a hunk of stale bread. I nibble the bread, but my stomach rebels and I end up retching into the stained metal toilet.

I try to sleep on the uncomfortable cot, but my brain won't stop racing. For all I know, they already have Darius in custody.

I have no idea what time it is when the lock scrapes and the door opens. A glare of fluorescent light from the corridor illuminates Ramirez. He inclines his head to the door.

"Come with me."

I sit up from the cot and drag my legs to the floor. "Where?"

"We were going to book you for being in possession of a stolen vehicle, but it looks as if you lucked out."

Fighting off a wave of dizziness, I get to my feet. Ramirez steps aside. I half expect him to handcuff me, but he indicates that I should stop at a grate-enclosed room at the end of the corridor.

Another officer hands me a box with my backpack, wallet, shoes, and the plastic bag of snacks. I sign the papers he pushes across the counter, then walk into the main part of the station.

The clock is at 11:34, and sunlight burns through the glass windows. The light is sharp and painful after the dim cell. Ramirez gestures to a row of molded plastic chairs. "Wait there."

I sink into a chair, gripping the box so tightly my fingers dent the cardboard. I calculate that I've been here for almost twenty-four hours. A woman is staffing the desk, her head down as she stamps papers. She looks up and catches my eye. Her mouth twists with faint derision.

Male voices drift from one of the offices. My breath stops. Darkness spills across my soul like ink.

The door opens. Conrad Hawke steps out, followed by Ramirez, Burton, and another tall, heavyset man in a suit.

Conrad stops and looks at me, his strong, lined features softened into an expression of such tenderness that anyone would think he cared deeply for me. My whole body contracts in self-defense and terror.

"Gentlemen, again, you have my everlasting gratitude." With a smile, Conrad extends his hand to Ramirez. "Thank you for bringing my granddaughter back to me."

"May I speak with you alone?" I look directly at Officer Ramirez, willing him to recognize the fear I'm trying to keep in check.

Then the heavyset man approaches me, and latent memories kick to the surface—*a dark blue sedan, the city bus, the man who'd given me the creeps.*

He was the one. I hadn't been paranoid. I'd been *right.* Conrad had sent his henchmen after me back in New York, long before I knew Darius was still alive.

The man reaches out to take my box. I jerk away from him and step toward Ramirez.

"Officer Ramirez, I really need to speak with you in private," I say again.

For an instant—the blink of an eye—I see him hesitate. Then Conrad steps between us, his wide shoulders blocking the police officer.

"Let's go, Nell." He nods toward the door.

I tighten my fingers on the box. I could scream, try and run, cause a scene. But that might make Ramirez throw me back in the cell. If there's any hope I have left, it's that I have a better chance of escaping Conrad than I do a holding cell.

I think.

"She's in shock, I'm sure," Conrad says smoothly to the officers. "We'll be sure to get her the help she needs."

Turning, I manage to walk beside him out the door to the Mercedes SUV waiting at the curb. I can't speak past the fear clenching my throat, the ice solidifying in my veins.

The heavyset man opens the SUV door. Panic rips through me. I back up. Conrad grips my arm, his fingers digging in hard.

"Get in the car, Nell."

God in heaven.

My choices are a holding cell and possible arrest versus going with Conrad and dealing with whatever he's planning. He's already laid the groundwork with law enforcement, probably across the state.

Would they even believe anything I said? After all, Mr. Hawke has been looking for his missing granddaughter for almost two weeks. He's so relieved to have her back safe and sound.

The interior of the SUV looms like a cave. The heavyset man moves to take the box from me. I tighten my hold on it and shake my head, pushing past him to climb into the vehicle.

Crisp, cool air and classical music wash over me. I hear Conrad conversing with the other man, whom he calls Sampson, before he gets in beside me.

The door slams shut. A dark window separates the back from the driver's seat. Another door closes, and the SUV glides forward.

I stare out the window at the distant mountain ranges, blurred smudges of purplish-black like bruises against the hazy sky. The only advantage I have is silence. I will never say one word about Darius. No matter what Conrad does.

He doesn't speak either. The air-conditioning grows colder, prickling against my clammy skin. Conrad opens the refrigerated console and holds out a bottle of water. I shake my head.

"Where are we going?" I finally ask.

"Vegas." His tone is clipped, no longer grandfatherly and caring. "Had yourself a little adventure, did you?"

"I wouldn't call it that."

"People are worried about you."

"You did a great job pretending you're one of them. You should have been an actor."

He makes a noise of faint amusement. "You should have listened to me when I told you to stay out of it."

I don't respond, thinking he's probably right. On the other hand, I've spent a long time learning how to step in and take action when it matters the most. I refuse to cower any longer or to do what other people demand or even expect. I follow my own internal compass now, and I'll deal with whatever consequences that brings.

The SUV drives into Vegas, cutting a smooth path through the crowded, neon-lit streets before coming to a stop in front of a massive resort hotel and casino. Two more stocky men in suits arrive to open the car doors.

The instant the door cracks open, I have a flash of Darius kicking open the truck door and escaping his captors. In a surge of panic-fueled adrenaline, I lunge out of the car.

I don't make it two steps before a weighty hand clamps

down on my arm, and two huge men step in front of me, blocking me from anyone who might have seen my futile attempt to run.

"Don't make a sound." A low, guttural voice—not Conrad —hisses in my ear.

He pushes the barrel of a gun against my side. I still, my breath choking my throat.

One of the others prods me forward. Sampson takes my box out of the backseat.

Flanked by the three men and Conrad, I manage to walk into the marble-floored hotel with its multiple waterfalls and chandeliers hovering overhead like crystal helicopters.

I'm guided into a mirrored elevator, which sweeps silently upward like a needle slicing through cloth. The guard takes the gun away from my side, no longer needing to threaten me with it now that there's no one else around.

The penthouse—or what I assume is the penthouse because if we were up any higher, we'd be on a space station —is a huge multi-roomed suite with a wall of windows overlooking the Strip and beyond. Glossy stone floors, zebrawood paneling, and jade sculptures give the place a pseudo-Zen atmosphere.

"You can have your things back later." Conrad dismisses the guards with a flick of his wrist. The three hulks retreat, but continue to hover in the foyer. Sampson stands like a wall between me and the door.

I follow Conrad down a hallway lined with Japanese prints to a carved teak door. He pushes it open and ushers me inside.

"You'll find new clothes in the closet and dresser," he

says. "Take some time to clean up. Come out whenever you're ready."

He leaves, closing the door behind him. I listen for the click of a lock, but there isn't one.

I step into the room almost cautiously. The bed is about the size of an aircraft carrier. I pull open a black, inlaid wardrobe to find an array of clothes in different sizes with the tags still attached—dresses, skirts, blouses, T-shirts. The adjoining bathroom has a jetted hot tub and glass-enclosed shower with a rainforest showerhead.

Since I haven't showered in close to three days, I strip off my clothes and turn the water to hot. I step in and stand under the spray, then scrub myself down with the lemon-scented soap and shampoo. Though I don't like taking pleasure in anything Conrad Hawke provides, getting clean again restores some of my equilibrium.

I wrap myself in a fluffy white robe and leave the bathroom. My backpack is on the bed, the laptop missing and most of my things put back in the wrong places.

After digging through the closet, I dress in a pair of leggings that fit reasonably well and a green T-shirt. I put on my shoes and a sweater in the event that I have a chance to try and run again.

Scraping my wet hair back into a ponytail, I return to the living room. The smells of steak and butter drift from the formal dining area. Several silver-domed plates sit on the table, and Conrad is at the bar, mixing a drink.

"Sit down," he says without turning to face me. "You must be hungry."

I'm not, but I've barely eaten in over twenty-four hours, and I need to preserve all the strength I can for whatever comes next. I sit down and take the covers off the plates—revealing an exquisitely prepared filet mignon and poached lobster tails. I feel Conrad's gaze as I choke down a few bites that taste like sawdust.

He pours me a glass of wine from a bottle that probably cost more than my father's monthly salary.

My father.

The thought of him makes my heart stumble, as if it's tripped over an uneven piece of sidewalk. Ignoring the wine, I take a gulp of iced water.

Conrad pulls out a chair next to me and sits. "Where is he, Nell?"

"Who?"

He huffs out a laugh. "Let's not play this game. You won't win."

"That's the thing about games, though, isn't it, Conrad?" I shovel a spoonful of wild rice into my mouth. "You never know who's going to win."

"Actually, I do." He sips his drink. "What did you do with the files?"

"What files?"

Though his mouth curves into a humorless smile, his eyes harden. "I know that Krasnovian shithead sent them to you. A mistake he paid for with his life."

I try not to flinch at the mention of Savko, but I don't succeed. The bites of steak and lobster turn rancid in my stomach.

"No one's going to hurt you." Conrad regards me steadily. "Least of all me. But I strongly suggest you don't try and fuck with me either. Where is Darius and what did you do with the files that were stolen from my computer system?"

I drop my spoon and push the plate away. "Look, I don't know where Darius is. That's why I came to you in the first place, remember? As for the files, I never intended for anyone to steal anything. I was in contact with several people in Krasnovar, and one of them sent me a bunch of documents. I had no idea what they were or how they were supposed to help me find Darius, so I deleted them all. That's it."

"You downloaded them onto your laptop."

"So bring me my laptop. I'll show you there's nothing on the hard drive that belongs to you."

"We've already checked. It appears you transferred them to an external drive."

"I don't know anything about that."

"Why did you leave New York so suddenly, then?"

I shrug. "Spontaneous getaway."

Conrad rubs a spot between his eyebrows with his fore-finger, then gets up and retrieves a printed sheet of paper from the sideboard. He drops it in front of me and takes another swallow of his drink.

I pick up the paper, which has the word *Missing!* in red block letters at the top.

My hands shake. It's another screenshot of me from the motel security camera along with a description:

Female in her early twenties, long brown hair, approxi-mately 5'6", 135 pounds, wearing jeans and a red T-shirt. Last seen with a dark-haired male, late thirties or early forties, muscular build, approximately 6'3" or 6'4"—

A sharp realization clicks into place. While I'm sure the

woman at the motel called in a tip about me and Darius, there's no way the police jumped right on the case and sent out all kinds of alerts. I'm not a minor or a runaway.

No. What happened was that Conrad's henchmen unearthed the tip and the video screenshot—probably using facial recognition software or some high-tech search functions—which led to him contacting investigators and agencies about his "missing granddaughter."

And of course, his money spurred law enforcement into action. That was how he knew I'd been taken to the station by the Nevada state police.

The man is like a giant squid with massive eyeballs and tentacles that penetrate every crevice.

"The woman who called the hotline was mistaken." Meeting Conrad's gaze, I push the paper back toward him. "I was alone. I have no idea what man she was talking about. Maybe she'd been reading a romance novel and conjured him up out of her fantasies."

His mouth compresses, deep brackets carved on either side. He puts his hand on the paper and slowly begins to crumple it into his fist.

"All right, Nell." He pushes to his feet, his height and breadth throwing a shadow over me. "Get some sleep. We'll talk again tomorrow."

He turns away. My heart is pounding, my blood hot. I want to scream at him that he can't keep me here against my will, but the words would be useless.

Because he can.

CHAPTER 24

Nell

THAT NIGHT, I doze off for a couple of hours from sheer exhaustion and spend the remaining hours until dawn trying to come up with a plan. But to make a plan, you need tools and resources—and I have none. My laptop is gone. There's no phone. No computer. No intercom.

I can't even daydream about hitting Conrad over the head with a lamp and making an escape. Even if I succeeded in a knockout blow, I could never get past the Three Hulks who are always looming around the door and elevator.

I push my feet into a pair of tennis shoes and pick up my backpack before leaving the bedroom. At the very least, I can be prepared to run if I ever get the chance.

This time, the smells of coffee and bacon drift from the dining area. Conrad is sitting at the table, his gaze on a tablet. He looks like he always does—dressed in an impeccably tailored white shirt and tie with his hair combed back, the steel-gray color emphasizing the hard angles of his face.

Without glancing at me, he points to the opposite chair.

I sit down, and a man in a crisp chef's jacket glides forward to pour my coffee and deliver plates of eggs Benedict and bacon. I thank him—it's not his fault he works for an asshole—and reach for the coffee cup.

There's a box close to the center of the table next to the overdone flower bouquet. For some reason, unease ripples through me. The box is a couple of feet square and made of faded, paisley-printed cardboard with a scuffed blue lid.

I glance at Conrad. He's watching me, his cup held close to his mouth.

"Open it," he suggests.

"Is something going to jump out and scare me shitless?"

He chuckles. "Open it and find out."

I push the china plates and silverware aside and drag the box toward me. I pull off the lid and peer inside.

No fake exploding snakes or spiders. There is an old leather book and another smaller box—this one expensive-looking and covered in rich, blue velvet.

I take out the velvet box and open it. A gasp catches in my throat. Inside is an exquisitely crafted jeweled egg, as large as a mango.

The enameled surface is decorated with an intricate floral motif of silver and gold, each design inset with aquamarines, diamonds, and lustrous pearls. A carved gold band winds around the egg's center. The multitude of jewels both absorb and reflect the light, gleaming with such intensity they seem alive.

My breath grows shallow. I pick up the egg with great

care, almost as if I'm lifting a grenade. It's heavy, the weight settling into my palms. I don't need to be told that I'm holding a priceless work of art, that it's composed of real diamonds, pearls, rose gold, and platinum.

Slowly, I open the egg on its tiny hinges. A sapphire blue-bird—gold filigreed wings spread, diamond eyes glittering—rises from a nest of entwined silver and gold threads. On the interior of the eggshell, embedded in the floral motif, is a pattern of diamonds forming the letter *O*.

"Fabergé." Conrad sips his black coffee. "Commissioned, of course. It was my wedding gift to Odette."

My heart thumps so hard I feel the echo all the way through me.

"I guess she didn't take it with her when she moved back to Russia." I close the egg and place it gently back in the velvet box, unable to take my eyes off the mesmerizing surface of colors and light.

"She would have, if I'd let her." Conrad sets his cup down and wipes his mouth with a cloth napkin.

"So you kept it in a cardboard box instead?"

His mouth twists in derision. "The album was stored in the box. The egg has been locked away in my bank vault for the past thirty years. Until yesterday."

This is a game.

The kind Conrad Hawke plays so well, a game of power and manipulation.

Only I don't know the rules.

I take out the scuffed leather book and open it. A surge of both elation and pain fills my chest.

The pages contain dozens of faded, color photographs—a tall, elegant blond woman smiling into the camera alongside a beautiful girl of about nine wearing a flower-print dress. There are photos of them together, and more of the girl alone—at Christmas, on a carousel, onstage for a school performance.

And there are many photos of the girl with a dark-haired boy whose eyes snap with energy and whose smile lives inside my heart. There are pictures of them on bikes, wading in a creek, dressed up for a party, and playing with other children.

It's my mother's photo album—the one I hadn't even known existed until Darius told me about it in Grenville. The one we'd both thought was lost forever.

"Why did you keep this?" I ask.

Conrad shrugs. "I suspected it might be useful one day."

I stare at an image of my mother smiling into the camera. When I was eleven, she'd burned all of our family photos during one of her dark episodes. I only have one left, a picture Darius had taken of her and me at Volkov Bay.

I've never even seen photos of her as a girl. I've never seen many photos of Darius either; for me, he has always existed on the other side of the camera.

"Which one is worth more to you?" Conrad's voice breaks past my sudden disquiet.

I look up, catching the gleam in his eyes the instant before he conceals it behind impassivity. My whole body goes cold.

"Why do you want to know?" I counter.

"Choose one." He sits back, nodding to the box. "And you can have it."

Oh, you bastard.

I stare at a photo of Darius—a triumphant, grinning boy

holding up a fish at the end of a pole. I can see the man that boy will become—powerful, active, charismatic.

Slowly, I close the album and place it back in the box, then set the Fabergé egg on top. Though my heart feels like it's cracking, I put the lid on the box and push it toward Conrad.

"I don't want either one," I tell him flatly.

He laughs. "Yes, you do. But it appears I was correct when I said you're more like me than anyone else in this godforsaken family."

Though my skin crawls at the idea of being *like him* in any way, I suspect I might have won this round.

Conrad rises and approaches. "Where is he, Nell?"

"Did you think I'd tell you just because you offered me a gift?"

"No." He studies me, a faint smile rising to his eyes. "I thought you'd finally admit you know where he is."

"I didn't—"

Shit. I did.

So much for winning this round.

Conrad taps his finger against my forehead. "We can keep going, or you can tell me the truth. If you're especially helpful, I might let you walk away with both the Fabergé egg and the album. Those are the only photos of your mother as a child and young woman. The only photos of her and Darius, who is clearly rather…important to you."

Hot tears swell in my eyes. I clench my teeth so hard my jaw hurts.

"You can burn that box, for all I fucking care," I hiss. "I'm not going to tell you a damned thing. So you might as well get it over with and kill me now."

He clicks his tongue. "I'm not going to *kill you*, Nell. I thought you were above your mother's brand of drama. But you were institutionalized once too, weren't you? Your father certainly had a lot to contend with."

I blink hard, but a tear rolls down my cheek. I wipe it angrily away.

Once upon a time, I'd thought that being in love with Darius was like the exhilarating chaos of a whirlwind. It had been as momentous as the creation of the sun, the continents coming together, a collision of the moon and stars. I was in constant motion—falling, rising, spinning, crashing, soaring.

But I'd known, even in the middle of it, that I would never again be in a place of such safety. I'd learned that love can also give you the deepest, most profound peace.

I cling to that truth now, as I face the fact that I am totally out of my depth. I'm getting tossed around by turbulent waves, losing all sense of balance and control.

I can resist telling Conrad anything, but I can't anticipate his next move or try to evade his manipulative traps. I don't have the weapons to fight him.

He was right. We both know who will win this game.

He snaps his fingers at Sampson, who is standing like a granite statue near the door. The bodyguard comes forward and picks up the box. He takes it to another room and returns without it, stopping nearby as if awaiting further orders.

Conrad bends to look me in the eye, his features as tight as a shell. "Where are the files, Nell?"

"I don't know."

"All right." He turns away, gesturing sharply at his bodyguard again. "Sampson, get my bags. I'm going to pay Nell's father a visit."

Panic spears through me, swift and painful. I crumple a cloth napkin in my fist as if the action will stop me from flying at Conrad in a rage. "No."

He lifts his eyebrows. "You're not in a position to use that word."

"Leave my father out of this." I meet his gaze steadily, hoping he doesn't notice how hard I'm struggling not to shake.

"He and I have never met," Conrad replies with a shrug. "It's about time we do. I'm sure he's been as worried about you as I was."

A heavy sensation like a cloud of black smoke fills my chest. I imagine Banks in those fraught seconds between his CO's order and the bomb blast. Seconds that must have felt like years. Seconds in which he was forced to either kill a teenage boy or put an unknown number of others at risk.

Had he even had time to make a decision? Had he wondered if it was a real threat or a hoax? And what in the love of God had he thought or felt when the bomb exploded?

I don't think even a Darius Hawke photograph could have captured the unimaginable chaos Banks had experienced in that instant.

I tell myself I'm fortunate that I don't have to make a decision. I don't have to choose between pulling the trigger and looking away. There is no choice, no matter how violently every part of my body and soul resists the idea of betraying Darius, even for my father's sake.

But Darius can take care of himself. He always has. He knows what to do, and how and when to do it.

A man who has withstood torture will never be cowed by the likes of Conrad Hawke. Darius has more than enough weapons to fight his father, with or without me.

Gripping the edge of the table, I look at Conrad again. "I put the files on a flash drive."

He frowns. "Where is the drive?"

"Darius has it."

His mouth compresses. "And where is Darius?"

"He was…he and I were heading to Los Angeles when the police stopped us."

"How did you find him?"

"I didn't. He found me. He'd escaped the bombing in Varaz and made his way to Moldova before coming back here."

"Why did he come back?"

"He suspected I might be in trouble."

Conrad regards me for a moment. "You knew the contents of those files were confidential."

"I thought they might be, but I didn't know what they were."

"Why didn't you come to me?"

I stare at him. "You'd made it clear you wanted nothing more to do with me."

"I made it clear I wanted you to stay out of things that were none of your business," he replies sharply. "I *warned* you. Why the fuck didn't you listen?"

"You know why!" I struggle to keep my tears from overflowing. "I love Darius. I wasn't going to stop until I'd found him. And I didn't mean to take your confidential files or whatever they are. I just wanted any information that might have helped me find out what had happened to him. And even if I had considered telling you I'd gotten the files, you said we were finished. What was I supposed to do?"

His jaw tightens. "It sounds like you wouldn't have done anything if Darius hadn't stepped in."

I hitch in a breath. He's probably right. I might have held on to the files for another couple of days before throwing the flash drive away. As my instincts had been telling me to do.

But then what? Conrad would still have known that Savko sent me the files. He'd still have come after me to get them back. He wouldn't have believed I'd trashed them, even if I had.

"How did Darius know you had the files?" he asks.

I stare at the plate of now-congealed eggs and cold bacon. I will not implicate Patrick.

"Darius finds things out," I say with a shrug. "He has a huge network of contacts and resources. Plus he and Savko were good friends."

Conrad drums his fingers on the back of a chair. "So Darius discovered you had the files. He knew Savko was dead. He suspected you might be in trouble. And he came back to New York to rescue you from my evil clutches."

"That's about the size of it, yes."

"What's his cell number?" Conrad asks.

"I don't know. He'd gotten a new burner phone. I can't remember the number."

"Where have you been all this time?"

"On the road." I glance at him. "How do you know we haven't copied the files or sent them to anyone else?"

He gives a short laugh. "The files are all embedded with tracking codes. We knew immediately where they'd gone after they were stolen from the system, which is how we traced them to you. There's been no activity on any of the files since then."

I remember Banks warning me and Darius not to transfer the files because of potential tracking codes. Which means Darius now has the only existing copy of them outside of the Hawke Financial system.

Which also means the files must contain something extremely incriminating if Conrad wants them back this badly. It has to be more than the fact that he's invested in Krasnovar's mining industry.

"That's all I can tell you," I finally say.

"Where in Los Angeles were you and Darius going?"

"There's a computer conference in Hollywood this weekend. He'd wanted some sort of internet muffling device."

"Likely he's taken a detour now that you've gone missing." Conrad straightens, pushing back his cuff to look at his watch. "Sampson, call down for the car. We're going to get Henry Fairchild."

I jerk my head up. *"What?"*

"I need an insurance policy." Conrad pulls on his suit jacket. "We'll endeavor not to hurt him."

Fresh panic floods me. "But I told you everything!"

"Yes, and it took you longer than I'd anticipated." He takes his cell phone from the table and slips it into his pocket. "However, as I said, you do have a spine."

"What are you going to do to my father?" I stand, shoving my chair back so hard it topples over with a crash. "I told you what you wanted to know. And you...you said..."

Conrad meets my gaze, his eyes gleaming with a combination of triumph and what looks like pity. "Did I?"

It feels like an earthquake is rumbling inside me, cracking my bones, breaking my self-control. A horrifying realization pushes to the surface.

I'd thought Conrad and I were making a deal. I'd tell him the truth in exchange for him leaving my father alone.

But he'd never promised any such thing.

"Here's some advice, Nell." He steps closer, the triumph replaced by a strange shadow of regret. "Never make assumptions. And *never* give someone what they want unless you know exactly what they're giving you in return. In fact, always get the terms in writing first."

"You son of a bitch." I bolt toward him in a rage, my hands going for his eyes, but before I get even two feet, Sampson hauls me into an immobilizing grip. I struggle wildly, kicking and trying to break free, but it's like being trapped by iron bars.

"Lock her in the bedroom," Conrad orders.

Tears of fury blind me. I can't breathe. I'm about to explode with rage, even as my soul turns to ice.

If he uses my father against both me and Darius, this might be it.

Game over.

CHAPTER 25

Darius

I COULD FLUSH him out like the shit he is. Log in to my email, take out cash with my debit card, use my registered cell phone, rack up a few purchases on my credit card. Throw down the bait leading him straight to me. Then hook and flay him alive.

Though it's tempting, he'd send his thugs after me first. And they're not the ones I want.

I try not to think too much about Nell. She's always there, a riptide under the surface, but if I speculate about where she is or if she's okay, I'll lose my mind. Not now, not when I need to be at full throttle.

The Nevada sun bakes the land, creating cracks and fissures in the desert. I drive through Arlington, the town where I assume the police took Nell after the rest stop.

In the hopes that maybe they let her go, I take the risk of

stopping at a few places—a diner, a grocery store, a gas station—to ask if they've seen a woman with her description.

But no. Nothing.

In another one-road town close to the Utah border, I use one of the library's computers to search public crime reports and arrest records. I bring up the trafficking center website, which includes a link to the FBI's "missing persons" section.

I scroll through dozens of bulletins with photos of men, women, and children—all displayed next to their physical stats and descriptions of what they were wearing when they were last seen. Many of them first went missing years ago.

I don't think Nell has been reported as missing. She was considered a suspected trafficking victim, but not a missing person. Unless her father or one of her friends reported her. Maybe that's why the police didn't arrest her.

My insides twist. I navigate to a page listing missing persons who are believed to be in Nevada, then scroll through more photos and descriptions.

Halfway down the page, a photo of Nell appears—an image captured from the motel security camera. I click on it.

A dedicated *Missing* page loads, displaying her description and the details of her last sighting. But a large red X covers the word *Missing*. Next to it, in a bigger font, are the words *Found Safe*.

What the fuck?

I scroll down the page and reread the details. Next to the security camera shot is another picture that wasn't sent in to the trafficking site—a photo I haven't seen before.

Zooming in, I stare at the second photo. It's a shot of her from the chest up. She's looking directly at the camera, unsmiling. Her hair is pulled back, her lovely face dusted with makeup, and she's wearing a crisp white blouse and a navy suit jacket. The scar from the landslide is visible on her forehead. The photo was taken recently.

A chill races down my spine. I know where she's sitting. The security offices of the Hawke Financial building are stark and antiseptic, but I'd recognize them anywhere. I also recognize the type of headshot—the security team takes "visitor identification" photos to run through facial recognition programs and to keep on file.

There's only one place anyone in law enforcement could have obtained that photo—from the Hawke Financial security team. Or from Conrad himself.

He's the one who reported her missing.

I grab the mouse and navigate back to the top of the page. *Found Safe.*

He's also the one who "found" her.

But she sure as hell isn't safe.

CHAPTER 26

Darius

IT'S A VOLCANO INSIDE ME—THE thought of Nell with my goddamned father. I have to keep the molten rage contained, though I'm ready to rip apart the Hawke Financial head-quarters to get to her.

If that's where they are.

I walk back out to the car. Heat thickens the air, dry and oppressive. If Conrad picked Nell up from the police station —which is likely—he might not have taken her back to New York yet. Or maybe he didn't intend to, not when he knows she didn't leave the flash drive there.

I pull a spiral-bound atlas out of the glove compartment and flip the pages to Nevada. I locate the tiny dot indicating Arlington.

Once she was identified as Nell Fairchild, the police

would have pulled up the contact information on her missing person's report and called Conrad right away.

Sir, we have good news. We've found your—

My teeth grind together. When Conrad reported Nell as missing, he'd have needed to establish a family connection. And the most logical one—the one that's loosely true, if sickening—is that Nell is his step-granddaughter. Knowing him, he'd have told the authorities she was his granddaughter, then promised them a massive reward if they found her.

And they did.

Fuck.

Where did he take her?

I stare at the thin lines winding over the state map like veins. Sweat rolls down my temple. I twist open a bottle of lukewarm water and take a swig.

Conrad would avoid small towns and possibly even airports. He wouldn't want Nell to be recognized by anyone else. He sure as hell wouldn't give her any opportunity to escape or call for help. He'd have her flanked by a wall of bulky security guards at all times.

He also wouldn't want to draw any attention to himself. Much less allow anyone to find out he's kidnapped his step-granddaughter and is chasing down his son to retrieve a flash drive holding hardcore evidence of his crimes. Driving a convoy of Mercedes and Cadillac SUVs through desert towns—with an entourage of henchmen—would generate more interest than Conrad Hawke wants.

But there's one place in Nevada where expensive cars and bodyguards don't draw much attention. Where money buys privacy and "no questions asked." Where Conrad could lock Nell in a tower behind multiple doors, and everyone around him would look the other way.

I toss the atlas back into the glove compartment and get behind the wheel. Vegas is five hours away. I make it in three.

After parking on a side street, I walk to the Strip. Neon lights flash and blink against the glass-fronted shops, casinos, and high-rises. Vehicles clog the street.

My father has never been a recreational gambler—the stakes are too low in a casino—but for him it's been a convenient place for anonymity and to reward loyal partners and employees. He always stays at the luxury Palazzo Resort, where the staff have learned to bow, scrape, and cater to his every whim.

Even kidnapping.

I wait in the front garden of the Palazzo near the massive, ornate fountain spewing recycled water. The parking lot is full of cars, the valets scurrying around to help dislodge passengers from Bentleys and BMWs.

Dusk crawls over the sky. The lights get brighter. Stars evaporate under the glare.

I keep waiting, changing location a few times to avoid attention. Hours pass.

Finally, close to eleven at night, a Mercedes SUV pulls up to the front of the hotel. The glass doors slide open again. Attendants, valets, and doormen all straighten and step forward. Two big guys in suits lumber out and down the steps, followed by Conrad Hawke.

My spine tenses. I fold my arms, digging my fingers into my biceps to stop myself from charging at the fucker like a battering ram.

He looks the same as he has for most of my life—sharp suit and tie, steel-colored hair, that innate power—but he's smaller somehow. Diminished.

Nell isn't with him. The hotel's doors glide shut.

One of the valets holds open the SUV door. Conrad disappears inside. The bodyguards spread out and get into their respective seats before the car leaves.

My blood seethes. This confirms it.

He's here. And Nell, the only person besides me who can give him what he wants, is locked in the penthouse.

Every instinct, every cell in my body, fights to go to her, to battle anyone who gets in my way, to tear the place apart.

Hold on, Nell.

Feeling like I'm moving through tar, I turn and walk away from the hotel.

Conrad will try and force Nell to talk, to give me up, to confess where we've been, what we did with the flash drive, how much we know.

She'll fight with everything she has not to surrender. She'll rage and yell and tell him to go fuck himself. She'll be a supernova in her fury.

But Conrad has spent a lifetime twisting and manipulating people. Breaking them down. He can find a person's weak spot with one sharp look. He knows how to deploy every game, maneuver, con, strategy, and trap to get someone to do his bidding. He's a master of his craft.

And I'm still his son. I've spent years watching him. I know his next move.

He'll go after Nell's biggest vulnerability, forcing her hand by attacking the man she loves most in the world.

This time, that man isn't me.

CHAPTER 27

Henry

Made it safe and sound. *Tons of people here! Love you.*

Fern's text is accompanied by a heart. Henry responds with *Have fun—I miss you already.* Then he spends a good two minutes searching for a heart emoji on his phone. After failing to find it, he adds a little picture of a penguin and sends the message.

He picks up the tray of iced coffees and leaves the student union. Though it's true that he already misses Fern, her absence is giving him plenty of time to finalize his plan. She'll be at the comic book convention in Seattle for three days, and he'll have everything in place by the time she comes home on Sunday evening.

Home. Maybe he's trying to take his and Fern's minds off their concern about Nell, but the past couple of weeks have only solidified his conviction that he wants Fern *at home* with him all the time. Their home. Whether they're worrying, talking, laughing, making love, or just watching TV, he needs her in his atmosphere like the earth needs the sun.

He walks toward the history department. It's a hot afternoon, the air still heavy with the laziness of late July. Summer school classes are over, and the campus hasn't yet begun to crackle with the anticipation of fall.

Although Henry always enjoys the start of the new school year, he appreciates the summer break from curriculum planning and grading papers. Normally he'd spend the month of August working on his book, but this year there's too much crowding his mind. For the first time in years, he couldn't care less about the Roman Empire.

He distributes the coffees to his colleagues before getting his briefcase from his office. He never leaves campus early, but he's anxious to get home and check his landline phone for messages.

He has a call in to Darius's friend Patrick about Nell, but Patrick hasn't responded yet. No surprise, given that he, too, travels frequently to remote parts of the world. If Henry doesn't hear back from Patrick by tomorrow, he'll call again.

As he walks to the parking garage, he takes a few deep breaths to try and ease his anxiety. For days—again—he and Fern have been unable to stop worrying about Nell. After a phone call from Clover a couple of days ago, also on the topic of Nell, Fern had stayed up all night scouring the internet for any potential clues about Nell's whereabouts.

Even though she understands this has to do with Darius, she's been upset with Henry for not calling the police. He's battled more than one headache trying to decide if he's doing the right thing by *not* contacting them.

But he can't shake the notion that Nell doesn't want, or can't have, police involvement. That he'd be putting her in danger if he called them. He has to trust his instincts. He *will* trust in his daughter.

On the way home, Henry stops at a gift store to place an order for multicolored balloons that spell out *Will You Live With Me?* He orders a bouquet of red roses from the florist and a cake from Fern's favorite bakery.

He'll pick everything up on Sunday afternoon a few hours before she's due to get home. He's also planning to hang framed vintage comic book posters in the living room and place Superman and Wonder Woman cardboard standees on the front porch to greet her arrival.

Fern might not want to officially marry him, but they can still be a "married" couple without the legal paperwork. And though more than anything Henry wants her to be his wife, he'll be blissfully happy waking up with her every morning, knowing she'll be here when he comes home from work, and not having to text each other every day to see if he's going to her place or she's coming here. Living together is the perfect compromise for the marriage issue.

And once Fern realizes paperwork is not that big of a deal, maybe she'll finally decide she does want to say the words *I do*.

He pulls into the driveway of the house and goes in to check his landline phone. His heart sinks. No messages. His fear for Nell is a hard knot in the pit of his stomach.

It had been the same way when she was in Varaz, but at least then, he'd occasionally been able to talk to her. He'd trusted Darius to look out for her. Hell, he'd been enormously relieved that the other man was there. And Henry had known where Nell was.

Now? He has no idea.

He checks his cell phone again. No texts or calls from her.

I need just one message—one or two words letting me know she's okay.

He tosses his phone on the desk in his office. As he leaves, his gaze catches the photo of Katherine and Nell that sits on the mantel.

His chest constricts at the sight of his serious daughter with her glossy brown pigtails, her pinafore dress, her hands folded neatly in her lap. She was such a quiet child, her intelligent gray eyes watchful, as if she were always measuring her life in relation to what else might be out there.

Henry had been spellbound by Katherine, entranced, but he'd never understood her. He'd understood their daughter though—the comfort Nell found in her own inner world combined with a strange unexplainable urge for something more, something bigger.

He'd never fulfilled that longing for himself—never lived in Rome or joined archeological expeditions or walked the Camino de Santiago. He'd never boarded a ship to search for Plato's lost city of Atlantis.

But whatever dreams he'd once had had fallen away the instant he'd looked into the eyes of his infant daughter. Nothing else mattered. He'd vowed he would live his life to protect and love her.

He'd tried. Failed more often than he cared to admit, but the promise and the intention were always there.

Now he has no idea—doesn't want to know—how he'd

survive this break with his daughter if Fern wasn't at his side.

He goes into the kitchen, appreciating the reminders of Fern—the paintings she'd put on the walls, the snapshots she'd stuck to the fridge, little scribbled notes left on the counter.

As he takes a glass from the cupboard, he hears a thudding noise come from the back garden. He sets the glass down and goes to investigate. He's been having problems with squirrels nesting in the old oak tree—which isn't a big deal except that he suspects they might be getting into the rafters of the house.

Pulling open the back door, he steps onto the porch and peers at the tree. No movement in the branches, but they're getting close to the windows of Nell's attic room.

Time to trim them back again. He'll get to it sometime this weekend before Fern gets home.

He turns toward the garden shed. He'd better get his old shears sharpened; if he leaves them at the hardware store tomorrow morning, he can pick them up before Saturday.

The crack of a heavy twig splits the air.

Henry stops.

A tall man comes around the side of the garden shed, his hands up at chest level in a nonthreatening gesture.

Shock bolts through Henry, taking his breath.

"Henry," says the man with whom he's shared the better part of a lifetime.

Henry can only stare at him. Part of his brain disconnects from the truth and assesses Darius clinically—the shadows under his eyes, his messy hair, the multiple days' worth of stubble covering his jaw. He's wearing faded jeans and an open, long-sleeved shirt over a navy T-shirt—all creased with wrinkles like he's been sleeping in his clothes.

Henry blinks. His disbelief fades. A hot rage flickers in his gut.

As if sensing it, Darius takes a step back. "I know you want to kick my ass."

"No." His voice sounds like a saw. "I want to kill you."

"I know." A dark shadow crosses Darius's face. "But right now, I need you to come with me."

Henry shakes his head. He hadn't heard that right.

Darius glances at the house. "Where's Fern?"

"In Seattle, at a comic book convention."

"Good."

Henry has no idea why Fern's absence is *good*, but he recognizes the conviction in the other man's voice.

Aside from looking run-down, Darius is the same. Henry still sees the big, unruly sixteen-year-old who'd come out of nowhere to dispatch the assholes who were using him as a punching bag. He still sees the grin on Darius's face when he'd introduced Henry to Katherine.

He still sees the man with whom he's shared countless drinks, sports, talks, dinners, and plans. They've gone camping together, fixed cars, shot hoops, played poker, challenged each other to a thousand stupid contests from eating hot peppers to downhill ski races.

His oldest friend. Even when Henry's parents had written him off, Darius was still there. Always.

He swallows convulsively, his hands clenching and unclenching.

His daughter.

God.

His *daughter.*

"N-Nell." He hates the unevenness in his voice, but he can't help it.

Tension locks through Darius's muscles, as if he's been trying to keep it contained.

"She's in trouble," he says. "That's why I'm here. You need to come with me."

"The fuck I do." The rage boils up again, coating his vision in a red mist. "Where is she?"

"With my father." Darius narrows his gaze past him at the driveway. "And not by choice."

Henry struggles to process that. Darius steps closer, and Henry senses not only his tension, but a leashed urgency that feels as if it could explode any second.

"Henry, I swear on my life I'm not lying."

"Your life doesn't mean a damned thing to me." The words snap out of him like a whip.

Darius flinches almost imperceptibly, but Henry sees it. He smothers an unexpected flicker of regret.

"I swear on Nell's life," Darius says, and there's a pleading note in his voice that Henry has never heard before. "On Katherine's. On my mother's."

Henry pulls in a breath. His mind races with fear, confusion, anger.

"Get your phone." Darius indicates the house. "I think Nell is okay, but we have to move fast. They're coming after you next."

Darius *thinks* Nell is okay.

The thought spurs Henry into movement. He turns to the house and goes inside.

Darius follows, his boots ringing against the old weathered steps of the porch. "Pack a few clothes. Whatever you need for a day or two."

Henry gets his phone and wallet from his office, then climbs the stairs to his bedroom and throws some clothes into a bag. His anger has frozen into sharp, cold flames scraping his chest.

He no longer trusts Darius. He doesn't want to go anywhere with him. He doesn't even want to breathe the same air as the other man.

But Darius knows where Nell is.

She's in trouble. But she's with Conrad Hawke? What the—

"Henry." Darius pushes aside the bedroom curtain and looks toward Dearborne Street. "Let's go."

Henry zips his travel bag. Darius grabs it from the bed and strides to the staircase.

Henry glances out at the black SUV rumbling up the driveway from the street. The tinted glass windows only reveal several shadowy figures.

He follows Darius out the back door. Seconds later, they're hurrying across the grass, past the oak tree, and into the unkempt wooded lot that surrounds the house.

Henry has to jog to keep up with Darius's pace. He glances back once to see a burly man stalking around to the yard.

They come out onto a dirt road where a beat-up old sedan is parked. Darius tosses Henry's bag into the backseat and gets behind the wheel. Henry slides into the passenger seat, his phone tight in his hand.

Darius reverses into a sharp turn and drives away from the house, the car engine rumbling. He navigates through downtown Grenville to the highway onramp pointing north.

And then Henry knows where they're going.

They drive in silence. The air is dense and leaden. Henry's chest burns. Darius grips the wheel hard, his knuckles white.

"I'm sorry," he finally says.

"To hell with you." Henry stares out the front windshield.

"It wasn't…" Darius's throat works. He flexes his hands. "I didn't coerce her."

Henry's gut twists. He knows that statement is true. He wishes he could believe Darius capable of the worst. He'd never want a violation to be inflicted on Nell, but it would be easier if he could think of Darius as a monster.

He supposes it's a measure of his own perceptiveness that even now, he can't. It would rip another hole in his heart to think that he'd been blind to Darius's true nature for so many years.

Which is yet another reason why Henry can't reconcile everything that's happened. How was it even possible for Darius and Nell to—

"Jesus." He shakes his head with a hollow laugh. "You were the best man at my wedding."

It's the only thought that unravels, as if it expresses all he wants to say. Maybe it does.

Darius doesn't respond, but his body is rigid, as if in defense. Like he's fighting something from the inside.

Good. Let him suffer. Henry hates Darius now, the man he'd loved like a brother for so many years.

But to bring his daughter back…he will walk through fire.

CHAPTER 28

Darius

VOLKOV BAY IS cold and drenched in fog, as if it has its own weather system.

I unlock the door of the beach house, smothering any memories of the last time I was here four years ago. After opening the windows to let out the dusty air, I flip the main circuit breakers on the electrical panel and turn on the water supply valve.

Henry stands by the door, unmoving. I know he has a shitload more hate and betrayal to unload. I've never seen him this angry, this tightly contained, as if it's all bubbling inside him like a pressure cooker. But his rage will have to wait.

"What are we doing here?" he asks. "Why is Nell with your father?"

"Just a sec, and I'll explain everything." I head outside again to grab a bag of groceries from the car.

When I go back in, Henry has moved into the living room, his gaze passing over the sagging bookshelves, the dusty ship-in-a-bottle, the fishing net. I unpack the food and take out a bottle of scotch.

"Want a drink?" I ask.

"Sounds like I need one."

I pour the scotch and set a glass on a table near him, then sit down in the armchair.

"So explain." He folds his arms, eyeing me narrowly.

"My father has been financing a terrorist organization for the past six years." I lean forward, resting my elbows on my thighs. "The People's Liberation Front, the same group who took me hostage. That's the reason he didn't pay my ransom. He cut a deal with them instead, and let them keep me as leverage for their other demands."

Henry is silent for a second. Then he looks away and takes a swallow of the drink. "How did you discover that?"

"Through some documents and photos Nell obtained. If it weren't for her, I might never have found out."

"Does she know?"

"Not all of it, no. Not yet."

He stares at the liquor and shakes his head. "How did she get that kind of information? And how did you end up back here anyway? She said you'd turned yourself over to the PLF."

"I did." Though I don't like reliving it, I tell him the whole story—from the siege of Varaz to our attempted escape to how I managed to get out of Krasnovar. I explain how Nell ended up with the Hawke Financial documents and why I couldn't get back to New York fast enough after Savko's death.

"I knew it wasn't good." I deflect a rush of remembered fear. "All I wanted to do was protect her."

"Why didn't you just give the damned flash drive back to Conrad?" Henry puts the glass down with a hard click. "You didn't have to take off like a bat out of hell. With my daughter."

"Yeah, I did. Even if I'd given the drive back, Nell had seen the documents. She didn't know what they were, but Conrad wouldn't have cared. She'd breached his walls. He'd already killed one man over the files. He wasn't going to let Nell walk away."

Fear glints in his eyes. "But he has her now. Have you seen her?"

I shake my head. "I saw him. They're in Vegas, or at least, they were. I knew he was coming after you next, and I think he left her there and went to Grenville alone."

Henry picks up a shell from Nell's display box. His hands are shaking. "What is he going to do to her?"

I can't respond. I wish I could say, *Nothing.*

But I'd once thought my father's evil had a limit. That he possessed at least a thin moral center. There had to be a point beyond which he would never go.

I no longer think that. Which means he could do anything to Nell.

"I don't know," I tell Henry. "But whatever it is, she's fighting like hell."

His expression darkens. "Fern and I both knew something wasn't right. She wanted me to call the police."

"Why didn't you?"

He shrugs, rubbing his thumb over the shell. "I figured there was only one reason Nell would drop off the face of the earth like that. She had to be with you."

My chest constricts. He must have been out of his mind with worry. Not only over Nell's safety, but the fact that he knew she was with me.

"What do we do?" He drops the shell back into the box and spreads out his hands. "How do we get to her?"

I push to my feet. He's not going to like this. "I'm going alone. You need to stay here."

His eyes widen. "What the hell? Why?"

"Because Conrad is after you. I needed to get you out of his target range. He doesn't know about Volkov Bay. You'll be safe here."

"I'm not staying at the *beach* while my daughter is a prisoner," he snaps. "I'm going with you...where? Back to Vegas?"

"Yeah." I check my watch. It's close to four. Chances are Conrad will stay in the Bay Area overnight. He'll scour all of Grenville and surrounding areas looking for Henry before driving back to Vegas.

Which means I need to haul ass to get there first.

"How do you know Nell is still there?" Henry asks.

"I don't." I grab a bottle of water and pick up the car keys. "But she's not with him, so it's the next logical guess. He can keep her locked up pretty tight at the Palazzo."

His mouth compresses, another flash of fear crossing his face. Ignoring a stab of regret, I stride to the door. "Avoid using your phone. I'm not going to call you until I have her safe, so it might be a while."

"I'm going with you."

"And put Nell at more risk?" I yank open the door. "I don't have time to argue. Stay here. I'll contact you as soon as I can, Henry. I promise."

Though my promise is worthless to him now, he doesn't follow me to the door. He stands there watching me leave, the late-afternoon shadows streaming through the windows.

A few seconds later, I pull out of the driveway and start back over the mazelike roads to the highway leading south to San Francisco. Fog and storm clouds are rolling in from the ocean, obscuring the sun behind a curtain of gray. I'm not five minutes into the drive when the engine clunks. The noise jars the car. Smoke billows from under the hood.

"Fuck." I pull over and pop the hood. I should be grateful the old car has gotten me this far, but I need it to last for the nine-hour drive to Vegas.

After checking the engine, I start the car again. The engine grinds, but starts. Could be any number of things—alternator, fuel gauge, transmission—none of which I can fix without tools and parts. If they're even fixable on this beater.

I get the car turned around and drive slowly back to the house. The smoke thickens, the grinding and clunking noise getting louder.

A stream of curses runs through my head. The closest sign of civilization—an old restaurant—is a good ten miles away. I could walk it in the time that it would take a taxi to get here.

But how the hell am I going to get ahold of another car? I can't use my credit card or ID—Conrad knows I'm alive, but he still doesn't know where I am.

And now that Henry is with me—

I pull into the driveway, and the car rasps to a halt.

When I open the front door, Henry startles and pushes up from the sofa. "What are you doing back here?"

"Car broke down." I toss my bag on the table and eye the landline phone. I'd told Henry that Conrad doesn't know about Volkov Bay or the house, but I can't put anything past my father. Though I've evaded him so far, he has a lot of tracking technology at his disposal.

"So now what?" Henry frowns, his face pale. "How are you going to get anywhere?"

"Good question." I pick up my new burner phone, which indicates that there's a voicemail.

I haven't yet contacted Patrick from this phone, so aside from Nell, Banks is the only one who has the number. I call his cell.

He answers on the first ring. "Jesus, what took you so long?"

"Just got your message."

"I finally found him." Banks almost sounds like he's punching the air in victory. "He checked into a hotel in San Francisco. Place called the St. Francis."

I'm not surprised. Conrad would send his men to small-town Grenville to abduct Henry, while he waited in a luxury penthouse for their return. Keeping his hands clean.

This could work to my advantage. If Conrad is in San Francisco, and *if* Nell is still in Vegas, I'll have a better chance of getting to her without him nearby.

"Hawke?" Banks says. "Did you hear me?"

It takes me a second to remember that Banks doesn't know I saw Conrad coming out of the Vegas hotel. He also doesn't know I figured out that Nell is with him.

"Yeah," I say. "Thanks."

"No leads on Nell yet." His voice sobers.

I want to tell him what I've discovered—if for no other reason than to assure him he doesn't have to keep looking for her—but Nell was right. I've put Banks at risk, and while I suspect in some ways he's been enjoying the hunt, I'm not taking another chance.

He might not be a target right now, but he could be. The guy who tracked us to Banks's cabin might have been the only one who knew about it, but that's a futile hope at best. Whatever Conrad Hawke's men know, Conrad knows.

"Okay," I finally say. "Thanks again. I'll keep looking."

He updates me on Poe's condition—an all-clear from the vet during his follow-up, and the stitches will come out in another week—before we end the call.

"Who was that?" Henry is watching me, eyes narrow.

"An old friend." The word *friend* is surprisingly easy to say. "He's been helping us out."

"What are we going to do about Nell?"

"There's a restaurant about ten miles away. I'll have to—"

"The Fisherman's Hook."

I look at him. I'd almost forgotten the history of Volkov Bay, the number of times the Fairchilds came here to visit. The countless evenings we drove to the Fisherman's Hook for fried shrimp, coleslaw, and beer. Nell always had a basket of fish and chips followed by key lime pie.

I'd taken her to the Fisherman's Hook for breakfast the morning after we—

"So what about it?" Henry asks impatiently.

I shake my head. "I have to walk over there to call for a taxi."

"Call for one here."

"It'll take longer by the time they navigate the roads." I glance at the clock. "And I don't want to use the landline."

"So you're going to rent a car?"

"I have to." I don't have a choice. If renting a car alerts Conrad's security team to my location, so be it. I need to get Nell. I'd promised her I'd always come to her. No way will I break that promise now.

I open a drawer in the kitchen and riffle through old advertising fliers and brochures before finding a few taxi service cards. I stuff them into my backpack when my phone buzzes again.

I pull it out of my jeans pocket, expecting Banks. Instead, it's a number I don't recognize. But the 212 area code is all I need.

Pushing the sliding glass door open, I step onto the deck and shut the door behind me. The phone buzzes again.

I answer the call. "You hurt her, I'll fucking kill you."

"You're not in a position to be making threats," Conrad replies. "But I'll give you credit. You're good at playing dead."

"How did you get this number?" Behind me, I hear Henry open the door. I move to the edge of the deck, not wanting him to hear any part of this conversation.

"Nell told me you got a new burner phone," Conrad says. "At first, she couldn't remember the number. Then she did."

"Where is she?"

"It's amazing what you can recall when there's a gun at your head," he remarks. "But you already know that, don't you?"

Rage shreds my insides. He doesn't even have to hurt Nell for me to kill him.

"Where is she, you piece of shit?"

"Right here," Conrad says.

My blood freezes.

"Do you want to talk to her?" he asks.

For a second, I can't speak. Can't push anything past the constriction in my throat.

On the other end, there's a shuffling noise, then a quick intake of breath that I'd recognize anywhere.

"Nell."

"Darius?" Her voice is faint, thick with tears. "Oh my god, is that you?"

"It's me." I grip the phone so hard it might break. "Are you all right?"

"I'm so sorry. I tried not to tell him anything...I *didn't*, not at first, but then he—"

"Nell...baby, it's okay. Are you all right?"

"No. I mean, yes, if you mean...I'm not...not hurt. But he said he was going to—"

Henry grabs my arm. "Let me talk to her."

"Dad?" Nell's voice rises. "Dad, are you there too? What are you—"

The airwaves go dead.

"Nell?" I force down a wave of panic. "Nell!"

Nothing. I hit the button to redial the number, but it rings without a response or voicemail pickup.

Shit. I smother the urge to throw the fucking phone into the ocean.

My vision blurs. I drag my sleeve across my eyes and haul in a breath.

Get to her. Now.

Turning, I meet Henry's gaze. He's watching me, his expression stark and strangely penetrating.

"What did she say?" He steps closer. "Is she okay?"

"She's alive." That's all I can tell him. All I know.

He grabs the phone and scrolls back to the number. He calls again, to no avail, then hands it back to me with a muttered curse. I yank open the sliding glass door and go back inside.

"What did Conrad say?" Henry shuts the door behind him, his eyes like stone. "Where is she?"

"He's in San Francisco, not Vegas." My chest is raw, drenched in thick, black smoke. "The connection was clear, so I don't think she was on a video call or another cell. She has to be with him."

Henry lifts his gaze. "San Francisco is less than two hundred miles away."

But Nell is under Conrad's control. She might as well be two thousand miles away.

My phone buzzes again. I access the call, suppressing the urge to say Nell's name.

"You got to Henry first," Conrad says. "You'll end up regretting that. I wanted him so I wouldn't have to hurt her. He was my insurance."

"Put Nell back on the phone."

"She's...indisposed."

I swallow a flame of rage. I want to reach through the phone and strangle him.

"You have something that belongs to me." Conrad's voice hardens. "And I have something that belongs to you. What are we going to do about this?"

"You can have the fucking flash drive. But if you even look at her wrong, I will rip you apart."

"You need to be in the same room as me if you're going to

do that," he replies dryly. "If I don't have that drive in my hand by midnight, you won't like what happens to her."

My jaw tightens to the point of pain. It's not an idle threat. I know that all too well.

"So come and get it," I tell him. I'd rather meet him in the city—or at least a more well-populated area—but without my car it'll take too damned long to get anywhere. And I don't have the time to waste.

"Where are you?" he asks.

"Volkov Bay. I'd come to you, but I can't be there before midnight. And I know you don't want a scene at your high-end hotel. You can bet your ass this will be one."

He gives a short laugh. "Where the hell is Volkov Bay?"

"Look it up. There's a house on the edge of the beach. I'll be there. Make one wrong move, and every file on that drive goes to the FBI, Interpol, and the UN. I'll send it to the press and a dozen other agencies. You'll know which ones from the tracking codes."

"She'll have a gun to her head. If anyone is there but you, I'll pull the trigger myself."

"Fuck you." I end the call.

Henry is staring at me. "He's coming here? When?"

"Soon."

I look out the front window at the dark, purple-black sky. I have the home turf advantage. But Conrad has Nell. The one person, the one entity in the universe, who can break me.

And my father knows it.

CHAPTER 29

Nell

DARIUS'S VOICE is inside me, like a symphony still resonating in the air long after the last note has faded. The echo of it, the knowledge that he's close, eases some of my fear.

He got to my father first. Darius knew what Conrad would do next, and he cut him off at the pass. The triumph of that maneuver gives me a new burst of sorely needed courage.

I pace from one end of the sleek, polished bedroom to the other. I've come to despise high-rise buildings and pent-houses with their massive windows that look down on the world. Aside from being trapped, I don't like being so elevated, so removed from anything tangible.

Up this high, even if it weren't a prison, there are no trees, no grass, no wildflowers. From the bedroom window, I can see the circle of the San Francisco Bay, the dense billow of fog, but I can't feel or smell the cold salty wind. I want my feet to be on the earth, not up here in a structure of glass and steel where nothing is solid or secure.

I don't even know what day it is, though I've been keeping track of time by making marks on a scrap of paper. It's been almost four days since I was at the rest stop with Darius.

Last night, Sampson and two of the other hulking hulks —Isaac and Marko—"accompanied" me to the cave-like SUV in front of the Palazzo. We drove for hours overnight, reaching San Francisco at the break of dawn this morning.

When I saw Conrad again, his polish had eroded, exposing a cold, rusted anger whose source I didn't—at the time—understand. There were no more probing questions over steak and lobster. No more stupid games involving Fabergé eggs and old photo albums.

No.

This time, Sampson stood behind me, one meaty hand on my shoulder to pin me into a chair. With his other hand, he pressed a gun to my temple.

I'd thought of Darius. My father and Fern. Alexei and Sofia. I'd remembered an animated short Clover made about a girl who discovers she can fly. I'd pictured myself in Harmony Square playing Shepherds and Sheep with a group of laughing, energetic children. I'd imagined the taste of doughnuts with blackberry jam.

But all of that was overpowered by the resurgence of raw terror. The memory of Darius on the dirt road, bloody and bruised. The soldiers surrounding us with their AK-47s. Alexei bleeding in the back of the truck, Jacob at his side.

Lenkov's hands on me, the barrel of a rifle pressed to my head.

I'd seen Darius in the courtyard of his prison as his captors pulled the trigger on an empty chamber.

The only bit of information I hadn't yet given Conrad was Darius's phone number. When Sampson cocked the gun and the metallic click echoed through my brain and into my bones, I'd told him the number and prayed that somehow Darius would want his father to contact him. That he'd want to know where Conrad was. That he had a plan.

Conrad had given a nod of satisfaction. A man accustomed to winning, even when the rules have changed. Even when it's no longer a game.

I fold my arms and stare out the window. This high up, I can't even see any people on the street below.

Behind me, the door clicks open. Conrad stands in the doorway, his big frame almost filling the space between the jambs. I tighten my arms around myself.

Despite knowing my father is with Darius—and that there is no safer place in the universe—I'm still terrified for both him and myself. I've been forced to admit I'm no match for Conrad Hawke. Neither is my temperate, scholarly father.

But Darius is. I seize that knowledge like a rope that will drag me out of this suffocating quicksand.

"Get ready." Conrad rakes his gaze over my wrinkled jeans and T-shirt. "We're leaving in fifteen minutes."

"Where are *we* going?"

He leaves without a response, shutting the door behind him. Though my mind fills with horrific speculations about where he might be taking me and what he might be planning to do, I gather my few belongings and zip my backpack.

A short time later, our merry little band of misfits—a vile, corrupt financier, me, and the Three Stooges with Curly pushing a gun into my side—descends to the hotel lobby.

Aside from deferential nods and murmurs of, "Mr. Hawke," the staff and other people keep their eyes averted. Though I'm again tempted to cause a scene—cry *fire* at the very least—the thought of the potential repercussions is enough to stop me. There's a slight chance I might succeed, but a much bigger chance that I'll fail—and likely not survive the fallout.

A convoy of three SUVs is waiting at the front steps. They're not normal vehicles—they're specially outfitted with security technology designed to prevent unauthorized persons from getting in...and out.

More than once on the drive from Vegas, I tried to open the car door, to throw myself onto the side of the road if I had to—but the instant I touched the handle, an alarm sounded. After that, two of the hulks sat on either side of me for the rest of the trip. I'd felt like a bug being squashed between two huge fingers.

This time, Conrad gets into the back with me. Several more big men approach from the parking lot and occupy the third vehicle. Backup hired guns, I assume.

The door slams shut. I hate the sleek, polished interior of the car with its artificial air and stink of leather. The tinted bulletproof windows block out all natural light.

Without warning, panic can set in, throwing me back to the hours I was trapped under piles of rock and mud. When I couldn't escape, didn't know if I would survive.

I stare out the window, trying to focus on the solid reality of other people, the trees, the cars. The SUV glides toward the Golden Gate Bridge.

As soon as we cross the bay into Sausalito and start heading north, I wonder if we're going to Grenville. Are my father and Darius there?

Conrad had been right behind me when I'd talked to Darius yesterday. He'd heard me asking for my father. He knows he's with Darius.

But then Conrad had grabbed the phone and left the room. I'd assumed he'd called Darius again, but I didn't hear their second conversation. It had to have been about the flash drive.

Did they come to some kind of agreement? Is that what this is about?

We continue north on the highway. I grip my hands together. My heart races. The SUV passes the turnoff into Grenville and keeps going.

Then I know where Darius and my father are.

CHAPTER 30

Darius

THE BATTERY in the old clock on the wall died long ago, but I can almost hear it ticking down the minutes.

Henry paces to the windows and stares out at the fog and storm clouds encroaching on the white-capped ocean. Dusk is approaching, throwing a metallic haze over the cove.

"Why midnight?" he asks. "Is that when Conrad turns into a pumpkin?"

I almost laugh. "It's his way of drawing the line. I'd chalk it up to a supervillain move if I didn't know that he carries through with his threats."

Henry glances at me, his expression sobering. He's heard plenty of stories about Conrad's threats and retribution, from forcing Katherine into various institutions to locking us in closets to dumping me off at the side of a road in a snowstorm. Henry knows I overheard Conrad telling my mother she'd never see me again if she left him—which was the reason she never did.

He knows about the time Conrad threatened to kill Katherine's pet hamster. Two days later, he threw the live little creature into a fire while we stood there and watched. Katherine's screams almost shattered the windows.

No. *Midnight* is not an idle threat.

"Did you ever meet your grandparents?" Henry asks.

I look up. "No. Why?"

He shrugs. "People like Conrad get twisted early on. It's happened throughout history. Dictators often have child-hoods filled with abuse, trauma, violence, abandonment. There's a reason they end up the way they are. I figured Conrad's parents might've provided a clue."

"They both died when he was young." I sit back and drag my hands over my face. "House fire. He and his little sister both escaped, but she died later of her injuries. Conrad was raised by his grandfather, who started Hawke Financial. From what I know, he considered Conrad the chosen one who'd take over the family empire, but he was also an iron-fisted tyrant. I'm sure he was violent and abusive. So, yeah. Conrad didn't have it easy. But we all have shit to deal with. Not everyone who's suffered ends up murdering people for profit and power."

Henry acknowledges that with a nod. "Or sacrificing their only son."

We both fall silent. I look at my watch. Almost two hours since I spoke to Conrad. If he left San Francisco right away, they should be here soon.

I shove to my feet and go into the kitchen. Every nerve is on high alert. Impatience claws right under my skin. I want

Nell back. Now. Safe and unharmed. The force of that need is overpowering.

I also want my father to pay for what he's done—to Nell, to me, and to countless other people killed by the PLF. I want him to pay for the genocide of ethnic minorities who were targeted by the former dictatorship—the same government Conrad wants restored to power.

I want him to pay for the people who've suffered and died in the violent PLF coup *that he supported and financed.* Conrad Hawke is responsible for tearing Krasnovar apart right when its people were starting to recover from the civil war. God knows how long it will take for them to rebuild again.

Yeah, I want him to pay.

And I have the power to take him down. To cut the PLF's funding off at the source, which could destroy their whole operation. Without weapons and supplies, they can't keep fighting. It's what I've been working on for years—a way to stop the PLF and other terrorist groups from inflicting violence and murder.

If Conrad loses all rights to Krasnovar's mines—which he will if the PLF and dictatorship fail in the coup—then those mines could be returned to Krasnovian companies, stimulating the economy with a lucrative industry.

And once other countries learn about the substantial lithium ore deposits, Krasnovar's international standing would improve. There would be more employment, income, trade deals. After years of suffering, the Krasnovian people would finally have a chance.

I'm the one who has to make the decision. Which isn't

really a decision at all, no matter how complicit and guilty I'll be.

I will never sacrifice Nell, not even for the cause of an entire country. Not even to see Conrad Hawke pay for his crimes. Nothing can force me to put her in the line of fire.

If that decision—one person over many—sends me to hell in the afterlife, then I'll greet the devil and pay my dues.

But here, now, there is no choice. All I want is to give Conrad the flash drive and haul Nell back into my arms where she belongs.

I feel Henry watching me, as if he knows what I'm thinking. I look up to meet his gaze. Over the past few hours, his initial anger has shifted into fear and worry, but I know it's still there, waiting to be unleashed again when this is all over. When his daughter is safe.

"I'm sorry I hurt you," I tell him. "But I'm not sorry I love her."

From outside, heavy tires crunch over the gravelly dirt road.

CHAPTER 31

Nell

THE SUV STOPS in front of the beach house, followed by the other two vehicles.

My breath is shallow, my heart racing. As we approached the coast, the sight of Volkov Bay, like a pool of silver mercury roughened by the wind, created a surge of hope. Familiar ground. I'm no longer on Conrad's turf, no longer trapped miles above the earth.

The house sits on the edge of the dunes, the old structure stark against the charcoal sky. Storm clouds billow on the horizon.

Knowing that Darius and my father are so close…it's all I can do not to smash the car window to reach them. Then the window darkens as two massive figures move in front of it.

The passenger door opens. Isaac reaches out to grab me,

his grip encircling my entire arm. Sampson's gun is drawn. Conrad gets out on the other side.

Four other men exit the third SUV and fan out in various positions like they're executing some kind of battle strategy. All of them are holding handguns and no doubt have more weapons concealed beneath their jackets.

The cold salty air brushes my face. Waves push and roll against the jagged rocky cliffs.

I inhale deeply, letting the ocean enter my bloodstream. Despite the encroaching storm, the air is that peculiar blue-gray just before twilight. Lights burn from inside the beach house.

The door opens.

I swallow a cry of—I don't even know what. Relief, fear, hope?

Darius steps onto the porch. A half-dozen guns point in his direction. His sharp gaze passes over the other men and stops on me. I take an involuntary step toward him, feeling his presence and strength like a jolt of electricity.

Isaac tightens his grip. Sampson lifts the gun. The cold barrel presses against the side of my head.

Darius holds up his hands to chest level, palms out. "No need for that. I have what you want."

"Good." Conrad approaches him, stopping halfway to the door. "Where's Fairchild?"

"Inside." Darius locks his gaze on his father. The lines of his body are tense, his eyes hardening to ice. "We're leaving him out of this."

Conrad twists his mouth. "Are we?"

"He doesn't have anything you want." Darius looks at me again. "Nell, you okay?"

My throat is so tight I can't speak. I nod. The gun presses harder into the side of my head. Terror prickles my nerves. I pray Sampson's finger doesn't slip on the trigger. Or that Conrad doesn't issue a "fire" order at random.

"Where's the drive?" Conrad asks.

"In my pocket." Darius slants his gaze back to his father. "I'm going to reach down and get it."

"You're not going to move." Conrad snaps his fingers at Marko. The bodyguard moves closer to Darius. The other men continue to pin him with their guns.

Darius remains still as Marko approaches and searches him for a gun or hidden weapon.

"He's clean, boss," Marko says.

Conrad nods. Darius reaches into his jeans pocket and takes out the flash drive. Marko extends his hand.

My heart thunders. The beat is so loud in my head it almost drowns out the crash of waves.

Darius drops the flash drive into the guard's hand. Marko backs up and gives it to Conrad.

"Let her go." Darius's voice is steel.

"You're not giving the orders." Conrad gestures to another man by the third SUV. "I need to verify this is what I want."

The other man takes a laptop out of the SUV and puts it on the hood of the car. Conrad inserts the flash drive into a port and turns the computer on.

Time stretches taut, like a rubber band on the verge of snapping. I fix my attention on Darius, letting the sight of him soothe the worst of the terror. The porch light shines against his dark hair and etches shadows across the planes of his face.

He's wearing an open, long-sleeved shirt over a T-shirt, and I imagine pressing against his chest. I can feel his arms close around me, pulling me back into his fortress. I can almost smell the citrus of his soap and the warm, clean scent of him that has always been such a comfort.

Only minutes now. Seconds, maybe. I'll survive this. He's so close. His gaze is on me too, our eyes locked across the distance. I can almost hear him telling me to hold on.

Conrad checks the contents of the flash drive for what feels like hours. Finally he straightens and pulls the drive out of the port.

"Let her go," Darius repeats.

Conrad closes the computer and puts the flash drive in the pocket of his suit jacket. It starts to rain, heavy drops splattering onto the sand and driveway.

He opens the SUV door, setting the computer on the seat. His movements are strangely slow and deliberate, like he's taking his time.

Which doesn't make sense. Don't we all want this little transaction to be completed with swift efficiency? Don't we all want to get the fuck out of here?

"Conrad." Darius steps forward, his eyes narrowing.

"Sorry, son." Conrad shrugs. "You both know too much now." He points at Isaac. "Put her back in the car."

"No!" The word explodes out of me. I break away from Isaac so hard and fast my arm twists in his grip.

Darius shouts. My other arm hits Sampson's, catching him off guard. The gun barrel knocks against the side of my head. I dart to my right, away from the men.

In a blur, I see Darius hit the ground and reach one arm behind the concrete planter box.

A gunshot blasts. Isaac grunts, his body stiffening before he falls to his knees. He grabs for me. His fingers clutch at empty air.

In this instant, no one is gripping my arm or holding a gun to my head.

Go.

Gunfire starts, bullets thudding against the house, cracking the windows. Panic rakes my chest. I run, swerving around the SUV and behind the old sedan parked in the driveway. Staying low, I head for the pathway leading to the beach.

My father.

I need to get to him. Skidding to a stop, I duck behind the garbage and recycling bins next to the garage. Cobwebs stick to my face. My hands scrape the bricks securing the bins against the wind. I wedge into the dark, cold space as far as I can.

More gunfire. I block threatening images of the siege, of Alexei collapsing against me, his blood staining my hands. I close my eyes and fight for calm.

Darius.

Barely breathing, I creep forward just far enough to peer around the corner of the house. He's crouched behind the planter, firing his Glock with deliberate aim.

But his targets have all rushed to protect Conrad and get behind the SUVs. Isaac is hunched over, clutching his chest. Blood spreads over his shirt.

Conrad holds up his hand. The men stop firing, but keep their guns pointed at Darius.

"I'd suggest you give it up, son," Conrad calls from behind the biggest SUV. "You're not getting out of this alive. In case you missed it, you're outnumbered."

Darius's sharp, "Fuck you, Dad" makes me want to cheer in spite of my outright terror.

Before Conrad can respond, Darius bolts out from behind the planter and runs to the other side of the house. In a blur of motion, he fires again.

One of the men behind the third SUV grunts and grabs his shoulder. His gun clatters to the ground. Another hailstorm of bullets splatter against the planter and the siding.

Darius disappears into the shadows.

"Get them both," Conrad snaps. "Her father too. I want the girl alive. Kill the men, if you have to."

My heart jams into my throat. The remaining five bodyguards split up. Two of them run after Darius. The third stands at the road, guarding the front. Sampson and Marko rush in my direction.

I push back behind the garbage cans and squeeze into a tighter ball, trying to make myself as small as possible. The men thunder past me to the beach pathway.

I struggle to pull in a breath. The rain is coming down harder. I have to get to my father. I don't know if he's still inside. I don't know where Darius went.

If I can make it to the side door of the garage, that will be my best bet for getting into the house. I don't want to be trapped inside, but my father is in there because of me. I can't—won't—leave him.

In the distance, men are shouting. Another gunshot. Wincing, I start to edge my way out of my hiding place. A shadow falls over me.

I look up. Conrad Hawke.

No.

The word erupts in my brain again. *No fucking way.*

His eyes are granite. The exterior lights carve his face into deep grooves. Rain plasters his hair to his forehead.

"Get out of there," he orders.

I edge my way out from behind the bins, my breath coming in short, hard bursts. My fingers brush against one of the crumbling old bricks. Slowly I curl my hand around it, hoping to God he doesn't notice. His gaze is on my face, cold and unyielding.

"Get up." He reaches down to grab my arm, which still hurts from wrenching myself out of Isaac's meaty grip. Conrad clamps his hand in the same place Isaac was holding.

"Stop grabbing me." I glare up at him, twisting my bruised arm. "I'm sick of being manhandled. Let go of me, and I'll come with you."

Impatience hardens his features, but he loosens his grip. My heart thumps hard. I start to rise slowly, pretending like my legs are stiff. I clutch the brick. Halfway to standing, I bolt to my feet and lift the brick at the same time.

With a strength that seems to come from the earth itself, I swing the brick in a wide arc and smash it against the side of his head. The impact jars my entire arm.

His eyes widen in shock. Then he grunts and collapses to the ground, one hand coming up to clutch his head.

Triumph surges through me.

"Here's some advice, Conrad." I drop the brick. "Always get the terms in writing first."

Before he can regain his senses, I reach into the pocket of his suit jacket, grab the flash drive, and run. I skid to a halt at the sight of the men prowling around the back of the house and the sand dunes.

Shit. I can't go around the front because the fifth thug is guarding the road. I flatten myself against the side of the garage.

"Psst."

I look up. My father is hovering in the shadows of a copse of trees and tall sea grass. He glances at Conrad, then motions me forward.

I edge closer to him, gripping the flash drive in my sweaty palm.

My father extends his hand. I grab it. His fingers close around mine.

We can't go to either the front or back of the house. If we turn to the left, we'll end up on the open expanse of the beach and the sand dunes.

My father tightens his grip. There's only one direction we can go. But it's a place where we still stand a chance.

We turn at the same time and run down the pathway leading to the ocean. He diverts at a fork on the path and takes the narrow, steep trail cutting like a vein between the massive granite rocks. I follow, clutching his hand.

The sheer walls rise up thirty feet on either side of us. A shot blasts in the distance. We hurry down the rocky path to the sea caves hidden in the cliff.

CHAPTER 32

Darius

STAYING LOW, I run through the rain and enter the house via the side door.

Henry isn't here. I knew he'd get out as soon as the shots started outside. I hope to God he reached Nell. I've heard a few more gunshots, but the four men are still prowling the beach and rocks, so they haven't found her yet.

I grab a sheathed paring knife from the kitchen and push it into my boot. I need any extra weapon I can get. In the hallway, I pull down the attic hatch and climb up just as the back door smashes in, wood splintering.

I close the hatch. Two of the men stomp inside, guns firing, bullets hitting the walls. They know what'll happen to them if they don't deliver.

I crawl across the shallow attic space. From below, more

shouting, the crash of furniture overturning, then the door slamming again as the men leave.

After pushing aside the cobwebs covering the old smudged window, I look outside. One of the men is dead, lying on the sand dune like a beached sea lion. I'd gotten him straight through the chest.

There are four left, including the guard at the front. The third guy is coming toward the house. The other two— Sampson and Marko—are heading toward the cliffs surrounding the bay.

Unlatching the old rusty lock, I open the window just far enough to edge the barrel of the Glock outside. With one shot, I take out the guy coming toward the house. Sampson and Marko turn and start firing up at the attic. They can't see me, but they sure as hell know I'm here.

I shoot at Sampson. The bullet flies past him. Just beyond, on the narrow trail leading down to the caves, I catch a glimpse of Nell's blue shirt before she's swallowed up by the cliff walls.

Yes.

Relief surges. The caves are her best bet for escape— especially given the open expanse of the beach and the fact that she's blocked on all other sides. Nell knows the layout of the caves and where to go. She can follow the tunnels all the way to the outlet that opens onto the western part of the shore.

But where the hell is Henry?

Conrad's voice rises from outside. He comes around the corner of the house. Even from a distance, I can see blood trickling down his temple. The rain washes it away.

"You fucking idiots." He thrusts his finger at the trail. "*Get them.* If we have the girl, we have my goddamned son."

The two men swerve and run toward the narrow trail. Conrad follows.

Them. Henry must be with her.

I shove back to the attic hatch and lower the ladder.

All three fuckers are moving in on the Fairchilds from the beach. If Nell and Henry can get to the cave tunnel and the western outlet before the tide comes in, they'll be okay— as long as all the guards are out of the way.

One more to take down. Then I'm going after her.

CHAPTER 33

Nell

THE VOLKOV BAY cliffs are like another world—granite arches and piles of rocks rise from the turbulent water like lumbering sea creatures, and the cave entrances yawn like huge mouths. We make our way over the slippery rocks, pausing only long enough to get a foothold.

The storm is picking up, throwing waves against the base of the rocks. A narrow promontory juts out into the bay. Once upon a time, this terrain had been like a second home, and while I haven't been here in years, these ancient geological formations haven't changed.

Ahead of me, my father stumbles, one foot slipping off the rock.

"Dad!" I reach for him as a wave crashes against the cliffs, the spray hitting me like a thousand stinging bees.

My father and I grab arms, steadying each other. My

heart pounds. Aside from the icy temperature and storm, between rogue waves and powerful riptides, neither one of us wants to end up in the ocean.

Still balancing each other, we manage to get across the rock formations. After rounding another corner, we reach the cave closest to the trail and duck into the damp, dark shelter. We stop to catch our breath. A layer of freezing water shifts and pitches across the sand.

My father pulls his keys from his pocket and turns on a small pen flashlight. The light gleams against the stone walls, illuminating pockets of algae and white calcite.

His face is haggard, his angular beard emphasizing the shadows under his eyes. My throat closes over. We reach for each other at the same time. It's our tightest embrace ever.

"Are you all right?" Keeping his voice low, he pulls back to look me over. "You're causing me a lot of worry these days, young lady."

I manage to smile through my tears. "Maybe I should have gone to library school after all."

He squeezes my shoulder and shakes his head, his eyes gentling. "I think you ended up where you were meant to be, in some ways. Though I'd appreciate it if you'd stop risking your life. Speaking of which…"

With the flashlight beam concealed by his hand, giving us just enough light to see, we hurry farther inside. A deep niche, sheltered by another stack of rocks, is in the depths of the cave. We crouch behind it, letting the cave conceal us from view.

Though we're far from safe, I welcome being back in this place that was always so filled with wonder. I was never allowed to come here alone, but I'd spent hours exploring the rocks and tunnels with Darius. He would only let me go into the tunnels that had been mapped, and not even geologists and scientists know how far the maze extends into the cliff.

He'd explained that the caves were formed by the force of the sea over thousands of years. Waves eroded the fault lines in the cliffs and created the hollow caverns and tunnels honeycombing the interior.

He'd told me about how pirates used to use the caves as hiding places for smuggled goods. I'd always thought of the caves as protective, never dangerous, and it's fitting that we've found shelter here now.

Darius will know we came here to both hide and escape. If any of the thugs are still on the beach, he'll dispatch them before we reach the outlet. I touch my father's arm.

"We should keep going. It's only a matter of time before they figure out where we went."

He nods, turning the flashlight back on. We rise and start toward the tunnels, which diverge in two directions—right and left, or as Darius used to say, "heads or tails?" My father and I go into the right-hand tunnel.

Another gunshot blasts, the echo earsplitting in the chambered room. We start to run.

We turn a corner to a narrow, hilly corridor that leads to a small chamber. We're forced to slow down, balancing on the slippery incline.

"Over here!" Sampson shouts.

My heartbeat kicks up. I glance over my shoulder. We quicken our pace, holding on to the walls for balance.

The tunnel widens into a room the shape of an egg—my former "secret hideout" where I'd make up games with shells and bits of driftwood. Stalactites drip from the ceiling and the limestone looks like puddles of melted bronze.

"Dad, this way." I tug on his sleeve, leading him into another tunnel that curves toward the western outlet.

I stop. The tunnel is blocked by a pile of broken rocks.

"What…" My father stops behind me. "Shit."

"How could that have happened?"

"Earthquake, most likely." He closes his hand on my arm. "We have to go back."

"No, we can go this way." I pull him toward a narrower tunnel leading in the opposite direction. He resists.

"That's not mapped," he hisses.

"Well, it's either an unmapped tunnel or an asshole with a gun," I snap. "If we go back the way we came, we'll run right into him."

"Not if he took the left tunnel at the main chamber."

"And if he didn't?"

"And if we get lost and can't find our way out?"

"Darius will find us."

His mouth thins, as if relying on Darius for anything is anathema. I yank away from him and stalk back the way we came in. If nothing else, we might be able to hear Sampson approaching.

We make our way back to the main chamber. The storm is at its peak, rain pounding against the ocean's surface and pushing heavy waves against the rocks.

The water in the cave is almost knee-deep now, soaking our shoes and jeans. Even if we had taken the unmapped section of tunnels, we'd still have to contend with the threat of flooding.

We don't encounter a sign of Sampson, but when I start

to turn the corner into the main chamber, a gasp catches in my throat.

Conrad and Marko hover at the entrance, their big frames silhouetted against the metal-gray sky.

My father pulls me into the niche. Thank god he'd thought to turn off his flashlight before rounding the corner.

We crouch behind the rocks. My breath sounds like a chainsaw in the cavernous room. I pray Sampson doesn't come bolting in from the other tunnel. We're totally exposed to his view.

"Where the fuck did he go?" Conrad peers into the darkening cave as if there's any chance of him seeing what he wants to see.

He's holding a gun now. We've driven him to get his hands dirty. Despite his willingness to let his henchmen do all the work, I have no doubt he knows how to use that gun.

Icy water splashes around our thighs. My father and I lock gazes, sharing the same realization.

We're trapped, and the water is rising too fast.

CHAPTER 34

Darius

THE RAIN IS RELENTLESS, the wind lashing the tall sea grass. Ducking behind one of the SUVs, I creep up behind the guy guarding the front of the house and latch my arm around his neck.

He grunts, shoving his foot back to try and catch me in the knee. I move just in time, tightening my hold. I wrap my other arm around his head and twist until bone cracks. His body goes limp. He falls.

Isaac, the first one I shot, bled out beside the first SUV. Two left, plus Conrad, and they're all down in the caves. I run back to the beach.

Dusk is turning into night. The wind rips across the ocean's surface, pushing increasingly heavy waves onto the rocks and the shore. It's a cold, punishing wind, the spray knifelike.

I cross the sand, circumventing tangled piles of seaweed. The outlet from the cave tunnels is embedded in the rocky western slope of the cove. During low tide, it opens onto a narrow but short hill that leads to the safety of the beach. During high tide, it's submerged in the ocean.

The tide comes in fast to Volkov Bay, as the waves sweep over the narrow inlet to the caves. Right now, the rising water covers the hill and is approaching the lower half of the cave outlet.

The storm is speeding up the process, like a faucet filling a pot. If Nell and Henry don't get out now, the water will flood the tunnels. Even faster than usual.

I deflect a stab of panic. Nell should be on the hill or even on the beach. There's only one reason why she wouldn't have made it to the outlet by now.

She couldn't.

Turning, I run across the beach to the trail leading down to the cave faces. The ocean is already encroaching on the rock stacks and arches. Waves crash against the base of the cliffs, sending up geyser-like sprays.

The other two cave mouths are shallow with few places to hide and only unpassable connections to the tunnel system. I wade into the water and try to look into the caves, but it's too dark to see. No sign of Conrad and his thugs.

I pull my gun out and move closer. A faint light flickers— Conrad's cell phone flashlight. It illuminates him and Marko, both standing like stone guards at the largest cave entrance.

Nell and Henry are still somewhere in there. The water is thigh-high and freezing, the undercurrent strong.

How far did they go? Are they trapped in Nell's secret

hideout or were they forced to venture into the unmapped tunnels?

I aim the gun at Marko's head. Squeeze the trigger. A gust of wind shoves me off balance. I'm too late to stop the movement of my hand. The gun fires. The bullet skims past him and ricochets off the cave wall.

He and Conrad turn. Marko swings his gun around and fires. I dodge to the right, blocking myself behind a rock stack. Another bullet zings past. If Nell and Henry are close—

I shove my gun into my waistband and plow forward, slogging through the icy water and tackling Marko before he can fire again. He stumbles backward and hits the cave wall.

His gun falls into the water. Conrad shouts. Another gunshot. I smash Marko's head against the wall and turn, bringing my arm up to knock the gun out of my father's hand.

"You sonuvabitch." In the darkening light, his face is a gray mask of fury.

He swings, catching me on the jaw. A sharp pain radiates through my skull. Despite the weight of the water, I fire off a few jabs that slow him down. Marko clamps a heavy hand on my shoulder.

"Darius!" Nell's voice, edged with warning.

I turn and break away from Marko. Another bullet hits the cave wall—Sampson, wherever the hell he came from.

Marko smashes the back of my knee. My leg buckles. I go down, the water hitting me with the force of a blast. All the breath whooshes out of my lungs.

I manage to move so my father is between me and Sampson. Marko hits the back of my head. Stars explode behind my eyes. My father snaps something at him. Marko grabs my neck and shoves me under the water.

My mind goes blank. Arctic saltwater floods my eyes and mouth. My chest burns. The guy's big hand is a fucking vise. I grab for the knife in my boot, but can't reach it.

While I still have air in my lungs, I fumble around on the ocean floor. Sand billows into the waves. The edges of my brain darken.

Then my fingers brush the metal of my father's gun. I grab it, wedging the barrel against Marko's leg. Praying the gun will fire under the weight of water, I pull the trigger.

A bullet drives into Marko's leg. He releases my neck and staggers. His blood swells through the water.

I shove upward and break the surface, gulping air. The gun falls out of my frozen hand. Marko collapses against the wall, half-submerged.

My father advances, slamming a fist against my temple. The blow is almost anesthetized by the frigid cold. I get to my feet, my clothes soaked and heavy. I need to stay close to him so Sampson can't get a clear shot at me.

"Kill him, you asshole," Conrad shouts at Sampson.

Pulling up my old fight training, I clench my fists and lunge at my father with three sharp hooks to the jaw. He curses, spitting out blood.

The gun goes off again. I can't follow the path of the bullet. Sampson grunts. From the corner of my eye, I see his shadow scuffling with…Henry? Nell?

I grab my father's shoulders and headbutt him, making sharp contact with the bridge of his nose. His head snaps back. I plow forward and immobilize him in a headlock, tightening one arm around his neck.

"You have no idea how much I want to strangle you," I hiss in his ear.

He barks out a laugh. "Yes, I do."

I squint into the depths of the cave. Marko is losing his battle against the rising tide and sinking fast.

Sampson shoves through the water. He's got one hand clamped on Henry's arm and the gun pointed at his head.

I tighten my grip on Conrad's neck, cutting off his air. "Tell him to let Henry go, or you're dead."

"You'll kill me anyway."

"Maybe. Or I might let you live so I can see you locked up on charges of corruption, terrorist financing, and war crimes."

A wave courses through him—a combination of shock and cold.

"Yeah, I know, Conrad. You've been funding the PLF all this time so you could get your hands on Krasnovar's mines. You didn't pay the ransom because you were cutting a deal with them. That included letting them use me as a pawn for their other demands, didn't it? Want to know how I found out? Those photos of the factory bombing came from a spy in the PLF, a guy who actually works for an intelligence agency. You thought you were getting them from one of your PLF buddies, didn't you? Surprise. You were duped."

He shoves his elbow back into my ribs, but the contact barely makes an impact. The cold is sapping his strength.

"Let him go!" I yell at Sampson.

Conrad nods at his bodyguard. Sampson releases Henry, pushing him so hard he stumbles against a stack of rocks.

Behind him, Nell flies out of the darkness, making a huge jump and landing on Sampson's back. She wraps her arms around his neck and holds on like an albatross. Sampson growls in anger and tries to throw her off. She doesn't let go.

I shove my father away and plunge through the water toward them. The water is more than waist-high now, rising swiftly to chest level. Sampson flails to get Nell off, unable to get a shot at me.

Grabbing his arm, I wrench the gun from his hand and lodge it against his breastbone. I pull the trigger. He chokes, stiffening.

Nell drops away from him, staggering backward toward her father. Sampson collapses and sinks underwater.

I turn. Conrad is lurching toward the cave entrance, his movements slowed by the rapid waves.

"Stop," I order.

He flounders, the ocean splashing around him. He's soaked through, his face white with cold, his gray hair plastered to his forehead. If he weren't such a shitbag, I might pity him.

Or not.

I fire the gun, purposely missing. The bullet shoots past him and drops into the water. Conrad flinches and tries to speed up, to get back to the trail.

I could kill him. But I want to see him suffer. To be publicly vilified. To live out the rest of his days in a cell. Time for him to find out what that's like.

"Next time, I won't miss," I warn him.

He wobbles to a stop, his body swaying as he tries to maintain his foothold in the undercurrent and the pounding rain. He grabs the side of the cave archway. His glare slices through the darkness.

"A real man would've already killed me," he snaps. "You

were always such a fucking disappointment."

"I wanted to do a hell of a lot more than just disappoint you." I start toward him, gun aimed.

We have to get out of here. The tide is getting rougher, almost to chest level—at my height. Nell will be close to submerged. She and Henry are still next to the wall, and he's pushing her up onto a higher ledge.

Behind Conrad, a colossal swell rolls in from the open ocean. Like a sea monster charging under the surface.

I stare at it for a second. Fear bolts through my chest. There's no fucking way we can—

"Nell! Henry, hold on!"

The swell rises, expanding into the size of a mountain before breaking. The wave crashes down with a thunderous roar, shoving the ocean violently toward the shore, the cliffs, the caves.

The water surges and collides with the rocks, sending up geysers of salty spray. I drop the gun and manage to get my arm around a column, bracing myself against the impact.

Conrad's eyes widen in shock the second before the wave crashes over him. He goes under, arms thrashing.

Some latent instinct pushes me forward to try and get to him. He bobs to the surface, choking and spitting up saltwater.

Our eyes meet. I've never seen him look so terrified. I've never seen him look scared at all.

"Darius…," he gasps, spewing out more water. "Son…"

The water shoves me back a few steps. I lunge against the current. The ocean retreats, pulling the massive swell back into the bay.

And taking Conrad with it.

He screams, struggling to get back into the cave, to find secure ground. But there is none. He's caught in the powerful undercurrent, his panicked fighting useless against the savage force.

I fight my way forward.

"Help!" he yells. "Help…"

He goes under, the waves closing over him swiftly, erasing any evidence that he was there at all. The cold sinks into my bones, freezing everything inside me.

He comes to the surface again farther in the distance, still visible despite the storm, but it's too late. The ocean drags him out to the bay and down into the cold, submerged deep.

Nell. Henry.

My heart jolts back to life. They're huddled by the cave wall, dripping wet and shaking violently. Nell is halfway up on the ledge, and Henry is still in the water up to his chest. I slog my way toward them.

Without wasting energy trying to explain—it's obvious we have to swim out, which is a dire prospect given what we just saw happen to Conrad—I reach up and grab Nell around the waist, hauling her down to me. Her skin is ice, her teeth rattling and her whole body trembling.

I tighten my arms around her hard, trying to give her whatever body heat I have left. "Hold on."

She clutches my wet shirt. I look at Henry. His mouth is a grim line, his eyes burning.

"Get my daughter the hell out of here," he orders hoarsely.

"I will. You too." I peel off the long-sleeved shirt I'm wearing over my T-shirt and fasten it around my waist, then tie one sleeve to Nell's wrist. I ask Henry to give me the leather belt he's wearing. For extra security, I push the belt through several loops on both my jeans and Nell's before latching the buckle. If she loses strength, we'll still be attached to each other.

"Hold on to me," I tell her. "Swim as much as you can. We'll stay close to the surface. I won't let you go."

She nods, shivering. I extend my hand to Henry. We grab each other's wrists, and the three of us start through the turbulent water.

The cave is submerged in storm water and the increasing tide. The trail leading down to the caves is flooded now. I don't want to risk going back that way; a rogue wave could smash us against the rocks.

The ocean floor falls away. Still gripping Henry's wrist, I start to swim around the western slope of the cliff to the beach. On my other side, Nell starts to kick. The cold is a sharp, physical pain, the leaden water like a tornado.

Rain lashes down. We struggle against the undertow, the force trying to drag us all out into the ocean. Seaweed whips around us, a tangle of slimy ropes.

Henry's fingers start to loosen on my wrist. I tighten my grip. He's a strong swimmer—or at least, he once was—but these conditions are apocalyptic. For every foot toward the beach, we're pulled three feet backward. The water and rain are so frigid it's like swimming through needles.

Nell is holding on, but her kicks are getting farther in between. I will the shirt and belt to keep us latched together. Her arm brushes mine, giving me a surge of strength.

I keep going, muscles aching, the saltwater stinging my eyes, throat, nose. The current is ferocious, like a massive creature with sharp teeth determined to drag us into its lair.

Henry is faltering, becoming a deadweight. I yank his wrist in a silent order not to give up. If he does, he'll take me and Nell with him. The shirt and belt ties won't last long in this tide.

He pulls up beside me. With our hands linked, we each only have one arm to propel us through the water. But when he comes parallel to me, we start a front crawl in a rhythm, both lifting our arms and kicking at the same time.

Progress. I drag in short, desperate breaths every second I break the surface. Henry gasps and coughs. *Arms, kick, arms, kick.*

I lose track of time. I stop thinking. The shore seems miles away. But every time I squint through the storm, it's still there, the house hunched on the dunes like it's waiting for us.

We're going to make it. Any second now, I'll put my legs down and feel solid ground. Any—

Henry's grip breaks away from mine.

"Henry!" I shove up to the surface, spitting out water.

Shit shit shit.

The current carried him back, and now he's ten feet behind us.

"D-Dad…" Nell's voice is a death rattle.

I have to get her to the shore. I have to get Henry.

Those two thoughts spear through me. I plow against the water toward the shore. I stop, feeling for the ocean floor. As soon as my feet touch the ground, I grab Nell and haul her into my arms.

I stumble up the slope to the beach, putting her down as soon as we're away from the water's edge. She falls limp, her body heaving.

I yank the knife out of my boot and slice through the shirt and belt ties, then I turn and plunge back into the blade-sharp ocean.

Henry is struggling to reach the shore, his movements increasingly frantic. I shove my way through the current, kicking as hard as I can.

No way, Henry. You're not going out like this. I won't let you.

I keep going in his direction. He's almost motionless by the time I reach him, his head barely above water. I pull him toward me, turning him onto his back and clamping one arm around his chest.

"Nell," he chokes.

"She's safe." I grip him harder and start back to the shore.

The rain pounds down in icy sheets. Nell is a smudge of blue and gray on the beach. I propel myself forward with one arm and heavy kicks, finally finding the slope where I can stand.

Nell stumbles toward us and grabs Henry's other arm. We stagger back to the beach, dragging him with us. He collapses, coughing up water, his hands clawing the sand.

"Is he all right?" Nell gasps.

I drag in deep, painful breaths. "He will be."

She stares at me, almost as if she's just realizing what happened. We're both shaking, soaked, frozen to the bone.

I hold out my arms. She steps into them, pressing her face to my chest.

And the raging of the earth falls silent.

CHAPTER 35

Nell

THE CERAMIC MUG has a bright yellow smiley face and the phrase *You're Awesome!* The coffee, Banks informed me, is a medium roast blend called Tanzania Peaberry. When I'd told him he could make even canned coffee taste like the nectar of the gods, I swear he'd actually blushed.

Noon sunlight falls through the forest, and the leaves create little dancing shadows over the ground. The campfire is out, the logs dusted with ash and still emitting the smell of burned wood.

Poe snuffles around at my feet, vacuuming up the crumbs of my doughnut. He's not back to full-force yet, but he's doing well and was so happy to see me and Darius return yesterday that he popped a stitch—which thankfully was easily fixed since his wound is healing properly. The vet assured us he's on the road to a full recovery.

I rest my hand on the dog's head. He licks my arm.

My chest is still tight with a thousand emotions I don't quite know what to do with—love, overwhelming gratitude, apprehension, hope. I don't know what happens next, where we go from here, but I would not change an atom of what I've shared with Darius Hawke.

The aftermath of our terrifying ordeal four days ago had been chaotic and exhausting. Police and investigators swarmed the beach. The ocean spit Conrad back onto the shore the following morning.

Between him and the bodies of the other men, the investigators had endless questions and procedures to enact. Darius also called in high-level UN officials and FBI agents, all of whom are familiar with his counterterrorism work.

After close to forty-eight hours, Darius had insisted that my father and I both be allowed to return to Grenville, but I hadn't wanted to leave him. When Fern called to say she'd been able to get a flight from Seattle, my father rented a car to drive home.

"I'll come back soon." I'd stood outside with him next to the car, not wanting us to separate with any recrimination or blame. Not again.

"I know." With a gentle smile, my father embraced me. "And I know you don't want me to tell you what to do, but I'd still appreciate you not risking your life again."

"I won't, I promise." I hugged him tightly. "I've had enough adventure for a very long time."

He released me and looked past my shoulder to where Darius was approaching from the beach.

Wariness filled the air. My stomach knotted.

"Henry." Darius extended his hand.

My father looked at it, then curled his own hand into a fist. Without warning, he drew his arm back, twisted, and hit Darius hard across the jaw, forcing him to stumble back. I clamped a hand to my mouth to hold back a gasp.

"Damn." Darius blinked in shock and rubbed his jaw. "I didn't know you had such a strong right hook."

"You're the one who showed me how to throw one." My father grimaced a little. "Just took me twenty-five years to find a reason to use it."

He held out his hand, and they shook.

Though I knew a "strong right hook" wouldn't resolve their conflict about Darius's and my relationship, something appeared to settle between them. And given what I've learned about men needing to deal with their shit through physical means, I suppose it was a start.

Shortly after my father's return to Grenville, the investigators had gathered enough solid intel on Darius to allow both of us to leave. Darius told the UN officials he would take the flash drive to an expert who could determine if the contents were still readable after their immersion in saltwater.

He and I drove to the Black Hills to get Poe, to fill Banks in on everything that had happened, and to see if he could salvage the flash drive.

The police investigators are still prowling around Volkov Bay, but Darius's lengthy, complicated explanation of corporate crime and international terrorist financing, not to mention the influence of the UN, seems to have convinced them that this is a matter best left to higher-level law enforcement and authorities.

Poe nudges my leg. I dig into my backpack for a dog

biscuit. He grabs it out of my hand and settles down to happily crunch away.

The cabin door opens, and Banks clomps out. With his shaggy beard and ripped T-shirt, he's become a comforting rather than an alarming sight. Darius follows, both of them still talking as they approach.

"Any luck?" I ask.

"Luck?" Banks glowers at me. "You don't need luck when I'm around."

"Sorry." I hold up my hands. "How did it go?"

"He salvaged it all." Darius hands me the flash drive and sits beside me.

"Really? The entire contents?"

"It was pretty waterlogged, but yeah." Banks lowers himself into a chair and scratches Poe's ears. "All the documents and photos were intact. We just sent them to the FBI, the United Nations' Security Council, and the International Criminal Court."

"You think there's a chance this could go to the ICC?" I ask.

"More than a chance," Darius says. "If a corporation funds people who commit war crimes, they're both guilty and complicit. Hawke Financial should be charged right along with Conrad."

"Can he be tried posthumously?"

"No, but his company and reputation can be." Darius picks up a stick and pokes at the burnt logs. "The investigation has already started. Once they overturn all the rocks, God knows what—or who—will come slithering out. Hawke Financial seems to be the main funding channel for the PLF, and without money, they can't survive. Plus, we'll have more evidence after we learn about the Granite Intelligence infiltration."

On our drive to South Dakota, he'd explained how he learned that Conrad had obtained the factory photos directly from the PLF—a discovery that helped him untangle the truth about his father's financing of the whole organization.

The hidden watermark on the photos had proven they came from the PLF, though Conrad obviously hadn't known they'd been marked by a Granite Intelligence agent who'd infiltrated the organization.

It had taken me no time at all to guess that the spy was likely the PLF soldier called Tarek. The whole time we were confronting Lenkov and the soldiers, Tarek had been strangely unthreatening. Though he'd carried an AK-47 and extra ammunition, he hadn't had the hard edge of violence that the others did. When we'd reached the PLF encampments at the base of the mountain, Tarek had ordered the other men not to touch us or risk Lenkov's wrath.

I also remember feeling an odd relief that Tarek was the one who'd accompanied us to Kolchava. His presence had been almost reassuring compared to the other soldiers, and now I understand why.

"Going after Hawke Financial is cutting off the head of the snake," Banks philosophizes. "Darius also sent the details to his journalism contacts. Enough pressure from the media, and both national and international investigators will be forced to step it up."

And Krasnovar might finally recover. Though the Krasnovian military and the PLF are still battling across the northern province, the fighting has decreased considerably in both the south and the west.

I don't know how long it will take before this mess with Conrad affects the PLF's actual operations, but if they lose the war, there's no way they can regroup and rearm without financing. Maybe they won't even be able to continue fighting for much longer. Plus, now that the international justice systems are about to learn of the PLF's structure, there will be a worldwide effort to shut them down for good.

Darius, of course, will spearhead the effort. I can't wait for the day when he finally gets retribution for what the PLF —and Conrad Hawke—did to him.

Though in many ways, he already has.

Feeling his gaze, I look up. His expression is both warm and pensive. Since we left Volkov Bay, I've frequently caught him watching me. Sometimes like he still can't believe I'm real.

"We should get going." He stands and extends his hand to me. I slip my palm into his, letting him pull me to my feet. "Long drive back."

I start to collect the coffee mugs, but Banks waves at me to leave them alone. Poe lumbers up, as if he knows he's coming home with us.

"Banks." I turn to him. "Thanks."

A faint grin appears behind his beard. "Nell. You're swell."

I laugh, even as sudden tears sting my eyes. Before he can protest, I close the distance and hug him tightly. He tenses in surprise for a second before folding me into his tree-trunk arms.

"Really." I ease back and pat his wide chest. "Don't keep

your exceptional knife-slinging and coffee-brewing skills hidden away up here forever. Come and visit…"

My mind trips and stumbles over the word *us*.

"…me," I finally say. "My father would like to meet you, though you and he are about as different as night and…a banana split."

He frowns. "Which one am I?"

"A woolly mammoth."

He chuckles but makes no promise. Letting me go, he nods to the rented car. "Go on, get out of here."

Darius holds out his hand, and they exchange a hand-shake before Darius goes to get our travel bags.

Banks crouches, putting his face close to Poe's. He rubs the dog's head and murmurs something in his ear. Tail wagging, Poe licks his beard.

I turn away before I actually do start crying. Darius holds open the back door of the car, and Poe trots over to climb inside. A few minutes later, we're heading out of the forest toward the highway.

I turn to wave at Banks through the rear window. He lifts both arms in farewell. I watch him until the trees close between us, and he's gone.

CHAPTER 36

Nell

ON OUR DRIVE back to Grenville, Darius and I stop overnight at a halfway point in Utah. Rather than a luxury hotel in the city, he's booked us a cottage on the grounds of a historic inn that overlooks a wide expanse of sky and red-gold desert hills.

The one-room cottage is charming—decorated with watercolor paintings, dried-flower bouquets, and patchwork quilts. Poe has his own fluffy dog bed and a beef bone gifted to him by the innkeeper.

Darius and I order room service and sit outside on the deck to eat. The sunset and clouds unfold over the horizon like a tapestry.

Remember this, I tell myself. *When you are an old woman working in your studio that smells like paint, pencils, and chalk, when you are baking blueberry muffins for your grandchildren, when you are pondering the superpowers of dream weaving, when you are teaching young artists to trust their creative instincts...remember the colors of this desert and this sunset and the inside of your heart.*

Terracotta, cream, burnt orange, coral, pink lemonade, sage, peach, crimson.

And him, of course—my beautiful protector, a mountain and a forest with his dark hair the shade of midnight, a few strands of silver capturing the light, his black stubble and bronze skin, the mutable deep brown of his eyes.

Stone, chestnut, ash, mahogany, stars.

I take a long breath, pulling all of it into my blood, inviting it to become part of me.

Darius and I haven't talked about what happens next...at least, not with us. We've been too caught up in what's happening at the moment.

Now that the immediate chaos has calmed, Poe and I are going to stay with my father for some much-needed peace and quiet. Darius will return to New York to deal with Conrad's estate and the ongoing investigation.

I remember my little daydream of he and I taking a romantic road trip through small towns. Antique shops, specialty bakeries, farmer's markets. Just us rolling along and discovering whatever we want.

We could do that now. Keep going. Tour the southwest, drive into Louisiana, stay in New Orleans. Then make our way back...where?

Home? I don't even know where that is anymore.

No, that's not true. *He's* my home. I just can't live there.

"You're quiet." He pushes his plate away and sits back, his gaze on me. "You look like you're thinking very hard."

I shrug, twirling pasta on my fork. "Still a lot to think about."

A shadow crosses his face. I put my fork down and reach over to squeeze his forearm. I don't want him to have shadows or ghosts anymore. From now on, forever, he deserves only light.

"I love you," I say. "That's one thing I don't need to think about. It just is. It always will be."

He smiles faintly, sliding his hand to mine. Our fingers entwine. He tugs me up out of my chair and closer to him, and then his chest is against mine, our bodies pressing together without a space or seam between us. Everything in me softens and yields. He slips his hand under my chin and lifts my face at the same time that he lowers his.

My heart catches. His kiss is as warm as sunshine, as light and soft as a baby chick. And right now, I want it exactly like this—not fierce or wild or edgy. Just him and me and the endless desert and the sky all pink and frothy like a layer cake.

He brings his hands up to the sides of my head. I slide my arms around his waist, loving his taste, his strength, the sheer pleasure of everything he is.

He caresses my lips with his, urging my mouth open, drinking me in. Slowly he backs me up through the open door and into the room with its vanilla-scented potpourri and little dishes of wrapped chocolates.

He eases away from me, his eyes darkening as he lowers me onto the bed and runs his hands over my breasts. One by one, he unfastens the buttons lining the front of my blouse and presses kisses on my bare skin. I thread my hand through his hair and down to his jaw, his stubble like fine sandpaper against my palm.

"Come here," I whisper.

He braces himself above me, lowering his mouth to mine again. I love the weight of his body pressing me into the bed, the engulfing strength of him. Our mouths are still locked together as he pulls the blouse from my shoulders and tugs down the cups of my bra, baring my breasts to his touch.

Anticipation flares through me, lighting my nerves. I arch upward into his hands, against his groin. With a half laugh, half groan, he eases away only long enough to divest me of my skirt and underwear, pushing them into a heap at the foot of the bed.

"Not fair." I tug the front of his shirt.

With a slow smile, he pushes away and stands. He's wearing black trousers and a long-sleeved, crisp white shirt open at the collar to reveal the strong column of his throat. A black leather belt circles his waist, the silver buckle gleaming. He unbuttons his shirt much faster than he did mine and lets it drop to the floor.

He takes my breath away. The sunset blazes through the window behind him, spilling a honey-cherry light across his broad shoulders and burnishing his dark hair with gold. The scars marking his skin are striking evidence of both his battles and his victories.

I wiggle to sit on the edge of the bed and unbuckle his belt. His erection pushes against the front of his trousers and along his thigh. I take off his belt and unzip his pants, unable to prevent a little sigh of anticipation at the sight of his hard length. I lean forward to take him in my mouth, the taste of him jolting through me, but this time, he doesn't let me linger.

Pushing his hand into my hair, he urges me back onto the bed and slides his hand between my legs. Heat unspools in my belly. However long I live, I will never experience anything like Darius Hawke's touch—the slow, expert rubbing, the unerring precision, the way he knows exactly what I both want and need.

I pull him back down to me, the friction of our skin lighting fires in my blood. Our mouths meet again, hot and open. He levers himself above me, his eyes burning into mine, fathomless as the sea.

With a groan, he eases into me. I hug my legs around his thighs and wrap my arms around his shoulders, cleaving every part of myself to him.

Thought falls away. The world is only the flex and pull of our bodies, the increasing rhythm of his thrusts, the arch of my hips.

When the bright thread shatters into bursts of glitter, he grips my hair and swallows my cry, pushing so deep inside me that our pleasure merges into one and becomes endless. I tighten around his shaft, loving the way his muscles contract the instant before he comes, his release sparking a fresh wave of sensation.

I press my face against his shoulder, my arms locked around his back, absorbing the weight of him on top of me, the slickness of our skin. Our breathing eases.

Slowly he rolls onto the bed and pulls me closer. I rest my head on his chest, gazing out the big picture window at the fading sunset and the stars just beginning to open their eyes.

Tomorrow, we'll be back in Grenville. I think of the young woman I'd been four years ago, when my world had stopped at the town's borders. In no universe or fantastic dream could I ever have imagined Darius and I would be here now, like this.

I burrow against his side. "When do you leave for New York?"

"Wednesday morning." He rubs my shoulder.

"How long will you stay there?"

"About a week." He picks up a few strands of my hair, studying them in the waning light. "Depends on how long it takes to deal with my father's estate. The lawyers will handle most of it. And he cut me out of his will a long time ago, so there's probably not much I need to do."

I lift my head to look at him. Given what I know about Conrad Hawke, it's not a surprise to learn he'd disinherited Darius. In fact, that might be the least malicious thing he'd ever done.

"What's going to happen to his estate and all his money if it doesn't go to you?" I ask. "You're his only heir."

He shrugs. "I hope he left it all to charities or a worthwhile cause. He never did any good in his life, but maybe he will in his death."

I'm doubtful, but at least it's still a possibility.

"And after New York, what are you going to do?" I ask.

He twists my hair around his fingers and rubs it with his thumb. Unease tightens my throat.

"Darius?"

"I'm going back to Krasnovar." He lets go of my hair, his expression darkening. "The PLF is still trying to gain control of the north, and General Balakin hasn't surrendered yet. Plus there's the whole mess with the mining rights and companies. Since I know more than most people about the PLF's structure and now their funding channels, I'm the one who needs to make sure they're dismantled from the inside."

I move away from him, getting off the bed and reaching for my robe. Tears sting my eyes.

I'd expected him to work with the UN and other organizations on taking down the PLF. I'd expected him to eventually return to his photojournalism work. I hadn't expected him to go back into the conflict and directly deal with the whole mess—and his captors—again.

"Nell." Regret weights his voice. He pulls on his trousers, tension flexing through his back like wire.

I walk outside to the deck, grateful for the cooler air. I shouldn't feel anything but pride in him for his determination and resolve. He's been working for years to obliterate the PLF—and now he has all the tools he needs to succeed.

And of course if the PLF is destroyed, who knows how many acts of terror will be prevented? How many lives saved? The positive impact will be vast and untold.

But Darius's reasons are also intensely personal. Both his father and the PLF tortured and permanently scarred him. Conrad Hawke was responsible for the PLF's attempted coup, which led to countless deaths and destruction. Darius will be the one to rectify his father's crimes, no matter the cost to himself.

I pull in a breath and wipe my eyes on my sleeve. It's selfish of me, this combination of both frustration and deep sorrow. But how will he ever know any light if he keeps going back endlessly into the dark?

He settles his hands on my shoulders. I feel his body heat even though there's still space between us.

"Will you be able to get to Telina?" I swallow to conceal the hitch in my voice. "To see Alexei and Jacob?"

"I'll try to, yes. First thing."

Hope rises under my lingering sorrow. Patrick had left a message on Darius's voicemail letting him know that despite our hopes about the refugee camp database, Alexei still has no word on Sofia, Tomas, and Marcus. But Darius might have resources that they haven't yet tried.

"Nell, I have to—"

I turn to face him, holding up my hand. "I know. I'm not asking for an explanation or a list of reasons. I know why you're going back. I understand."

He studies me, his eyes dark with some undefinable emotion that feels too complex for resolution. "I'm sorry."

I shake my head, suddenly unable to stop the pain from breaking through. "I might understand, but I still hate it. I can't stand the thought of you putting yourself at that kind of risk again—and with *them*. What if they're still out for revenge? What if they abduct you for the third time? Or not even that...what if they just kill you on sight? Now more than ever, they'll want you dead."

He steps away from me, resting his hands on the porch railing, the muscles of his shoulders bunched and tight.

My heart thumps. I hadn't intended to outline all my fears—and those aren't the only ones—but after all we've been through, I can't fathom him going right back into the terror.

And yet, that's how he lives. I've always known that.

"I don't have a choice," he finally says.

"That's not true. You didn't have a choice when you were a hostage. You didn't always have a choice when you were a child. But ever since then, you've always had a choice."

"Nell, you know what my father was responsible for. How can I not fix it?"

"I'm not trying to change your mind." I wrap my arms around my waist. "I know you. I know how much good you'll do in Krasnovar"—*if you're not killed*—"but that doesn't mean I'm not scared for you."

I'll always be scared for him. And I don't want to live in fear anymore.

"But this is what you do." I rest my hand on his forearm. "You don't have to apologize for being who you are. Especially not to me."

He looks at the railing, his hair falling in a rumpled mess over his forehead, his eyes shuttered and opaque. "You're the only person I want to apologize to. Because I can't give you the life you deserve. And even if I could, what happens later? When you're sixty and I'm over eighty?"

I blink. "Then we'd have had almost *forty years* together. How many people have that kind of luck?"

He doesn't respond. He thinks he's already used up his allotment of luck. His grip on the railing is so hard it looks like he might crack the wood.

"Darius." I edge closer to him. "What I deserve—what anyone deserves—is the life we create. And I can figure out a way to do that for myself."

I look at the mountains and the early night sky, like a bucket of navy-blue paint has spilled over the desert. "I'm going to stay in Grenville for a few weeks, then I'll move back to New York. I guess we can see each other when you get back from…wherever you are. Whenever that is."

His mouth compresses, as if he can't even picture that scenario. Neither can I.

The little seed is still buried in my heart, but it hasn't yet started to grow. I'd once thought it might—one day, with enough care and sunlight.

I'd believed in the possibility that Darius and I could have a future together. With our new symmetry, the even scales of who we are, I'd thought we had a chance at a different kind of life. He could pursue his work, and I would wait for him to come back while figuring out my career, my art, and my goals apart from him.

But I can no longer see that reshaped future.

Even if I stay in New York while he continues to battle the PLF or goes on assignment, even if we text and call every day and have intense, passionate reunions whenever he comes home, even if I avoid the news and try not to think too much about where he is and what he's doing, even if he can't talk to me about his work—we would both know.

Now that I've experienced firsthand the horror of war—and still only a tiny fraction of it—I wouldn't be able to help picturing him in the midst of the violence. Seeing people shot, maimed, burned. Praying he won't be next.

I've changed so much, learned so much, that I can't bear the pain of such risk. Not when I know to the core of my being how valuable life truly is. But I also never want to be the one who takes him away from his objectives, his drive, the wrongs he considers it his duty to *fix*.

And he would have a perpetual sense of guilt, of concern about me, a tug-of-war between wanting to do his life's work and wanting to be with me. He might not even be the photographer he once was.

Even if the PLF is destroyed for good, even if he decides he's had enough of war and chooses to become a wildlife photographer or a sports photographer, even if I go with him while he takes pictures of Arctic penguins and lions on the Serengeti…he'd feel like he was taking me away from my own career pursuits and from the parallel life he thinks I should live—the one with a fictional nice husband, two cute kids, a house with a picket fence and an art studio out back. And I'd be the one responsible for forcing him to stop doing what he's done for almost twenty-five years, the job he's best at.

And even if we say we're okay with everything, the dissatisfaction would fester because neither one of us would believe the other when we promise that we have everything we want.

Which is so fucking sad. Because we trust each other with our lives, our hearts, and yet we can't seem to trust each other with our promises.

Even if he abandons his counterterrorism work or chooses to do it full-time instead. Even if he takes a government appointment or a position at the UN. Even if I insist on going wherever he goes. Even if we keep it casual—living our lives separately while being lovers whenever we get the chance.

Even if…*all of that.*

Even if—

What else is there? He opens a photography portrait studio while I keep looking for an arts-related job? He takes ordinary assignments from wire services—political rallies, elections, the occasional human-interest story? I struggle to sell my art, to have a gallery show, to publish a graphic novel?

We both give up everything else and get regular jobs like regular people and find our own house in the suburbs with a white picket fence? We move back to Grenville and live next door to my father?

In no scenario will either one of us be fully at ease and without self-blame and guilt.

And yet—I chose this. I wanted him. I knew he was complex and challenging and that he would never fit into any kind of conventional life. That right there is just one of the reasons I fell so hard in love with him. And why I'll always stay exactly where I fell. There's no rising and flying away from Darius Hawke.

I shift my gaze back to him. He's standing closer now, so close I can see the ring of black surrounding his irises, the texture of his skin, the bullet scar on his shoulder. I reach up and run my finger around the edge of the raised, jagged circle.

"Remember when you said you'd always come to me?" I ask.

He nods. Darkness clouds his eyes and carves deep lines around his mouth.

"And I said I'd always be here for you." My vision blurs. "I'll keep that promise. If you ever need me, I'm here."

"Nell—" His voice cracks.

"Darius, we're part of each other." I stroke my hand across his chest, stopping right over his heart. "I knew you before I was born. We share the molecules of life and time and whatever else makes up the universe. And we've both always known—even back in Grenville—that life is the opposite of a fairy tale. I told you once that I'd take whatever you could give me, and I have. Greedily and with both hands. I also know when it's time to stop taking."

He puts his hand on the side of my neck, the weight of his palm like the force of gravity keeping me from spinning off the earth.

"I love you." His confession is raw, like he knows it's the last time he'll ever say those words. "I'll never love anyone else."

I wipe my cheeks and shake my head. Neither will I, but I can't tell him that. It's not what he wants for me.

He pulls me into his arms, folding me against him. I press my face to his chest. His heartbeat is heavy and rhythmic, his warmth and strength endless. He tightens his grip in a way that makes me feel as if he'll hold on forever.

What a strange thing love is. Breaking your heart by filling it with so much.

I ease away first, sliding my palm over the taut skin of his abdomen. The little seed buried inside me isn't going to grow. Sometimes they don't. I'll have to plant different seeds instead. Tidy, contained petunias instead of flourishing wildflowers and dragon lilies.

Slowly I turn and go back inside. From his bed beside the window, Poe lifts his head, his ears perking as I kneel to ruffle his fur.

Darius stands at the railing, his arms folded, his gaze on the distant mountains. Shadows move across his back like wings.

The sky is turning from blue to black, the light surrendering, darkness falling. The bright, vivid display of the horizon will reappear tomorrow morning—honey, vermilion, apricot, ruby.

No, it won't be the same as it was today or yesterday. Nothing is ever exactly the same. But the sun and clouds will return, rolling across the sky and bringing the colors back again.

CHAPTER 37

Darius

Six weeks later

MONSOON SEASON. The New Delhi streets are crammed with cars, pedestrians, taxis, rickshaws, bicycles.

There's constant motion, as if everything is spurred along by the threat of a downpour and the incessant noise. Horns, engines, street vendors shouting, music blaring from radios in open-air stalls, cheers over a televised cricket match.

The air is thick with the smells of exhaust, sandalwood incense, spices, smoke, oil and fried dough from the *chaat* stands. The early September heat burns down from the sky and up from the greasy asphalt.

It's a good place to be. The chaos keeps other thoughts

submerged. After Vidya had shown me all her latest work on watermarking digital photographs, she'd invited me to stay with her family longer.

"You need a vacation," she'd said. She's probably right, but I have to get to Geneva for a meeting with members of the UN Security Council.

Then—Krasnovar again. I hope. I'd managed to get into the country after leaving New York, but because of the continued fighting in the northern province, I'd only been granted a two-day visa. Though I'd seen Alexei and Jacob, I hadn't been able to look into the refugee camps or the whereabouts of their family. I also hadn't had time to get near the PLF forces again or investigate anything more about their strategy.

"Sahib, sahib!" A boy of about ten wearing a torn shirt and shorts, his dusky feet bare, runs up to the outdoor table where I'm sitting. With a wide grin, he points to the camera next to the paper *chaat* plates and bottle of mango-flavored soda. "Picture, sahib."

A half-dozen other children gather behind him—all in ragged, faded clothes, all smiling and giggling. They probably haven't seen an actual camera before. And with the proliferation of cell phones, it must seem like an antique. I pick up the old Nikon and remove the lens cap. The kids push closer, like I'm performing a magic act.

I snap their photos, capturing their wide smiles and dark eyes. I haven't taken many photos in the past few weeks. The ones I have taken are uninspired and bland.

The boy makes an eager gesture with his hands, like he's clicking the shutter. "I take?"

"Sure." I loop the heavy camera around his neck and

show him how to look through the viewfinder, adjust the focus, press the shutter button, and view the image.

With a grin, he turns to his friends and snaps a group photo. Then he hurries down the street, pausing to take pictures of anything and everything—a dog pawing for scraps, a sleeping rickshaw wallah, a pile of lemons at a fruit stand.

His friends follow, clamoring for a turn. In seconds, they're swallowed up by the mass of people and vehicles. I let them go. Maybe my camera is in better hands with them.

I pick up the mango soda. The bottle is sweating but still cold. I take a long drink, then get up to order another plate of *puri* shells filled with spiced potatoes and chickpeas. I return to the table and sit for another hour, eating *chaat,* drinking overly sweet soda, swatting at flies.

The activity of the street doesn't make Nell go away— nothing can do that—but it gives me a distraction. She's still in Grenville. Last I heard from Lindsey, she's planning to visit New York for a week or two next month in preparation for her move.

I don't know when I'll go back. Can't imagine setting foot in the city, knowing she's there and not being able to see her.

Well. Keeping myself away. Because I still don't trust myself with her unless I'm protecting her. Because I don't know how to be with her in…life. After the storms. In the sun.

I pull out my phone and scroll through the messages. I open an email from my lawyer that she sent last week. Papers to sign. Tax forms to file. Accounts to transfer.

I read her message again, still trying to process the sight of my mother's name, the unexpected discovery of what she'd done for me. The foresight she'd had in knowing my father and I would face each other down on the battlefield. The evidence that she was always on my side, even in death.

"I tried to take care of you, Darius. The best I could."

You did, Mom.

I haven't thought about what to do next. Conrad's lawyers have been dealing with his estate. Turns out he'd split the bulk of his money among his friends and associates. Some of it he'd left to charities that Hawke Financial had been involved with, and the rest went to his alma mater.

He had, to my surprise, not removed me as beneficiary of either his Manhattan apartment or his house in the Hamptons. I've already put both on the market and will donate the proceeds to the Freedom Foundation—the hostage support organization I'd intended to be the recipient of my book royalties.

Since I terminated the contract and didn't write the book, it's a consolation that I can still do something for them. And using Conrad's money to help former hostages feels right.

"Sahib!" The boy runs back through the crowd like a fish darting through water. He holds up the camera to show me the images on the screen.

I look over them all, pausing to tell him which ones I like the most. He gives me a thumbs-up. The other kids hold out their hands for their turn. I give the camera to a little girl, and the boy tugs on my hand, urging me to stand.

For the next couple of hours, I accompany their little group through the crowded streets as they take pictures and show me their images. Despite our language barrier, we manage to have discussions about photography and how to frame a shot. I buy them plates of *chaat,* curry bowls, and bottles of Frooti. They gobble the food down like they haven't eaten in a week. Probably they haven't.

When the boy—Rohan—hands me the camera and points to the dark rainclouds gathering overhead, we part ways. I give them all the cash I have in my wallet, which isn't enough and won't do anything except buy them another few meals. They distribute the money among their group, then rush away, their bare feet swift and agile on the hot asphalt.

I watch them go. When they've disappeared into the commotion again, I head toward the neighborhood where Vidya's family lives. Rain starts to fall—a drizzle that will become a torrent in seconds.

My phone buzzes. I step under a grocery store awning and open a message from an editor at the *World News* service. Guerrilla fighting in Venezuela—drug trafficking, political opposition, assassination attempt, deadly clashes at the border.

You going?

I stare at the question. I need to get back into Krasnovar. But this time, because I'll be working directly with the government, I have to stick with legal entry—which means waiting for another visa approval. And I can't do nothing while I wait.

I type the word *yes* and hit send, then walk back out into the storm.

CHAPTER 38

Nell

WOOF.

My father's text is accompanied by a blurry photo of him and Poe—well, the upper half of Poe's face and my father's chin. He and Poe have not only bonded over tug-of-war and steak, they've also apparently discovered a love for selfie photography.

With a smile, I type, *Miss you both. See you Wednesday.*

I slip the phone into my bag as the subway train squeals to a halt at the 86th Street station. Navigating through the crowd, I climb up to the street. The October morning air is brisk and cool, the never-ending bustle of Manhattan both familiar and welcome.

Though I'm only here for a week, I've already gotten leads for several jobs, applied for at least a dozen more, and put in info requests for pet-friendly apartment rentals. If everything goes as planned—and this time, I'm convinced that it will—I'll be able to move back here with Poe before Thanksgiving.

In-between job and apartment hunting, I've seen my friends and caught up on all their latest news and adventures. Last night I had dinner with Jonah, who is now an official architect with Fountain Architecture Group in Chelsea, and he had the grace not to ask for details about why my relationship with Darius "didn't work out."

Lindsey tells me Darius has been busy in the two and a half months since we parted—first with his father's estate and the investigation, then in Krasnovar, then with counterterrorism meetings and reports.

He's also been in India, Geneva, and Paris. A few weeks ago, Alexei messaged me that Darius hadn't been able to stay in Krasnovar for long due to his visa, and there was still no word about the rest of Alexei's family.

I've gotten back to contacting relief and refugee organizations in the hopes that I can be of some help. The number of refugees throughout the world makes it a daunting prospect at best, but I've learned how to be a very loud squeaky wheel when it comes to hierarchies and red tape.

Hazel and Brian, my old friends from Global Rebuild, have both moved on to working for different nonprofits— Hazel with a group that provides meals to impoverished communities, and Brian with a healthcare NGO—but they both sent me names and contact information for people who can give me some leads.

After dropping off applications at several Manhattan stores and restaurants, I stop at the Art Institute to see the exhibits and say hello to several former professors. As I'm leaving the main building, my phone buzzes.

I unlock the screen, expecting another blurry Poe-Henry selfie. Instead it's a text from Lindsey—*are you on your way?*

I respond with *be there in half an hour.*

Lindsey had invited me over for lunch this afternoon—and while I've often been the recipient of her and Tom's generous hospitality, she'd been oddly insistent that I have to come over this exact Friday and be there exactly on time.

I take the bus to their Lower East Side brownstone. Lindsey has assured me she'll have shifts available for me at Pen and Paper when I move back to the city, though with a few promising possibilities as an art program coordinator, a youth arts instructor, and an assistant designer, I might not need to take her up on her offer.

As I approach their house, I notice that the curtains in the front window are closed. Strange, considering it's such a beautiful day, and their front room is delightful when the sun is pouring in.

I walk up the ramp leading to the front door and ring the bell. The curtains flicker.

From behind the entryway window, I see Lindsey coming to the door. She opens it and wheels back to let me in. "How were things at the Institute?"

"Busy as usual." I take off my lightweight jacket and hang it on the rack. "It's fun to go back and see what current students are doing."

"Come in." She maneuvers her wheelchair around and gestures to the interior of the house. "Tom is getting the food organized. I invited someone else, if you don't mind."

"Not at all. I was—" I stop, my heart suddenly jumping.

A tall, handsome man, his left arm wrapped in a cast and sling, comes out of the front room. A wide grin brightens his bearded face, and his eyes are sparkling.

I put a hand to my mouth, swallowing a gasp of shock. *"Alexei?"*

"The one and only." With a laugh, he comes forward, his right arm extended.

"What...how did..." I shake my head in disbelief. Tears spring to my eyes.

"Sometimes miracles can happen, yes?" He wraps his arm around me, and I reach up to return his tight embrace.

"I can't believe it." I pull away and wipe my eyes, looking him over from head to toe. "How are you? What are you doing here? How did you get here?"

He and Lindsey exchange a conspiratorial wink. She looks incredibly pleased with herself.

"Lin, how—"

"Go on in." She tilts her head. "Alexei has a lot to tell you."

Still grinning, he steps aside and waves me into the front room.

I walk past him...and stop again in shock. Then I start crying in earnest.

Sofia, Marcus, Jacob, and Tomas are all standing in front of the curtained windows, beaming at me with such delight that their smiles could power the entire northern hemisphere.

"I can't believe it." Though I repeat the words as I hug them all, both laughing and crying at the same time, in this moment, there is nothing I believe more.

Lindsey hands me a box of tissues after I've finally calmed down. Jacob and Tomas are still jumping up and down, gleeful over their wildly successful "surprise of Nell."

"It's so wonderful to see you." Sofia takes my arm and leads me over to a sitting area of sofas and chairs.

A round table bears trays of cheese, crackers, and fruit. Jacob and Tomas look pleadingly at their mother—apparently having been instructed to wait before digging in. Sofia gives them a nod of assent, and they descend on the food.

We sit down, and Alexei explains how Darius helped them all find each other again and come to the States.

With the strict visa requirements, he hadn't been able to stay in Krasnovar for long periods of time and sometimes couldn't get into the country at all. For the past month, he's been staying in the Moldovan capital, pressuring both the Krasnovian embassy and the US consulate to grant him a longer visa term.

While in Moldova, he got in touch with a friend who was covering the influx of Krasnovian refugees who'd crossed the border to escape the fighting in the northern province. With a lot of string pulling, Darius was able to access the database of displaced refugees. Marcus, Sofia, and Tomas were listed among them.

Since there had still been substantial fighting in the north, it wasn't safe for them to try and return to either Varaz or Telina. So Darius had then fought to get Alexei and Jacob out of the country.

After learning that Alexei's arm still hadn't healed properly, Darius had managed to procure him a medical visa for treatment with a renowned specialist at George Washington Hospital. He'd also gotten tickets and temporary visas for the rest of the family—and they'd been reunited at the airport in Brussels before getting on the flight to Washington DC.

"I have had second surgery." Alexei indicates his sling. "Bone fragments had to be removed. But it is recovered now."

"Papa has to do this." Jacob waves a cracker up and down in a demonstration of Alexei's arm exercises.

"Two times a day." Tomas reaches for another olive.

"He is on the road." Sofia smiles at her husband, her eyes shining. "Darius also gave us our wedding photos, and we cannot wait to share them with Alexei's mother and sister. When we go back, we will stay with them near Saldem."

I glance from her to Alexei. "You're going back?"

"Yes, of course." Alexei appears mildly surprised by the question. "Why would we not?"

"I...it's just that there's still unrest and fighting."

"Krasnovar is our home." Sofia shrugs, as if that explains everything. Maybe it does.

"We leave three days from now," Alexei says. "We came to New York just this morning. We wanted to see you, and of course we had not yet taken a bite of the Big Apple."

"It's delicious," Tomas says—a remark that sends Jacob into peals of laughter.

"Darius gave us the contact information for his good friends Lindsey and Tom, and they helped us make arrangements." Sofia reaches over to squeeze Lindsey's hand. "Now we are fortunate to have them as our good friends too."

"I think Darius is still in Moldova." Lindsey looks at me, as if she knows I'm wondering. "Or he might have left by now. We haven't heard from him since last weekend. He was trying to get back into Krasnovar, but if he couldn't get another visa, he planned to take an assignment somewhere else. That's why he didn't come with the Rostovs."

"Do you know where he was planning to go?" I ask.

She shakes her head.

I let out my breath slowly. I'd turned the world upside down trying to find Darius after I'd left Varaz. Now I have to live with the possibility I might never know where he is. Again.

"What's the situation in Krasnovar now?" I ask. Though I've kept up with recent news, I haven't been able to trust any official sources to provide the true story.

"The democratic government remains stable and has been confiscating the weapons and equipment of the PLF," Marcus says. "The fighting in the north has begun to subside, but it remains to be seen when we can return to Varaz."

"I must get back to the museum as soon as I can." Alexei leans forward, his elbows on his thighs. "There is much damage to assess, and I want to learn the condition of Bram Castle."

His dedication doesn't surprise me. Even after all that's happened, he's determined to return to his life's work. Not unlike someone else I know.

"What about the command chain of the PLF?" I ask.

"General Balakin was killed in a skirmish near Telina," Marcus says. "After his death, the People's Liberation Front began to rapidly break down. They are…"

He makes a motion with his hands like he's smashing a bug.

"Many PLF soldiers have been arrested," Alexei adds with a frown. "And many of the officers will be charged with war crimes."

"Have you heard about anyone else from Varaz?" I ask. "Josef or Lara? Anna? Ivan?"

Alexei and Marcus exchange glances. A tangible dismay falls over the room. My stomach twists.

"Lara and Josef are both fine," Alexei assures me. "She is with her sister near Telina, and he is in Polvik. Anna was in a refugee camp, but has been reunited with her family. We have not yet found Mr. Becherov, but others are safe."

He explains the whereabouts of several families, the nuns, the men who'd been working on reconstructing the building exteriors.

But—

"Ivan?" I ask.

Alexei shakes his head and reaches out to put his hand on my arm. "He was killed in Varaz."

Sorrow constricts my throat. I will never forget that first dinner I had with Alexei at the Koroleva Café when Ivan had served us all his best dishes, and Alexei had told me my name means *shining light.*

"He was taking shelter in library when PLF began shooting through window." Marcus's brow creases. "Mr. Rustin and the Goncharovs also died there."

They hadn't been the only ones. Marcus and Alexei relay the fates of numerous others who were killed either during the siege or as they attempted to leave the province.

Such sadness and cruel loss. Now I understand the pull Darius has always had for telling people's stories. Why shouldn't the world know about the big, boisterous café owner who'd welcomed everyone into his establishment as if it were his home? As if we were family.

After Tom calls us into the dining room for lunch, he

pours glasses of wine, and we toast Ivan and the others who have lost their lives. Marcus and Alexei then proceed to tell entertaining stories about Ivan that have us all laughing—which is exactly what the café owner would have wanted.

For the next few days, I forgo my job and apartment searching to spend time showing the Rostovs around New York. We visit the zoo and museums, get last-minute tickets for *The Lion King*, eat ice-cream sundaes at Serendipity's, ride to the observatory decks of the Empire State Building, and take the ferry to Staten Island and the Statue of Liberty. Jacob and Tomas are all at once thrilled, overwhelmed, and exhausted by the activity.

All too soon, we have to part again. I accompany them to the airport. Amidst more hugs, tears, and promises to stay in touch, the Rostovs prepare to board a flight that will take them back to their wounded but resilient home country.

As they make their way to the security line, Jacob tugs on the hem of my jacket and crooks his finger. I crouch and look into his incredible dark eyes.

"Make sure you keep practicing checkers," I tell him. "When I come to Krasnovar again, I'm going to challenge you to a championship match."

"You need this to win." He holds out his hand.

A piece of gray sea glass—the one Darius and I had found on the beach at Volkov Bay when I was a girl, the one he'd carried with him for four years, the one he'd given Jacob to bolster the boy's courage in the midst of the siege—sits in his palm like a raindrop.

I pick it up and rub my thumb over the surface. Somehow it feels as if the little stone contains the essence of everything we've all endured.

Broken from its moorings, the piece of glass twisted and spun through the turbulent sea. And on the journey, the ocean waves polished the glass, smoothed its rough edges, gave it a different shape and texture. So the sea glass is both what it once was and something entirely new.

"You keep." Jacob nudges my hand back toward me. "For protection, Mister Darius said. And for good luck."

I look at him, my heart filling with a thousand emotions. "Don't you need good luck anymore?"

He shrugs. "You keep."

"I'll keep it for now." I close my hand around the glass. "But I promise to bring it back to you. That way, we're certain to meet again."

"Soon," he says.

"Yes." My throat tightens. "Soon."

He smiles and hugs me, then hurries to catch up with his family.

I watch as the five of them walk away, all turning to wave goodbye before they disappear into the crowd.

CHAPTER 39

Nell

I'LL BE *at the airport to pick you up, but Poe will be waiting for you at home.*

A photo accompanies my father's text—Poe gnawing on a beef bone the size of a bowling pin.

Did that come from a buffalo? I text back.

Either an elk or an extra-large cow, he replies.

With a chuckle, I relay my flight information for the following morning and promise to text again before takeoff. I drop my phone back into my bag and continue walking.

The leaves of Central Park are red and gold against the dusky blue sky. Dog walkers, cyclists, and pedestrians crowd the walkways and grass, all out enjoying the brisk, late-afternoon air.

I leave the park and make my way down 5th Avenue, glancing at glossy storefront window displays en route to the Museum of Modern Art. One more stop before I take the subway to Alice's apartment and pack for my flight back to California.

After showing my museum membership card at the front desk, I spend a couple of hours wandering the floors and drinking in the paintings and sculptures. I've always loved these artists wildly—the rebels, adventurers, and romantics.

But now I understand them in ways I hadn't before. I know what it feels like to *feel* so much that you don't know how your single, small existence in the universe can contain it all. I understand the desire to change things, whether through one's ideas or actions or vision.

I'll always have the impulse to create art, that indefinable urge that makes me pick up a pencil and draw even if no one else will ever see the final product. It's part of my soul. I love watching figures and objects take shape under my hand, and I still harbor a little dream of one day seeing Winsome Swift grace the pages of her own graphic novel.

But something fundamental has changed deep inside me. My world has expanded so much that I want to do more than work in a studio and seek out exhibitions, publications, and freelance work. Of course, I'll be grateful for whatever job I'm offered, but that little seed is still there, buried inside me.

Maybe it didn't have anything to do with Darius after all. Maybe it was meant to grow just for me. He and I couldn't reshape our future together, but I can reshape my own. I don't yet know how, but the possibility is there. I just need to learn how to cultivate and take care of it.

I continue walking through the galleries. Outside, the sky

begins to darken as twilight approaches. I glance at my watch. Almost half an hour before the museum closes.

I climb the stairs to the fifth floor and navigate to the gallery housing the artwork of nineteenth-century painters. Visitors are drifting out of the rooms, turning to each other with questions about dinner and plans for the evening.

There are just a few people in front of Van Gogh's *The Starry Night.* I wait until they've left, then I sit on a bench to look at the turbulent night sky, the brilliant golds and blues, the stars that spin right in the middle of my heart.

The Starry Night had inspired my own drawings of nocturnes when I was in the institution. I'd thought of Van Gogh in his Saint-Rémy asylum, looking out the window just like I was doing.

Like Darius had done in his cell, though at the time I hadn't known we were looking at the same stars. And when I came home again, I'd returned to my little cove on the rooftop above my bedroom where I could look at the night sky and remember that even in the darkness, there was so much beauty.

I move closer to the painting, letting my gaze trace the thick combs of paint, the curved lines of the cypress tree, the lights of the village.

Be clearly aware of the stars and infinity on high, Vincent had once written to his brother. *Then life seems almost enchanted after all.*

The back of my neck prickles. A security guard walks past. I step away from the painting and slide my bag over my shoulder.

As I turn away from the nocturne whirlwind, my heartbeat increases, as if it knows before I do that my world is about to tilt wildly off balance.

I stop. Darius is standing less than twenty feet away, his feet planted apart as if he, too, has stopped suddenly.

Electricity sparks between us. The current arcs into me and lights my blood.

I take a breath, trying to absorb the shock of his tall, beautiful presence. To keep my ever-present love for him locked behind my guard. I hadn't really believed we would *never* see each other again, but I also haven't hoped for or dreamed about our reunion. I couldn't. Not when—

Almost as if shaking himself out of a trance, he starts walking toward me. I can only watch him approach, my pulse thumping with every step he takes.

His gold-flecked brown eyes…closer. His thick dark hair. Closer. His wide chest and shoulders, his well-shaped mouth, his…*everything.*

"Nell." In his voice, my name sounds like a smooth pebble dropped into a pool of deep, clear water.

He stops in front of me—almost within touching distance. I want to close that distance so badly my bones almost hurt from the effort of staying where I am.

"Darius." I swallow past the constriction in my throat. "What are you doing here?"

"I had a layover at LaGuardia for a flight to Venezuela. I thought…I didn't know if you'd still be in New York."

"I'm leaving tomorrow morning." I flex my hand on the strap of my bag, struck by the fact that while he looks like the same man I have loved for so long, something has changed. There's a relaxed set to his shoulders, a different light in the depths of his eyes. Like he's done with all the battles he's ever fought. Like the war inside him is over.

"When does your flight to Venezuela leave?" I ask.

"It already left."

"Was the first flight delayed? Is that why you came into the city?"

"No." He takes a step closer, his attention so focused on me it's as if he's studying one of the paintings on the walls around us. "I didn't get on the second flight."

"Oh." I catch his scent—citrus, fresh autumn leaves, him—and my knees weaken. "Why not?"

"I didn't want to. I..." He pauses, lifting a hand slightly toward me before dropping it back to his side. "I'd intended to. I was in Krasnovar, and my fifth visa expired so I had to leave again. While I was waiting for another approval, I was going to use the time to get back into the field because I thought I couldn't do anything else."

I stare at him. That statement hardly makes any sense. "Darius, there's nothing you *can't* do. You're capable of...everything."

His mouth tightens slightly. He looks away.

This time, I step closer to him. "How can you not know that?"

"Because I've failed at the one thing I want to do the most." He shifts his gaze back to me, his eyes dark. "Which is to be with you."

My heart gives a wild leap, even as the cloud over it still lingers. "You haven't failed. My relationship with you will always be the most cherished part of my life. Of *me*. Just because it didn't last doesn't mean it failed. Lots of beautiful things don't last. Fireworks. Christmas trees. Sunflowers."

"But those things aren't gone forever. They come back."

I smother a sudden rush of hope. I want so badly to believe he means *us*. Though I can envision a life without him, it's not one I would pick—if I had the choice. I will always, forever, endlessly, throughout time and across universes…choose him.

But we both made our choices already. Didn't we? Even I couldn't work out all the tangles and complexities of our lives together, no matter what the scenario.

"Nell." Darius pauses, as if he's struggling to figure out how to say what he wants to. "When I was in India, I let this group of children use my camera. I've always carried a few point-and-shoots with me because kids are often interested in photography, but this time, they used my Nikon. And later, when I was looking at the photos they'd taken— whether it was a dog or a bicycle or each other—I realized they were all about how these kids see the world, what it looks like through their eyes, what's worthy of their attention."

He gives a rueful shrug. "Which I know sounds obvious, but I started thinking I've spent all this time, all these years, telling people's stories and trying to make their voices heard when they should be the ones telling their own stories."

"That's a lovely thought." A book of Darius's photography flips through my mind—countless images of pain, loss, and violence, and also of hope. "But one of the reasons you're so good at what you do—telling people's stories—is that you do for them what they either can't or are unable to do for themselves."

"But what would it take for them to be able to tell their own stories? To make their voices heard?"

"I suppose they'd need a way to do it. An avenue or a path."

"Exactly." He takes another step toward me, and now all I'd have to do is lift my hand, and I would touch him. I curl my fingers into my palm.

"I thought about that for weeks, the whole time I was in Moldova and working with the refugee organizations," he says. "And then in Krasnovar, when I was investigating all the connections between the mining rights and the PLF... rather than documenting the effects of the war myself, I wanted to know how the Krasnovian people would do it. So I gave my camera to them. Kids, parents, teenagers, senior citizens. They took hundreds of photos. Told hundreds of stories."

"That sounds incredible." I wonder if that's the reason for the new light in his eyes. Maybe seeing how other people view the world has made him realize he doesn't need to shoulder the weight of responsibility all the time. He doesn't have to seek out darkness.

"Are you going back?" I ask.

"I hope so, but not to investigate the PLF again," he says. "Their ranks are decimated, and international tribunals are collecting evidence to prosecute the leaders. The mining rights issues are with the courts right now. Needless to say, they no longer belong to Hawke Financial. I took the job in Venezuela because I've been waiting for another visa approval to go back to Krasnovar."

"So did you get the approval? Is that why you decided not to go to Venezuela?"

"No." He puts his hands in his coat pockets, his gaze steady on me. "I was supposed to be ready to get back to work, charged up like I've always been before an assignment. But I wasn't. I didn't want to run into the front lines or toward the killing and bloodshed like I've done for over twenty years. This time, there was only one place I wanted to run."

"Where?"

"Back to you."

A breath escapes me. The hope grows stronger, unfurling warmth through my entire body. It's the feeling of tender leaves opening, of tiny shoots breaking free and growing into bright blossoms.

"But..." I struggle to remember the reason I need to protect my heart. "What about all that stuff you said about not having a choice?"

Regret shadows his features. He lifts his hand, brushing his fingers gently against my cheek. "You're the only woman I've ever chosen. The only one who chose me. For so long, I thought my life couldn't change, but then I realized it already had. You changed my life. You changed me. I can't have a future without you."

I didn't have only *one* buried seed. I must have had a thousand because they're bursting open at the same time, flooding me with all the colors, all the light.

The struggle I'd had to envision a possible scenario for us falls away. Because after everything we've been through, *being together* now feels like it might be the easiest thing in the world.

"I want to be with you, Nell," Darius says. "I want a life with you, even if I don't know what that looks like yet."

"Oh, my love." I press my hand to his strong chest. "That's one of the amazing things about being alive. We don't always know, but we can do it anyway. It's like having an empty canvas and a box filled with paints and pencils. Sometimes you have no idea what you're going to end up with, but you have this impulse, this fire inside you to create something new. And so you start. You just start."

The jingling of keys resounds through the gallery, and a security guard pokes his head into the room. "Sorry, folks, we're locking up in about five minutes."

We give him a wave of acknowledgment, and he continues on his way. Darius turns toward the door and extends his hand to me.

Life doesn't seem enchanted after all. Life *is* enchanted.

I put my hand in his, and we both hold on.

CHAPTER 40

Nell

THE WEDDING ARCH glows with autumn flowers and illuminated garlands. String lights twinkle around the trunk of the oak tree, and rust-colored paper lanterns hang from the branches. The setting is a magical fall fairyland, and the house on Dearborne Street feels warm and alive.

As twilight descends, close to fifty guests gather to sit in the chairs alongside the grass aisle, which is lined with wooden lanterns, each one harboring a lit candle, and bouquets of dahlias, asters, and eucalyptus leaves. Pachelbel's "Canon in D" drifts from the speakers set up on the back porch.

Turning from the window of the office, I touch my father's arm, indicating it's almost time. He nods and straightens his tie. He looks very handsome in a classic,

tailored gray suit and waistcoat with an elegant rose boutonniere attached to his left lapel.

I slip my arm into the crook of his elbow. We walk
outside, past the oak tree to the wedding arch and a small
raised platform where the officiant is standing.

Darius is waiting next to the platform. Like my father, he
looks exceptional in his gray suit and boutonniere, his thick
hair brushed away from his—for once—clean-shaven face.
Poe is at his side, freshly washed, brushed, and wearing a
gray bow-tie with a miniature boutonniere attached to his
collar.

As my father and I approach, Darius winks at me, his
private smile sending a wave of pleasure through my heart.
Poe approaches, sniffing at the folds of my dress. I give him a
quick fur-ruffle and ear-scratch.

After squeezing my hand, my father walks over to stand
in front of the archway. I follow, taking the best man's—*best
daughter's,* he'd called it—position at his right, while the
groomsmen Darius and Poe line up on my other side.

The music changes as the back door opens. The guests
rise and turn to watch Clover approach. She comes down
the aisle, her plum-colored silk dress shining in the lights.
Flashing me a quick smile, she takes her place at the left side
of the archway.

Then Fern appears, stunning in a simple, ivory lace gown
and holding a bouquet of fall flowers and foliage. As she
descends the steps and starts down the aisle, my father clears
his throat. Darius passes him a handkerchief.

Fern gives my father a radiant smile as she approaches.
He steps forward and whispers something in her ear before
they both turn to face the officiant.

The ceremony is simple and heartfelt—my father and Fern exchange their own written vows, and Clover and I join them in creating a unity vessel of sand. We each pick up a small jar of colored sand and, together, the four of us pour them into an elegant glass vase. The fine-grained sand blends into one bright, multicolored column.

The guests—my father's colleagues and grad students, Fern and Clover's friends and coworkers—applaud and whistle loudly as the married couple make their way back down the aisle, glowing with happiness.

After Simon, the official wedding photographer, takes more photos of the wedding party, the reception begins in earnest. Everyone moves to sit at the round tables extending over the yard, and the caterers open both a buffet and a cocktail bar. A few of the men move all the chairs around the perimeter of the fence, so the backyard becomes a big dance floor.

Music swells—everything from "Uptown Funk" to "All of Me." After dancing with my father, then Fern, Simon, Clover —my new stepsister—and two of my father's grad students, I take a quick break to check in with the caterers. They assure me that the service is going beautifully and there is plenty of food.

My father is standing by the bar, disheveled and flushed with contentment. I reach out to straighten his askew boutonniere.

"Congratulations, Dad."

He smiles. "It was a good wedding, wasn't it?"

"The best. You couldn't have done better. But then, neither could Fern."

"Nell." He puts his hand on my shoulder. "I hope..." He

pauses. "I hope you know—that you've always known—everything I've done in life, even if it was misguided, has been for you."

"I know." I reach out to embrace him as any tiny cracks still left in my heart smooth over. "We've had a lot of rough waters, but never once have I doubted your love for me. Never once have I doubted you'd always be there, no matter what challenges I threw at you. And I was right. You're my anchor."

His eyes glitter. He eases away from me and reaches for his drink. "So next Saturday is your flight to New York?"

"Yes, after you and Fern get back from Hawaii. Poe is going to miss you when we leave."

"I suspect Fern has her eye on a dog at the shelter already."

"*Fern* does, hmm?" I nudge his arm. "You know you can visit whenever you want."

"I know." He takes another sip. "I meant to tell you I got a call from one of the Hawke Financial lawyers yesterday. Our home phone number was the only one he had on record. He said something about a music box or some kind of jewelry box—he didn't give me many details—and a photo album that used to belong to Odette."

My heart thumps. "What did he say about them?"

"They'd been found among Conrad Hawke's possessions, but they were on a list of things that had legally belonged to Odette and were included in her will," my father explains. "She'd distributed the items to different people, but she'd left this box and the album to your mother. And since you were Katherine's designated beneficiary, they now belong to you."

I shake my head. "The...the jewelry box and the photo album? They're mine?"

"I guess so." He shrugs and puts the glass down. "I don't know if Katherine even knew anything about the will, or maybe Conrad kept it from her. But apparently it's all legit. The lawyer said you have to sign some papers before taking possession of the items, but you can do that in New York. Sorry I didn't tell you sooner. There were so many last-minute wedding things going on yesterday that it slipped my mind until now."

"It's okay. I'll call the lawyer." I can't fully process this revelation—at least, I won't until I actually have the Fabergé egg and the photo album in my hands. But even the idea that somehow those two items would find their way back to me...

"There you are." Fern walks over, her smile encompassing both of us. She puts her hand on my father's arm. "Sorry for interrupting, but can I steal you away? My friend Gina and her husband have to leave early, and I don't want to miss a photo with them."

"Of course." My father touches my shoulder, and he and Fern head off in search of Simon.

I watch them go. Fern hasn't told me what finally changed her mind about marriage, but I'm sure it had to do with my father's close call. Sometimes courage comes from fear of what might have been—and since the worst hadn't happened, she realized that what they have together really is the best.

A comic book expert and a Roman history scholar. Who knew it would have turned out so perfectly?

I pour myself a glass of spiked apple cider and sit on one of the chairs by the fence. The air is alive with joy.

The children of several guests form a conga line on the dance floor. Patrick O'Hare is dancing with Ms. Meadows, and the way they're looking at each other makes me think they might rekindle the romance that fizzled out after Patrick's contract ended at Monarch High.

The caterers bring out more food. One of the Comic Castle college workers is demonstrating how to balance a spoon on the tip of his nose to an appreciative audience of history professors. Fern and my father are standing with her friends by the oak tree, all four of them laughing so hard about something that Simon gives up trying to pose them and instead snaps photos of their sheer merriment.

I glance up to see Darius approaching, his tie loosened. The multitude of lights glows off his dark hair. He smiles at me, his eyes crinkling at the corners.

My heart gives a happy little leap. Sometimes I still can't quite believe it—that he and I have come to a place of peace, of resolution—and then I catch him watching me or coming toward me, and any lingering disbelief vanishes.

Every time he looks at me, his expression is filled with such tenderness, such undying warmth and love, that where once I struggled to envision a scenario in which we could be together—now, I can't imagine one in which we're ever apart.

"Hey." He stops and brushes his knuckles briefly across my cheek.

I consider telling him about the Fabergé egg and the photo album, but decide that can wait until later.

Taking his wrist, I press a quick kiss against his palm

before he lowers his arm back to his side. Though my father has mostly come to terms with our relationship, Darius and I are both aware that acceptance isn't always an easy, straightforward road. So while we make no secret of being in love, we also don't engage in overt displays of affection when my father is nearby.

"I saw you dancing with everyone but me," Darius remarks.

I arch an eyebrow. "Well, everyone but you asked me to dance."

"I was keeping Poe from pestering the caterers. But now he's had his dinner and is patiently waiting for dessert." He holds out his hand. "Will you dance with me?"

"Always." I slip my hand into his, and he leads me to the dance floor, where "Best Day of My Life" is underway.

We dance the way we did at the Friendship Festival in Varaz—with energy, pleasure, and happiness. But this time, there are no lingering questions, no uncertainties or doubt. This time, there's only us and our limitless future.

As the music slows into the melodic rhythm of Elvis's "Can't Help Falling in Love," Darius pulls me into his arms. I lift my head to look up at him, unsurprised to find him watching me.

I stop and take his hand, leading him off the dance floor. "Come with me."

"Where?"

"I want to show you something."

"What about the cake?"

I toss him a grin over my shoulder. "Oh, I'll give you cake."

In response, he discreetly pats my rear as I go up the

steps and into the house. The caterers are bustling around the kitchen and going back and forth through the side door. Still holding Darius's hand, I climb the stairs to the second floor.

"This is getting more and more promising," he remarks.

"Hold that thought." I lead him up the narrow staircase to my former attic bedroom and open the door.

All the furniture is the same, and several of my old drawings are still tacked to the walls, but my personal belongings are gone. I let go of Darius's hand and cross to the dormer window. After jiggling the tight lock, I unfasten it and push open the window. Music, lights, and conversation drift into the room from the party below.

"This isn't what I was hoping for," he says, though he and I both know he'd never disrespect my father and Fern by having a secret rendezvous with me in the house.

"It might end up being more than you were hoping for." Grasping the window, I lift myself onto the sill and lean out.

"Nell." Darius takes my arm. "What are you doing?"

"Don't worry." I kick off my high-heeled shoes and grab hold of a branch on the oak tree. "I've done this a thousand times. Put your foot on this thick branch right here, and hold on to this one. Follow me."

I climb out into the tree. Below me, the noise and music rise upward in waves. Even though I haven't been out here in years, I don't have to think about where to step in order to reach the roof. It's almost as if the oak tree is lifting me into place.

Grasping the branches, I make my way onto the roof and balance across the ridge to my secret hollow between the sloping sides.

Darius is right behind me, and he pauses on the ridge. The ambient light illuminates his faintly puzzled look. "What are we doing?"

"Come here." I lie back on the slope of the roof, indicating the space next to me.

He sheds his suit jacket and climbs down. After draping the jacket across my shoulders, he stretches out beside me. I slip my arms into the warm sleeves and point upward.

It's a clear night, and the stars spill like powdered sugar across the sky. The moon is a delicate, ghostlike crescent in the west.

"Remember when I told you I used to come onto the roof to look at the stars?" I ask. "This is the place. No one could see me, but I could see the whole sky. Whenever I came here, no matter how bad things were, I always felt like maybe they'd turn out okay. One day."

He settles his hand on my thigh, right where my scars still mark my skin. The warmth of his palm flows through the material of my dress.

"And they have." I turn to face him, letting my gaze trace the strong lines of his features. "They've turned out far more than just *okay*. It's amazing, isn't it? What can happen if you hold on to hope."

With a murmur of agreement, he slides one arm around me. I nestle closer as his body heat warms me to the tips of my toes.

"I love you, Darius."

"I love you, Nell." He wraps the length of my hair in his hand and gives it a gentle tug. "Because of you, I believe in more than I could ever have imagined. I want to look at things the way you do. You are what the world should be. You make me want to…"

He stops and shakes his head, like he doesn't have the right words. But I know what they are because he makes me want to do the same thing. He ignited the urge the moment I first saw him standing outside the house over four years ago. Now that flame will never go out.

"To find the light," I whisper.

And together, we have.

He looks at me for a long moment, then lifts my face gently and presses his lips against mine. I sink into his warmth, his strength.

Time no longer matters. We only need to treasure what we have right now, this lovely knowledge that we've both found everything that had been lost or missing.

He slides his hand to the back of my neck, bringing me closer, deepening the kiss. Above us, the stars unfold and spin into forever.

EPILOGUE

Nell

Six months later

EVENING SUNLIGHT SPARKLES on the Mediterranean as if a bucket of gold glitter has spilled over the azure-blue water. A horseshoe-shaped beach hugs the wide cove, and the harbor is lined with colorful fishing boats bobbing in the water like drops of paint.

The Greek village of Arkenos spreads over a low, tree-covered mountain alongside the coast—a panorama of whitewashed houses with red roofs, narrow cobblestone streets, and hidden archeological treasures. Trails flourishing with wildflowers lace over the hills, and a twelfth-century Byzantine monastery sits above the town like a benevolent nursemaid guarding her charges.

Poe and I wander the main street past the Orthodox church and rows of cafés and shops. I especially love the groceries with their bounty of food—ripe tomatoes, olives soaking in barrels of brine, thick honey the color of sunshine; plump, juicy figs, pomegranates, and mangos. In the months we've been here, I've sampled it all and then bought more for seconds and thirds.

After purchasing a package of crumbly feta cheese, we cross the town square, which is lined with shopkeeper stalls and tables. Today is market day, and vendors have been out selling everything from handwoven cloth to porcelain dinnerware, lamps, and antique clocks.

I stop at one of the stalls and purchase a cobalt-blue vase, disappointing the shopkeeper with my refusal to haggle over the price, despite his best efforts.

"*Efharisto.*" With a smile of thanks, I tuck the wrapped vase into my bag and continue walking.

I'm warm from being in the sun most of the afternoon—Poe and I had hiked up to the monastery, and I'd spent a few hours sketching scenes of Winsome Swift in the Mediterranean landscape. She's found a new life here in this home of mythology, and she and I have been creating a new story about her triumph over a malevolent sea monster and her struggle to reconcile both the magical and conventional sides of her life.

I carve out the time to work on Winsome's story and illustrations in between my other activities. Tomorrow morning, I'm going to teach a group of elderly women the basics of figure drawing, then I have a lunch date with

Darius, then I'm going to help Mrs. Varelas weed her garden.

I'm not at all surprised by how quickly Arkenos has become home to both me and Darius. Nowhere in the world is it easier to take a deep breath.

Poe trots alongside me as we navigate through the streets to a wood-and-stone building at the end of the road. Rickety paper-covered tables are scattered under an awning on an outdoor patio, and lights twinkle around the windows.

Inside, a bar curves along one wall, wooden tables and chairs fill the two rooms, and rustic, fishing-themed folk art decorates the whole place.

A few locals are already seated at the bar, but the bulk of the crowd will arrive after the shops have closed. Long into the night, the taverna will resound with music, laughter, and stories.

"*Kalispera,* Nikos." I wave at the older man polishing glasses behind the bar.

"*Kalispera,* Nell. You stay for dinner?"

"Not tonight, thank you. I picked up our dinner groceries this morning."

He points his chin to the back of the taverna. "Make him cook for you."

"I will, indeed."

I walk into the second room, where Darius is spreading paper cloths over the tabletops and setting them with silverware. He's wearing cargo shorts and a T-shirt, with a dishtowel slung over his shoulder. I pause to admire the sheer beauty of what several months in Arkenos has done for him, both inside and out.

His hair is longer, brushing the back of his collar, with

lighter streaks bleached by the sun. His skin is tanned a deep bronze, and his formidable muscles are even stronger now from all of his physical activity—whether it's hiking the multitude of trails, helping the fishermen pull in their catch, or building a bookshelf for Mrs. Panagiotou.

But as beautiful as his outward appearance is, the easy relaxation and peace radiating from the center of his being makes him infinitely more captivating. He's quick to laugh. He'll sit for hours at the taverna or the café or the market, listening to people tell their stories. He hangs out at the harbor, discussing the day's work and the weather with the fishermen.

He's bought cameras for the local schoolchildren and taught classes on how to use them. He helps out at Nikos's taverna, often setting up and serving the afternoon guests. Sometimes he stays into the evening, but Nikos usually sends him home to be with me, or together, Darius and I join the crowd for dinner, card games, conversation, and dancing.

Despite our many endeavors, we find each other often throughout the day, whether we meet for lunch, go hiking, explore the old ruins, or sit and drink coffee while making plans for the future. And at night, we're never apart.

He turns to catch me watching him. With a smile that never fails to make my heart skip a beat, he crosses the room.

"Cute freckles." He taps his finger against my nose, then greets me with a warm kiss. I press my hand to his chest, drinking in his scents of lemon, sea salt, sunshine.

"Are you ready to go?" I ask.

"As soon as I finish setting the tables, yeah." He pats my

hip and turns back to pick up the tray of silverware. "Mrs. Panagiotou brought me a *portokalopita* as thanks for the bookshelf. We can have it for dessert."

"Yum." I love the traditional orange custard pie. "Poe and I will wait outside for you."

After he's finished, we walk farther up the hill to a two-story, whitewashed house overlooking the harbor and flanked by olive trees. Potted plants in fat, terra-cotta pots line the steps, and old wooden shutters frame the windows.

Though the house is weathered—peeling paint, chipped tiles, a sagging roof—Darius and I had both fallen in love with it on sight. The windows frame expansive views of the harbor and the sea, a garden and terrace extend out from the back, and a trail in the yard leads in two directions to the beach and the hills.

We go into the high-ceiling kitchen, and he refills Poe's food and water dishes. I take the cobalt-blue vase from my bag.

Every morning, Darius puts a bouquet of wildflowers on the table for me, and it's about time the pretty blossoms live in something nicer than a chipped glass jar. I put today's bouquet in the vase with some water and place it back on the table.

As Darius sets up the grill on the terrace, I get the food ready—sea bream caught this morning, fresh tomatoes, fragrant lemons, and the block of sharp feta I just bought. While he grills the fish, I make a salad and a sauce of lemon and olive oil, then slice a loaf of crusty bread and pour glasses of wine.

We eat outside on the terrace, as we always do if the

weather allows, watching the sunset, the sea, the boats floating in the harbor.

"I have something for you." He takes a wrinkled, opened envelope out of his pocket and pushes it across the table.

It's addressed to both of us, postmarked Varaz, Krasno-var. I pull out the sheet of paper and glance over it, my breath catching.

"Really?" I look at him. "We're going?"

"We are. I'll book the tickets for next week. After we have a better idea of the situation, we'll be able to start bringing in supplies and staff."

I squeeze his hand. "I'm so proud of you."

He laughs. "Of me? You've done more than I have to get this off the ground."

"No, I haven't. And it was your idea."

When he'd first brought up the possibility of creating a foundation dedicated to bringing the arts back to cities that are recovering from war, I'd been all-in—even though I knew nothing about running a foundation. But I'd plunged into learning, and together, we filed the paperwork, established a board of directors, and founded the Creativity Collective.

Working in conjunction with both UNESCO and nonprofits helping towns with practical rebuilding, the Creativity Collective will give people the tools, supplies, and funding needed to address human rights issues and to foster peace through the arts and storytelling.

Along with a compilation of data and statistics proving how the arts support reintegration, we'd explained our philosophy in the Creativity Collective's mission statement:

Our core belief is that artistic freedom and creative expression are essential building blocks of a stable, peaceful community.

If we can help bring the arts back to life in cities that have been ravaged by war and other conflicts, people will rediscover the power of their own voices, honor what is important to them, and amplify the message that art is a dynamic, transformative tool for recovery and reconciliation.

Darius has already contracted with several major technology companies to supply cameras, tablets, and internet access to schools in war-torn and impoverished regions so children can both connect with the rest of the world and visually tell their stories.

I've contacted my former professors to network with artists for classes and workshops, my friends Alice and Cecily are spreading the word through the New York dance and arts communities, Jonah is sourcing ideas from his architecture firm, and Clover and Simon are both recruiting support from animation and film directors. Fern is brimming over with ideas, and my father has been emailing us his research about the histories of the cities and towns on our list.

Darius and I have rented a warehouse in New York, and it's already filled with art supplies that we plan to ship to schools and town centers. By working with other organizations, we can also ensure that people first have their basic needs of food, shelter, and safety met before starting our programs.

Darius is funding the Creativity Collective with the substantial trust his mother left for him—a windfall he hadn't known about until after his father died. When she was pregnant with Darius, Victoria Hawke had created a trust fund for him containing stocks, mutual funds, and shares of both Hawke Financial and two other companies that her father had owned. She'd done it all without Conrad's knowledge.

Victoria had continued adding to the fund until her death, and over the years, the accounts have all skyrocketed in value—leaving Darius with far more money than he'd ever anticipated.

Though Conrad had apparently learned of the trust after Victoria's death, he hadn't divulged its existence to Darius. But Darius's lawyer said the terms were so tightly locked that not even Conrad's legal team had been able to break them. And so now the entire trust fund belongs to Darius.

He's investing a large percentage of the money into the foundation, ensuring that it will be self-sustaining. The rest of it, he's set aside for us to visit different towns and cities so we can work to organize the Creativity Collective programs, while returning to our Arkenos home in between our travels.

My inheritance is also secure; the Fabergé egg is now in my safety deposit box in California, and I keep the photo album on a table in the sitting room.

It's no coincidence that both Odette and Victoria separately made plans to guarantee that their offspring would receive what was due to them. Darius and I come from intelligent, strong women who had found ways to subvert Conrad Hawke's power despite his attempts to control them.

In the end, they'd won. And so have we.

Now, Darius and I can return to Varaz to launch our programs and help the people and town we've both come to love so much. Though Darius had started a photographic history of Varaz when we were there, he's now planning to turn the idea over to the residents so they can tell the story of the town in their own words and images.

"Alexei says they've started repairing the museum." Darius indicates the letter. "And he can't wait for you to arrive so you can help him with the artwork again."

With a smile, I read the letter. Alexei and his family returned to Varaz a few months ago, and he was happy to report that the damage to both the museum and the castle weren't as bad as he had feared. About half the town's residents have also returned, and the government has been providing funds for both aid and rebuilding.

"He says UNESCO has already contacted him about grants too," I tell Darius. "That's promising."

He nods, rising to pick up our plates. "With the news about the PLF's defeat and the Krasnovian lithium mines making headlines, I think they'll be getting quite a bit of international aid and investments soon."

It's all good news, and I hold on to the hope that things will only get better.

"What about my father and Fern's visit?" I ask as we clean up the kitchen.

"We'll be back before they get here." Darius sets the dishes in the drainer and dries his hands on a towel. "I'll let him know."

We haven't seen my father and Fern since their wedding, and they've made plans to visit next month. In addition to

Arkenos, my father wants to take Fern to Athens and Crete, and they've invited us to travel with them for a few days.

After enjoying slices of the custard pie, we take Poe for a walk along the beach before returning home to review all the organizational paperwork for the Creativity Collective and to make our travel plans.

Poe will be able to come with us to Varaz, but if it's not possible for him to travel with us, he'll stay with Nikos, whose huge family and cadre of grandchildren all adore our loyal, beautiful, resilient dog.

Close to midnight, Darius and I climb the worn stone stairs to our bedroom. Moonlight spills like cream through the windows and over the iron-framed bed. He pulls me into his arms the instant I step toward him, a movement as smooth and natural as flowing water.

Our lips meet, gentle kisses slowly turning hot and deep as we shed our clothes and sink onto the bed. He strokes my sun-warmed skin. I bury my hands in his thick hair and arch against him. We fit together like a letter sliding into an envelope.

So easy. After all we've endured, all the battles we've fought and challenges we've faced—it's now so blissfully easy.

He's found his peace out of the storm. I've found my truth in the world and in myself. There is nothing wrong. We no longer need defenses, fortresses, or locks. All we need is this wide-open space we've found, this intense, unrestrained love, this life together in which we can both take flight.

ABOUT THE AUTHOR

Born and raised in California, *New York Times* and *USA Today* bestselling author Nina Lane now lives in Wisconsin where the winters are freezing and the cheese is exceptional. Mom to two teens and a neurotic dog, half her life consists of laundry, Girl Scouts, horses, and football, while the other half is filled with hot, swoony alpha heroes and the women who bring them to their knees.

Nina is a fan of popcorn, print magazines, working out, and checking the weather daily with her meteorologist husband. She holds a PhD in Art History and an MA in Library and Information Studies, but considers writing epic, emotional romances her one true calling in life. Thus, she is grateful and ecstatic to be able to bring the stories in her head to life for all her amazing fans.

www.ninalane.com

facebook.com/ninalaneauthor
instagram.com/ninalaneauthor
amazon.com/author/ninalane
goodreads.com/ninalane

THE SUGAR RUSH SERIES

Sweet is the new sexy.

From the Stone family patriarch down to the youngest bad boy, follow the lives and loves of the Sugar Rush men and the women who bring them to their knees.

THE WHAT IF SERIES

First we fell in love. Then we fell apart.

Shattered by decade-old tragedy, two lovers fight the secrets that could destroy them.

THE SECRET THIEF

"This book is a work of art."

A woman fleeing scandal. A town's mysterious recluse.

Lust and secrets collide in this provocative romance.

THE DARING HEARTS SERIES

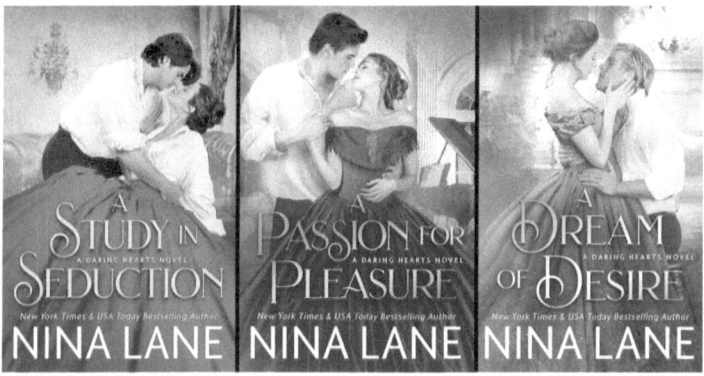

In bustling, colorful Victorian London, powerful lords and unconventional women battle scandal and secrets as they risk everything for love.

NINA LINDSEY BOOKS

Enjoy my heartwarming, sexy-sweet Nina Lindsey books set in Bliss Cove, a town where love sweeps in on the ocean breeze.

WE FOUND LOVE

After Trevor's meteoric rise to fame in the chef world tears them apart, Kate escapes to a small seaside town to heal her broken heart. Determined to prove they belong together, Trevor seeks Kate out in Bliss Cove and risks it all for a second chance.

LOVE WALKS IN

Shaking off her past mistakes, Aria Prescott is determined to start a new life with her latest venture, the "Meow and Then Cat Café." Then property developer Hunter Armstrong swoops in to take over the whole district. Who will win this war of both homes and hearts?

AND I LOVE HER

An expert on the hot, wild tales of mythology, Callie Prescott leads a tidy life. And that, thank you, is exactly how she wants it…until action hero Jake Ryan arrives in town and wants some close-up action with the brilliant, beautiful professor.

LOVE ME TENDER

Rory Prescott and tavern owner Grant Taylor make a deal — she'll be his date to his brother's wedding if he'll let her stay short-term in his cottage. But what happens when this fake relationship becomes passionately real?

WORDS OF LOVE

When chirpy reporter Brooke Castle gets trapped in a snowstorm with grumpy bookstore owner Sam Donovan, the fire isn't the only thing heating up the cabin.

BOOK OF LOVE

High school literature teacher Grace Berry has no time for romance. But when sexy, award-winning author Lincoln Atwood comes into her classroom, Grace is eager for his lessons in love.

www.ingramcontent.com/pod-product-compliance
Lightning Source LLC
Chambersburg PA
CBHW020508260626
47156CB00006B/1915